ALEC

A SLATER BROTHERS NOVEL

Stacey, Thanks for taking a chance on Alec! :)
- L.A.

L.A. CASEY

Copyright © 2014 L.A. Casey
All Rights Reserved.

All rights reserved. No part of this book may be reproduced in any form or by any electronic or mechanical means including information storage and retrieval systems-except in the case of brief excerpts or quotations embodied in review or critical writings without the expressed permission of the author.

The characters and events in this book are fictitious or are used fictitiously. Any similarity to real persons, living or dead, is purely coincidental and not intended by the author.

Cover Design: Mayhem Cover Creations
Literary Editor: Jennifer Tovar
Formatting: Mayhem Cover Creations

DEDICATION

My Lasses.

My family.

My friends.

My readers.

This is for you.

TABLE OF CONTENTS

CHAPTER ONE	1
CHAPTER TWO	19
CHAPTER THREE	33
CHAPTER FOUR	55
CHAPTER FIVE	70
CHAPTER SIX	89
CHAPTER SEVEN	104
CHAPTER EIGHT	114
CHAPTER NINE	120
CHAPTER TEN	127
CHAPTER ELEVEN	140
CHAPTER TWELVE	154
CHAPTER THIRTEEN	169
CHAPTER FOURTEEN	179
CHAPTER FIFTEEN	190
CHAPTER SIXTEEN	198
CHAPTER SEVENTEEN	218
CHAPTER EIGHTEEN	230

CHAPTER NINETEEN	237
CHAPTER TWENTY	242
CHAPTER TWENTY-ONE	253
CHAPTER TWENTY-TWO	264
CHAPTER TWENTY-THREE	272
CHAPTER TWENTY-FOUR	276
CHAPTER TWENTY-FIVE	287
CHAPTER TWENTY-SIX	296
CHAPTER TWENTY-SEVEN	319
CHAPTER TWENTY-EIGHT	329
CHAPTER TWENTY-NINE	343
CHAPTER THIRTY	350
CHAPTER THIRTY-ONE	353
CHAPTER THIRTY-TWO	360
CHAPTER THIRTY-THREE	364
CHAPTER THIRTY-FOUR	370
CHAPTER THIRTY-FIVE	375
CHAPTER THIRTY-SIX	390
CHAPTER THIRTY-SEVEN	401
CHAPTER THIRTY-EIGHT	421
CHAPTER THIRTY-NINE	433
ACKNOWLEDGMENTS	443
ABOUT THE AUTHOR	445
OTHER TITLES	446

CHAPTER ONE

"Miss Daley? Open up! I know you're in there, your car is outside in the tenant car park!"

I groaned at the sound of the loud voice, and flicked my eyes open then quickly re-closed them. It took a few moments for me to be able to keep them open, and when I could, I couldn't see very well. I squinted through the darkness waiting for my eyes to adjust to the minimal lighting. When I could finally see, I quickly narrowed my eyes at the fat snoring male beside me. I shoved him hoping to knock him off the bed, but instead of falling off like I'd hoped he only farted and rolled over in my direction then placed a big sloppy kiss on my mouth.

"Storm!" I shouted and wiped at my mouth and tried not to heave, but the smell of Storm's breath made that very hard.

Storm lazily got to his feet, stretched and made some weird noises then proceeded to belly flop on top of me until I gasped for air. Storm, my two year old German Shepherd, needed to be put on a diet or one of these days the fat baby was going to smother me in my sleep.

"Off!" I gasped and shoved at his large body with both of my hands.

Storm did as ordered and got off me. But he didn't get off the bed, instead he just rolled back over to his side - yes, my dog had a side of the bed - which was just typical. The only time he willingly moved was if it was breakfast time, lunch time, dinner time or pretty much any time he knew there would be food in it for him.

"You pathetic excuse for a guard dog," I muttered as the banging on my apartment door started up again.

Storm replied with another fart that had me opening the windows before I left my bedroom to proceed down the hallway to open my door. I stubbed my toe on one of Storm's doggy toys as I walked and cursed the person on the other side of the door for making me get out of bed - it was the middle of the night for God's sake!

"I'm comin', keep your knickers on!" I shouted when I reached my door and began unlocking all the locks. There were five of them in total because in the area where I lived, one lock was not enough. I switched on my hall light and jumped when the bulb blew, coating the hall in darkness once again. I sighed as I turned to my front door, even though I was pretty sure I knew who was on the other side, I still looked through the peephole just to be safe.

When I confirmed the noisy menace at my door was in fact my neighbour, I unlocked the final lock and pulled it open then harshly glared at the man who was stood before me. Mr. Pervert - his real name was Mr. Doyle - was a middle-aged man who was the CEO at Perverts 'R Us. The man was a major creep, and I hated that I answered the door to him dressed in nothing but my nightdress because it gave him free rein to ogle me with his ever-roaming eyes.

"Can I help you, Mr. Per-Doyle?" I asked, biting my tongue so I didn't laugh at almost calling him Mr. Pervert out loud.

He snapped his eyes up from gawking at my legs to my face and cleared his throat as he lifted his hand - a hand that contained one single envelope. I simply stared at the envelope for a moment then flicked my eyes up to Mr. Pervert and found his eyes weren't on my face anymore. I knocked on the outside of my door with my free hand which made him jump with fright and me inwardly snort. When his eyes were once again on mine, I nodded to the envelope in his hand and then raised my brows in a silent question.

He cleared his throat again before he said, "I've been away the last few weeks and found this in my mailbox when I got home a few moments ago. It is addressed to you, but has my apartment number on it instead of yours."

I wanted to punch him. I used the light from the hallway outside of my apartment to look back inside and lock my eyes on the clock hanging on the wall behind me, it was twenty past three in the morning.

Couldn't he have just waited till morning before he delivered it to me?

The bloody eejit!

I sighed as I turned back to Mr. Pervert, who was back to looking at my body. I reached out and gripped the envelope and gave it a little tug until Mr. Pervert released it.

"Thanks, I appreciate you goin' out of your way to make sure I get me post." I faked a smile and then pulled the hand that now held the envelope away until it was tucked safely behind my door - along with the rest of my body - so Mr. Pervert couldn't see me anymore.

He blinked a few times and looked at my face, because it was now all that he could see.

"It was no problem at all, sweetheart."

Sweetheart? No!

I smiled and nodded my head as I inched my door closed. "Good night."

"Good-" I closed the door before he could finish his sentence.

I shook off my shivers then I relocked all of the locks and closed the bolt at the top of the door. I breathed a sigh of relief when I heard Mr. Pervert's footsteps trot back across the hall and into his own apartment where he closed the door behind him. I looked at the envelope in my hand and decided to open it because I was curious as to what was inside it. I couldn't see very well because the hallway was still dark but I knew it wasn't a bill, it didn't feel like the envelope bills came in, it was thicker. From what I had seen it looked nicer than a bill envelope. Fancier.

I headed into my kitchen that also doubled as my sitting room and flicked on the light. I tossed the envelope on the kitchen table and went to the counter drawers to look for my envelope cutter. I found it after only a second of looking, but had to put it down when I heard my phone ring from my bedroom. I furrowed my eyebrows in confusion.

Who the hell would be calling me at twenty past three in the morning?

"Aideen," I said out loud and headed in the direction of my bedroom.

Aideen Collins was my best friend. She was the closest thing I had to a sister and I loved her dearly, but she had her moments when she royally pissed me off. Ringing me at half past three in the morning was one of those moments.

When I got to the phone in my bedroom and pressed answer I said, "You'd better have a good reason for ringin' me at this hour Aideen Collins or I am goin' to kick seven shades of shite outta you!"

I heard a deep, rumbling chuckle.

"She *does* have a good reason, so you don't need to kick any shade of shit out of her," a male voice replied, it made me jump with fright because I wasn't expecting it.

"Who are you? Where is Aideen? Why do you have her phone?" I asked then gasped and shouted, "If you have hurt me friend in any way I'm goin' to fuck you up!"

The stranger laughed this time and said, "Is that a promise, kitten?"

Ex-fucking-cuse me?

"Where is Aideen? You better tell me right now or I'm gonna-"

ALEC

"Fuck me up? Yeah, I got that part," he chuckled again then before he could say anything else I heard a different male voice speak, "I asked you to ring the girl's friend, Alec. What the hell is taking so long?"

I mentally made a note of the name Alec in case I had to call the Guards.

"I'm talking to her friend, but I haven't been able to tell her the point of my call. She is too busy threatening to 'fuck me up' if I have hurt the girl," the lad who called me laughed.

I was mad and also scared as to where Aideen was and who these foreign guys were. I knew they weren't Irish or even English - their accents sounded too different - but I couldn't pinpoint where they were from because there was a lot of background noise. It sounded like music.

"Just tell her what I told you to say so she can get here already," the second lad said to the one who called me.

The lad who called me sighed and said, "Keela, I'm calling to let you know your friend Aiden was in a fight and we need you to come pick her up. She told me to call you."

"Her name is Aideen not Aiden, it's pronounced Ay-deen," I said then widened my eyes when I comprehended the rest of what he had just told me. I screamed, "Is she okay? What happened? Who hurt her?"

"Calm down, hellcat. She is fine, we just need you to come and collect her. I'll explain everything once you get here."

"Where is 'here'?" I snapped as I moved around my room pulling on my shoes. I grabbed my car keys from my bedside table as I held my phone to my ear with my shoulder.

"Playhouse Nightclub, it's right beside the Tallaght bypass-"

"I know where it is, I'll be there in five minutes," I said and hung up on him.

I gripped my phone and car keys in my hand as I closed my bedroom window. I told Storm to stay put, but it feel on deaf ears because he didn't move an inch or even wake up. I ran down my hallway and unlocked the locks and the bolt on my door then flung it open and sprung into the corridor. I closed my front door, locked it, then ran like a bat out of Hell down the hallway, down four flights of stairs and out into my apartment complex's car park. I sprinted towards my car and only realised I was in my nightdress when a cool breeze hit me and made me shiver.

"Fuck!" I snapped as I unlocked my car, got into it and started the engine.

I didn't think of changing my clothes, I just thought about getting my shoes on and then getting out to my car. I wasn't going back inside to change. I had to get to Aideen and make sure she was okay before changing clothes even became an option. It was okay though, I didn't show off any valuables. The nightdress was just a little short, it was black so I didn't have to worry that it was see through, at least I got lucky with that. The weather was good tonight as well, it was cool but not windy or raining. I would just have to hold the hem of my nightdress down when I got out of my car to keep it from rising up in case I had to run anywhere.

I pulled out of the car park and straight onto the main road and headed towards the nightclub. I was wide awake now, but the stinging in my eyes didn't go amiss. I had only been asleep for four hours before Mr. Pervert woke me up. Before that I hadn't slept in twenty-seven hours. I worked in my local supermarket, Super Value. I was broke and I needed all the hours I could get, so yesterday I worked an eleven hour shift and instead of going straight to bed when I got home, I dove straight into writing and pulled an all-nighter.

I have always had a passion for bringing the stories in my head to life on paper - or on a laptop screen. I only ever dabbled in silly little things here and there, never a full length novel. Luckily for me Aideen - literally - gave me the kick up the arse I needed and said I should just 'go for it' because I wouldn't know if my writing would be a success if I never put it out there. After my wake up call, which was three weeks ago, I knuckled down and started writing my very first book. Yesterday, even though I was shattered, I was completely in the zone and I just had to write. I had so much inside me for my story that if I didn't get it out of my head soon I was going to explode. So I wrote, wrote, and wrote some more. The lack of sleep and the stinging in my eyes from staring at my laptop was kicking my arse now though because I felt like death and I was pretty sure I looked the part too.

When I came to a red traffic light I pulled down my visor and looked in the little mirror and winced. Scratch that, saying I looked like death would have been kind. The sclera around my green eyes looked like a road map to Hell, that's how bloodshot they were. My fiery red hair was slightly greasy, and pulled up into a disastrous looking bun. I glanced down at my long bare white legs and shook my head.

Why did I have to be so tall?

If I were shorter, this nightdress would be longer and less exposing!

I angrily pushed my visor up when the traffic light changed to green and sped to the location of the nightclub Aideen was at with these men. I got there in less than five minutes because the green lights were with me, and there was little to no traffic on the roads thanks to the early hour. I turned into the nightclub car park entrance and looped around until I saw two huge males looking down at a small woman sitting down on the path a few meters away from the nightclub's entrance. It was Aideen, I just knew it. I parked my car across from them, jumped out, and slammed my door before I took off running towards Aideen.

When the sound of my feet hitting the pavement could be heard both men looked up at me, but didn't say anything as I reached them. Once I was next to them, I dropped down to my knees and pulled Aideen into a hug. I ignored the slight stinging in my knees from the concrete ground digging into my skin and held Aideen tightly.

"Are you okay? What happened?" I asked then pulled back from the hug so I could look at her.

Aideen looked back at me and I gasped at the sight that greeted me. She had a small cut over her eyebrow and her right jaw was swollen.

"Some bitch jumped on me," she grumbled.

"Who?" I snapped. "I'll fuckin' kill 'er!"

I was surprised that I sounded like I could actually follow through with my threat.

I was not a fighter.

I mean I could stand up for myself when needed, but I wasn't exactly Mike Tyson.

I have been in one fight in my entire life, and that was only because my younger cousin Micah punched me in the face when we were kids to see if my blood was blue. She told everyone I was an alien from outer space with blue blood and the only way to prove I was a human was to punch me and make my nose bleed. I agreed because I didn't think it would hurt that much - I was wrong, very wrong, because it hurt like hell.

After Micah punched me and red blood streamed from my nose, we confirmed I was in fact human. I jumped on her then because I was in so much pain and decided that she needed to be punished for hurting me. Instead of dishing out a hiding, I received a black eye and a chipped tooth. Micah kicked my arse and it was the first and only fight I have ever been in. Regardless of my inability to bring the pain, if anyone hurt Aideen or Storm, I would go Bruce Lee on those fuckers.

That was a cold hard fact.

Aideen smiled at me and pulled me in for another tight hug. "I know you would, but I just want to go home now. Can I stay with you?"

Was that a serious question?

I shook her. "Of course, you bloody eejit."

Aideen laughed and so did the males who stood over us. I don't know how, but I forgot they were next to us. I quickly stood up and pulled Aideen with me. She wasn't exactly drunk, just a little tipsy. I didn't have to balance her or anything, but I still kept a tight hold on her just in case.

"This is Alec," Aideen said and lazily pointed to the man on the right who was openly looking me up and down, "and Kane." I tightened my hold on Aideen when I looked at Kane, the man on the left. He was just as tall and as muscular as the arsehole who was looking at my body, but he was scary looking. He had a large scar that curved around the left side of his mouth and some claw like scars going from his right temple and down through his eyebrow leaving gaps in the hairs like they were styled that way.

"Hi," I said lowly and avoided direct eye contact.

"Kane came to me rescue when Alec's girlfriend hit me," Aideen said and smiled at Kane, who smiled right back at her.

"She was my lay from last week, not my girlfriend... and I apologised for her actions," Alec said with a sigh.

I ignored Alec, the eejit who just spoke and looked at Kane when he smiled and felt myself instantly become relaxed. He didn't look scary when he smiled like that. I frowned though when the rest of what Aideen said settled in my brain. Before I knew it I let go of Aideen and shoved Alec in the chest as hard as I could. He wasn't expecting it so when I shoved him he lost his balance and fell back onto his arse with a grunt.

"That is for your bird hurtin' me friend and if I find out who the slut is I'm gonna fuckin' kill 'er!" I bellowed.

Aideen pulled me back by the arm and begged me to stop while Alec looked up at me with wide eyes before he looked to Kane, who stared down at him also with wide eyes and his mouth agape. A few seconds passed until they both burst out laughing like what just happened was the funniest thing ever. I saw red and tried to go for Alec again, but Aideen moved herself in front of me and pushed me back by the shoulders.

"I told you bro, she is a fucking hellcat!" Alec cackled as he gripped onto Kane's outstretched hand and was helped to his feet.

Kane continued to laugh as he shook his head. "I wish the twins had seen that, Dominic would have helped her hit you while Damien recorded it."

I had no idea what or whom they were talking about, but I pointed my finger dangerously over Aideen's shoulder at Alec and snarled at him.

"Keep laughin' pretty boy and I'll scratch up that face of yours!" I warned.

Alec stepped forward, a grin tugged at his mouth. "I'm finding myself highly attracted to you right now. Would you like to come home with me since you're already dressed for bed?"

I dropped my jaw in shock, and so did Aideen who spun around and shoved him in the chest, but didn't manage to knock him to the ground. "Knock it off! I appreciate you both helpin' me, but I won't have you treatin' me friend like she is one of your old clients, Alec. She is a good girl!"

Clients?

What the hell did *that* mean?

Alec grinned at Aideen before he flicked his eyes to me. "Oh, I'm bettin' there is a bad girl deep inside her somewhere. I'll just have to use my fingers, mouth, and cock to bring her out to play."

What. The. Fuck?

"Who the hell do you think you are?" I snapped.

He grinned and gave me a wink as he said, "Alec Slater, your next - or only - great fuck."

Was he for real?

"You're about to be Alec Slater - murder victim - if you don't shut that hole in your face!"

Kane cracked up with laughter as he reached for Aideen's arm and pulled her into him and away from me. "Please, don't interfere. I've never seen a female, besides Bronagh, backtalk him like this before," he said to Aideen then brushed her blonde hair out of her eyes. The action caused her to melt into a puddle by the way she sagged into him.

I rolled my eyes at her then looked at Alec who had inched

closer to me before I growled, "Try touchin' me, and you won't ever be able to have kids. I'm warnin' you."

Alec grinned and folded his arms across his board chest; it caused all his muscles that I could see to contract and tense. He settled on staying put, but openly raked his eyes over my body, mainly my legs, and it made me feel very uncomfortable.

"Stop lookin' at me you dirty bastard!" I growled.

Alec flicked his eyes up to me. "Why would you come outside dressed like *that* if you didn't want people to look at you?" he asked.

I clenched my hands into fists and took a step towards him. I had to tilt my head back a little bit because he was a lot taller than my five foot eight inches and when I realised that fact I felt intimidated, but I was not ready to back down.

"I came outside dressed in me nightdress because me friend needed me and gettin' dressed didn't cross me mind when you rang me, you bloody eejit."

He flashed his teeth at me when he smiled. "You sound like my bro's girl, she calls me an eejit a lot too."

I looked him up and down, my lip curled in disgust. "She must be kind 'cause there are a lot of words that would suit you much better. Batty boy would be two of them," I snarled then turned in Aideen's direction and found her kissing Kane. Not just smooching, she was completely necking with him. I walked forward, grabbed her arm and tugged her not so gently next to me.

When she was next to me I squeezed her arm and snarled, "Do you not remember the stranger danger film we watched when we were in school?"

Aideen gave me an are-you-serious look before she snickered and shook her head. "They aren't dangerous. Kane *saved* me from danger."

I pointed over my shoulder. "Yeah, and batty boy's bird *put* you in danger so let's go."

"I get the feeling that you're calling me gay," Alec said from behind me.

I set my jaw and continued to tug on Aideen as she frowned over my shoulder and said, "She is callin' you gay, but she doesn't mean it as an insult or anythin'. She's not homophobic, she just said it because she hoped it would piss you off."

Seriously?

"You aren't supposed to tell him that, Ado!" I snapped.

"Ado? I like that nickname," Kane's voice purred from my right.

He pronounced Ado so proper.

Ay-doh.

I pushed Aideen behind me, ignoring her complaints as I fixed Kane with a glare that wavered the longer I looked at him. "Listen, thanks for helpin' me friend after she got hurt, but she isn't goin' to thank you with some personal pole dancin' so give the flirtin' a rest."

Kane raised his eyebrows as he looked over my shoulder and asked Aideen, "You're a stripper?"

"No, I am a teacher," Aideen scoffed. "No pole dancin' means no shaggin'."

Kane laughed then. "Your friend is *banning* you from having sex with me?"

"Yes," Aideen and I said in unison.

"And you're going along with it?" Alec asked Aideen as he rounded on us and leaned back against the same car Kane was leaning on.

They looked like a pair of fitness models and noticing that pissed me off.

"Yeah," Aideen sighed. "She is pretty big on no sex with strangers and... so am I."

Kane's eyes bore into Aideen's and then he smiled as he said, "Pity."

"Uh huh," Aideen agreed with a sad sigh.

I rolled my eyes and said, "I'll stop off at the late night shop on the way home and buy you some batteries for your vibrator to get you through the night. You will be grand."

"Keela!" Aideen gasped and smacked my arse, it made me yelp and jump.

Both of the lads laughed at what I said and shook their heads as they continued to look at us. I got annoyed and said to Aideen, "Maybe they could apply to Perverts 'R Us, they fit the bill with those stares."

Aideen laughed and smacked my arse again.

"Excuse me?" Alec said.

Aideen was snickering as she said, "Keela's neighbour, Mr. Doyle, is a man who stares a lot so she named him Mr. Pervert and imagined him bein' the CEO of a company called Perverts 'R Us."

I narrowed my eyes when the two hyenas started laughing again - they seemed to do that a lot.

I angrily reached behind me and grabbed Aideen. "We're leavin'. I have to go home to Storm."

"Storm?" Alec questioned.

"Storm is her-"

"Boyfriend." I smiled as I cut Aideen off and gave her a go-along-with-me look. She looked back at me and I could see the amusement in her eyes as she nodded her head and looked back at Alec.

"Storm is pretty protective of her," she said.

Alex cocked an eyebrow. "If he is so protective then how come he let you come out here alone while dressed like *that*?"

He made it sound like my nightdress was skimpy!

I snarled and made a move forward to set him straight but Aideen put herself between Alec and myself before saying, "Storm is very hard to rouse durin' the night. He probably didn't even hear her leave, but he is still a great... lad."

I inwardly snorted.

"Yeah, and he will kick your arse for even suggestin' we have sex!" I stated.

Alec popped his head around Aideen and grinned at me. "I'm a lover, not a fighter."

Good news!

"You better back off then because one more crude comment and *I* will fuck you up, never mind Storm!" I snarled.

Alec bit down on his bottom lip and grinned at me, I knew he was thinking crude things so I glared at him which made Kane snort.

"Can we keep her? I like hearing someone put you in your place, the fact that she is a female is even better. You don't affect her bro, you're losing your touch." Kane chuckled and playfully shoved Alec when he settled back beside him on the car they were leaning on.

Alex continued to grin at me as he spoke to Kane, "It's still early, don't shoot me down so quickly, bro."

"I'll fuckin' shoot you," I murmured making Aideen snort as she reached for my hand.

"This has been... interestin'. However, Keela is right, we better get goin'."

"Thank you, Jesus," I cheered making Kane snicker before looking to Aideen.

He grinned at her and said, "I guess I'll see you around, Ado."

I narrowed my eyes at him. "I'm the only one allowed to call her Ado."

Kane flicked his eyes to me and smiled. "I like you."

I flushed but forced myself to stand up straight as I said, "Well, I don't like you or your pervy friend-"

"Brother. I'm his pervy *brother*." Alec cut me off making Aideen snicker.

I shoved her and glared at Alec before I looked back to Kane, who still looked at me with an amused expression. I cleared my throat and said, "I don't like you or your pervy *brother*. You're both clearly nothin' but trouble if the people you pal around with attack girls for no reason. You're both very fuckin' rude as well!"

I turned and grabbed Aideen's hand and took off walking away from the brothers and in the direction of my car.

"What? No goodbye kiss? *Now* who is being rude!" Alec's voice called out after us making Aideen cackle.

I grunted. "Fuck you!" I shouted without turning around.

"Name the time and place, kitten," Alec called back which caused Aideen to break out into a full on laugh.

Kitten?

I fumed in silence as I all but hauled Aideen across the dark car park and into my car. "Name the time and place, kitten," I mimicked Alec's voice which caused Aideen to laugh harder as she buckled her seat belt.

I buckled my own seat belt then started up my car. I pulled out of the space I was in and quickly drove out of the car park. I don't think I calmed down enough to breathe normally until we were on the Tallaght Bypass.

"Can you believe him? What a fuckin' dick!" I spat.

Aideen snorted. "I found that entire conversation hilarious."

I shook my head. "Well you shouldn't have. Look at your face, Aideen!"

Aideen sighed. "I know, but it honestly wasn't their fault. We were just havin' a good time when out of nowhere this girl jumped on me."

I gripped my steering wheel so tight that my knuckles turned white.

"Why were you even with them?" I spat.

I wasn't angry with her, I was just angry that she got hurt by some bitch.

"I wasn't even with them. Tonight was the first time I met them. I was out with Branna. Tonight was a small twenty-first birthday party for Bronagh. Branna, Ryder, Nico, and Bronagh just left. I was sat with Kane and Alec when a drunk girl came over and accused me of bein' Alec's latest shag. Alec laughed at the girl but didn't deny it so she jumped on me."

I grunted.

Branna Murphy was Aideen's friend and has been her friend since they were in preschool. Aideen is a few years older than me so she has known Branna longer than she has known me. I'm a grown woman, I'm not at all jealous of their friendship. Branna was cool after all. Her sister Bronagh was great as well, I was two years older than Bronagh, who turned twenty-one today. I had been invited to go out with everyone tonight, Aideen hounded me to go, but my body was beat, so I declined the invitation.

My thoughts calmed me down enough for me to loosen my white-knuckle grip on the steering wheel but I still shook with anger. "You should have let me punch 'em."

Aideen chuckled then lifted her hand to cradle her face. "You would have broken your hand! Did you see how big he was?"

I grunted and nodded my head. "His brother was even more muscular. Do they live at the gym or somethin'?"

Aideen snickered. "Branna said they have a gym in her house. 'Member I told you she moved in with Ryder and the oldest twin, Nico, moved in with her sister?"

I nodded my head.

"Branna didn't just move in with Ryder, she moved in with Alec and Kane as well. She said there is a gym room where the sittin' room should be and that they all work out a lot. You should see Nico; he's twenty-one and the lad is ripped. He is a fighter or somethin'."

I glanced at her wide-eyed. "Why the hell are you hangin' around walkin' tanks, Aideen?"

Aideen burst into a fit of giggles that made me grin even though I was mad.

"They are lovely - big and scary - but lovely."

I shivered when I pictured Kane's face, calling him lovely was not a word that I would use to describe him.

"How do you think Kane got those scars on his face? They are kind of severe."

Aideen sighed. "I've no idea what happened to him but he is

still gorgeous!"

"You like his accent as well, right?" I questioned.

Aideen purred, "Oh my God. I could listen to him talk all day! He could make me wet by just sayin' 'Hello'!"

I rolled my eyes. "I swear you think with your dick."

Aideen cackled. "You mean vagina?"

"Yeah, I mean vagina but sayin' dick sounds better."

Aideen continued to laugh then hissed a little and covered her face with her hands. I glanced at her every so often during the five minute drive back to my apartment complex. I parked in my usual spot, then Aideen and myself got out of the car. After I locked it we quickly scurried across the car park and into my apartment building. We took the stairs two at a time until we got to the fifth floor where my apartment was located. I opened my hall door with lightening like speed because I didn't want to be caught by Mr. Pervert again dressed in just my nightdress.

Luckily, we got inside with no one seeing us. Aideen and I then went into the bathroom where I got out my first aid kit while she pulled her dress off then pulled down her underwear and sat on the toilet.

I was opening an antiseptic packet when I glanced up at her through the mirror and snorted, "Do you reckon lads do this?"

Aideen opened her eyes and lazily smiled at me as she said, "Willingly go to the toilet with another lad in the room? Nah, they would call each other gay."

I chuckled and looked back down to the first aid kit while Aideen finished up on the toilet. I turned when the toilet flushed and waited for her to wash her hands before I began cleaning her face up. She was four inches shorter than me now that her heels were off, so it made holding her head still a lot easier.

"Ow!" Aideen suddenly hollered which earned a bark from my bedroom.

"Go back asleep you fat shite!" Aideen shouted when I swiped the antiseptic wipe over a small cut above her eye.

I hissed at her, "Leave him alone, he isn't fat. He just has a thick coat!"

Aideen laughed through her hissing. "Yeah, a thick coat of blubber."

I gave her a firm look. "Don't slag me baby when I'm cleanin' you up. Me finger might slip and jam into your eye."

Aideen gave me a wary look and closed her mouth which made me inwardly grin as I finished cleaning up her face. When I was finished, she went into my bedroom to get some of my pyjamas to wear while I went into the kitchen to get a glass of water. I turned on the kitchen light then moved to the sink and filled up a glass and quickly gulped down the water. I looked to my left and noticed the envelope Mr. Pervert gave to me earlier, still unopened on my kitchen table.

"Storm, get off the bed... or at least move over!" Aideen's voice shouted from my bedroom.

I roughly rubbed the back of my neck and sighed. I glanced at the envelope once more before I shook my head and walked over to the kitchen light switch and flipped it off. I turned and walked towards the sounds of growling and shouting coming from my bedroom and decided that dealing with Storm and Aideen was enough to deal with for one night.

Whatever was in that envelope could wait until morning.

CHAPTER TWO

I woke up and felt like I had the mother of all hangovers even though I hadn't touched a drop of alcohol the night before. It was a lack of sleep hangover that I would nurse throughout the day and I instantly felt like a grump because of it. I was never what someone would call a morning person, but waking up with a headache sealed the deal that I would be a grouch.

I whined when I heard shouting coming from the kitchen followed by barking that didn't help the pounding that had taken up residence in my head.

It was too early for this shite.

"Those bloody two," I grumbled as I kicked the bed covers from my body.

I sat upright and gently shook my head to try and clear it then stood up and stretched until my back cracked. I dragged my feet as I walked out of my room, down the hall and into the kitchen. I crossed my arms over my chest and yawned as my tummy rumbled from the delicious smell of a fry up being cooked. You cannot beat sausages, rashers, eggs, and pudding for breakfast on the weekend, there was nothing better. I leaned my shoulder against the kitchen wall and watched the scene before me with mild amusement.

"Listen to me you big fat baby, these rashers are mine and Keela's. You aren't allowed to have any!"

Yes, Aideen was in a battle of words - sort of - with Storm.

Storm growled at Aideen and stepped closer to her; she had a butter knife in her hand and pointed it directly at him. "Try it and I'm warnin' you, I'll be fryin' dog meat!"

I laughed which got both Aideen's and Storm's attention. Storm forgot about Aideen when he heard me, this was apparent when he jumped and barked as he came running in my direction. I audibly grunted as he collided with my legs then laughed when he stood up and placed his front paws on my shoulders and licked my face. He was a big dog, when he was stood up on his back legs he was the same height as me.

"Down, good boy." I chuckled when he dropped to all fours and continued to rub his head against my leg.

I looked up at Aideen, who was glaring at Storm. "I hate him."

I grinned. "I think he reciprocates that feelin' wholeheartedly."

Aideen grinned then turned and flipped the rashers in the frying pan and added some fat sausages.

My mouthed watered.

"What were you both fightin' for *this* time?" I asked after I swallowed down the saliva in my mouth.

Aideen huffed. "He keeps tryin' to jump up and grab the food when I'm not lookin'. He is a greedy, fat fucker."

I looked down at Storm and rubbed his head. "Sticks and stones baby boy, sticks and stones."

Aideen snickered and shook her head at me. I moved over to her and leaned in close to her so I could study her face. She had a bruise on her cheekbone, and her lower lip was bruised and swollen as well.

I frowned. "I hope the bitch that did this gets the runs while wearing white."

Aideen burst out laughing, and it made me grin.

"Me too." She chuckled as she continued to cook our breakfast.

I washed my hands in the sink, dried them and yawned as I moved over to the kitchen table. I rubbed my eyes and slightly shook my head at all the magazines that were spread out all over the table. Aideen had a thing about magazines; she couldn't just read one at a time, she had to have at least ten in front of her to choose from.

ALEC

"You do know that you can download magazines directly onto to the Kindle I bought you right?" I murmured.

I scratched the back of my head as I looked over the magazine covers deciding on which one to read myself.

"I know, but I like holdin' them in me hands when I read," Aideen replied as she switched off the cooker and dished up our food.

I looked at her and glared at how fresh and alert she was.

"It's a little bit weird that you don't get hangovers," I said as she placed my plate in front of me.

Aideen sat down across from me and shrugged. "I'm just lucky, I guess."

I nodded and reached for the ketchup that was currently placed on top of the magazine that Aideen was looking down at. I opened the bottle and poured a decent amount of sauce onto my plate then got up and went to the bread bin.

"How is your diet goin'?" Aideen then asked with a grin before she popped a piece of pudding into her mouth.

I glared at her as I sat back down. "This is my cheat meal, I only have one a week so leave me alone."

Aideen held her hands up. "No judgment," she said around the food in her mouth.

"You're a knacker!" I snapped.

Aideen chuckled as she swallowed down her food. "Sorry."

She wasn't sorry in the slightest.

I grimaced in disgust. "You were raised by wild dogs."

Aideen grinned. "It not *my* fault me ma died givin' birth to me brother and left me with three older brothers, a little brother, and a father that are all cavemen."

I snorted. "Don't play the me-ma-died-givin'-birth card, you won't get any sympathy from me. You had a brilliant upbringin', a lot better than mine and *my* ma is alive and well."

"Unfortunately," Aideen murmured making me exhale a large breath.

Aideen sighed then and said, "I'm sorry Kay, that was mean. I know she is your ma, but God, I want to smack her sometimes for the way she treats you."

I shrugged my shoulders. "Don't think about her. Just do what I do and pretend that she and me crazy family don't exist."

Aideen snorted as I popped some pudding into my mouth.

"Not likely, your uncle is the reason why I masturbate."

I began to choke on the pudding in my mouth so Aideen jumped up and rushed to my side. She whacked me on the back three times, and the force of her pounding caused my ribs to rattle. The food came up from my throat and landed on my plate in front of me.

"I'm fine," I retched.

I closed my eyes and forced myself not to have a coughing fit, the rest of the food that I had just eaten would be all over the floor in seconds if that happened.

"Are you okay?" Aideen asked, her voice high pitched and panicked.

I didn't reply to her. I focused and took breaths in through my nose and out through my mouth. After a few seconds I blinked my eyes open and nodded my head at Aideen. "I'm fine," I rasped then reached for the glass of juice Aideen filled for me to have with my breakfast.

After another minute passed I got up from my chair, moved to the sink and filled up a fresh glass with water then downed it in one swallow.

"I'm sorry, I didn't mean to almost kill you," Aideen said from behind me.

I coughed a little then turned to face her, I folded my arms across my chest and raised my eyebrows at her. "Tellin' me you masturbate over me uncle while I'm eatin' isn't goin' to cause anythin' other than death, Ado."

Aideen had a ghost of a smile on her face as she scrubbed her face with her hands. "He *is* hot though, I can't help it."

I shivered. "Brandon is me uncle, me blood... stop it."

Aideen laughed. "It's a pity he is your uncle, I never get to see him. Can you imagine if he was *your* da and not Micah's?"

I nodded my head and said, "Yeah, I can, I'd be a spoilt bitch who threatens everyone with daddy."

Aideen shrugged. "If your da was here and he was the boss man of a dangerous organisation you would probably boast about it as well."

I snorted. "Not likely, I was told to never to pay any attention to anythin' I heard when I went to Micah's house and Micah was told the same thing. To this day I don't know what me uncle is involved with and I'd like to keep it that way. He is me favourite family member, knowin' he does bad stuff would mar that. I'm more than happy with bein' in the dark, besides it's probably nothin' like you think.."

Aideen stretched and said, "Yeah, I get that but if Micah *does* threaten everyone with her da when she stumbles into trouble, he doesn't follow through with her threats. I remember Gavin tellin' me Micah battered Bronagh Murphy a few years ago outside school and when her fella, Nico, warned her off and knocked Jason around nothin' happened to him by Brandon's hand because he is still walkin' around."

I felt my stomach lurch at the mention of his name.

Jason Bane was a prick and his last name represented him completely because he was the bane of my existence. He was not only a disgusting human being but he was a scumbag who used his looks and charm to get what he wanted in life. For a time, I was something he wanted. I closed my eyes as the memory of our first encounter flooded my mind.

"Is this seat taken?"

I looked up at the lad who spoke to me and shook my head but didn't speak. He was a man is his early twenties, he was tall - taller than my five foot eight. His hair was jet black, his eyes were dark blue and his lips were plump and the colour of a rose. He wasn't even pale, he actually had a slight tan. I was quite possibly staring at the hottest person I have ever seen in my entire life.

"What's your name, gorgeous?" the hot stranger asked me.

I looked over my shoulder to see if there was some sort of model sitting behind me that he could be talking to. When I spotted no one around me I settled on the fact that he was in fact talking to me.

I cleared my throat. "Um, Keela... Keela Daley."

The stranger smiled. "Nice to meet you Keela Daley, I'm Jason Bane."

I felt myself flush when he stuck his hand out in my direction. I lifted my hand and placed it in his. Before I could shake his hand he lifted mine to his mouth and placed a light kiss on my knuckles.

Oh... My... God!

"It's nice to me you too," I said, my voice hesitant.

Jason smiled at me. "So tell me, what is a gorgeous girl like you doin' sittin' all alone at a bar on a Friday night?"

I could still feel the flush in my cheeks but I forced myself to smile and not appear as awkward and as nervous as I felt.

"I'm waiting' on me friend, she is meetin' me here soon."

Jason grinned at me. "In that case I'll just have to stick around and keep you company until she arrives."

I felt my belly flutter with butterflies.

I licked my lips and said, "Oh, that's okay. You don't have to sit here with me."

"But I want too."

I widened my eyes. "You do?"

He did?

"I do," Jason said and gave me a firm nod.

Oh, wow.

"Um, okay then." I smiled.

He signaled for the bartender then. "A pint of Bud for me please, and for the lady..."

Jason looked from the bartender to me and my heart jumped, he was buying me a drink! No one has ever bought me a drink before.

"Vodka and coke, please," I said a little breathless.

Jason turned back to the bartender and asked, "You get that, man?"

The bartender nodded then went about making our drinks.

"Thanks for the drink." I smiled when Jason turned back to me.

Jason waved me off. "Don't give it another thought."

I did just that and said, "So, what brought you here tonight?"

Jason jammed his thumb over his shoulder and I followed his thumb to a group of lads seated across the pub. "Me and the lads decided to come here for a few pints before we headed out to a club. I spotted you at the bar and had to come say hey in case I never got the chance again. It's not everyday someone as gorgeous as you crosses paths with someone like me after all."

What?

Seriously, what?

"Are you jokin'?" I blurted.

Jason raised his eyebrows. "No, why?"

I shook my head. "Because you're gorgeous."

I wanted to die when a huge smile almost spilt Jason's face in two. "I'm glad you said that because I think you're gorgeous, too."

I was starting to sweat, that's how flushed I was.

Jason chuckled at me and changed the subject to more mundane things and after a while a lad from his group of friends came over and nudged him. "We're headin' off, man. You comin'?"

Jason kept his eyes locked with mine as he said, "Nah, man. I'm good here."

His friend chuckled and winked at me. "Yeah, I thought you might say that. See you tomorrow. Bye, gorgeous."

Two males called me gorgeous tonight!

Two!

"You don't have to stay here with me. I'm sure me friend will be along-"

"I want to stay here with you and I'm kind of hopin' your friend doesn't show up. I want to keep you all to myself."

Oh, my God.

As if on cue my phone rang and because I didn't have an inkling of what to say back to Jason I quickly got my phone from my bag and answered it.

"Where are you?" I asked Aideen when I answered.

"I'm leavin' in five minutes. I got stuck with runnin' night detention at the school," Aideen replied in a huff.

"Take your time, I've got company," I said making Jason grin as he drank the remainder of his pint.

"Male or female?" Aideen questioned.

"Male."

"Can he hear what you're sayin'?"

"Yes," I replied then held up one finger to Jason indicating I would be only a minute longer on the phone, he nodded and smiled at me.

"Is he hot?"

I inwardly rolled my eyes at the question but said, "Like you wouldn't believe."

Aideen screamed so loud that I pulled my phone away from my ear with a hiss. "I'm not comin', you stay with him and have fun. You hear me, Keela? Fun!"

I was mortified, the entire bloody pub could hear her.

"What do you mean you aren't comin'?"

Jason smiled and he leaned forward and brushed his finger over my exposed knee. I tensed and locked eyes with him, my breath quickened and my pulse spiked.

"Go have fun! Call me if you need me!" With that said Aideen hung up. I wanted to crawl through my phone and slap Aideen silly, Jason could be a murderer for all she knows!

I looked away from Jason and to my phone with a frown. "Me friend isn't comin'"

Jason grinned at me. "Don't worry, I'll look after you."

I smiled at his flirting and said, "How do I know you're capable to look after me?"

I gasped as the stool I was seated on was suddenly yanked towards Jason, his right hand moved to my waist and his face was a hair's breadth away from mine.

"I'm more than qualified for the job," he said then flicked his *tongue over my bottom lip. "Trust me."*

I did trust him and trusting that arsehole was the biggest mistake of my life. I frowned at my thoughts and Aideen noticed, she sighed and rubbed her bruised cheeked.

"I'm sorry Kay, I shouldn't have mentioned Micah or him. I forgot."

I shrugged. "Don't be sorry. I'm goin' to have to get used to hearin' his name, he *is* marryin' Micah after all."

Aideen scoffed. "I can't believe he used you to get back at Micah when they broke up and now they are gettin' married. I hate the fuckin' pair of them."

"I hate them too."

Aideen shook off her anger and retook her seat at the table but she shot back up when she looked at her plate. I laughed when I realised what had just happened.

"You bastard! You fat, greedy bastard!" Aideen bellowed as she searched the room for Storm.

I glanced at the table and shook my head, both mine and Aideen's plates were cleared of food and Aideen was on a mission to wring Storm's neck. He knew that as well because he was hiding from her.

"Where are you?" Aideen hollered making me burst out laughing.

Storm was a big dog, a really big dog, so the fact that he could hide in my tiny apartment cracked me up. I laughed even harder when I heard my bedroom door close. Aideen legged it from the kitchen and ran down the hallway to my bedroom door. I walked to the room after her and continued to laugh.

"I can't believe you ate our breakfast! You're a greedy fucker of a dog!" Aideen hollered to Storm who was now lying on my bed.

He raised his ears at Aideen's shouting but other than that he did absolutely nothing, and it only served to make Aideen even more furious because of it.

"I fuckin' hate him! He is literally like a man, a fat useless man."

Storm farted in response and it had Aideen and myself fleeing my room - me still in a fit of laughter and Aideen bursting with anger.

"Why do you baby him so much? He is a pathetic dog Keela, he is literally good for *nothin'*!"

I shrugged. "He doesn't have to have a purpose in order for me to have him, Ado."

Aideen threw her hands up in the air. "You got him as a *guard dog*."

I smiled. "He guards his food, that's worth somethin'... right?"

Aideen stomped into the sitting room and angrily sat on the settee. "You're unbelievable!"

I chuckled as I fell onto the chair next to her. "You still love me though... right?"

Aideen shrugged. "I'm fifty-fifty right now."

I nudged her and said, "Bitch."

Aideen snorted and relaxed into the chair. "So... last night was crazy, huh?"

Alec Slater's smug face flashed in my mind and I tensed.

"Yeah, crazy."

Aideen cleared her throat and said, "I can't believe you physically assaulted someone."

I turned my head and gaped at her. "What?"

Aideen shrugged. "You pushed Alec to the ground. He is like six foot somethin'. He's really tall, even compared to you, which is sayin' somethin' so I don't know how you managed to get him on the ground."

I held up a finger and said, "First of all, I pushed him, I didn't pound on him which doesn't count as physical assault." I popped up a second finger. "Secondly, I caught him by surprise which is why he fell so easily, he wasn't expectin' it." I stuck up a third finger. "And lastly, I did it to defend you. His misses did that to your face!"

Aideen reached up and touched her face, hissing a little before

ALEC

she lowered her hand. "She was an old shag of his, not his misses."

I huffed. "Same difference, she was still linked to him."

Aideen sighed. "They did help me though, Kay... Kane especially."

I groaned. "Stop it. Don't be thinkin' he is some kind of hero, the lad looks like trouble."

Aideen frowned at me. "That's very judgemental, Keela, just because he has scars means he is trouble?"

I opened my mouth but closed it.

Aideen smiled at me so I glared at her making her laugh. "I know you're just angry because I got hurt. I love you for it but there is no need to be angry at the Slater brothers for it."

I grunted. "Okay, fine, I won't be angry at them for that but I *will* be angry at Alec for the things he said to me."

Aideen nodded her head. "I don't blame you, he was crude and a complete dickhead."

I raised my hands. "Thank you!"

Aideen laughed then. "I can't believe how rowdy you got. I have never seen you act like that before, you're usually a little pushover."

I frowned and slumped my shoulders a little. "I am with me family because it's easier to just be quiet around them, but you got hurt and I got mad... I couldn't help it. Besides, it's not like I murdered anyone."

Aideen grinned. "You threatened it enough."

I glared at her. "Shut it."

She cackled a little making me grin. I yawned and then stretched before looking at the kitchen table. I stood up and moved into the kitchen. Aideen cleared off the table and put the delph in the sink, she washed them then left them on the draining board to dry.

I focused on the kitchen table and began to stack up the magazines. When they were in a pile I looked at the table and stopped for a second. I picked up the envelope that Mr. Pervert dropped off last night and sighed as I turned it over and ripped it open, not caring about the contents inside.

I turned the card in my hand over when I pulled it from the envelope. I opened the pretty cover and read the first line. I dropped the card on the table and stepped back.

"Oh my God!" I said, starring down at the table.

"What?" Aideen asked as she came into the kitchen, I pointed at the card without looking away from it.

She moved around the table, picked up the card and read it. "No fuckin' way!"

I nodded my head.

"They invited you to their *weddin*? The evil fuckin' bastards!" Aideen growled.

I felt a little dizzy so I pulled out a chair from my kitchen table and sat down before I leaned my head forward and placed it on the table and let the tears come. "Why would they do this to me?"

"Because they are evil, pure fuckin' evil!"

I cried hard when Aideen began to read out loud the wedding invitation to Micah's and Jason's wedding. She stopped midway, ripped the invite up, got her lighter from her purse and lit it on fire. I sat up straight and stared at her when she walked to the sink, dropped the burning innovation into the sink then poured water on it. The fire alarm went off from the smoke so Aideen stood up on a chair, pulled the battery out of the alarm on the ceiling then got down and opened the windows in the apartment to air it out.

I didn't move as she did all this, I could only sit there and cry.

"I still can't believe I didn't recognise Jason, I'm so stupid. When he pulled me at the pub last year I thought he really liked me. He was with me for six weeks just to get back at Micah for cheatin' on him. That bastard made me fall for him and he knew it!"

Aideen moved in front of me and kneeled down. "You had never seen Jason in person, you don't go round to Micah's house at all. The most you had seen is pictures of him on Facebook. He dyed his hair black and hit the gym since his school year ended. He isn't the same person that's on his profile picture, he looks very different so this is not your fault. He played you, that fucker took your virginity for fuck's sake!"

I sobbed as I leaned forward and wrapped my arms around Aideen and squeezed.

"We will just pretend you never got that invite, okay? We'll be here all day, I can arrange all my course work for the students who are attendin' summer school this year and you can write some more of your book. What do you say?"

I groaned and pulled back from our hug. "I can't even think about writin' at the moment. I just want to go to bed and not get up ever again."

When Aideen slapped me across the face, it me took a few seconds for the pain and realisation of what she did to hit me. "What was *that* for?" I snapped and lifted my hand to my now throbbing cheek.

"For gettin' yourself into a slump over a prick who does *not* deserve it!" Aideen stated.

I frowned and continued to rub my cheek as I said, "Sorry."

"Don't be sorry, not for *anythin'*. Okay?"

I nodded my head and hugged Aideen again and when we separated I said, "I have to go to the weddin'. You know me ma will come round here and pester me for life if I don't. If I go and sit down in the back of the church and reception she won't care."

Aideen growled, "I hate your ma."

I smiled making Aideen chuckle.

I sighed. "I just wish I didn't have to go single, that will only make the entire day worse."

"The entire week actually. The weddin' is in the Bahamas and you leave in the next few days."

"What?" I screeched.

Aideen nodded. "That's what the invitation said."

"Fuck!" I groaned and hung my head.

We were silent for a moment until Aideen dramatically gasped which made me jump.

"What?" I asked.

She looked at me and said, "You're goin' to kill me, but I have a solution for you so you won't be attendin' the weddin' as a single woman."

I raised my eyebrows at her. "Yeah, what's that then?"

"Not that, more like *who*?"

I furrowed my eyebrows. "*Who* then?"

Aideen smirked as she said, "Alec Slater."

CHAPTER THREE

"What about Alec Slater?" I asked Aideen with my eyebrows raised.

Aideen gave me an are-you-serious look then sighed. "He could be your date to Jason's and Micah's weddin'. *Duh*!"

For real?

I burst out laughing. "Yeah, *right*!"

Aideen shoved my shoulder. "I'm dead serious, this is what he does. Well, not *exactly* what he does but it's close enough."

I felt my eyes roll with confusion. "Ado, I've *no* clue what you're talkin' about."

Aideen pinched the bridge of her nose and blew out a long breath before she focused on me and said in a low voice, "Alec is a male escort, Keela."

I held Aideen's stare for a few seconds before I cracked up laughing again. Aideen grunted and slapped at my arms to get me to stop laughing, and after a minute or so it worked.

"I'm not jokin'!" Aideen bellowed.

I was still chuckling a little as I said, "I don't believe you."

Aideen folded her arms across her chest. "Keela, I swear on me life that I'm *not* jokin' with you. I'm dead serious. Alec *is* a male escort."

My shoulders stopped moving and my chuckles slowed until no more sounds of laughter came from my mouth. I blinked as I looked at Aideen, her face didn't hold any hint of a smile like she was playing with me and that freaked me out more than a little.

"You're serious?" I asked my voice a whisper.

Aideen nodded. "Yes, I didn't believe at first because Branna told me one night when she was drunk, but when I said it to her the next day she flipped out and made me promise never to tell anyone."

I gestured between Aideen and myself. "What's this then?"

Aideen snorted and waved me off. "You're me best friend, so you don't count."

That's Aideen's logic for you on a plate.

I chewed on my bottom lip as I tilted my head back and looked up at the ceiling. "Okay, I believe you, but I don't see how Alec bein' an escort helps me. I was in his presence for only five minutes and I already can't stand him. He is dickhead."

Aideen laughed. "So? Alec is gorgeous, and havin' someone like him on your arm will be the ultimate fuck you to Jason and Micah. Jason *hates* Dominic Slater, so chances are that he hates his brothers as well. Come on Keela, just think about how pissed he will be that you're with a Slater at *his* weddin'."

I could picture Jason's face twisted in anger and it brought a smile to my face.

"Okay, I agree that it *would* be great to rub someone Jason hates in his face, but I don't think Alec will agree to it. I mean, I pushed him to the ground and called him a batty boy."

Aideen waggled her eyebrows at me. "There is only one way to find out if he will be your date."

"Which is what?"

Aideen winked. "You ask him."

I sat up straight. "You want me to ask him to be me date to me cousin's weddin' after what I said and *did* to him last night?"

"Yes," Aideen replied instantly.

She was unreal!

I groaned. "And if I say no?"

Aideen shrugged. "I'll ring and ask him for you."

The evil cow!

I gasped. "You wouldn't dare!"

Aideen devilishly smirked. "Try me, Kay."

I slightly whimpered, "I hate you."

"I love you, too."

I closed my eyes and thought this over.

Did I like what I knew of Alec Slater so far?

No.

Did I want to be around him for a week if he accepted an offer to come to the Bahamas as my date to Micah's and Jason's wedding?

Hell no.

Did I want to actually see him again after our first interaction last night?

Heaven and Hell no.

Those points aside; did I want to have someone who looked like him posing as my boyfriend to my family and Jason?

Yes. God, yes!

I smacked my hand against the table when I came to my decision. "Fine, I'll ask him."

"Success!" Aideen cheered.

I snickered at her then watched as she jumped to her feet.

"Easy tiger, why so jumpy?"

Aideen moved closer to me, grabbed my hand, and pulled me to my feet. "Go get a shower, we're goin' to get this done in the next hour."

Excuse me?

I felt my insides churn. "*Today*? Can't this wait until Monday?"

Aideen shook her head. "No, you leave for the Bahamas within the week and we have to go shoppin' for your holiday clothes so you'll look gorgeous at all times. Then we need to book your flights and call your job and tell them you're sick and will be off for a week. We have a lot to do, and I won't have you lookin' anythin' other than stunnin' at that disgrace of a weddin'. We also need Alec on board as soon as possible."

I swallowed down the bile the suddenly rose up my throat.

"Oh, God... I don't think I can do this."

Aideen grabbed my arm and pulled me out of the kitchen and straight into the bathroom. "You're just takin' a shower, that's it. One step at a time."

"Yeah, but–"

"Stop talkin'," Aideen cut me off. "Take a shower, and don't over think this."

With that said she up and left the bathroom leaving me alone in the room. I groaned as I began to undress. I turned on my shower and waited a minute for it to heat up. When I was sure the temperature wouldn't give me hypothermia I stepped under the flow of water and closed my eyes.

I didn't move from under the water for a few minutes because I was thinking, as you do when you're in the shower. I thought about what I was going to do and say when I came face to face with Alec. I couldn't exactly think of what to say after my encounter with him last night so I decided to just wing it. If I thought about it too much I wouldn't go and that would piss both myself and Aideen off, because once I gave my word on something I wouldn't back out.

I wasn't a chicken shit, I would one hundred percent go through with this and ask Alec to be my date to this farce of a wedding. The worst he could say was no. Plus, I've seen him once in my entire life and he has lived near my area for more than three years. It's not likely that I'd run into him anytime soon if he rejected me.

I hoped not anyway.

Twenty minutes after I entered the shower, I exited it sopping wet but extremely clean. I scrubbed myself raw making sure no dirty or dead skin was left behind. I moved to my sink and looked into the mirror; I rubbed the steam away and looked at my body. I didn't look below my chest because I hated my stomach, I had this little kangaroo pouch thing that *never* went away no matter how hard I dieted or how long I worked out in the gym!

I sighed as I grabbed my toothbrush and toothpaste, I applied the paste onto my brush, wet the brush then went to town on brushing my teeth. I was a bit OCD when it came to brushing my teeth. My teeth were very crooked when I was younger so my mother got me braces and when I had my braces removed and found I actually had lovely straight teeth, I made sure to take extra good care of them. They were my favourite feature about myself, I liked my smile.

After brushing my teeth and gargling some mouthwash, I grabbed a towel off the rack and dried myself down. I used the same towel to towel dry my hair then dropped it onto the floor to soak up my footprint puddles. Yeah, I used the one towel for everything. I hated when Aideen showered in my apartment, she used three towels just to take one shower and that pissed me off. A lot.

Next up was my moisturiser, I grabbed my favourite tub of strawberry body butter and rubbed it all over my body, then I did a little bit of a naked waving dance to help it dry faster. I probably looked like a dope, but it was effective and that's all the mattered.

When I emerged from the bathroom wrapped in a towel I was pounced on by Aideen. "Come on, I've got an outfit picked out for you."

She pulled me down to my bedroom by my arm and I stumbled a little when she let me go. I balanced myself and looked to my bed where Storm was passed out cold again and snoring.

"He is worse than a man."

Aideen snorted. "I would say he portrays males perfectly."

I snickered as I moved towards Aideen who was now practically inside my wardrobe. "I've picked out this blue knee length dress and a white pair of Converse for you to wear. It's on the end of your bed."

I looked at the dress and nodded my head in approval. I bought it a few weeks ago in Pennys for the summer months because it was a great length and fitted nicely.

"It's lovely but me boobs aren't big enough to fill it out though."

Aideen grinned. "That's why God invented the push up bra."

I gave her a get-real look. "God didn't create push up bras, man did."

Aideen shrugged. "True, but God planted the idea in man's mind. Put it on."

I chuckled, and dropped my towel. Aideen was already turned and back inside my wardrobe looking for my right Converse since the left one was already on the floor. I put on the bra then grabbed a pair of white knickers from my underwear drawer. I pulled my dress on over my head and looked down at my chest just as Aideen turned around and gave me a thumbs up.

"See? Instant jugs."

I snorted and held my hand out for my Converse. Aideen wrinkled her nose at me and shook her head before moving to my chest of drawers. She opened the bottom one, and grabbed a white pair of ankle socks.

"I *hate* when you don't wear socks with shoes, it's disgustin'."

I stuck my tongue out at her as I took the socks from her hand, I put both of them on then put on my Converse and stood up. I did a little twirl.

"What do you think?"

Aideen tilted her head to the side as she looked at me and frowned. "You've lost weight, your love handles are virtually gone."

I clapped my hands together like a happy seal. "Best news ever!"

Aideen shook her head. "No, it's not, you shouldn't lose weight as fast as you are. Are you eatin' three full meals a day?"

No.

I wasn't starving myself, but I tried my best to limit my food intake if I could help it.

"Yes, mother," I teased.

I didn't tell her the truth because Aideen wouldn't understand, she would just nag me about 'not eating properly'. I didn't hold it against her though because she cared about me and was only looking out for me, but she didn't know what it was like growing up with a mother like mine. One who scrutinised everything you put in your mouth and made you feel like crap about yourself. I barely loved my ma, she is not a nice person. Not even to me and I was her only child.

Aideen smiled at me as she believed my lie. "Well, lucky you. All your hard work is paying off, the Jason fat is nearly all gone. Woohoo."

I snickered and high fived her.

When I found out who Jason was and that he wasn't my partner, and that he used me just to upset my cousin, I comfort ate and put on three and a half stone. Aideen called it my Jason fat. That nickname alone gave me the boost needed to lose the weight. I didn't want any part of Jason connected to me, *especially* Jason fat.

I moved to my chest of drawers and opened the top drawer. I took out my hair dryer and hair straightener before I sat on my bed then handed them to Aideen. She plugged the hairdryer into the outlet on my wall and spent the next ten minutes blow drying my hair. My hair wasn't very long. It fell to my mid back when it was straight and it wasn't very thick, so luckily it didn't take long to dry.

"I'm gonna put loose curls down the end of your hair, it looks gorgeous like that. We need you to look hot so it persuades that sexy fucker to be your date in case he hates you after last night."

I raised my eyebrows. "Hell no, if he says no then that is his final answer, no ask the audience, fifty-fifty, or phone a friend. I won't beg or try to persuade him in *any way*."

Aideen grinned. "Yes, ma'am."

I glared. "That also means you won't try to persuade him either."

She put the straightener down and held up her hands. "I won't do anythin', I swear on the Bible."

I rolled my eyes. "That means nothin' to me, you're goin' to Hell and you know it."

Aideen snickered as she grabbed some heat protection spray and put some on the ends of my hair. She waited a few minute for it to dry then picked up the straightener and started to wrap the ends of my hair around the hot plates before she pulled. When she released my hair the ends of it sprung into loose curls, it made me smile because I loved this look on me just as much as Aideen did. It was a nice change considering I wear my hair in a ponytail or up in a messy bun most of the time.

"Hair is done, make-up is next. We're keepin' this pretty face as natural as possible."

Fun.

"Do whatever you want to me."

Aideen tapped my nose. "Open with that sentence when you speak to Alec and you're guaranteed to have him as your date to the weddin'."

The dirty bitch!

I burst out laughing making Aideen smile as she got my small makeup bag from my chest of drawers and brought it over to me. I closed my eyes as she picked out the makeup she would be using on my face and just relaxed while she went to work. She got my foundation, powder, and blush done in less than five minutes because she went very light on everything. She spent a few extra minutes doing a very light brown smoky eye on my eyes, but once that was done I was good to go.

"Perfume?" Aideen questioned.

I shook my head. "No thanks, I have strawberry moisturiser on so I smell nice and fruity."

Aideen leaned in and inhaled deeply.

"Nice."

I playfully shoved her away from me. "Come on, let's go and get this over with before I get nervous."

Or more nervous.

"I'm good to go, baby," Aideen cheered.

Storm barked from the bed so Aideen stuck her finger up at him before she skipped out of the room. I shook my head at her then moved around to Storm. I rubbed his head then kissed it. "I'll be back it a little while, bud."

Storm groaned and stretched then rolled over. I chuckled as I stood up and walked out of my bedroom. I left the door open for him so he could have access to his water and food. I topped off both before I followed Aideen out of my apartment.

"I took him out on a quick walk to go the toilet earlier, and the fucker almost bit my hand off. I'm never doin' it again."

I laughed as I locked up my apartment door and headed down the stairs of my apartment complex with Aideen on my heels. When we were out in the car park I groaned in delight as I felt the heat of the sunlight caress my skin.

"I bloody love the summer."

Aideen sighed, "Me too, babe."

We got into my car and rolled down the windows straight away because the inside of my car was boiling hot. I started my car then pulled out of the car park and onto the road.

"Where am I drivin'?"

Aideen cracked her knuckles. "Upton."

I glanced to her before refocusing on the road. "He lives in Upton? Is he rich?"

Aideen shrugged. "Branna said they are well off."

I snorted.

They are more than well off if they lived in Upton. That was probably the poshest part of Tallaght. Well, if Tallaght had a posh part then Upton would be it. Aideen and I didn't speak as we drove the ten minute drive across two estates until we entered the ever clean and peaceful Upton.

"I'd love to live here," I murmured as I slowed down enough to look around.

"Me too, it's so quiet."

I nodded. "I could get so much writin' done if I lived here."

Aideen glanced at me. "How *is* your book comin' along?"

I shrugged. "It's comin' along grand, I'm about forty-four thousand words into it."

Aideen whistled. "I can't believe you can write so many words.

I struggle writing a text with more than twenty words."

I chuckled as I pulled up in front of the house Aideen pointed out to me.

"How do you know this is their house? Have you been here before?" I asked Aideen as we unbuckled our seat belts and got out of my car.

"No, but Branna said it was a four story house that has a white post box on the wall next to the hall door."

I looked to the house and spotted the post box Aideen spoke of and blew out a big breath. I felt sick now that I was here in front of their house.

"Come on, let's get this over with," I muttered.

"Lose that attitude and think positive, clear your mind," Aideen said from behind me as I walked into the garden and up the steps that led to a porch.

"Okay, yoga weirdo," I said making Aideen chuckle.

I bit down on my bottom lip as I read *Slater* labelled across the white post box next to the hall door. I closed my eyes then opened them again as I pressed the doorbell.

For a whole ten seconds nothing happened so I shrugged and said, "Looks like no one is home. Oh well, I tried. Let's go."

Aideen grabbed my arm as I tried to turn away from the door. "Oh, no you don't! Have patience and wait!"

I grunted and folded my arms across my chest while Aideen rang the bell again.

"Coming!" a male voice from inside the house hollered a few seconds later.

"Fuck!" I whispered making Aideen snicker.

A few seconds after I spoke the hall door to the Slater residence opened. I had already seen what Alec and Kane looked like and this man was neither of them.

Nope, I was gazing upon another God.

A God who had on shorts that fell to his knees and a vest top that was stretched over his torso. Tattoos where inked on his body, *lots* of tattoos. He was nothing short of a masterpiece. Easily over six feet tall with short dark brown hair, bright grey eyes and plump lips.

"Aideen," the man smiled revealing straight white teeth.

This really wasn't fair.

He was simply beautiful.

"Hey Ryder," Aideen chirped then glanced to me and whispered, "He is the eldest."

Ryder heard Aideen and smiled at us. I mentally, and probably audibly, sighed because he was so fucking good looking that it almost hurt to look at him and this was Alec's *eldest* brother?

These lads will only get better with age, let me tell you!

"Branna isn't here right now and-"

"Oh, we aren't here to see Branna. We're here to see Alec. Well, me friend is here to see Alec."

Ryder's eyes fell on me, he glanced to my stomach then to my face. "You're not pregnant, are you?"

I flushed every shade of red imaginable.

I looked fucking pregnant?

"No!" I stated, appalled that he even asked that question.

Ryder quickly cleared his throat. "You don't *look* pregnant, that came out wrong. Having a girl show up here looking for Alec is extremely rare so I'm a bit worried. He never tells his lays' where he lives."

His lay?

I felt my eyes practically fall from my head. "I did *not* have sex with your brother!"

Ryder bit down on his bottom lip and ran his hands through his trimmed hair. "I'm *so* sorry, this is coming out all wrong. You don't look like Alec's usual lay, I mean, you're gorgeous but his girls' are usually blonde and-"

"Jesus Christ, Ryder, just stop talkin'! You're diggin' yourself into a never endin' pit here," Aideen angrily snapped.

Ryder jumped a little at the volume of Aideen's shout, but

nodded his head and focused on me. "I'm *so* sorry."

I just nodded my head to him not knowing what to say so I stayed silent. He blew out a long breath before he turned around and shouted, "Alec, a woman is here to see you!"

A few moments passed by until I heard a door open, a few light footsteps then a whisper, "If she has blonde hair, a mole on her left cheek, and huge tits, close the door right fucking now."

I felt my face twist in disgust as I shook my head, he was such a fucking dick.

"I don't have blonde hair, a mole on me cheek or big tits, it's safe to come out!" I shouted.

Ryder grinned at me, but tried to hide it by rubbing his hand over his mouth. He then stepped to the right and allowed Alec to fill the doorway. I was embarrassed and mad over what Ryder said to me, but I forgot about that when my eyes landed on Alec.

Shirtless Alec.

Shirtless Alec who had a large dragon tattoo that covered his right arm and part of his chest *and* possessed six pack abs as well as the ultimate V line.

Did all of these brothers have bodies and tattoos like this?

"*Keela?*" Alec said, clearly surprised that I was on his doorstep.

"The Keela that put you on your ass last night? *That* Keela?" Ryder murmured to Alec.

"Yeah, *that* Keela. Don't worry, she is calm and won't hurt Alec again, promise," Aideen chirped making both of the brothers chuckle and me bristle. I glared at her, but the bitch paid me no attention.

I cast my head down and cleared my suddenly dry throat.

"Can I speak to you?" I asked when I looked back up at Alec.

I narrowed my eyes when I found his eyes on my legs instead of on my face. "Eyes on me face buddy, me *face.*"

Alec lifted his head and flicked his eyes across my face. "And what a pretty face it is."

Really?

I groaned out loud. "Did you really just say that? That was beyond pathetic."

Alec grinned while Ryder snorted and murmured, "Kane was right, she isn't affected by you."

"All in good time bro," Alec muttered back.

Seriously?

I could *hear* them talking.

"Are you goin' to leave two lovely ladies stood outside on your porch or are you goin' to invite us in?" Aideen asked with a beaming smile.

Ryder quickly nodded his head. "Right, sorry, come on in. Branna shouldn't be too long so you can hang with me and my brothers while Alec and Keela talk."

Aideen was happy with that and headed into the house with Ryder on her heels. I wanted to slap her silly, she just bloody abandoned me in my time of need. Some best friend she is!

"You're the last person I expected to see today, kitten. How did you know where I lived?" Alec asked me as he leaned his shoulder against the doorframe.

I shrugged. "Branna told Aideen and Aideen told me."

I let my eyes wander everywhere except for his body and face, he didn't like this though because he reached out and gripped my chin with his fingers and lifted my head until I was looking at him.

"Why won't you look at me?" he asked.

I shrugged. "Because."

He smiled and dropped his hand. "Because what?"

Because you're the hottest person I have ever seen.

His brothers were fine as hell but Alec was in your face hot! *That* hot!

I shrugged again. "Just because."

Alec chuckled and folded his arms across his chest. "To what do I owe this unannounced pleasure, miss?"

I rolled my eyes and said, "Daley."

"Miss Daley." Alec smiled.

I stared at his smile before I looked down and mumbled, "I need to ask you somethin'."

"Okay, but look at me when you do it."

I felt my heart pound against my chest as butterflies filled my stomach. "Look, it's hard enough to swallow my pride and ask a stranger this question, a stranger who I had an argument with less then twelve hours ago."

Alec regarded me. "You physically assaulted me less than twelve hours ago as well."

I snapped my head up and fixed a deadly glare on him. "Are you tryin' to piss me off?"

A thoughtful look fell over his face as he scratched his chin. "You clearly aren't shy when you're angry, I'm helping you relax."

I clenched my hands into fists. "I'm not shy at all."

"Then ask the question that you came here to ask me," he challenged.

I glanced at my surroundings and said, "Can we not do this inside?"

Alec raised his brows as he gave me a once over, but did as requested and pushed away from the doorframe and strightened to his full height. He then turned to his side and gestured me into the house with his hand. I swallowed and turned to my side so I could slide past him. While I shimmed by him I locked eyes with his pecs then looked up to his handsome face.

"Hi," he smiled down at me, revealing deep identical dimples in his cheeks.

Why did he have to have dimples? *Why?*

I let out a big puff of air and replied, "Hey."

A sly smile curved his mouth as he shook his head. Once inside his house I fully looked him over. He had his hair back in a bobbin, but the strands from the front of his head escaped the tie and hung loose. I clenched my hands into fists so I wouldn't brush them out of his face even though I *really* wanted to.

"We can talk here or in my bedroom, which do you prefer?"

His bedroom?

My legs shook and nearly buckled from under me.

"Here," I squeaked then quickly cleared my throat. "Here is fine, thank you."

Alec fully smiled at me so I looked down to my fingers and said, "I need help with somethin' and Aideen told me you are more than qualified help me with it."

"Clarify 'it'."

I felt my face heat up, so I covered my face with my hands. "God, this is so bloody embarrassin'."

Alec didn't say a word so I closed my eyes and blurted, "She told me you're an escort."

Silence.

A long period of fucking silence.

Oh my God.

I wanted to die.

"I'm retired," Alec replied after ten seconds that felt more like an hour.

I looked up at him and found his face completely passive.

I shifted my stance a little and licked my suddenly dry lips.

"Oh, so you can't help me then?" I frowned.

Alec titled his head to the side and looked at me for a long moment.

"No, I can't. I don't deal in that business anymore. You will have to find another guy."

I felt my heart jump.

"But I don't want your, um, *regular* services. You don't have to do anythin' sexual or anythin' like that, I swear," I blurted out then tensed up when Alec's face turned to stone.

"Sexual? I was an escort, Keela, not a prostitute."

I shrugged my shoulders in confusion. "Are they not the same thing?" I asked, quizzically.

I regretted my question as soon as the words left my mouth because Alec's jaw set and his face hardened even more than it already was. He was glaring at me, and was clearly angry but I couldn't help but notice that he looked so bloody hot when he was mad.

"I'm s-sorry," I stuttered. "I didn't mean to offend you. I just don't know the difference. I thought escorts-"

"You thought escorts were paid money to fuck people, right?" Alec cut me off.

I swallowed, nervous over his clipped tone.

"Um, well yes, I did," I replied honestly.

Alec shook his head and muttered something under his breath before his fixed his eyes on mine. "Escorts provide companionship to a person, sex is optional, but *not* the baseline. Prostitutes are paid for sex and only sex, that *is* the baseline."

I wondered how many times he had to explain that to people who knew about his previous job.

I swallowed feeling awful that I assumed the worst in him.

"I apologise for bein' naive."

Alec shrugged uncaring. "It's okay, but I still can't help you. I'm not in that business anymore."

I felt my stomach drop at the rejection. I was mentally prepared for it, but it still wasn't a nice feeling.

I nodded my head to Alec and looked down to my fingers. "I understand, sorry again for offendin' you, I didn't mean to pass judgement. I know I probably came off as a bitch last night but I am a nice person and I wouldn't purposely try to hurt your feelin's. I'm not like that. I'm very sorry."

I heard Alec hiss as he inhaled.

"Damn kitten, don't be getting upset on me." I looked up at him and he growled. "Put that pouty lip away otherwise I'm going to bite it."

I didn't even realise I was pouting, but I sucked my bottom lip into my mouth on a gasp and bit down on it.

Alec's lip twitched as he scrubbed his face with his hands. I took the momentary break from his gaze to clear my throat and gather myself.

"I'll go and get Aideen so we can leave-"

"Out of curiosity, what did you want an escort for?"

"I'd rather not say, it's embarrassin'."

"You didn't want me to take your virginity, did you?"

I snapped my head up and hurt my neck a little doing so. "*What*? No, that is *not* what I came here for!" I angrily snapped.

I felt heat spread across my chest and up my neck then onto my face. "First your brother thinks I am pregnant by you and now you think I am virgin? I'm *not* pregnant and I'm *not* a damn virgin!"

Alec raised his eyebrows and looked a little shocked. I ignored him and his expression, as I turned my body then shouted, "Aideen! Move it, we're leavin'!"

I felt a rush of air touch my skin seconds before a body molded into my back and arms came around my waist. "Now wait just as second, kitten. I jumped to conclusions, but so did you. Give me a break here - I'm not being a dick, I'm just trying to understand what you would need an escort for."

I opened my mouth to snap off a snarky reply, but nothing came to me because Alec was right. I relaxed a little and he must have felt it becuase he moved back away from me, giving me back my space.

I was about to reply to Alec when I heard movement and mumbling in the room behind the doors across from me. Without a second thought I walked to the double doors and opened them. Three large males fell forward taking me to the ground with them.

A mountain of muscle was crushing me, most would say this was the ideal way to die, but not me!

"Can't breathe," I wheezed from under the bodies.

"Get off her!" I heard Alec bellow.

Courses of the word 'sorry' were offered as I was dug free from the mountain of muscle and helped to my feet. I took in a few deep breaths and groaned in delighted as oxygen filled my lungs.

"Fuck, that hurt me chest."

"Do you think something might be broken?" Alec asked as he appeared in front of me, placing his hands on my bare shoulders.

I shook my head and took a few more breaths. "No, I'm fine. I just couldn't breathe, and it burned."

Alec looked to his right and said, "You almost smothered a woman."

"Sorry," three voices said in unison.

I got control of my breathing then looked to my left and saw a frowning Ryder and Kane as well a frowning younger man who looked similar to Alec.

"Which brother are you?" I asked him.

"Nico," he replied at the same time all three of his brothers said, "Dominic."

I looked to the lad and asked, "What am I callin' you, Nico or Dominic?"

He shrugged and grinned at me. "You can call me whatever you want, gorgeous."

I raised my eyebrows at him and couldn't help but smile a little, his forwardness and the way he held himself was kind of charming. I observed him with my eyes which he fully appreciated, judging by his smile which revealed dimples that matched Alec's.

"I'll call you Nico," I replied, smiling wide myself now.

I settled on Nico since that was the name he said when I asked his name. His name was obviously Dominic, but if he wanted to be called Nico, I would call him Nico.

"And you are?" Nico asked, keeping eye contact with me.

"Keela," I said and blushed.

His stare was very intense and I couldn't help but flush under it.

"*Kee-lah,*" Nico purred. "Beautiful name for a beautiful girl."

Alec used his hands, which were still on my shoulders, to push me behind him as he stepped forward towards his younger brother.

"Boy, cut that shit out or I'm knocking your ass out," Alec snarled to Nico.

ALEC

I looked around Alec's body and watched as Nico, Kane, and Ryder all dropped their jaws and gaped at Alec. I furrowed my eyebrows, why did they look so shocked? Did brothers not threaten physical beatings to each other over random things all the time?

"Are you okay?" I asked them.

Nico was the first brother to compose himself, before the other two quickly followed suit.

"We're fine," Ryder assured me.

I stepped to Alec's side and curtly nodded to Ryder which he frowned at. "I *really* am sorry for what I said to you earlier Keela. It was a dick move just to assume something like that. Forgive me?"

I gave him a genuine smile and nodded my head because he looked a little distressed that I was still upset with him, and it just confirmed that he was a good man if a stranger could do that to him.

"Where you all listenin' to the conversation I had with Alec?" I asked the brothers.

One by one they hung their heads in shame and nodded. I found the sight hilarious, but I didn't laugh. They were huge men but they were acting like a bunch of little lads who were caught with their hands in the cookie jar before dinner.

"Great, now I'm even more embarrassed," I muttered.

"What do you need an escort for? Don't you have a boyfriend?" Kane suddenly asked me.

My stomach fell out of my arse when he asked that question because I forgot all about pretending that Storm was my boyfriend.

"Oh Jesus," I groaned and covered my face with my hands.

"Yeah, what was his name again? Thunder?" Alec sarcastically asked making Kane snicker.

I uncovered my face and looked at Alec with my eyes narrowed. "Storm."

"Ah yes, Storm. Why can't *Storm*escort you?" he asked, a grin tugging at his lips.

He was such a dickhead, he knew I didn't have a boyfriend.

"Because I don't have a boyfriend. I only said that Storm was me boyfriend last night to stop you from chattin' me up because I didn't want to have sex with you. I *still* don't want to have sex with you. I just need your help, but you said you can't help me so I'll be goin' now. Aideen!"

Aideen suddenly appeared walking down the hallway that I think led from the kitchen, she had a bottle of Bulmers in her hand and a smile on her face.

I pinched the bridge of my nose and shook my head at her.

"Really? It's not even the afternoon and you're drinkin'?"

Aideen shrugged her shoulders. "It's hot outside. The heat does things to Irish people, it forces us to drink!"

I gave her a 'really' look which made her smile and take a sip from her bottle.

"Whatever. Keep the bottle, we're leavin' now. Alec won't help me."

Aideen frowned as her shoulders slumped. "Dammit, who the hell can we get to be your date to that weddin' now?"

"Whose weddin'?" Nico asked Aideen.

I gently shook my head at Aideen and gave her the don't-say-a-word look. Any other female around the globe would know that look and not say a word, but not Aideen, she had too big of a mouth to keep anything to herself.

"Keela's cousin, Micah, is gettin' married to her dickhead of a fella next week. Jason, Micah's fiancé, fucked Keela over a few months ago. Since she has to attend the weddin', we wanted someone to go with her that would show Jason she can do miles better than him. I thought Alec was the man for the job, but apparently I was wrong."

I put my face back in my hands when Aideen finished speaking and wished the ground would open up and swallow me whole.

"Wait, you're related to Micah Daley?" Nico asked me.

I uncovered my face and found he was looking at me with wide eyes as he awaited my answer. "Yeah, Micah is me cousin. Do you know her?"

"Unfortunately, I do. She was in my homeroom in the final year of high school."

I nodded my head in understanding.

Nico looked closely at me then and studied me with his eyes squinted. "She was a brunette in school, but I've seen her around town and she has red hair now. You look similar to her."

I shrugged. "Her hair is dyed red, mine is naturally this colour. I'm not like her at all, she is a bitch of epic proportions."

Nico grinned. "You don't need to convince me she is a bitch, I believe you."

I chuckled.

"What did Jason do to fuck you over?" Ryder questioned me when I looked at him.

I sighed and rubbed my neck awkwardly, embarrassed that I was revealing this information to very hot strangers.

"He pretended to like me, took me out on dates and such to made me think we were a real couple, but really he was only usin' me to get back at Micah for cheatin' on him. It's all really fucked up, they worked shite out and are gettin' married and because we're family I have to go their weddin'."

Kane frowned at me. "Why not tell them to shove their wedding up their asses?"

I chuckled a little. "Because me ma would be on me case about it. Goin' to the weddin' and keepin' out of the way is much better than dealin' with my mother if I don't go. She is the Devil."

"Amen," Aideen said and made the sign of the cross, which Kane found funny.

I sighed, but kept a bright smile on my face. "Yeah... Well it was nice seein' you again Kane and Alec, and lovely meetin' you two lads. Have a nice day."

I nodded for Aideen to walk out with me, but when I turned to leave a large body blocked my way.

"Turn around and walk into the kitchen," Alec said, staring

down at me, his gaze hard.

I swallowed. "What? Why?"

He kept eye contact. "Because I need to iron out some details with you if I'm going to be your escort to your cousin's wedding."

CHAPTER FOUR

I stared at Alec and felt like I swallowed my tongue. A few seconds passed by until I found my voice and said, "But you said that you aren't in that business anymore and that you are retired-"

"Do you want my help or not?" Alec cut me off, his tone clipped.

I bit the inside of my cheek, and nodded my head because I really did want his help. No scratch that, if I wanted to show Jason and Micah that life after Jason was better than ever, I *needed* his help.

"Then turn around and walk into the kitchen, I want to talk to you in private. Just the two of us."

I have no idea why I didn't backtalk him for giving me an order. His tone left no room for argument though, so I kept my mouth shut turned and walked by Nico, Kane, Ryder, and Aideen on my way into the kitchen. I heard the kitchen door close after me, and knowing I was in a room all on my own with him made me nervous.

Very nervous.

"Do you want a cup of tea?" Alec asked from behind me.

I raised my eyebrows and turned to him.

Out of everything I expected him to say, that sentence was *not* it.

Alec shrugged his shoulders at my shocked facial expression. "Bronagh and Branna always tell me to 'put the kettle on' when they need to have a serious conversation, I figured you might want one before we talk."

Were we about to have a serious conversation?
Uh-oh.

"Um, sure. I'd love a builder's cuppa, please."

It was Alec's turn to raise his eyebrows then.

"What the hell is that?"

I chewed on my bottom lip for a moment, released it and said, "You know, a cup of tea with loads of sugar?"

Alec looked at me like I was stupid before he shook his head and turned to the counter where he picked up the kettle and filled it up with water from the tap. He placed the kettle back on the holder when it was full and flipped the switch on. He turned to face me then as he leaned back against the counter with his arms folded across his chest and looked at me, his eyes fixed on mine.

I shifted my stance a few times then dropped my gaze to Alec's nose instead of his eyes because I was a little unnerved that he wasn't blinking as he looked at me. I lowered my gaze to his mouth just as a smirk curved it and his dimples dented his cheeks.

I cleared my throat and said, "I'm just goin' to sit down."

I turned and moved to the kitchen table and made a huge deal of looking at my surroundings as I sat down just so I wouldn't have to look at Alec or his sexy dimples.

I didn't like him - he was hot all right, but he seemed to have the personality of a goat, and I didn't like goats.

Whether I liked him physically or not, it didn't calm my nerves when he looked at me. His gaze was intense and even though I wasn't looking at him, I could feel it piercing me. I waited a solid minute before I spoke.

"So what 'details' do we have to go over in order for you escort me to me cousin's weddin'?" I asked as I looked directly in front of me.

Across from me was a sliding glass backdoor. I could see out into a large back garden that was neat and tidy with a beautiful bed of flowers down the back that was topped off with a stunning deck that looked only half varnished.

"In order for me to escort you to your cousin's wedding, I need to draw up a contract-"

"Hold up, buddy. A contract? Is this conversation about to get *Fifty Shades of Grey*?"

Alec frowned at me. "That kinky porn book women love?"

I nodded my head and watched as his face changed from expressionless to beatific as he laughed and moved over to the kettle when it whistled letting us know the water was boiled.

"No, it's not about to get fifty shades of anything, Keela. Contracts with my clients are routine."

"Alec, I'm not your client. What I am askin' of you is a favour, *not* a business deal."

Alec looked over his shoulder and gazed at me with a look of confusion across his face. "Why don't you tell me what you want from this 'favour' so I get a better understanding of things then."

That seemed fair.

I nodded my head as he turned back around and began to make me a cup of tea.

"Well, much wouldn't be required of you. I just want you to pretend to be me boyfriend... That's it."

Alec turned back in my direction with a black mug in his hand. He carried it over to me, and placed it on top of the coaster that was already placed on the table in front of me. He took a seat across from me, clasped his hands together and placed them on the table in front of him. My eyes lingered on the light blue bulge of veins running down his arms; the veins were noticeable, but could be easily overlooked thanks to the stunning dragon tattoo that covered Alec's left arm, half of his chest, and part of his neck.

I only then realised that Alec was still topless and I was openly gawking at his chest and arms. I quickly looked up to Alec's face and instantly glared at the smugness that was visibly plastered across his face.

"Can you put some clothes on?" I asked.

Alec raised his eyebrows. "Does my being topless make you

uncomfortable?"

No, it makes me drool.

"Yes, it does."

Alec smirked. "Though shit. It's hot out, so I'm skins for the day."

I frowned. "I don't even know what that means."

Alec clicked his tongue at me. "Irish people."

"*American* people!" I fired right back making him chuckle.

"So, you just want me to be your boyfriend?"

Nice subject change.

I licked my lips, and nodded my head. "Yes, you just have to make it believable that we are a real couple."

Alec smiled suggestively. "How would you like me to make it *believable*?"

Why did he say that word like it was something dirty?

I felt myself flush, and I hated it. "Stop tryin' to embarrass me."

Alec pushed his hair back from his face and said, "I'm asking a legit question."

"Just act like a lovin' boyfriend; hold my hand, kiss my cheek-"

"Open a door for you then smack your ass when you walk by?"

I rolled my eyes. "I'm bein' serious."

"So am I."

I groaned, and placed my head in my hands. "I just want me family to think we're a real, happy couple. That's *it*."

Alec chortled. "Trust me kitten, this will be the easiest job I've ever done."

I uncovered my face, and raised my eyebrows at him. "It will?"

Alec nodded, still smiling wide. "Yep."

Perfect!

I smiled also. "So does that mean you will escort me to the weddin'?"

I had my fingers and toes crossed, hoping he would say yes.

Alec laughed at me. "If you abide by my conditions then yes, I will."

I frowned and uncrossed my fingers and toes. "What *are* your conditions?"

Alec held up his index finger.

"Number one, absolutey *no* falling in love."

Oh, he had a sense of humour!

I couldn't help the snort that erupted out of me then or the laughter that followed it. Alec's eyes narrowed as I snorted again mid-laugh which of course only made me laugh harder.

"I'm being serious Keela," Alec growled, no trace of humour on his face or in his tone.

Oh, crap, he was serious!

I laughed harder then, and quickly fanned myself. "I know, that's why... I'm laughin'... so hard."

Alec stared at me blankly and unblinking, so I forced myself to relax until my laughter subsided. "Okay, so I'm not to fall in love with you. Got it, what's number two?"

Alec rolled his eyes and said, "Number two, you treat me as a person and not as the hired help."

I frowned. "I will always treat you as a person... I can't treat you like hired help even if I wanted because I'm not payin' you."

Alec clicked his tongue at me. "You could pay me in sexual favours."

I raised my eyebrows then gave him a get-real look and said, "You will get paid with *nice manners*."

Alec smirked. "The rest of my conditions might make you a little uneasy then."

I sat up straight as a shiver ran down my spine. "What are they?"

Alec lifted his arm and rubbed the back of his neck. "You sure you want an honest answer to that question, kitten?"

I nodded my head and ignored the bulge of his bicep even though it whispered for me to take a peak.

Alec shrugged and said, "I want to fuck you."

I was about to laugh, but Alec's tone and facial expression shut me up before I even made a sound. I did nothing but stare at him for a few moments before I opened my mouth and said, "Why aren't you laughin'?"

"Because I'm not joking."

I widened my eyes in sheer horror. "You *better* be fuckin' jokin'!"

Alec sat back a little and raised his eyebrows and hands. "I don't joke about conditions for a contract."

I smacked my hands down on the kitchen table. "This is *not* a contract, this is a *favour*. You don't get paid for it with anythin' other than a *verbal* fuckin' thank you."

Alec folded his arms across his chest. "So I'm to be your boyfriend *without* receiving the privileges or benefits of having a girlfriend?"

Seriously?

"Yes! This is all only *pretend*!"

Alec shook his head. "Nah, that's a no-go for me. We're going to hash that out right now, if you want me to be your boyfriend then I want some privileges at least. I'm a man - I have needs."

Oh my God!

What the hell was this?

I rubbed my temples with my fingers. "What exactly do you want from me, Alec?"

If he said he wanted to fuck me again I was going to smack him.

"I like physical intimacy. No feelings or emotional bullshit, just the physical stuff. I like holding hands, kissing, cuddling, hugging, and fucking. If I'm to be your pretend boyfriend then this is what I want, it's not asking for much."

Not asking for much?

NOT. ASKING. FOR. MUCH?

Men!

I was mad that he wanted to have sex with me, but I couldn't help but also feel a little flattered because men who looked like

Alec *never* peeked in my direction, let alone look in it. Flattered or not, I was also extremely disgusted that sex was *all* he wanted from me. I wasn't expecting anything to come from this arrangement, but to be told someone wanted me for my body, and my body alone, was *not* a mistake I would make twice in my lifetime.

My heart was hammering against my chest and my stomach contents were rolling around inside my belly.

"Shaggin' is *not* on the table at all so you can get it out of your head right now."

I could not believe he even suggested that he get laid as a condition to escort me to Micah's wedding!

Alec grinned. "We'll see."

I growled, "What do you mean 'We'll see'?"

"I mean we will see."

Fuck that and fuck him!

"We won't see anythin'! I change me mind, I don't need your help," I snapped and stood up from my chair. I pushed it into the table then turned and walked towards the door, but Alec's arms stopped me as they surrounded me.

I was more than a little shocked that he was behind me again - I didn't hear him move from where he was sitting.

"You came to me for help, not the other way around, kitten. You don't have anyone else who can help you or you wouldn't be here... Like it or not, you *do* need my help."

I shrugged out of his hold, then spun around and placed my hands on my hips. "I'm *not* shaggin' you. If that is a deal breaker for you then so be it, I won't sleep with you in order for you to escort me to the weddin' as me boyfriend. I don't care how good lookin' you are. I'm *not* that kind of girl!"

A smile stretched across Alec's face as he looked down at me. "You think I'm good looking?"

Of course his bloody mind would focus on *that* part of my sentence.

I narrowed my eyes to slits and glared at Alec which made him lightly chuckle and hold his hands up in front of his chest like he was surrendering.

"I want to fuck you, no doubt about it, kitten, but it doesn't have to be a condition since you're so against it. In fact, since you're dead set *against* it, I'm going to make you a bet instead."

I raised my eyebrows and stared at him curiously.

"What kind of bet?" I questioned.

"A sexual kind of bet."

He lost me.

"What?"

Alec smirked. "I bet that before anyone says 'I do', I'll have you on your back with your legs spread wide as I pound away between your thighs."

I felt my jaw drop open.

"And *you* will be the one begging *me* to suck and fuck *you*."

My eyes widened to the point of pain.

"Are you serious?" I asked my voice a whisper.

Alec nodded his head.

I laughed, and I laughed hard.

"You've got yourself a bet, laddie."

Alec didn't realise it, but he was setting himself up for disaster with this bet because I was the almighty queen of self-control. I fucking had this!

Alec tilted his head and smiled at me as his dimples earned an inward sigh from me.

"My updated conditions are that we sleep in the same bed and that I can kiss you, touch you, and cuddle with you whenever I want."

The sneaky fucker!

I deadpanned for a moment, but then smiled wide. "You think by doin' all that I will willingly want to shag you?"

Alec shrugged his shoulders, but had a ghost of a smile appeared on his face that confirmed my suspicions.

"Fine, we can sleep in the same bed, but you *have* to wear

pyjama bottoms."

Alec held up his hand. "I sleep naked, always have and always will."

I clenched my hands to fists. "You *will* wear pyjamas. I'm not backin' down on this, playboy."

Alec blinked at my insult. "Playboy, really kitten?"

I hissed, "Stop calling me kitten!"

Alec shook his head and said, "Nah, I like it. You're small and vulnerable like a cute little kitten."

Puke.

"If kitten is staying then so is playboy," I warned.

Alec laughed and shrugged his shoulders. "I've been called worse, *kitten*."

I narrowed my eyes. "I really don't like you."

"Give it time, and you will like me plenty."

Cocky bastard!

I shook my head and refocused on *my* condition. "You *must* wear pyjamas when you are in the same bed as me, do you understand me?"

Alec smirked down at me. "I like you giving me orders."

"Does that mean you will follow them?" I asked hopefully.

He laughed. "Let's not get too hasty, kitten."

Fucker.

"I'm not backin' down on this, wearin' pyjamas is a condition of *mine*."

Alec raised his eyebrows and folded his arms across his bare chest.

"Is that so?"

I swallowed but firmly said, "Yes, it *is* so."

Alec smiled and let his eyes roam over my face until they landed on my eyes. "Fine, pyjama pants in bed."

Small victory won!

I smiled happily. "And as for the kissin' and touchin' - we will have to build up to that happenin' freely. I don't know you, and I refuse to get intimate on any level, even if it *is* fake, with a stranger."

Alec scratched his chin then took my arm and lead me back to the kitchen table where we retook our seats.

"Okay, that sounds fair."

I was bouncing a little on my seat as I asked, "So you will be me pretend boyfriend, and escort me to Micah's and Jason's weddin'?

Alec laughed at my happiness. "Yeah, kitten. You've got yourself a fake man."

I clapped my hands together. "I can't wait to see Jason's face, this is gonna be so feckin' good!"

Alec's lip was curved as he watched and listened to me. I gradually stopped moving, and speaking, and busied myself with drinking some of my now lukewarm tea. It tasted so good that I groaned out loud.

"Oh my God. You make a *perfect* cuppa tea."

Alec shook his head. "All that sugar will rot your teeth."

Dentists could perform miracles nowadays so I didn't care.

I shrugged. "I need this, this is how I stay sane."

Alec laughed then looked at his nails and picked out some dirt from under them. I inwardly snorted at how feminine he suddenly looked then heard a bit of a thud coming from outside the kitchen door. I furrowed my eyebrows as I stood up and walked towards the door and pulled it open.

I jumped back and screeched when Nico's large body fell forward and crashed onto the ground. Alec burst out laughing from his seat while I stared wide-eyed at Nico on the floor with my hand held over my chest.

"I *told* you she had super hearin'!" Aideen's voice shouted from another room in the house, I guessed she was in the sitting room.

Nico grunted and groaned as he pushed himself to his feet, I gripped his arm to steady him in case he dropped again.

"Are you okay?" I asked, worried.

"He is fine, don't be fussing over him. It serves him right for eavesdropping."

ALEC

Nico growled and snapped his head in Alec's direction. "I was *not* eavesdropping. I was coming in to get some water-"

"Explain why you were pressed up against the door and fell when it was open then?" Alec cut Nico off with a wicked grin.

Nico narrowed his eyes then opened his mouth to speak but closed it and huffed which made Alec snicker.

"Get your water and leave, little brother. I have things to discuss with my *girlfriend*."

Nico eyebrows got lost in his hairline that was how far up his eyebrows shot.

"Girlfriend?"

I flushed every shade of red and glared at Alec. "He means *fake* girlfriend."

Alec shrugged and grinned at me. "I'm getting into character, baby."

I curled my lip in disgust; I *hated* that pet name.

"Don't call me that."

Alec snapped his teeth at me. "Fine, just kitten then."

I folded my arms across my chest. "How about callin' me Keela, since that's me name."

Nico snorted from my left, so I looked to him as he said, "Just call her Keela, I never hear the end of it if I don't call Bronagh by her name."

I smiled at him. "What do you call her if not her name?"

Nico looked down to me and gently clocked my chin with his knuckles. "I call her my pretty girl."

I melted and audibly sighed.

"That is the cutest thing I have *ever* heard in me entire life."

"Besides my pretty girl and her sister, you're the cutest woman I have ever seen in *my* entire life."

Oh my goodness.

Nico smiled at me and as I focused on his dimples I involuntary leaned closer to him only to be blocked by a large back that was suddenly pressed against my face.

"Five second warning to back off or I'm putting you on your ass, *little* brother."

I frowned at Alec's back and contemplated pinching it, did he not see that Nico was only playing with me?

"Bro, what the hell has gotten into you, since when do *you* threaten *me*? Since when do you threaten *anybody*?" Nico asked Alec, his tone laced with shock.

I looked around Alec to Nico who glanced at me, a tentative smile on his face.

"Stop flirting with her. I don't like it," Alec hissed, his tone filled with anger.

Holy shite!

"Jesus Alec, calm down. He was only messin' with me, you bleedin' weirdo."

Nico blissfully laughed then and looked to Alec and said, "I like her."

"I like her more and more each time she insults him," Kane's voice suddenly spoke.

"Fucking hell... deja vu," Nico muttered and rubbed his temples.

I glanced to my left when Kane entered the kitchen and I smiled at him as he headed straight for the fridge. He was wearing a vest top that was coated in sweat. With his arms bare I could see that he has some thick purple scars as well as some light pink ones covering sections of his skin. Nico was topless and in a pair of shorts just like Alec was. I found myself looking from brother to brother, but focusing my gaze on Alec's back. It was rippled with muscle and perfectly tanned with a few light freckles splashed across his shoulder blades.

Before putting any thought into it, I reached out and ran my index finger up his spine and stopped between his shoulder blades. Alec's body completely tensed and it caused me to freeze. I quickly pulled my hand anyway as he spun around to face me then he grabbed my hand and growled down at me.

ALEC

He lowered his head to my ear and whispered, "If you touch my back again be prepared for a hard fucking, *kitten*."

I hated that his words both infuriated me and turned me on at that same time.

"You dirty bastard! If you say anythin' like that to me again I'll... I'll..."

"You'll what, kitten?" Alec asked his voice teasing.

I clenched my jaw shut and settled on glaring at him because I couldn't think of anything to say.

"She will kick your ass from the looks of things," Kane snickered then left the room with the food he gathered from the fridge.

Alec smiled, but didn't look away from me. He instead reached out and brushed a loose curl out of my face and tucked it behind my ear. My breath caught and my lower region tingled.

"You're a real man, you know that?" I murmured.

"I'm *all* man, baby."

I rolled my eyes. "No, I mean you're a *man*, man. Like a caveman."

Alec frowned. "Is that a bad thing or something?"

"Yes and no," I replied.

He continued to frown at me then lifted his hand and rubbed his hands together. "I don't understand what you're saying. Is it bad or is it good? Be straight with me."

He wanted me to be straight with him?

Did he have all day?

Nico looked at Alec with raised eyebrows then shook his head and said, "Wrong thing to ask a woman. I'm giving you a crash course in what I like to call the Man Bible, it contains all the secret meanings to what women actually mean when they speak. So listen to me very clearly. It is almost impossible for males to understand it, but a lucky handful of us know the true meanings of words women use as weapons and I am about to impart this wisdom on you, bro."

I folded my arms across my chest and waited for Nico to speak,

I was just as eager as Alec to hear what he had to say.

"The first word is 'Fine'. When a woman says this during an argument, she knows she is right and that you are very wrong. She is *not* fine - you're *not* fine, *nothing* is fine."

I snorted because that was true.

Alec frowned. "But what about if she is wrong-"

"Alec, stop. Do *not* talk back when she says something is fine, wait until she is calm to mention she might be wrong. I usually wait a week for Bronagh to calm down before I mention things about past fights."

Smart lad.

"Okay, fine doesn't really mean fine, got it. What else, love doctor?" Alec sarcastically asked, but Nico ignored him and powered on.

"Second word is 'Nothing'. By the might of God Alec, when a woman says nothing is wrong, *something* is definitely fucking wrong."

Alec nodded his head and flicked his eyes to mine. "I'm starting to believe *that* one."

I gave him a look that caused him to grin as he looked back to Nico.

Nico then held up three fingers. "The third word is 'Whatever'. This is another way for ladies to say fuck you."

I snickered making Nico grin as he popped up an extra finger. "The fourth is a sentence. When a woman says 'It's okay, don't worry about it,' you *do* worry about it. You worry a lot because she is thinking of a way to make you pay for whatever you did wrong."

Alec raised his eyebrows and looked very confused. "Wait. They don't mean it's okay, and that I *don't* have to worry about it? Why would they say that if they don't mean it?"

Nico shrugged. "I think it's some sort of mind trick. They use that sentence as an illusion that things between you are okay, but when you least expect it, they will strike like a cobra and wound your soul."

Alec sat back and huffed. "Why can't they just say what they mean instead of giving words a double meaning?"

Nico shrugged. "I know the real meaning to certain things women say but I don't understand *why* women give them a double meaning, that it beyond my area of expertise, bro."

Alec grunted. "I don't like this."

I bit down on my lip so I wouldn't laugh out loud. I was enjoying this so much that I made sure not to make a sound so they would continue on with the conversation.

"Okay, listen very carefully to this two worded sentence. I'm serious Alec, if you're going to remember *any* of what I just said remember this - it might just save your life," Nico said this so dramatically that I sat forward when Alec did.

"When a woman tells you to 'Go ahead,' you do *not*, under *any* circumstances go ahead. You retreat to a safe distance and observe the situation *very* carefully. She is daring you to do something, *not* giving you permission."

I did laugh then and Nico smiled as he watched me.

Alec chuckled a little and shook his head. "I guess you laughing means all of that was bullshit?"

I wiped under my eyes and said, "No, the opposite, it was spot on correct and that's why it's so funny."

Alec got a deer in the headlights look and stared at me for a moment before looking back at Dominic. "We need to have a *serious*conversation, bro."

CHAPTER FIVE

"Dominic!"

I jumped with fright as a loud female voice bellowed out Nico's name. Aideen was in the bathroom, Alec was getting something out of his room, the rest of the brothers were out in the back, and I was sat in the kitchen waiting by myself. That was until Bronagh Murphy stormed into the kitchen like a woman on a mission.

"Oh, hey Keela," Bronagh said when she found me at the kitchen table.

I waved. "Hey, Bronagh-" I cut myself off when I saw her face. She had a black eye and her cheek was very swollen. "What happened to your face?"

Bronagh shrugged. "There was a bit of an altercation last night in the club. I sort of got tricked into a cage fight."

Um, what?

I stared at Bronagh. "You got *tricked* into a cage fight?"

Was that even possible?

Bronagh nodded her head. "Yeah, it's a long and very weird story."

I got the feeling she didn't want to tell the story so I nodded my head and kept my mouth shut.

"So... what's up?" Bronagh asked after a few moments of silence.

I cleared my throat and said, "Nothin' much, just waitin' on Aideen and Alec. She's in the toilet and he is gettin' somethin' out of his room."

Bronagh grinned. "You might be awhile, Alec takes forever

when he is doin' somethin'."

I tutted. "Great."

Bronagh smiled then looked out the window that was over the kitchen sink.

"How long have they been out there?" she asked me without looking away from the window.

"About twenty-five minutes. Kane and Ryder are tryin' to build a dog house and Dominic is watchin'."

"That's because he is a lazy bastard," Bronagh answered making me laugh.

"He said he was tried from mattress dancin' with you last night... and then again twice this mornin'," I teased.

Bronagh gasped as she snapped her head in my direction.

"He did not!"

I nodded my head. "He did. I smacked him for you because if that was my lad tellin' his brothers private things like that, I'd want someone to smack him too."

"Thanks, but you didn't hit him hard enough," Bronagh muttered.

"What do you mean?"

"He is still conscious."

I burst out laughing and it got the attention of the men out in the back.

"What's so funny, red?" Kane asked when he opened the back door.

"Bronagh," I said.

"Bronagh?" Kane repeated.

Bronagh moved into Kane's view and said, "Bronagh."

A genuine smile stretched across his scarred face. "Hey, bumble bee."

"Bumble bee! Is Bronagh back?" Dominic shouted from the back.

"Yes she is," Bronagh replied.

Dominic sprung up from his seated position and in a flash was next to Ryder, helping him with the half built doghouse.

"Don't even try and act like you were helpin', you pathetic sack of shite."

I smiled when Kane and Ryder burst out laughing.

"Caught by the misses," Ryder said in a Dublin accent and shoved Dominic making him stumble to the right.

Dominic waited a good five seconds before he turned to face the house with a beaming smile on his face.

"Hey, pretty girl. I missed you-"

"Save it, I don't wanna hear your bullshit today."

"Oh," I said aloud then laughed when Kane looked at me with an expression on his face that said he wanted to laugh too.

"It's not bullshit, babe. I did miss you."

Bronagh folded her arms across her chest. "You promised Tyson's house would be ready by the time I got back from signin' up for me... classes."

I momentarily wondered what classes she was talking about.

"It's nearly ready," Nico said and scratched his head.

"Yeah, no thanks to you."

Nico sighed before he turned to Ryder and said, "I'll finish it."

Ryder smiled and said, "Pussy whipped."

"So? It's a pussy of gold."

"Dominic!" Bronagh bellowed.

I smiled as she swatted at Kane and Ryder, who were laughing as they passed her by. They got some water then ventured off somewhere in the giant house.

"Where is your dog?" I asked Bronagh.

"In the sittin' room on his bed," Bronagh said then whistled so loud it made me wince.

Things were quiet for a moment then the noise of nails on the floor could be heard, as well as heavy panting. I widened my eyes when a puppy barged into the kitchen.

"Oh my God. Look at the size of him, he so feckin' cute!" I gushed when the little Husky waddled in my direction. He couldn't have been older than eight weeks; he was so chubby and small that I felt myself melt into a puddle.

"His name is Tyson."

"Hey Tyson," I cooed in a baby voice. "You're gorgeous. Yes you are, ah yes you are."

"Where did you get him?" I asked Bronagh as I rubbed Tyson's head.

"Dominic got him for me birthday yesterday." Bronagh beamed then messed with Tyson's ears making the puppy lightly groan in delight at having his head and ears scratched.

"Happy belated birthday," I said making Bronagh laugh.

"Thanks."

I turned my attention back to Tyson, picked him up and sighed. "I love him already. I love Huskies, they are my second favourite breed."

Bronagh asked, "What's the first?"

"German Shepherds." I gave Tyson to Bronagh then got my phone from my pocket and showed her the screen saver.

Bronagh's eyes widened. "Omigod, he is huge! So beautiful!"

I beamed. "His name is Storm and he is two years old."

Bronagh cuddled Tyson to her. "I don't want him to get big."

I laughed. "Trust me, I don't blame you. Storm refuses to sleep anywhere but in me bed. I babied him too much I guess."

Bronagh snorted. "Dominic won't let Tyson sleep with us because last night he bit his fingers and toes when he saw them touchin' me in bed, it was brilliant."

I smiled and looked towards the backdoor, Nico looked like he was having trouble with getting the roof of the doghouse positioned correctly. Bronagh opened the door and Nico's loud mumbling could be heard, she had a ghost of a smile on her face which indicated to me that she was about to do something to piss Nico off.

"You're doin' that wrong!" she called out.

Nico froze and the muscles in his back tensed. "Get back inside the house and close the door. Now," he growled without turning around.

I raised my eyebrows and looked at Bronagh, who didn't move a muscle.

"The doorway needs to be bigger, he is goin' to be a big dog Dominic," Bronagh said with an upbeat chirp to her tone.

"Bronagh Jane Murphy, I will paddle your ass so hard that you won't sit down for a week if you don't get back inside that house. You were just on my case about building the damn thing, so let me build it my way."

I blew out a breath and licked my lips only to receive a flick on the ear that made me jump and snap my head to the right. I tilted my head all the way back so I could look up at the person who flicked my ear.

I narrowed my eyes when they landed on Alec's face.

"What was that for?" I hissed at him.

"You were drooling over my little brother."

Untrue.

I scoffed and turned back to watch the amusing scene that was Bronagh and Nico.

"I thought you said you wouldn't get mad at me over me suggestions anymore?" Bronagh said to Nico.

Nico dropped his hammer, stood up to his full height and turned around. His body was perfection, ripped and tan beyond belief.

I licked my lips. "Okay, *now* I'm droolin' over your little brother," I whispered to Alec, who moved behind me and growled as he put his arms around me and placed his chin on my head.

"You're lucky you're sitting down."

I smiled. "Why?"

"Because I would smack your ass if you weren't."

I gasped and pinched the arms that were around me.

"What the hell is this?" Bronagh asked Alec and me.

I didn't know what to say so I kept my mouth shut, Alec on the other hand didn't have the same problem.

"Keela is my girlfriend."

Bronagh blinked in confusion then looked over her shoulder to Dominic when he came up behind her.

"Alec said he has a girlfriend. I think he is sick."

Dominic smiled. "Keela *is* his girlfriend."

Bronagh brows furrowed as she looked back in our direction.

"I don't understand... you were single when I left the house this mornin'."

Dominic laughed as he put his arms around Bronagh's waist. "This just happened thirty minutes ago."

"It was instant love, Bronagh. She took my breath away, I had to make her mine."

I rolled my eyes at Mr. Dramatic behind me and focused on Bronagh as I said, "We're fake datin', Bronagh."

"I'm sorry, you're *what*?" she asked.

I chuckled. "Sit down and I'll explain."

Bronagh did as asked and for the next ten minutes I explained everything to her about Jason, Micah, and my situation with them and how I needed Alec's help.

"That's messed up," Bronagh said when I finished speaking.

I laughed. "That's one way of puttin' it."

Bronagh looked to Alec who was now sitting next to me. "How the hell are you gonna pull off bein' someone's fella? You're the biggest slut I know."

I looked away from Alec so he wouldn't see me smile.

"Have a little faith, bee. I'll treat Keela like the queen she is."

I rolled my eyes at the same time Bronagh rolled hers and Dominic found it funny.

"Two words, bro - *good luck*."

Myself and Bronagh smiled as Alec waved Nico off. "I've got this, how hard can being a boyfriend be?"

I looked to him in awe. "You've really *never* been someone's boyfriend before?"

Alec scratched his neck. "No... work always got in the way of potential relationships."

What did that mean?

"I don't understand-"

"Keela, do you wanna come out back with me? It's roastin' in here."

I looked to Bronagh when she spoke and nodded my head because it *was* really warm in the kitchen.

Alec leaned away from me when I got up and went out to the back with Bronagh and I laughed when Tyson waddled out behind us. I was about to close the backdoor when I glanced up and froze when I found both Nico and Alec smiling at Bronagh and myself.

"Why are you smilin' at us like that?" I asked.

Nico then glanced to Alec and said, "She's straight to the point, I like her more than I did before."

Alec smirked. "I like her too, *all* of her."

I scrunched up my face in disgust when he openly molested me with his eyes.

"Stop it Alec, I'm not havin' sex with you."

Alec snapped his teeth at me. "I said I like you, I didn't ask you to fuck me."

"It's all you're short of doin' playboy, but you might as will give it a rest - sex is not on the cards for us."

"Challenging me in front of my little brother and his girl is *not* a smart move, kitten."

I snarled, "Call me that one more time and I swear to God I will-"

"Fuck me up?"

I clenched my hands into fists, and blew a huge amount of air through my nostrils.

"I'm going to punch you in the face before this day is up, I can feel it."

Alec yawned. "I think I can hold my own against you, kitten."

I glared at him and it made Bronagh and Dominic snicker.

I looked behind me to Bronagh and asked, "What's so funny?"

"Would you believe me if I said the conversation you just had with Alec is very similar to one I had with Dominic in our school corridor three years ago?"

I turned to face her. "You couldn't stand his cocky arse either?"

Bronagh grinned. "Yeah, I could barely stand him even when I got with him. We had to work through a lot of shite to get to where we are now."

Nico grunted from behind me. "You can say that again."

Bronagh looked to him. "It was worth it though."

I turned to my side and watched as Nico bore his eyes into Bronagh's, he stared at her until Alec cleared his throat and ruined their moment. Nico looked to Alec and then to me and said, "So... you like dogs, Keela?"

I looked to Bronagh, who was snuggling Tyson into her chest and said, "Yeah, I have a German Shepherd."

"You have a dog?" Alec asked me.

"Yeah."

Nico moved towards me when I pulled my phone back out to show him my screen saver of Storm. "He is a big boy."

I frowned. "It's just his coat, he isn't fat."

Nico flicked his eyes down to mine and then took a step back. "You consider him your baby, don't you?"

"Yes."

Dominic took another step back. "I'm keeping my mouth shut, I know how violent women can be when their 'babies' are talked about."

Bronagh snorted and said, "You're so subtle, you can't even tell you're talkin' about me."

I snickered a little when Nico pulled a face at Bronagh over my shoulder. I moved my eyes to Alec when he walked towards me and then stopped directly in front of me to look down at me.

I cleared my throat. "Can I help you with somethin', lanky?"

Bronagh laughed which made me grin and Alec smirk.

"Nope, just want to get an idea of how short you are. You're tiny."

I gasped and shoved him in the chest. "I'm five foot eight, that is tall for a girl!"

"I'm six-four, to me, you're tiny." Alec grinned.

Bronagh huffed from beside me. "Oi, stud! If five-eight is small to you, what does that make me?"

Alec flicked his eyes to her and grinned. "A very pale smurf."

She dramatically gasped, and it made me laugh.

"You're lucky I'm turning over a new leaf otherwise I'd kick your arse!"

Alec held up his hands and smiled. "I mean no harm."

Bronagh glared at Alec until she passed by us with Tyson and headed back inside the kitchen.

"I'm not that small, am I?" she asked Dominic who was right behind her.

"No pretty girl, Alec doesn't know what he is talking about," Nico replied making me smile as they left the kitchen together along with Tyson who was still in Bronagh's arms.

"He knows when to agree with her," I commented.

"He should, they'll be together for three years next month."

"Long time," I murmured.

"Yeah."

I looked at Alec who was directly in front of me, but I had to take a step back instead of tilting my head all the way back just to look up at him.

"I'm goin' to get a crick in my neck lookin' up at your lanky arse if you keep gettin' that close to me."

Alec waggled his eyebrows at me. "I could always massage you."

"You mean massage my neck?"

"Yeah, your neck, too." He grinned.

"Thanks, but I'll pass, Casanova."

Alec chuckled then sighed when Kane called for him.

"Be right back."

"Okay... send Aideen in to me, will you?"

Alec nodded as he went back into the house. I went back inside and retook my seat at the kitchen table and stared into my half full cup of cold tea. A minute or two passed by until I heard Aideen's loud sigh.

"Where have you been?"

Aideen shrugged. "Talkin' with Kane."

I raised my eyebrows, but Aideen said nothing more about Kane or what they talked about.

"I'm hungry."

Shocker.

"We can go to Eddie Rockets when we're done here if you want?"

Aideen licked her lips. "Sounds good, but why can't we leave now?"

I shrugged. "Alec said he wanted to come with us so he could see where I lived."

Aideen frowned. "Why?"

"I honestly have no idea," I replied.

Aideen huffed and folded her arms like a chastised child, after a minute of listening to her grunting and mumbling to herself about how hungry she was, I snapped.

"Aideen, stop it!"

Aideen jumped with fright then reach over the table and slapped my arm. "Don't do that, I almost wet meself."

I laughed at her and rubbed my stinging arm. "Sorry, but please stop givin' out, *you* are the one who wanted to come here."

Aideen sighed. "I know, and I'm sorry. You know how childlike I get when I'm hungry."

I nodded. "Trust me, I know."

Aideen stuck her tongue out at me making me chuckle as I lightly nudged her with my arm and waggled my eyebrows. "I thought you would want to stay longer since *Kane* is here."

Aideen pursed her lips and shook her head. "I must have been off my head last night for even thinkin' about havin' sex with him.

He is hot as hell, but he is *way* too cocky for my likin'."

I raised my eyebrows. "Really?"

Aideen nodded her head. "Yeah, when you were in here talkin' to Bronagh and the lads, we were in the gym room and he asked me to come up to his room so he could fuck me. I mean, seriously? When is that ever okay to just come out and say that to a lady? I must have really given him the impression I was a slut last night."

Well yeah, you were all over him like a bad rash.

I blew out a large breath of air. "What did you say to him?"

"I told him I was a lesbian and the only reason I came onto him last night was because I thought he was a butch girl."

The fact that Aideen said this with a straight face and a dead serious tone caused me to burst out laughing which in turn made her laugh.

"You did not!" I gasped through my laughter.

Aideen nodded her head. "I did."

I fanned my face. "And he *believed* you?"

Aideen was still chuckling as she shook her head. "No, he didn't, but the longer I keep this facade up he will."

I wiped under my eyes. "You're mental."

Aideen shrugged. "You know that and I know that, everyone else will find out eventually."

I covered my face with my hands as my laughter started up again. I quickly uncovered my face a few moments later when a female voice was heard from out in the hallway.

"Bitches!" Branna's voice cheered as she entered the kitchen.

I looked to her and smiled politely while Aideen jumped up and bee lined for Branna to gave her a bone-crushing hug when she was near enough to do so. I winced at Branna's screech when she pulled back from the hug and looked at Aideen's face.

Aideen reached up and gently touched her face before launching into a recount of last night's events.

"I was so drunk I didn't even know, I'm so sorry!"

"Stop it, you were already leavin' with Ryder, it's not your fault."

Branna was fuming that Aideen got hurt, but found my interaction with Alec and Kane hilarious.

Branna glanced at me as I wiped under my eyes for the second time in the last few minutes.

"Are you cryin'?" she asked me, worry suddenly laced in her tone.

I nodded in Aideen direction. "Only with laughter, because this one told Kane she was a lesbian so he wouldn't chat her up."

Branna burst into laughter that made me snicker again.

"It was the only thing I could think to say at the time to throw him off."

I raised my brows. "Flat out tellin' him you weren't goin' to have sex with him was too hard to think up, was it?"

Aideen narrowed her eyes at me. "You're a bitch."

I shrugged. "That's true."

Branna snickered at mine and Aideen's banter and then nudged Aideen's shoulder. "I thought you told me in the club last night that you thought Kane was hot?"

Aideen sighed and moved towards the kitchen table with Branna. "He *is* hot, but I clearly gave him the wrong impression last night. I was obviously a little too forward with him and gave off a vibe that I was down to fuck, but I'm not. Now he thinks I'm a lesbian."

I laughed. "This is goin' to blow up in your face."

Aideen rolled her eyes. "It won't, I would make a brilliant lesbian."

"Do lesbians act a certain way or somethin'?"

Aideen shrugged. "I have no idea, but I'll just pretend I'm into the V and not the D. Kane will get the hint that I don't want his trouser snake eventually."

Branna and I burst out into laughter and it set Aideen off. After we calmed down, the growling from mine and Aideen's stomach could be heard which made Branna shake her head.

L.A. CASEY

"I have to go shoppin' today, there is zero food in this house. I live with horses who inhale anythin' that resembles food, so I don't have much to offer," Branna said as she moved over to the fridge and opened it.

"I have small tins of tuna?"

I perked up. "I'll have a tin."

Aideen curled her lip up in disgust. "You're a knacker."

I grinned and shrugged my shoulders. I looked to Branna when she brought over my tin of tuna and a fork. I thanked her and pulled the pin off the tin and peeled the lid off.

"I love tuna," I mumbled as I filled my mouth with a large forkful.

Aideen heaved which made Branna chuckle.

"What are you eating?" Alec's voice asked.

I turned my head and watched as he and his brothers strolled into the kitchen all topless - none of them own shirts apparently - and looking like the Magic Mike cast, only much hotter.

I swallowed my food and tongue, but quickly cleared my throat and held up my tin of tuna and said, "Tuna."

Alec grinned at me. "I like eating things raw as well."

I dropped my fork and my damn tin of tuna!

"Alec!" I snapped.

Alec laughed, his brothers laughed, Aideen, and Branna laughed.

I was the only person red faced and silent.

I picked up my tin of tuna and my fork and placed them on the table in front of me then glared at Alec. "I'm leavin' now. I'm not waitin' around any longer for you to finish off whatever you're doin'."

Alec smiled. "Relax, kitten. I was packing my bags, they are in the hall so I'm ready to go too."

I furrowed my eyebrows in confusion.

"*Why* do you have your bags packed?" I asked.

"This should be good," Ryder murmured.

Branna stood up and moved towards him which caused his eyes to solely focus on her and a smile to stretch across his face as she neared him.

I looked from them to Alec when he scratched his neck. "I'm moving in with you."

I stared at him blankly.

After a few moments I found my voice and said, "Can you repeat that?"

Alec rubbed his nose. "You want your family to believe we're a real couple and you said you wanted to take things slow so you can get used to me so... I'm moving in with you. By the time the wedding rolls round you will be *more* than used to me."

"She might hate you by the time the wedding rolls round," Nico muttered making Kane snort.

"I already hate him," I growled keeping my eyes trained on Alec who wouldn't make eye contact with me.

He opened his mouth to speak, but I held my hand up in the air keeping him silent as I got to my feet. "You're not movin' in with me Alec, and how fuckin' dare you just assume it would be okay!"

Alec sighed. "I barely have two days to get to know you. If you want us to appear as a real couple then I *really* have to get to know you."

"But why do you have to move in with me if-"

"Because this is an easier way to spend a lot of time with you. Think about it, I know you don't like me and that you think I'm a prick-"

"She would be right on that front," Kane snickered.

Alec continued talking as if Kane never spoke. "But spending a lot of time with me will get you used to me, thus you would be comfortable around me. I have no underlying motive here, I swear. I'm not looking to get lucky. I told you I'll make you beg me before I fuck you, remember?"

I felt my eye twitch as the brothers, and the girls cracked up laughing again.

"You're a cocky bastard, you know that?" I growled to a grinning Alec.

"I'm aware of it, yes."

It was impossible to insult him!

I folded my arms across my chest and stared Alec down, but his gaze never wavered.

I cracked and stomped my foot on the ground. "Fine, but you will follow me rules or you're out on your arse, you got that?"

"Of course, sweetheart."

Nico laughed and sang, "Alec and Keela sitting in a tree. K-I-S-S-"

I held my hand up cutting Nico off and focused on Alec. "Our 'relationship' is fake, you'd do well to remember that."

Alec bowed to me and sarcastically said, "Of course it's fake, my lady."

His teasing ticked me off.

"Kiss me arse!" I snapped as Alec straightened back up.

"Present it and I will," he replied almost instantly.

I gaped at him.

You aren't supposed to reply back with anything other than a 'fuck you' when someone tells you to kiss their arse, no self-respecting person replies back to a dare with another fucking dare!

"I'm itchin' to smack that smug look off your face, playboy."

I looked to Alec's brothers when they laughed. Nico patted a grinning Alec on the back and chuckled as he said, "I'm fuckface, and you're playboy, the Irish are creative and funny with their insults, you've got to give them that."

Alec smirked. "That's for damn sure."

I sighed and lifted my hands to massage my temples, the slight pounding of a headache was starting to bother me again. I groaned loudly when I heard the grim reaper ringtone suddenly blare from my bag. That's all me and my headache needed, a conversation with my mother.

"Here we go," Aideen murmured.

I dug my phone from my bag and answer it as brightly as I could.

"Mornin', ma."

"Don't call me ma, you're not a sheep."

Well, hello to you, too.

"Mornin', *mother*." I said with a roll of my eyes.

Aideen grunted. "You should call her ma for the simple fact that she hates it."

I motioned for her to shut up, and she closed her mouth but she wasn't happy about it.

"Why haven't you called me about Micah and Jason's wedding? I've given you three whole weeks to mention it and nothing!"

Three whole weeks?

Even if I got the invitation on time that was still very short notice to be invited to a wedding in a different country!

"I only got the invitation today, the post man delivered it to Mr. Doyle's post box by mistake."

My ma dramatically gasped. "That damn Post Office, I knew I should have hand delivered it!"

It doesn't even surprise me that she is so involved with Micah's wedding, she probably planned the whole bloody thing.

I cleared my throat. "You think? A heads up that they were gettin' married in the first place would have been nice as well, mother."

I heard my mother tut and it pissed me off.

"It was very last minute Keela, Jason only proposed to Micah six weeks ago."

I widened my eyes. "He proposed six weeks ago and now they are gettin' married in *one*? Is Uncle Brandon payin' for this?"

It must be expensive as hell booking everything on such short notice.

Aideen snorted. "Of course he is payin' for everythin'."

"Keela, that is none of your business."

That meant yes.

"I still think it's very soon for them to get married."

"Keela, you have got to get over Jason."

Was that a joke?

"I am over Jason! I don't care that he is gettin' married. I just care that I have to fuckin' be there when it happens!" I snapped.

"Keela Elizabeth Daley!" my mothered bellowed.

I groaned and hung my head. "I'm sorry for cursin' mother, but look at this from my point of view, please."

My mother sighed. "I understand it will be awkward and believe me I don't care very much for Jason Bane either, but you *will* be at your cousin's wedding. My pacemaker would explode if you were absent, do you hear me? You would kill me!"

Oh, Jesus overdramatic Christ!

"Mother! You can't say somethin' like that to me, I'm your child!"

I practically heard her roll her eyes. "And as my child you should be wary of my weak heart."

I face palmed myself. "I can't believe you would use your heart condition as a guilt trip to make sure I go to the weddin'."

"I've no idea what you're talking about."

I gritted my teeth, she spoke so clear and proper, not like me at all.

"You're unbelievable, mother."

My mother chuckled. "Thank you, honey."

It wasn't a compliment and she knew it.

"Anyway hun, the point of my call is to let you know that I assume you've taken a week off from work so I already went ahead and paid for your room at the resort. It is a single, I would have gotten a double for comfort, but it was the last room available. I did manage to get a bigger bed for you though. I'll send all the information to your email."

I frowned. "I can pay for meself, mother."

"Don't argue, everything is last minute so I am covering your flights and hotel. I am your mother, it is allowed for me to give a helping hand to my only child."

I shook my head, this was the only time in my life she has thought ahead when it came to me and did something nice, but it was only because it was for Micah's wedding. There was no doubt in my mind that she wouldn't have gone out of her way to make sure I was going to this wedding if it had been someone else's.

"Okay accommodation and flights aside, what are you going to wear?"

I sighed. "I don't know, Aideen is comin' shoppin' with me and Alec to get-"

"Who is Alec?" my mother cut me off.

I looked up then and remembered where I was. I was in the middle of the Slater's kitchen and they were all staring at me whilst still being shirtless.

"Who is Alec?" I repeated and locked eyes with said male.

He grinned and me so I narrowed my eyes at him as I said to my mother, "Alec is me boyfriend, did I not mention him to you?"

My mother's gasp was overplayed. "No! You did *not* mention a boyfriend!"

I slightly smiled at my mother's shock.

I shrugged even though she couldn't see me. "Sorry, it must have slipped me mind."

"How could something like that just slip your mind, Keela? How long have you been together? Is it serious? What does he look like?" My mother fired her questions at me.

"How long are we together?" I repeated out loud.

"Three months?" Alec suggested in a low voice.

I shrugged. "We're together three months."

Alec winked.

"Is it serious?" my mother asked, exasperated.

"We're pretty serious, he is actually movin' in with me today," I said then wished I hadn't as I watched all the Slater brothers grin and bump fists with Alec.

Aideen chuckled from across the table. "This is gonna be hilarious."

"What does he look like?"

What the hell did she care?

"He is very good lookin', God mother."

Alec's ego and head got bigger in that moment, I'm sure of it.

"I cannot believe you are moving in with a man who I've never even met! I am coming over soon to meet him!" my mother snapped and then hung up on me.

I pulled my phone away from my ear and looked at Alec who had his eyebrows raised. "She took the boyfriend news well?"

I shrugged. "As well as can be expected."

Aideen burst out laughing. "She wants to meet him, doesn't she?"

I nodded my head without looking away from Alec whose eyes widened a little.

I titled my head and beamed at him with an evil smile. "Tell me, Alec... are you ready to meet the Devil?"

CHAPTER SIX

"Women love me, Kitten. Your mother won't be any different so stop stressing."

I ignored Alec as I tucked my phone into my bag. Aideen had just messaged me that she finally got into her apartment. I dropped her off on our way back to my apartment, but there was a car fire being put out in the carpark of her apartment complex so of course she started to talk with the hot firemen. Myself and Alec didn't stick around so I made Aideen promise to text me when she got inside her apartment, just so I knew she was okay.

I walked up the stairs of my apartment complex and even though Alec told me not to stress over him meeting my mother, I couldn't help but stress. My mother would be coming to my apartment to meet Alec and if the entire place wasn't sparkling, I'd never hear the end of it.

I glanced over my shoulder to Alec who was walking up the stairs behind me. "Are you sure you don't want a hand with your stuff?"

Alec shook his head. "No, I'm good."

I shrugged then turned my head back around, I was a little breathless by the time we reached my floor. I opened the doorway to the hallway that lead to my apartment and gestured Alec in with his two duffle bags ahead of me.

Yes, he had two huge duffle bags, the man wasn't joking when he said he was moving in. He was moving everything he owned into my apartment.

Everything.

"What is your apartment number?" Alec asked from in front of me.

"Five-twenty," I replied.

Alec stopped outside my door then dropped his bags to the floor and turned to me. "You have five locks on your door."

It was a statement, not a question.

I looked to my door then back to Alec and said, "They are necessary."

Alec frowned. "Why do you live here if it's not safe?"

I sighed. "Because I don't have the money to live somewhere like Upton, that's why."

I brushed by Alec and fished my keys out from the end of my bag, when I found them I pulled them out and got to work unlocking my door. I was in the middle of opening the last lock when the noise of a door opening from behind me got my attention.

"Keela?"

Bollocks.

I put a smile on my face as I turned and moved around Alec's large body.

"Hello, Mr. Doyle."

Mr. Pervert's eyes dropped to my legs for a moment before they reached my face. "Hello, sweetheart."

I shuddered in disgust then jumped when I felt a hand come around my waist, Mr. Doyle looked down to Alec's hand and his jaw set.

"Who is this?" he asked without taking his eyes off Alec's hand.

"I'm Alec Slater, Keela's boyfriend," Alec answered in a tone that was firm yet smooth.

I watched Mr. Pervert slightly narrow his eyes as he lifted them and looked over my head. "I'm Henry Doyle, Keela's neighbour."

"You mean *our* neighbour."

I bit down on my lip when Mr. Pervert stepped back a little, I don't know whether he was shocked or intimidated.

"You're movin' in?" Mr. Pervert asked, his voice gritty.

Alec gently pulled me backwards until my back was pressed against the front of his body. I bit the inside of my cheek when his hand slide down from my waist and rested on my lower stomach. If I had a V line, his hand would had covered one side of it, that's how low his hand was.

Don't remove it.

"Yeah, I am," Alec replied to Mr. Pervert and I could tell from his tone that he was smiling.

The smug shite!

"Well... welcome to the buildin'," Mr. Pervert said in a forced upbeat tone.

"Thank you," Alec replied, his tone naturally upbeat.

Mr. Pervert tilted his head a little. "If you don't mind me askin', where are you from?"

Alec's thumb began to stroke my lower stomach through the material of my dress.

Don't remove it.

"New York," Alec replied then randomly kissed the top of my head.

"Ah, I see. Well take care, and best of luck to you both." Mr. Pervert smiled, glanced to my legs then turned back to his apartment and disappeared inside.

When the coast was clear I slapped Alec's hand, which caused him to yank it away from my body lightning fast. I swirled around and shoved him in the chest and he found funny.

I pointed my index finger at him. "*Don't* touch me like that again!"

A bored expression overtook Alec's face as he looked down at me. "I touched your stomach through the material of your dress, I didn't rub your bare skin so relax and breathe."

I felt my eye twitch as I moved around him and unlocked the final lock on my hall door. When I opened the door I glanced to my left and groaned, dog food was all over the floor and so was some water from Storm's water bowl.

"I'm gonna kill that bloody dog!" I hissed as I turned and marched down the hallway and into my bedroom.

As suspected, Storm was lying on his side of my bed with his legs stretched out.

He was snoring.

"Strom!" I bellowed.

Most dogs would jump up with fright or at least wake up, Storm didn't even lift his ears to indicate he heard me. He really was the worst guard dog in the history of guard dogs.

"Storm!" I snapped again as I walked to my bed.

I reached onto my bed and shook him awake. He opened his big puppy dog eyes and stared at me with what I could only describe as distaste.

Yes, he hated to be woken up.

"Don't look at me like that, get your arse up out of that bed right now or you're gettin' a bath."

He slowly moved then until he was sitting upright, he hated getting a bath and recognised the word I had to threaten him with when I wanted him to do something for me.

He really was like a human male.

"Come on, off the bed," I coaxed.

He stretched, yawned and then jumped off the bed. I looked down at him when I heard a growl erupt from him followed by a loud bark that gave me a fright. He was crouched down a little and looking behind me so I turned around and saw Alec leaning against the frame of the doorway looking between Storm and myself with an amused expression on his face.

"You named your fake boyfriend after your dog?" Alec asked, the light laughter in his voice not going amiss.

How embarrassing!

I felt myself blush. I was mortified that I was caught lying in the first place but it was even worse now because Alec knew who Storm really was.

"Shut up, Alec," I muttered.

He chuckled. "You're adorable."

Come again?

"I'm twenty-three, I'm not adorable."

Alec winked. "You're a *very* adorable twenty-three year old, kitten."

I pursed my lips then looked back down to Storm when he growled.

"Hey, enough of that, he is our new house guest."

I looked at Alec when he lowered himself down to his knees. He avoided eye contact with Storm and held out his right hand like his was offering something.

"Come here, Storm," Alec said then whistled a little.

Was he for real?

"He won't go to you, he hates everyone but me."

Alec ignored me and continued to call Storm to him. I folded my arms across my chest and sat back on my bed with a sigh. Alec continued trying to coax Storm closer to him and just as I was about to put a stop to it Storm suddenly took a hesitant step in Alec's direction and ceased growling altogether.

I felt my jaw drop open as his hesitant step turned into slow moving strides. When Storm was in front of Alec, he sniffed at Alec's outstretched hand and nuzzled his nose into his palm then allowed Alec to pet his head.

He actually allowed someone other than me to touch him.

"I don't fuckin' believe it!" I gasped.

"What?" Alec asked me without looking way from Storm.

"He doesn't like anyone apart from me, this is weird."

Alec shrugged. "I'm good with animals."

I looked at him in disbelief. "Are you a dog whisperer?"

Alec flicked his eyes up to me for a moment before looking back at Storm, but not before I noticed they were creased with amusement. "No, I just know how to act with animals. Did you see how I was down on his level, and not looking directly at him as I offered my hand to him? He could sense I wasn't a threat which is why he is letting me pet him now."

I scoffed. "Aideen isn't a threat, she has known Storm since I got him when he was a puppy and he hates her."

"Does she hate him?" Alec asked quizzically.

That would be a hell yes.

I nodded. "Yeah, they fight all the time."

Alec chortled. "How can a dog and a woman fight?"

I scratched my neck. "You'd be surprised what lengths a woman will go to just to argue with someone... or something."

Alec smiled and shook his head causing lose strands of hair to fall free of his bobbin. "Well, he can sense she doesn't like him so he has decided not to like her back. He can decipher whether he likes someone or not, dogs are very smart."

"I *know* that, Storm is very smart."

Alec looked up to me. "Easy, mama bear."

I bit the insides of my cheeks so I wouldn't smile.

"Look, let me just show you the rest this coffin sized apartment so you can get settled in while I clean up before me ma gets here."

Alec complied and got to his feet then gestured around with his hands. "Let the tour begin."

I cleared my throat. "Well, this is me bedroom."

Alec glanced around then focused his gaze on the bed, the bed that pretty much took up all the space in my room.

"A king? I like it."

I gave him a pointed look. "*Storm* sleeps with me so I need all the room I can get."

Alec pumped his eyebrows at me. "Sounds like you need-"

I held my hand up cutting Alec off. "I'm sure whatever was about to leave your mouth was crude, offensive, and would make me wanna slap you so save it and let me continue on with the tour."

Alec smirked at me then motioned with his fingers that his lips were sealed.

"Follow me," I chirped.

I breezed by him then stopped seven steps later and opened the bathroom door on my right. "This is the bathroom. I'm OCD about cleanin' it so leave the bathroom lookin' like it did when you entered it or I will hurt you, understand?"

Alec leaned his head in and glanced around then looked down at me. "I'll keep it clean, but out of curiosity how would you hurt me exactly? I'm not sure you could physically hurt me... your hands are tiny."

They were not!

I frowned. "Don't underestimate me playboy, I can be dangerous."

Lie, I couldn't and wouldn't hurt a fly.

Alec licked his plump lips. "You can go from kitten to hell cat in half a second, got it."

I blinked up at him. "Great, so we're clear on that?"

Alec smiled at me again and I couldn't help but stare at his mouth.

"Did you ever have braces?" I asked.

Alec slid the tip of his pink tongue over his pearly whites and made me want to do the same with my own tongue.

Calm it, girly.

"Yeah, when I was a kid I had to wear thick metal ones for about two years. It sucked, but it was worth it."

I sighed. "Your smile is very pretty. I don't know if I like it... It seems wrong for someone to possess a smile like that."

I wasn't trying to chat him up I was just being honest.

Alec regarded me with a thoughtful look before he gazed at me with amusement twinkling in his big blue eyes. "All my brothers have nice smiles, it's something we all got from our father. Dominic, Kane, and myself have dimples - we got those from our mother. You can see Dominic's dimples when he speaks, that's how deep they are, but mine are only when I smile. Kane has a dimple on his cheek when he smiles, but you can't see it unless you're close to him when he smiles because a scar cuts through it. Speaking of Kane, his smile is the one to watch out for, it changes how he looks when he smiles."

I ignored the comment about Kane's scars because I didn't want to be rude and ask how he got them.

I thought about his smile though, and nibbled on my lower lip. "I already noticed that. He is sort of scary when he isn't smilin', but when he is smilin'... Oh my God, he is stunnin'. I don't believe in one night stands, but if he smiled at *me*-"

"He *won't* be smiling at you," Alec cut me off, all traces of amusement leaving his eyes and features.

I frowned. "What has your knickers in a twist?"

"Kitten, when I'm in your presence I don't want to hear you talking about my brothers. Any of them."

When I am in his presence?

"Who the hell do you think you are? Jesus?"

Alec shrugged his shoulders. "I'm probably the closest thing on this Earth to Jesus, kitten."

What. The. Fuck?

"You vain piece of shite. How *dare* you compare yourself to-"

I was cut off when Alec burst into laughter; he bent forward smacked his left knee with his left hand and placed his right hand on the wall to keep him steady.

"Your face!" Alec roared with laughter. "You should have seen your face!"

I hated him.

I didn't know him that well but I hated him and I was allowing him to move in with me.

I have officially lost my fucking mind!

I grimaced as I turned around. "Pipe down and follow me."

Alec continued to laugh as he followed me down the narrow hallway.

I stopped when I entered the combo kitchen and sitting room. "This is the kitchen and the sitting room since there is no wall separatin' them. It's a small one bedroom apartment but it suits me fine."

ALEC

I glanced behind me to look at Alec who was glancing around.

"You make the place look even smaller," I muttered.

Alec chuckled. "It's fine, it is small but we can use that to our advantage."

I turned to face him. "Explain."

Alec grinned. "We will be in close quarters so getting to know each other and becoming comfortable with each other will be a breeze. That's what you want, right?"

I eyed him sceptically. "Uh-huh."

Alec had a ghost of smile on his face that broke into a wide grin when Storm came up beside him and brushed his head against his thigh. Alec reached down and rubbed behind Storm's ears then he bent forward and gave him a few strong pats on the stomach. I folded my arms across my chest and glared.

"Bloody traitor," I muttered lowly to myself.

I cleared my throat. "Okay, so I don't know what time me ma will be here at but this place needs to be spotless before she gets here."

Alec stood up, glanced around the apartment and looked at me. "It is spotless."

I scoffed. "There is dog food and water on the floor behind you."

Alec shrugged. "Okay, apart from the dog food and water on the floor, everything else is spotless."

I scratched my neck. "I don't think so, I have to hoover, wash down the kitchen counters, and bathroom, then straightened up my bedroom-"

"Hold up. You mother checks your bedroom when she comes over? How old are you thirteen or twenty-three?"

I groaned. "It sounds bad I know, but just havin' everything clean and tidy will make her visit less painful. Trust me."

Alec regarded me with a wary look but eventually complied. "Okay, what can I do to help make this visit from the she-devil less painful?"

He was going to help me?

That was a nice and unexpected surprise.

"You can rinse the dealf that Aideen left on the draining board next to the sink this mornin'. I don't like them sitting there all day, dust and such will gather on them. Get on that while I sort out me bedroom and the bathroom, okay"

Alec held his hand out to me, his fist tightly closed and said, "On it, boss."

It took a second for me to realise that he wanted me to fist bump him and when I eventually did ball my own hand into a fist and touched my knuckles against his, he audibly awed.

"Your fist is the size of a toddler's, that's probably the cutest thing I have ever seen in my entire-"

"I'll punch you in the face with my toddler sized fist if your finish that sentence, playboy."

Alec bit his lower lip then proceeded to salute me. "Aye, Captain."

I rolled my eyes. "Just rinse off the delph like a good little lad."

I brushed by him and smiled when I heard his dramatic gasp. "Little lad? I'm big *all over*, baby!"

"Yeah, I noticed how big your feet were," I called back down the hallway as I neared my bedroom.

"They are average size for a man my size!" Alec bellowed. "Besides, you know what they say about men with big feet, *right*?"

"Yeah, they wear big socks."

"Smartass!" Alec shouted making me laugh as I closed my bedroom door.

I shook my head still lightly laughing as I moved around my bedroom five minutes later. I opened my bedroom windows, stripped the sheets from my bed along with my pillowcases and put them into the wash basket in the corner of my room. I got fresh linens from my wardrobe and put them on my bed. When that task was don, I got the hoover from my wardrobe - yes, items besides clothing were stored in my wardrobe because my apartment was so small I had no hot press for storage - and hoovered my entire room.

I opened my bedroom door and hoovered the hallway then inside the bathroom and back out into the hallway until the cord belonging to the hoover halted my movements as I neared the kitchen entrance. I went back to my room and unplugged it from the socket on my bedroom wall and brought it out to the hallway. I left it there so I could bring it into the kitchen and sitting room when I was finished cleaning the bathroom.

I was about to ask Alec how he was getting on with the dealf when I heard him singing. *The* fucker was not only good looking, but he could sing and sing *really* well. His choice of song caused my eyes to roll though.

"Sex bomb, sex bomb, *I'm* a sex bomb-"

"*You're* a sex bomb!" I corrected the lyric cutting him off as I went into the bathroom.

Things were silent then and I didn't notice he entered the bathroom until I looked up into the mirror and saw him behind me.

"Did you just call me a sex bomb?" Alec asked his gaze locked on mine through the mirror.

I would have laughed at him if his gaze wasn't so intense.

"I was correctin' the lyrics," I said then blew out a breath. "You aren't goin' to jump me, are you?"

Alec cocked an eyebrow. "I'm sorry did you say jump me or *fuck me*?"

I gasped. "Alec Slater, don't be so crude!"

Alec's pretty smile stretched across his face. "Did you just chastise me, little kitten?"

I narrowed my eyes. "I did, and I'll kick your arse if you keep up that dirty talkin'."

"I'll keep the dirty talking up as well as something else *up* if you don't stop being so damn innocent."

I furrowed my eyebrows in confusion. "What makes you think I'm innocent?"

Alec deadpanned. "You just yelled at me for being crude."

I rolled my head on my shoulders feeling frustrated. "Just because I don't like you bein' crude doesn't mean I'm innocent."

"Prove it," Alec challenged.

I raised my brows. "How?"

Alec pumped his eyebrows at me and said, "Surprise me."

I cracked my knuckles. "Stop tryin' to bait me into doin' somethin' sexual with you. I'm not havin' sex with you now or ever."

Alec stepped closer to me molding the front of his body into the back of mine and covered my hands on the bathroom counter with his. He kept eye contact with me through the mirror as he did this then he lowered his mouth down to my ear and lightly blew on it making me shiver.

His breath on my ear caused my eyes to drift shut as shudders shot throughout my body.

"I told you I will fuck you kitten and trust me, I *will* fuck you, but not until you beg me," he whispered.

He words were sobering but I still kept my eyes closed.

"You have a better chance of teachin' Storm how to roll over than you do havin' sex with me, playboy."

I opened my eyes and winked to a now smirking Alec. I jumped and yelped when he slapped my behind then ducked out of the room when I tried to return the slap, only to his face instead of his arse.

"Don't be violent," Alec grinned as I followed him out of the bathroom and into the hallway.

He was walking backwards while I moved towards him.

"You know what they say; actions speak louder than words."

Alec laughed. "I don't think that quote makes it okay for you to hit me."

I shrugged. "You slapped me first."

I continued to advance on Alec. I wasn't going to hit him but I was going to make him pay and when he tripped over the hoover I'd left in the hallway and fell over onto his arse, my payment was received.

"That's karma, bitch," I sang then turned and pranced into the bathroom.

I could hear Alec grumbling to himself from out in the hallway which made me chuckle as I went about cleaning the bathroom. I tuned everything out as I cleaned the bathroom; the only thing that got my attention was Storm when he came into the bathroom.

"Hey beautiful," I cooed.

Storm rubbed his head against my leg then whined and cocked his leg before putting it back down on the floor. I shooed him from the bathroom as I quickly ran to my bedroom to get his lead from the hook on my bedroom wall. When I re-entered the hall I clipped the end of the lead onto Storm's collar and moved towards the hall door.

"Be right back, Alec."

"Where are you going?" Alec asked.

"Storm needs to go to the bathroom," I said then looked to the kitchen only to find it empty. I looked to the sitting room then and gaped at Alec's body lying across my sofa making it look smaller than it was. He was reading something.

A book.

"What are you readin'?" I curiously asked.

"That porn book we were talking about earlier at my house. This dude is my God! He just fucked this Ana chick while she was on her period-"

"Stop it!" I screeched. "Stop readin' and put the bloody book down!"

He was reading *Fifty Shades of Grey*.

I was both horrified *and* mortified.

Alec got up from the sofa, placed the book on the coffee table and turned in my direction.

"Why are you blushing?"

Him noticing my embarrassment only caused my already red cheeks to heat up even more.

"Oh damn, your cheeks are so flushed," Alec said and took a step towards me.

I held up my free hand. "Hold it right there, buddy. I've to bring Storm outside so just rinse the dealf like I asked you to do half an hour ago and if you have a minute clean up Storm's food and water on the floor. We're supposed to be a cleanin' team."

Alec bowed. "Yes dear," he said and moved out of the sitting room and into the kitchen.

I left the apartment and hurried down the stairs of my apartment with Storm before one of the neighbours caught me. The apartment complex doesn't have a ban on animals but if enough neighbours complain about one, the animal or the tenant has to go. Storm is a good dog, but I still don't want to give any of my neighbours reason to report me so that's why I whisk him in and out of the building without being noticed.

Once we got outside I headed in the direction of the park that was located directly across from my building. I never let Storm off his lead for the simple fact that he never comes back to me when I call him. I was terrified he would run out of the park one day if I let him off the lead and get hit by a car. So to keep him safe and my nerves tamed, I bought a lead that extends pretty far so he feels like he is roaming free whilst still being secured on the lead.

Storm relieved himself as soon as we got to the park; I grabbed one of the doggie poop bags that were located around different stations throughout the park to bag it up. When that nasty business was bagged and placed into the bin, we spent half an hour walking around so Storm could stretch his legs. When he was ready, we walked back to my apartment. All the way back I was cursing myself for forgetting my hand sanitiser, I wanted to wash my hands so bad.

When I made it back into my apartment building, Storm and myself hauled arse up the stairs and down the hallway of my floor. I heard laughter coming from inside my apartment so I stuck my ear to the door to see if I knew whom it was.

I fumbled with my keys to open the door, when it opened wide

Storm shot forward and because I had his lead in my hand, I was jolted forward and face planted on the ground.

Things went silent then.

"That looked painful," Alec's voice commented after a moment or two.

I groaned.

"She's fine, she can be very clumsy. Never mind Keela, let's talk about you Mr. Slater."

"Please, call me Alec."

"Okay, Alec."

I groaned even louder when I heard my mother's voice.

If there was a Hell, I was in it.

CHAPTER SEVEN

"Are you okay?" Alec asked me as he helped me to my feet.

I nodded my head and brushed down the front of my dress as I ignored the throbbing pain in my knees and chest.

"I'm okay."

I wasn't okay, I was pretty sure I cracked a bloody rib.

"Are you sure, kitten?" Alec asked me, worry laced in his tone as he rubbed the back of his fingers across my cheek.

The sign of tender affection did nothing for me, but when I glanced to my mother I could see the smile on her face as she watched Alec interact with me.

Did she like him?

"Hey ma, I didn't think you would get here until later," I said as I straightened myself up.

My mother cut her eyes to me. "Mam or mother, Keela, never ma."

I inwardly bitch slapped her.

She was one of the few Irish mothers who had a preference on what her child should call her.

"Sorry, *mother*," I mumbled.

She made me feel like a kid again and I despised it.

"Come sit so we can talk," my mother said and moved to the one seater settee which left me and Alec to sit on the two seater settee.

"How and when did you two meet?" my mother quizzically asked when we were all seated.

Fuck!

I swallowed my tongue horrified that I didn't even think to go over questions like this with Alec on the drive from his house so we would have the same answers.

I started to sweat.

"Um... Well... Um."

I jumped a little when Alec's fingers suddenly threaded through mine.

I looked at him and relaxed when he winked at me.

He had this... or at least he better have it.

"We met three months ago in a night club, Ms Daley. We hit it off straight away and went on a few dates after that night. Three weeks into dating I knew she was the one so I asked her to be my girlfriend and she agreed. The days sort of meshed together then and flew by and before we knew it, we decided to move in together. As you can see, we just started the process today since all of my stuff is still in my bags."

My mother glanced over to the apartment door and to the two large duffle bags next to it.

"Are you sure your things will fit in this box?" my mother asked, a grin on her face.

I clenched my free hand into a fist, I knew my apartment was tiny but no one else could hate on it except me.

"We will get somewhere bigger in time mother," I said, my tone clipped.

My mother hummed in response as she glanced around the sitting room.

She was probably looking for a spot that was untidy so she could rub it in my face.

It wouldn't surprise me.

"Alec, could you be a pet and go make me a cup of tea, please?" my mother asked Alec, smiling brightly at him.

I raised my eyebrows.

My ma didn't drink tea.

What was she up to?

"Of course, Ms. Daley." Alec smiled.

He turned to me and mumbled, "Don't slap me."

I wondered why he said that, but realised why when his lips connected with mine. Alec's free hand cupped my face as he slipped his tongue into my mouth that was open with shock. I quickly realised what the fuck was happening and bit down on Alec's tongue making him whimper.

I released his tongue then pecked his lips and smiled evilly.

Alec's eyes were filled with tears, probably from the stinging pain in his mouth and it made me smile.

"'Ucking 'itch," he muttered, and rolled his tongue around his now open mouth.

I yelped when I felt a pinch on the outside of my thigh.

Alec hid his grin and made a move to go into the kitchen, but couldn't move very far because I wouldn't let go of his hand.

"Um, Keela, can I have my hand back?" Alec chuckled, but started to squeeze my hand to the point of pain.

He was hurting my hand, but I slightly shook my head.

"Don't leave me alone with her," I murmured.

Alec pulled his hand from mine and gave me a stern look that made me itch to bite him again.

"Talk to your mother," he smiled.

Bastard!

He moved off into the kitchen and since my mother had her back to him, he made a show of sticking his middle finger up at me then pointed to his tongue and mouthed, "That fucking hurt!"

I rolled my eyes at him and turned my head to face my mother who was staring directly at me.

"Did you lose a bet?" she asked me.

I raised an eyebrow. "What?"

"Is Alec really your boyfriend or did you lose a bet?" she asked.

I hate that Alec could hear this because it made everything worse.

I don't think I have ever been more embarrassed by a question.

"Why would you even ask me that?" I asked, my head downcast.

"Look at him, he belongs on a magazine cover, Keela."

And that meant he couldn't be with me?

"Is it that impossible in your mind for me to have a good lookin' boyfriend without some sort of scheme bein' involved?" I asked, my voice filled with emotion.

Alec *was* my fake boyfriend as a favour to me but still, I could go out with a good looking person if I wanted to. It wasn't *that* farfetched of an idea!

"Of course you can go out with a good looking person, you're a very pretty girl Keela even though you *are* overweight."

Oh my God, I thought and slumped my shoulders.

Why did she *always* have to bring my weight into everything?

"I've lost more than a stone since you've last seen me ma. It's comin' off slowly but surely. Can you not tell?" I asked, curiously.

My ma gestured for me to stand up so I did. Then she twirled her finger around, I turned around as well so she could she all of me.

"You *do* look slimmer, and I really like that dress on you, it hugs your waist perfectly," my mother said, humming in appreciation.

I blew out a breath of relief.

Thank God for that at least, my diet and exercising *was* working after all.

"Thank you," I said then sat back down.

Things were quiet for a moment, and I didn't dare look in the direction of the kitchen to see what Alec was doing. I was happy being unaware of him right now.

"How old is Alec?" my mother asked.

I stared at her blankly and unblinking because I had no fucking idea what the answer was to her question. I cleared my throat then glanced at Alec who was looking at me and mouthing something, but I couldn't make it out.

"How old is Alec?" I repeated with a smile and glanced to him again.

He was now showing me his age on his fingers; he flashed his hands twice then held up eight fingers.

Twenty-eight?

I thought he was closer to my age; he didn't look near his thirties.

"He is twenty-eight, mother."

"Hmmm," she murmured then waved me off.

"About Micah's and Jason's wedding, if you check your email you will see all of the information about the wedding. It is in the Bahamas six days from today. You and Alec will be flying out on the twenty first of September, two days from now on Monday, and return home on the seventh, the day after the wedding. Your plane tickets are included in the email all you have to do is print them out. Print out your accommodation proof for the Pink Sands Resort as well so you get your room key when you arrive. Families from both sides have already been in the Bahamas a week, but since I don't like the heat I will only be flying out the day before the wedding."

I stared at my mother blankly, blinking.

She got Alec a plane ticket and added him to the room she got me at the resort already? But she only just found out about him!

"Ms. Daley?" Alec's voice said from our left.

I looked as he moved in our direction from the kitchen with a cup of tea in his hands.

"I appreciate you thinking of me and getting me a plane ticket and sorting out my accommodation but please let me reimburse you-"

"No, consider it a pre-wedding gift for you and Keela."

Ex-fucking-cuse me?

"Mother!" I screeched.

My ma smiled, evilly.

"This was a fun chat, it was lovely to meet you Alec. Thank you for taking a chance on my girl."

Oh my God.

"It was actually Keela who took a chance on me. Your daughter is too good for me Ms. Daley, but I plan to spend as long as it takes to be worthy of her," Alec said proudly as he sat next to me and put his arm around my shoulder while he placed my ma's cup of tea on the coffee table in front of her.

I could have squeezed him for saying what he did because the shocked look on my ma's face was priceless.

"I better get going. I will see you both the day before the wedding when I fly out. I expect you both to look the part, do not embarrass me Keela."

"I wouldn't dream of it ma," I said, my tone cold as ice.

My mother hummed as she stood up and straightened her clothes. "Lovely to meet you pet," she said to Alec then turned and walked towards the door of my apartment. She of course gazed down the hallway and into the kitchen for God's only knows what before she opened the door and left.

I groaned in relief and shrunk backwards into the settee.

"Thank God that is over with."

Alec nudged my knee with his. "It could have been worse."

I looked to him with raised eyebrows. "How could it have been worse?"

Alec grinned. "She could have walked in on me fucking you on the kitchen table."

Don't hit him.

"You're sick in the head, you know that right?"

Alec shrugged then looked to the coffee table. "Why did she ask me to make her tea if she didn't drink it?"

I sat upright. "She doesn't drink tea, I'm pretty sure she asked you to make it just so she could grill me with you out of the way."

Alec glanced to me. "I heard her talking to you about your weight and I want you to know she's wrong. You're not overweight; I think you're the perfect weight. You have a gorgeous body."

He thought that?

I flushed. "You're just sayin' that because I won't sleep with you and you don't like bein' rejected."

Alec winked at me. "You're correct, I don't like being rejected so that *is* part of the reason why I want to fuck you. But the other part, the *main* part, is because you're hot."

I frowned. "Am I supposed to be flattered?"

"Yes."

"You're a dickhead."

Alec laughed. "Is that the best insult you've got?"

"Give me awhile, I'll come up with some bad names that will shock you to the core."

Alec stood up. "I don't doubt that for a second," he said.

I scratched my arm and curiously asked, "How long was she here?"

Alec shrugged as he got my mother's untouched cup of tea and brought it to the sink. "About ten minutes before you got back."

I groaned. "What did she talk about?"

Alec shrugged, again. "She just asked where I was from, who and where is my family and what I did for a living."

I swallowed. "And what did you tell her?"

Alec glanced to me and grinned. "I told her the truth, that I am from New York and I came here with my four brothers and I am currently in-between jobs."

I blew out a breath of relief and it made Alec laugh.

"You didn't really think I would tell her what I previously did for work did you?"

I blushed. "You're very open Alec, I don't think I could ever be certain over what comes out of your mouth."

Alec stuck his tongue out at me then whistled loudly before calling Storm's name.

I gaped at Storm when he barrelled down the hallway from the bedroom and into the kitchen. I have to call him at least ten times before the fucker will even acknowledge me.

"How did you do that? He never comes to me when I call him the first time."

ALEC

Alec shrugged as he bent down and petted Storm's head. "Maybe it's the tone I call him in. I don't leave room for arguments."

I snorted. "That must only work with dogs then."

Alec glanced to me. "It works on humans, too."

"Not *this* human."

Alec smiled. "Wait till you warm up to me kitten, you will see just how persuasive I can be."

I felt like he was threatening me.

"It will be a cold day in Hell before you can persuade me to do *anythin'*, playboy."

Alec winked. "I'm going to thoroughly enjoy completing these challenges, one by one."

I snarled at him making him snicker as he got Storm's lead from the table and hooked it back onto his collar. I got up from the sofa and quickly moved into the kitchen next to Storm and held my hands up in front of my chest.

"I already brought him out, we did a few laps of the park."

Alec raised an eyebrow. "Yes, and I'm going to bring him out again. I want him to get used to me being here. I'll bond with him more on my own."

I swallowed.

That was so cute, but another walk for my baby was *not* happening.

"I get that and it's brilliant that you're thinkin' of him but I don't want him to go on another walk."

Alec tilted his head to the side. "Why?"

I sighed. "Because his breathin' gets bad when he does too much in one day, I don't want to push him."

Alec shook his head at me. "Keela, this may be hard for you to hear, but Storm-"

"Don't say it."

"Is-"

"Do. Not. Say. It."

"Fat."

I gasped and slapped Alec's arm. "You bastard, he is *right there*, he can fuckin' *hear* you!"

Alec bit down on his lower lip.

"He isn't fat either, he just has a thick coat of fur. That's all."

Alec beamed at me. "You have just overtaken bee on the cuteness scale."

Who?

"Excuse me?"

"Bronagh, we call her bee. She can be very cute, but damn kitten, so can you."

I growled. "I'm *not* cute and you're *not* bringin' Storm out."

Alec scrubbed his face with his free hand and said, "Baby, I'm not insulting the big guy. I'm just stating facts. He *is* overweight, and it's *not* healthy for him. I think we should start weaning him from big portioned meals, and bring him out more often."

Was he for real?

I placed my hands on my hips. "We? I just met you last night and you just moved in and became my fake boyfriend today, and now all of a sudden there is a *we*?"

Alec snapped his fingers at me - he literally put his huge fucking hand in my face and snapped his bloody fingers at me.

"We're a we now, get used to it kitten. From this moment until we get back from the Bahamas we are a unit, a duo, a fucking couple - fake or not - so yes we're a *we*."

I blinked.

Well, excuse the hell out of me.

"Whatever," I murmured and folded my arms across my chest.

Alec sighed. "It'll be easier if we look at this arrangement as an actual relationship instead of a 'favour'. Things will look more authentic at the wedding."

I sighed because he had a point.

"Okay, fine, we're a we."

Alec smiled in triumph and raised his free hand in the air. I chuckled and high fived him with my hand.

"I'll bring Storm out on a paced walk, I'll bring a bottle of water for him just in case he gets thirsty. You can get a start at unpacking my bags if you want?"

I turned around and glanced at Alec's duffle bags.

"I think you have more crap than me."

Alec laughed as he walked towards the apartment door.

"I *do* have a lot of crap."

He opened the door then and glanced back at me and said, "You can just put some of my things in the bedroom, but not everything since we're leavin' for the Bahamas in two days, it'll be easier to have everything where I am sleeping."

He closed the door then and left me staring at it like a dope.

He thought he was sleeping in my bedroom?

No.

Hell no.

CHAPTER EIGHT

"Oh. My. God! Will you *stop* kickin' me? I can't fucking take this anymore!"

Tonight was the first night living with Alec, it was the early hours of the morning and I was contemplating murder.

Yeah the fucker got his way and was sleeping in my bed simply because he refused to get out of it when bedtime rolled around. It took Storm an hour to give up whining and claim the settee as his after Alec wouldn't let him up onto the bed. My room isn't a big room and having a king sized bed doesn't leave much floor space. With the three of us in the bed it would have been cramped so Storm got his marching orders.

"Ow! For fuck's sake *stop* scratching me, Keela!" Alec's voice howled as he kicked at my feet.

I angrily kicked his legs away from mine with force. "I can't help it if you get scratched, your legs keep gettin' tangled up with mine!"

I pulled my right leg up the bed but my toesnails caught Alec's calf.

"Jesus Christ, you're the worst person to sleep with," Alec snapped as he sat upright on my bed.

Me?

I was the worst person to sleep with?

Was this freak having me on?

I sat up and shoved Alec in the shoulder with both of my hands. "Go sleep on the sofa with Storm then, this *my* bed anyway, you should be thankful *you* are even on it right now!"

ALEC

Alec humourlessly laughed. "Yeah, because I feel very fucking lucky right now sleeping next to Edward Scissor Feet."

Bastard!

I screamed as I dove on his back when he tried to get up off the bed. "It's not my fault I can't find me toe nail clippers, you had it last. I told you to leave my bathroom the way you found it, but did you listen? No!"

Alec coughed as my arm went around his neck. "I left the damn clippers in the untouched bathroom, you physco!"

He pinched my underarm, which of course caused me to move it away from his neck. Still angry and now in pain from being pinched, I grabbed onto Alec's hair with my hands.

Alec yelped. "My hair, let go of my beautiful hair!"

I fisted my hand around his shoulder length locks and tugged which caused him to hiss in pain. "Take back what you said about me feet and I will."

"Twenty-three Keela, you're twenty-three so start fucking acting your age- Ow! Okay, okay, I take it back. *Jesus!*"

I honestly don't care how childish it was, I smiled in triumph and let go of Alec's hair but before I had the chance to climb off his back he stood up from the bed taking me with him. He then threw me back onto the bed and turned and pounced on me. He got between my legs, grabbed my arms and pinned them above my head and put the tip of his nose on the tip of mine.

This all happened in the blink of an eye, I barely had a chance to do anything before I realised he was in my face.

"You pulled my hair," he snarled.

I glared at him through the darkness. "You insulted me feet."

"Your nails *are* like razor blades! How is that an insult when it's true?"

I struggled underneath him and squealed when he wouldn't budge.

"You're too heavy!"

"Oh, so now you're callin' me fat? How insensitive, Keela,"

L.A. CASEY

Alec snapped at me in a high-pitched badly mimicked Irish accent.

I grunted. "I feel like you're mockin' me."

Alec laughed then. "You're so fucking annoying."

I rolled my eyes. "*I'm* annoyin'? Maybe that's because I'm wrecked from virtually *zero* sleep. You're the worst spoonin' partner ever!"

He really was. It was impossible to get comfortable next to him.

Alec let go of my arms and got up off me, he moved to my locker and flipped on the lamp.

I flung my hands over my eyes. "What are you doin'?" I shouted.

"Addressing what you just said. I'm not the worst spooning partner, cuddling is just... not for me."

What?

I under covered my eyes and squinted until my eyes adjusted to the light.

"What do you mean?"

"I can only cuddle you until you fall asleep, but I can not fall asleep that way. I've tried it hundreds of times before with hundreds of different people and it just doesn't work for me."

Slutty much?

I frowned. "Why?"

Alec shrugged. "It's awkward and uncomfortable."

I'll give on the comfort thing because cuddling with him was awful, but I won't give on it being awkward.

"What is awkward about cuddlin'?"

"I have four problems with cuddling women and I shall list them accordingly."

"Here we go," I mumbled.

I was sorry I bloody asked.

Alec ignored me and popped his index finger into the air. "Number one, I always get a face full of hair when cuddling with a woman and I don't care how hot a woman is or if she has a pussy of gold, I do *not* like it."

Pussy of gold?
What. A. Pig!

Alec ignored my curled lip of disgust and stuck up a second finger. "Number two, my arm goes dead from a woman lying on it. That wouldn't normally bother me, but the pins and needles that attack my arm a few minutes after it goes dead *do* bother me."

I thought on that one and inwardly shrugged my shoulders - I had to give him that, it didn't sound nice at all.

"Number three," Alec said, his third finger now erect in the air. "I get an awkward boner when cuddling and don't know whether to fuck a woman awake or just lie there until it goes away. Most women would love to be fucked awake, but knowing my luck the woman I'm banging would probably scream rape and have me arrested."

I bit down on the insides of my cheeks so I wouldn't laugh.

Alec popped a fourth finger up. "Then there is number four, cuddling with *you*. You're the first person to share a bed with me without fucking me. Hell, you haven't even kissed me yet and we live together that makes everything *harder*. Pun completely intended."

"Correction, we kissed in front of me ma today."

Alec scoffed. "Firstly, I kissed you, you didn't kiss me so it still stands that you haven't kissed me yet. Secondly, it wasn't exactly a kiss because you practically bit my tongue off."

I lightly snickered as he placed his hands on his bare hips and stared me down.

"You need to change your ways of thinkin', think of me as a sister or as a best friend."

Alec curled his lip in disgust. "I can't think of you as a sister because I want to fuck you."

Wow.

"Jesus, are you always so bluntly crude?" I asked and shook my head.

"Yes, I am."

I groaned. "Well, cut it out. I don't know how many times I have to tell you that sex will *not* happen between us. You're hot, *very* hot, but Alec you're an arsehole as well."

Alec smiled at me. "We can fuck around my being an asshole-"

"You're impossible to get through to!"

I was going to punch him if he kept it up.

Alec chuckled. "I'm only playing with you."

I glanced to him and shook my head. He wasn't playing. He really did want to fuck me and the more I shut him down, the more he tried to seduce me. This was where my super self-control was extremely important. I won't give in and sleep with Alec or any man unless there is something between us. I'm well aware that way of thinking might mean I don't have sex for a very long time but I refuse to give myself to someone who only wants my body for a dirty romp, and that is all Alec wanted me for.

Sex.

"We live together in order for *me* to get comfortable with *you* so pretendin' to be a couple will be easier next week at the weddin'. It's already failin' in the bedroom because I cannot sleep with you anymore, it's horrible. I'm one more knee in the back away from becomin' murderous."

Alec narrowed his eyes at me. "Challenge accepted."

What?

"Alec, I'm *not* challengin' you-"

"Too late, I've already accepted the challenge so get back under the covers you're about to have the best night's sleep you've ever fucking had. You will be *so* well rested tomorrow you won't ever want to sleep without me again."

This was weird.

"There is somethin' wrong with you."

Alec jumped onto my bed. "Tell me something I don't know, kitten."

I forced myself to get back into my bed next to Alec.

"You know you could just stick to your side of the bed and I could stick to mine?"

"I tried that, you just keep rolling in my direction."

I grunted as I got under the covers. "Because it's me fuckin' bed," I muttered.

"What was that?" Alec asked.

I laid down and clenched my hands into fists as I pulled my blanket around my body.

"Nothin'," I growled.

Alec remained silent and so did I.

The continued silence allowed my eyes to drift shut. After what could have been one minute or ten I could feel myself start to doze off, but that went to shit when I felt a tugging on my hair.

I reached up to see what my hair was caught on when my hand grabbed another hand.

"Alec," I growled.

"I'm sorry, I thought you were asleep."

I didn't turn to him or release his hand as I said, "You waited until I was asleep before you pulled me hair?"

"I'm not pulling it, just running my fingers through the ends... I do it when I'm tired, it helps me fall asleep."

Oh my God.

I should not be finding this cute, I should not like Alec touching any part of me but dammit I did.

"Okay, you can play with my hair. Just try not to pull it, okay?" I murmured and released Alec's hand.

"Thank you," he said and I could hear the smile in his voice.

Knowing he was smiling made me smile and the realisation of that freaked me out.

I have to remain strong when it comes to Alec.

Very strong.

CHAPTER NINE

"Have you had sex with Alec yet?" Aideen asked me as I opened my hall door to her.

I yawned and rubbed my eyes as she pushed by me.

"Good mornin' to you too, sweetie pie," I said as I closed my hall door.

"Mornin'," Aideen sang. "Back to my question, have you shagged Mr. Slater yet?"

"I can answer that for you if you would like?"

I didn't look over my shoulder as Alec spoke but when I moved by Aideen I saw that her mouth was hanging open so I came to the conclusion that he was, once again, shirtless.

"Unfortunately Aideen, Keela's vagina is still unknown territory to me." Alec sighed making Aideen cackle.

I rolled my eyes as I ran the tap and filled up a glass with water.

"You're disgustin'," I said then downed my water and placed my glass in the sink then turned around. I picked up a tea towel then and threw it at Alec who caught it in his right hand.

"Put some clothes on, nobody wants to see your half naked body this early in the mornin'."

"I do," Aideen chimed in.

I glanced to Aideen with distaste. "Let me rephrase that, nobody with any *self-respect* wants to see your half naked body this early in the mornin'."

Aideen snorted, but didn't say anything while Alec jammed his thumb over his shoulder and said, "It's twelve-thirty in the afternoon, it's not morning anymore."

I felt my eyebrows jump as I flicked my eyes to the clock on the wall behind Alec.

"It's that late?"

Alec smiled. "I told you that you would have a great night's sleep."

He was correct but I wouldn't admit it.

"I didn't get to sleep until three or four this mornin' *because* of you so obviously I slept in."

I looked at Aideen when she snapped her fingers in my direction. "You didn't get to sleep until three or four this mornin' because of Alec? Girl, you better explain!"

Alec snorted. "It's nothing exciting, trust me."

I hissed at him then looked at Aideen. "He kicked Storm out of me room and made him sleep on the settee because *he* wouldn't sleep there. He also kicked *me* a lot durin' the night and I couldn't sleep until I addressed the problem."

"By addressing the problem she means scratching me to death with her razor like toenails."

Aideen cracked up laughing which only heightened my rising temper.

"Fuck you!" I snapped at Alec as I pushed by him and stomped to the bathroom.

I slammed the door behind me to block out Aideen and Alec as I searched for my fucking toenail clippers. I was enraged to find that they were on the counter just like Alec said they were. I angrily sat on the side of my bath and put my foot on the closed toilet seat and went to work clipping my toenails until they were a 'safe' length.

I hated that they *were* pretty long like Alec said.

"Keela, how long will you be before we can go?" Aideen's now chuckling voice shouted from the kitchen.

I furrowed my eyebrows in confusion.

We were going somewhere?

"Go where?" I shouted.

"Shoppin', *duh*."

Shopping?

"Shoppin' for *what*?"

I jumped when the bathroom door was suddenly flung open. I don't know why I covered myself with my hands, I wasn't naked but if I were, Aideen would have seen everything.

"Shoppin' for what you're goin' to wear to the weddin', you're flyin' out tomorrow. Seriously Keela, get with it."

I groaned and lifted my hands to scrub my face, shopping for clothes completely slipped my mind.

"I've three hundred fifty euros for everythin', will that be enough?"

I hoped it was enough, that's all I could spare from my savings without putting myself in debt.

Aideen waved me on. "Please, I can make that stretch easily."

I gave Aideen a look. "I want to look *nice* Ado, not cheap."

Aideen placed her hands on her hips as she said, "We're bringin' sexy back, but on a budget."

I laughed. "You're up for the challenge then?"

Aideen laughed. "I got this, Kay."

I smiled. "I trust you."

I laughed when Alec popped his head around the door frame which made Aideen scream with fright. He chuckled and dodged her swinging hands. He put his arms around her from behind and pinned her hands to her sides.

"Did I just hear you say you have three hundred fifty euros to clothe yourself for this vacation?"

"Death sentence - *not* a holiday, but yes you did hear that correctly."

Alec shook his head. "No girlfriend of mine will be on a budget when she goes shopping, this is on me."

I looked to Aideen when her eyes all but fell out of her head.

"Can *I* be you girlfriend, please?"

I rolled my eyes while Alec laughed and said, "Sure you can. I'll always be up for a threesome with you and kitten."

In your dreams, playboy.

"Ha-ha very funny but no, I'm not takin' money from you Alec."

"Why not?" Alec asked.

"Yeah, why not?" Aideen echoed.

Really, her too?

"Because I'm not a leech. I don't need a man's money, I take care of meself."

Aideen groaned. "Give it a rest Kay. Alec wants to help you so let him help."

"Yeah, let me help."

I narrowed my eyes to the blue-eyed baby then huffed.

"He will probably want me to have sex with him as payment for the money."

Alec deadpanned, "Keela, I already told you I won't nag you into fucking me. You will take that route to me when you're good and ready."

I felt my jaw drop open just as Aideen burst out laughing. Alec chuckled also then kissed the crown of her head, released her arms and then left bathroom.

I angrily folded my arms. "Can you believe the filth that comes out of his mouth?"

Aideen smiled. "Yes I can and if you want this to work out you had better keep *your* mouth shut and put up with him. He is doin' you a favour after all, now hurry up so we can leave already."

I sighed as I stood up from my sitting position on the side of the bath.

"That will be me greatest accomplishment," I said.

Aideen raised her eyebrows and asked, "What will?"

"Just keepin' me mouth shut."

"Make her stop! I can't go into another store, I just can't do it."

I looked at Alec and snickered. He looked like he was about to cry and drop to the ground from tiredness. It was currently six in the evening and we had been out shopping in Dublin City Centre for the last five hours. His tux and dress shoes were the first thing bought because it was straightforward and simple. Alec hung the tux that came in the body bag looking cover up in the back of his Jeep while Keela and I hit a few shops on Grafton Street.

I bought myself all the essentials for a foreign country holiday like bathing suits, towels, sun cream, flip flops, the whole works. When Alec found us in Pennys he too got items a man would need on a holiday to a hot country. His basket was *a lot* lighter than mine because he literally just bought one pair of slip on shoes, four pairs of neutral coloured shorts, four white t-shirts, four coloured t-shirts, a packet of boxer briefs and a toothbrush. He said he would just make do with whatever I have with me in case he needed anything.

I don't know how much he can make do with female products but I didn't question him because I was tired myself. I was ready to go home an hour into shopping, but Aideen was in her element so I didn't even mention the word home, she probably would have hurt me if I did mention it.

"How long before we can go home?" Alec shouted to Aideen who was a few steps ahead of us.

Aideen turned and smiled. "We have everythin'. We just need to go to the hairdressers and get Keela's *gruig* under control."

Alec's face scrunched up in confusion.

I laughed. "What's *that* attractive face for?"

Alec looked to me and asked, "What does *gruig* mean?"

"It means hair in *gaeilge*... in Irish."

Alec raised his eyebrows. "You speak Irish?"

I shrugged. "I'm not fluent, I know most of what Aideen says but I still get stumped every so often."

Alec glanced to Aideen then back to me. "Aideen's fluent?"

I nodded. "Her family is fluent and so is she."

Alec smiled then looked at Aideen. "What is kitten in Irish?"

Aideen laughed and said, "*Puisin*."

I rolled my eyes and folded my arms across my chest as Alec laughed.

"Oh, that's fucking perfect."

I glared at him. "I don't like bein' called kitten in English let alone in Irish so don't even think about it."

"I can't call you my little *puisin* then?"

I wanted to laugh, his accent and the pronunciation of *puisin* was adorable.

"No, you can't."

"We'll see about that."

I growled making him laugh.

"Aideen, how do you say pretty girl in Irish?"

"I would go with *cailin deas*."

"Spell that for me please," he said then took out his phone and tapped on the screen as Aideen spelt the words.

"What are you doin'?" I asked.

"Texting my brother what pretty girl means in Irish, it will help him out when he and Bronagh are arguing."

I laughed. "You think she will melt?"

Alec looked at me and nodded. "Bronagh will think Dominic went out of his way to find out what his term of endearment for her means in her native language. It will be an instant lay for him."

My face scrunched up. "You're so nasty."

Alec laughed. "I'm just looking out for my bro."

I rolled my eyes. "Whatever, let's just go get me hair done so we can get out of here."

"I second that."

Aideen waved us on so we followed her.

Alec nudged me as we walked. "We have all the materialistic things needed for this wedding, we're pretty much ready on that front. Storm is being doggie sat by Aideen, he will be thrilled about that by the way. All we need is you to be ready... are you?"

I kept looking ahead as we walk.

Was I ready to face Jason, Micah, and the rest of my crazy family?

"We will find out soon enough."

CHAPTER TEN

"Do you reckon someone is a terrorist on this plane?" I murmured to Alec when we took our seats in coach.

We were at Dublin airport and arrived here roughly four hours ago. I was a jittery mess from the moment we stepped foot through the entrance doors of the airport and I wasn't any more relaxed now that I was on the plane.

"Jesus, Keela. Lower your voice, you don't say things like that on a plane."

I ignored the hiss in Alec's tone and looked at my surroundings and at every face that was in my view. I jumped when Alec's elbow nudged my arm.

"What?" I snapped.

He looked at me and shook his head. "Why didn't you tell me you were afraid of flying?"

I licked my lips and looked directly at the back of the seat in front of me.

"Because I didn't know I was afraid until I stepped into the airport."

That wasn't a lie; I've never been on a plane before so this was all very unexpected.

Alec rubbed his face with his hands. "Do you feel like you're going to freak out?"

I looked to him with raised eyebrows. "What do you mean by 'freak out'?" I asked, quizzically.

Alec chewed on his lower lip before releasing it. "Do you feel like you're going to scream, cry or do anything else to cause a scene and have us removed from the plane."

I wanted to snap off a snarky reply, but I didn't simply because I didn't know whether I would do any of the things Alec just mentioned.

"I don't know."

Alec cursed and then leaned into me and said, "I don't have any sleeping pills or muscle relaxers on me, but the flight crew might have some. I'll go see if I can get you something to help you relax."

I suddenly panicked when Alec made a move to stand up so I reached out, grabbed Alec's hand and held it tight in mine.

"Don't leave me on my own!"

Alec tried to pull his hand from mine and when I wouldn't release it he grunted and leaned even closer in my direction.

"Keela, I will be *right back*. They won't take off until everyone is in their seat, I'm no exception."

He was right, they wouldn't take off unless everyone was secure in their seats.

I swallowed my nerves and slowly let go of Alec's hand. I glanced over the seats in front of me and up to the top of the plane where I could see the flight crew moving about.

I looked back at Alec and frowned. "Do you not need written permission for prescribed drugs on planes?"

Alec petted my head. "It's cute you think I need permission for something that I want."

I raised my eyebrows. "How are you goin' to get- Wait, Alec, you aren't going to chat one of them up... are you?"

He simply smiled at me then winked as he stood and slowly moved up the aisle. I was nervous, but not nervous enough to overlook the roaming eyes of my fellow passengers that clung to Alec as he moved.

"Oh, for God's sakes," I muttered.

This was ridiculous, he was hot but some of these women and men were halting their movements and focusing on Alec as he walked by was just stupid. I looked away from Alec and my fellow

ALEC

passengers and busied myself with buckling my seatbelt. I tried tightening it as much as I could but I was slowly suffocating myself and had to loosen it a little. I read the safety booklet that came with my seat and memorised where the exits on the plane where and where my life vest was just in case.

Okay. This was going to be okay.

I was going to be okay.

I smiled and felt myself relax a little until I overheard a conversation from the two men that were seated behind me.

"Did you hear they found the plane that went missing a few weeks ago?" one man said.

"Yes, it crashed somewhere in the ocean, everyone died on impact people were sayin'. I reckon the pilot was in on it-"

I stopped listening to the men and focused on the start of their conversation. A plane crashed into the ocean... and all the passengers died on impact!

Oh, fuck no!

I unbuckled my seatbelt and jumped up to my feet so fast that Usian Bolt would see me as serious competition. I looked up and caught Alec's gaze as he walked down the aisle and towards our seats.

"I have to get off this plane," I said, my chest rapidly rising and falling.

I didn't realise how fast I was breathing but when I noticed, I started to notice everything else. I was sweating, my stomach contents threatened to spill at any given second, and I really needed to take a wee.

"Kitten, look at me."

I shook my head and pushed at Alec's chest when he blocked me into our seats. He was deluded if he thought he was keeping me here. I'd climb over the seats to get off this silver dildo if I had to!

"No, I want to go home. I don't want to be here!"

I heard my voice crack and I felt tears sting my eyes.

I sniffled loudly and lowered my head. "Alec, *please*, you have to get me out of here."

"Baby, I've had a drink made up for you that will relax you in just a few minutes. I promise you will feel perfectly fine flying after you drink it."

I looked up to Alec and blinked. My blinking caused my tears to fall which Alec frowned over. He lightly smiled at me as he reached out with his left hand and used his thumb to swipe away my tears. I looked away from him and down to his right hand that contained a glass.

"What's in it?" I asked when I looked back up to Alec.

"Something to make you feel better."

I was wary of the drink, Alec, and this entire situation, but I decided to take the drink and sit down because when I realised the entire fucking coach section of the plane was looking at me I wanted to die.

"I'm so sorry, I didn't mean to react like that. I just got scared-"

"Hey, you don't need to you apologise to me or anyone else. Do you understand me?" Alec asked.

I nodded my head then lifted the glass to my lips and downed it in one go.

I smacked my lips together a few times before licking them, there was a nice fruity taste from the drink.

"No alcohol?" I questioned.

"No, you shouldn't mix alcohol with a sleeping pill."

Sleeping tablet?

"You gave me a sleepin' tablet?" I asked Alec, wide eyed.

"Yeah, I'm sorry but I figured it would be best for you to sleep for the entire flight."

"*You* decided? How about you let me make my own bloody decisions!" I hissed in a low voice wary of our close proximity to the other passengers.

Alec sighed. "You weren't very reasonable when you were trying to make a break for it off the plane, Keela."

I scoffed. "You seemed you make the best out of *that* situation though didn't you? Who did you finger fuck in order to get me that drink, huh?"

Alec burst out laughing, and so did the men behind me.

My ears burned as mortification flooded me.

"I hate you!" I growled.

Alec was still laughing as he said, "I like you, kitten."

He was a bastard!

I angrily folded my arms across my chest and looked out the window of the plane. This was quite possibly the worst seat for me to be sat in right now, but looking at the airport distracted me from Alec's stupid self.

I turned forward a few minutes later and leaned back into my seat as I watched the flight crew go through their safety drills. My eyes started to get heavy then and keeping them open became a real struggle.

Time seemed to fold then because suddenly the passengers were fully seated, the crew was in their own area safely strapped into their seats and the plane was moving.

Not only was it moving, but it was up in that damn air.

"Wow!" I shouted.

How did it take off without me noticing?

I all but flattened my face to the small window just so I could see outside.

"That's a big fuckin' cloud!"

I felt hands on me then and laughter in my ear as I was gently pulled back to my seated position.

"Rein it in kitten and close your eyes for me."

I looked to Alec whose face was blurry, all I could make out were his eyes.

"Your eyes are pretty."

The corners of his pretty blue eyes creased.

"Yeah? Well, I just happen to think you have pretty eyes too little kitten."

I giggled.

Yep, giggled.

"I like your voice," I murmured as I leaned forward.

"What else do you like about me?" Alec's voice asked from a distance.

"Abs," I answered, "and your ass."

I heard laughter, but it was far away.

Everything stopped and my mind went blank, the last thing I saw was a pair of pretty blue eyes staring down at me before darkness consumed me.

I was uncomfortable.

The mattress on my bed was either lumpy as hell or Storm's paws were underneath me and were digging into my back.

I wanted to tell him to move but my throat felt funny, like it was tingling.

I slowly blinked my eyes open and just as I was about to sit up I froze. I heard an annoying high-pitched giggle and it confused the hell out of me.

Who the hell was giggling?

I focused my eyes on my surroundings and after a few seconds I remembered where I was. I was on the plane heading to the Bahamas for Micah's and Jason's wedding. I was just waking up but I didn't remember falling asleep. I remember freaking out about flying on the plane then Alec giving me a drink.

A drugged up drink to relax me... or to knock me out.

I wasn't sat upright like I thought I was. I was leaning to the right on a hard surface. Without being fully coherent, I still knew it was Alec's chest that I was leaning on and that was why my back was hurting.

I was about to sit upright and stretch so my back would crack but the giggling that I heard before sounded again and it fully got my attention.

Let it be known that I have no claim on Alec, he is my fake boyfriend and is on this plane as a favour to me. I don't like him in that way or want him to feel trapped from flirting with other girls.

That being said, he should not fucking flirt with an airhostess when I am lying across his fucking chest!

"What is goin' on here?" I asked in my firmest tone as I pushed myself upright.

It was hard though because I had just woken up and my voice was crackling. I doubt I sounded like anything other than a chain smoker.

I wanted to smile when the airhostess who was leaning into Alec jumped upright like a fish out of water.

"Good morning, sleeping beauty."

How dare he try and be nice when he was flirting with the airhostess while I was sleeping on him.

He *was* a free agent, but hello, I was laying on him!

I cut my eyes to him and glared. "Keep your tongue behind your teeth before I cut it off."

Alec's eyebrows jumped. "You aren't a morning person, are you?"

Was I that obvious?

"No, and I don't like mornin' people... or mornin's... or people."

"Wow, I'm a lucky guy to have you, baby."

Sarcastic pig!

"Blow me."

Alec snorted then looked to the airhostess who was still frozen like a statue.

"Are you okay, sweetie?" he asked her.

Sweetie?

Puh-lease!

The woman snapped out of her daze and focused on Alec, the smile that overtook her face was so big that I felt sorry for her cheeks.

"I'm great Mr. Slater, thank you."

"I'm great Mr. Slater, thank you," I mimicked the woman's voice.

The woman abruptly excused herself so she could go back to work. I didn't say goodbye or watch her leave, though I'm sure Alec did.

"You're fuckin' disgustin'. You couldn't wait to try and join the mile high club with airhostess Barbie until a time when I am not sleeping on you?"

I cracked my back, folded my arms across my chest and looked straight ahead.

"Keela?"

I set my jaw. "What?"

"What makes you think I'm not already a part of the mile high club?"

I snapped my head to Alec, unfolded my arms and shoved him.

"You really *are* disgustin'!"

"Don't knock it until you try it."

I scoffed. "I don't think so, playboy."

Alec's laughter stopped and a growl took its place. "It was funny the first few times you called me that but stop it now, *please*."

I smiled as I looked out the plane window. "I don't think so, *playboy*."

I felt Alec's glare so I turned to look at him and smiled when I found him all but drilling holes into me with his eyes.

"If looks could kill, I'd be dead," I joked.

"My pretty eyes won't harm you, don't worry."

Conceited much?

"Did you just call your own eyes pretty?"

Alec devilishly grinned then and it made me slightly uneasy.

"No, you said I have pretty eyes."

Was he high?

"Are you in your right mind? I have *never* said you have pretty eyes-"

"Yes, you have. Right before you fell asleep. You said I have pretty eyes."

I felt my face heat up.

It was the shit he gave me to knock me out that said that, not me!

"Did I say anythin' else?" I murmured.

Alec leaned in close to me and whispered is a slow, seductive voice, "You said you like my voice, my abs, and my ass."

I audibly gasped. "I did not!"

Alec snickered. "You did."

I was mortified, absolutely mortified!

"I hate you right now."

Alec laughed at me and for a moment my embarrassment subsided and anger took over as I gave him the finger.

"That was just rude."

"Sorry, I can't help it."

"Oh, so your middle finger has a mind of its own then?" Alex asked with an amused look.

I glared at him and said, "Yeah, and she was just sticking up for me."

Alec burst out laughing which gained us some attention from people sitting near us. I side kicked him in the shin under the table, making him hiss throughout his laughter.

"Do you ever shut up laughin'? You're like a hyena!"

Alec was still lightly chuckling as he said, "I'm a happy person and if that makes me like a hyena then so be it."

I shook my head. "No one should be as happy as you thirty thousand feet up in the air."

"We're actually under ten thousand feet, look out the window and you will see. Can you not feel us descending?"

I focused on the movement of the plane and actually did feel the decent.

"That means we're nearly there, right?" I asked, hopeful.

I could not wait to get off this plane.

"Yep, we're nearly there. Are you excited?"

Was that a serious question?

"One nightmare ends when I get off this plane and another one begins when I step foot in the Bahamas. I'm *very* excited."

"Are you always this sarcastic?"

"Yes."

"I'm in for a wild ride with you, aren't I?" Alec asked.

I glanced to him and smiled. "You have no idea, buddy."

We were off the plane, thank God, out of the airport, again, thank God, and now on our way to the Pink Sands Resort where Micah's and Jason's wedding would be. You can thank the Devil for that one.

I was tensed up and angry in the car on the way to the resort until twenty or so minutes passed and we came to a stop outside of a strikingly beautiful hotel.

"Oh my Jesus," I whispered earning a snort from Alec, which I ignored.

"It is pretty nice I guess," he mumbled.

"Pretty nice? It's beautiful! I've never seen somethin' so beautiful before," I said in awe looking out of the window.

"It's only a hotel."

I turned and looked at him. "Look at the detail, the layout and the settin' of it. It's like a beautiful back drop," I stated then shook my head. "It might not be that nice to you but I've never been away before, so this is gorgeous to me."

I was about to turn away when Alec frowned at me. "You've never been away before, as in on vacation? Ever?"

I shrugged. "No, this is the first time I have ever left Ireland. I thought I told you that?"

Alec didn't say anything as we came to a full stop.

We both got out of the car, me with a smile on my face as I looked around to see Alec with a passive face on. I didn't care if he was cranky because he was tired, I was tired too, I know I slept on the plane ride over but I was still tired. But tired or not, I wasn't going to act like a bitch to him so he should quit acting like one to me.

I took off walking into the hotel not really caring about Alec behind me. I breezed through the hotel lobby until I came to large desk where a young man smiled to me. "Welcome to the Pinks Sands Hotel. How may I help you today?" he asked polity.

My tune suddenly changed as I smiled; I was so happy I was here. Obviously not for the reason I was here, I was just happy to be somewhere so beautiful.

"Thank you, I'm checkin' in."

"Name?" he asked.

"Keela Daley."

He tapped away on the computer then moved away and picked up a key off the wall. "Your room number is four-seventy-six, Miss Daley. You'll be on the fourth floor. Enjoy your stay and if you need anything the telephone in your room connects you to the front desk... to me."

I took my key, still smiling widely. "Thank you."

"You're welcome," he smiled back.

I turned and bumped into Alec, who was looking behind me with a grin on his face. "Hey babe," he smiled then, looking down at me.

I raised my eyes and looked around to see who he was talking to.

"Who are you talking to?" I asked, confused.

He snorted. "You of course. Did you get the key to *our* room?" he asked, happily.

What was going on here?

Why was he so happy all of a sudden?

I just looked at him then held up my hand that contained the key card to our room. "Great, let's get upstairs then," he chirped and took my suitcase before heading over to the elevator.

I stumbled after him and into the elevator, hitting the button for the fourth floor. "Are you high? Why were you being so boyfriendy?" I asked when I got inside.

He laughed as the doors shut and moved my cases back to my side. "Boyfriendy isn't a word and I just had to do that. That guy's face was priceless."

I raised my brow. "What guy? What are you talkin' about?"

Alec shook his head. "The dude at the desk, he was checking you out. Judging by the looks and grins he was giving you I could tell that he was into you, and when you turned around to talk to me he leaned over and straight out stared at your ass."

I gasped. "He did not stare at me arse, you're makin' that up!"

Alec snorted. "I'm not, he really was. He pouted when I asked about 'our' room though, funny stuff."

I glared at him then. "Why do you care if someone checks me out?"

"Because you're my girlfriend, at least while we're here anyway. The only person staring at your ass will be me."

Oh, lord.

"You're so weird."

Alec smiled, but his smile dropped when the elevator jolted to a stop.

He saw the look I gave him.

"I'm a little claustrophobic, I can't stay in small spaces for too long," he explained.

I laughed. "How can you stand bein' inside me apartment

then?"

Alec shrugged. "There is a lot of windows, I manage just fine."

I chuckled as I grabbed the handle of my suitcase and walked out of the elevator when the doors opened and down the hallway of the hotel looking for room four-seventy-six.

"It's weird not being on the top floor of a hotel," Alec mumbled from behind me.

Escorts must always get the best of everything.

"Sorry, this will be a huge downgrade for you."

He grunted from behind me. "I don't *need* the top floor, I was just saying."

"Okay," I chuckled then paused outside the door when we got to room four-sevetny-six.

I swiped my key card and opened the door. "Omigod, it's so feckin' cute!" I gushed and barged into the room.

"Omigod, Alec! Look at the view, *look* at it!" I yelled and rushed to open the double doors leading to the balcony. "I love this!"

I heard a chuckle from behind me but I ignored it. I didn't care if he thought I was stupid.

"It's so pretty," I jumped up and down and clapped my hands. "I am in complete and total love with this view."

"Are you going to have an orgasm? It sounds like you're building up to something earth shattering."

I turned my body around, still smiling. "Say whatever nasty little thing you want, you can *not* ruin my mood. This view just makes me happy."

And it did, something so irrelevant to most people – like dickhead Alec – made me very happy. I always did enjoy the little things in life.

CHAPTER ELEVEN

"So, now that we're here what's the plan?" Alec asked me as I finished unpacking my suitcase.

I placed all my clothes into the wardrobe, there was only one so Alec said he was cool with his stuff staying in his suitcase on the floor. I didn't argue with him and just did as I wanted and put my things away.

I glanced at Alec when he spoke and shrugged, "I know you're here so I can rub you in Jason's face, but I don't really want to go lookin' for them right now. If we bump into them or anyone I know that is attendin' the weddin' then so be it. But if we don't, I think we should just chill on the beach by ourselves since it's mornin' time here."

"That's fine by me. Once I can lie down, I'm happy."

I smiled. "You're tired?"

Alec was currently lying on the bed we would be sharing throughout this death sentence.

"I didn't sleep at all on the flight over here, I'm still on Ireland time, and it's evening time there."

I whistled. "Maybe you should have taken a sleepin' tablet yourself so you could have gotten some shut eye on the plane."

"Nah, I wouldn't have been able to look after you if I was out cold too."

I swallowed. "You didn't have to look after me, Alec."

He sat up on the bed and looked down at me from my position on the floor.

"I know I didn't have to, but I wanted to."

ALEC

That was so... sweet.

"Well, thank you. I appreciate it," I mumbled and looked down to my make-up bag, fiddling with the products so I could keep my head down and escape the embarrassment of Alec seeing my flushed cheeks.

He wanted to look after me!

I wanted to smile but kept my face passive and aimed down as doubt entered my mind.

I hated that I couldn't just accept his gestures of being sweet and genuine because in the back of my mind a voice told me he was only doing all this to get into my knickers. The more he buttered me up by being sweet, the easier it would be to slide my knickers off.

I wasn't being paranoid with my thoughts either, he has flat out told me he *wants* to fuck me and *will* fuck me by the end of this trip. I just have to keep my guard up to avoid that happening.

"Are you okay?" Alec's voice asked, which got my attention.

I cleared my throat. "Yep, I'm grand, just thinkin' about how Aideen is gettin' on with Storm."

"One of them might be dead - my money is on it being Aideen."

"Alec!" I shouted. "Don't say somethin' like that!"

Alec howled with laughter. "I'm playing, I'm sure they're fine and will be fine for the rest of this vacation. Don't worry about them."

Easy for him to say, he didn't know what Storm and Aideen were like when they were left alone for long periods of time. I dreaded to think of the damage that could be done, war could easily erupt between those two.

"Maybe I should call. You know, just to check in."

Alec lay back down on the bed and waved me on with his hand. "Go ahead then, mama bear."

I smiled as I crawled over to my bag and dug out my phone. I typed in Aideen's number and waited for it to go international. The phone rang a few times before Aideen answered.

"Hey, you arrived safely?" Aideen asked when she answered.

I grinned. "No, we died. I'm callin' to tell you that you get to keep Storm forever now that I'm dead."

Alec snorted while Aideen huffed over the phone.

"Over my dead body, he will be put in a kennel so fast you would turn in your grave!"

How lovely.

"Things aren't goin' well then?"

"He chewed my gym runners up, they are completely destroyed and in the bin. The fat fucker did it on purpose, I know he did."

I held back a chuckle as I said, "He is brave for puttin' his nose anywhere near your runners."

I heard her dramatic gasp then a firm, "Fuck you!"

I did laugh then. "Don't get your knickers in a twist, I'm jokin'."

"Sure you were."

I smiled. "Jokin' aside, is everythin' okay?"

"Yeah, he is fed and sleepin'. I'll bring him out for his second walk later."

Hold the phone.

"Second walk, what do you mean *second* walk?"

I looked at Alec when he sat up on the bed and before Aideen spoke, I knew exactly what she was going to say.

"Alec told you to bring him out twice, didn't he?"

"Yep, to help shift the fat fucker's fat."

I narrowed my eyes at Alec and growled at Aideen, "Stop. Callin'. Him. Names."

"I will when he stops eatin' me shoes and growlin' at me all the time. I'm the only one here to feed him so he better learn quick."

It was like I was talking to a five year old.

"I'm not arguin' with you. Just take it easy on him when you're out walkin'."

"Aye, Captain."

Smartarse.

"Thanks, look I'll ring you-"

"Have you had sex with Alec yet?"

Is that all she bloody thought about?

"No, I have *not* have sex with Alec and I *won't* be havin' sex with him either. You're worse than him for goin' on about it!"

I could *feel* Alec smiling as I spoke.

Aideen laughed. "Yeah, yeah. When you do finally buck him I want to hear *all* about it. Every sexy little detail."

She was a male inside a female's body.

"Goodbye, Aideen."

"Slan!" Aideen sang and laughed as she hung up.

"You should take Aideen's advice and fuck me."

How romantic.

"Put a sock in it, Romeo," I grunted as I folded my arms across my chest.

Alec lay back down on the bed and patted his stomach. "Feel free to straddle me at any given time."

I squeezed my eyes shut and convinced myself not to punch him in the nuts.

"Why did you tell Aideen to bring Storm out on two walks a day, he is *not* your dog-"

"Did we not discuss us being a *we* until this favour is fulfilled?"

I pinched the bridge of my nose. "We or no we, he is *my* baby and-"

"He is a dog, Keela, a *dog*."

I growled, "I've more respect for that *dog* than I do you, you piece of shite."

Alec laughed. "Nobody has ever shown me that many ounces of dumb fuck before."

What?

"Excuse me?"

Alec got up from the bed, stood in front of me and looked down. "I'm looking out for *your* baby. If you want him to live a long life take *my* advice and get him healthy."

I held my tongue.

As much as I didn't want Storm to be uncomfortable by testing his limits, I *did* want him to be healthy.

I slumped my shoulders and blew out a breath. "Yeah, okay, fine."

I looked down and closed my eyes. I smiled a little when I felt Alec's arms wrap around me. He snuggled me close to him and I was aware that I was pressed against his shirtless torso and I didn't mind it in the slightest.

"You give nice hugs," I murmured as I wrapped my arms around his waist.

"I know," Alec replied.

"You're so damn cocky."

"Say 'cock' again."

I laughed and pushed away from him. I moved to the window, squealed as I gazed out it then I twirled around which made Alec laugh. "You cannot be this excited over a view."

I stopped and gave him a look. "No disrespect to me country but it's nice to see somethin' other than the mountains. It's sunny here and the sea is two minutes from where we're stayin'. I'm surprised I'm not explodin' right now, this is me first holiday!"

Alec shook his head as he moved his suitcase against the wall next to the wardrobe. "That is wrong on so many levels. How did your parents not bring you on vacation when you were younger?"

I instantly frowned. "Me ma went away a lot, but I stayed home with Micah and her stepma and da because me ma said I wasn't allowed to flaunt around in a bikini unless I looked the part and-" I cut myself off, and blushed fiercely.

I cannot believe I almost told him how tight of a leash my mother had me on when I was younger.

"Where is your dad?" Alec asked me, overlooking the fact that I cut myself off mid-sentence.

"Me da? I don't know, I never met him."

Alec nodded his head but didn't say anything further.

Silence stretched for a few moments until I spoke.

"Do you want to come to the beach or just hang out here until the dinner tonight?" I asked, avoiding looking at Alec.

He didn't say anything other than, "Sure."

"Sure to the beach or to hangin' out in here?"

"The beach, obviously," he said glancing around the room like it was a joke to be asked to stay here.

I rolled my eyes; I loved the room, I thought it was great.

"Okay, well, you go get changed in the bathroom, and I'll get changed in here."

Alec nodded as he opened his suitcase and grabbed the first item on the top then headed into the bathroom. I opened the wardrobe and got what I wanted to wear then turned back to the bed only to stub my toe on Alec's suitcase in the process.

I let out a loud pitched scream.

"What's wrong?" Alec shouted, bursting from the bathroom with a tube of toothpaste in his right hand raised in the air like a weapon.

I fell back onto the bed gripping my foot. "I hurt me toe."

"We haven't being here five minutes, how did you hurt yourself already?" Alec snapped in annoyance.

I sat upright ready to give him a piece of my mind, but stopped dead in my tracks when I noticed a sculpted torso in front of me. I wasn't joking - a six pack of abs stared me directly in the face.

I swear one of them moved as well.

"Up here, sweetheart," Alec's voice said in an amused tone.

I snapped out of my trance and looked upwards pretty quickly. "I wasn't perving on you. Your body was practically in me face, and it still is so back up off me and give me some personal space."

Alec did as asked with a grin on his face.

I involuntary dropped my eyes then and read the words *Calvin Klein*. He was in just his boxer briefs!

"Oh my God!" I gasped as I flung my hands over my eyes and

dropped backwards onto the bed. "Cover yourself!"

Alec burst into belly rumbling laughter. "That brought back a flashback of my sixteen year old self stripping in front of a girl I was trying to seduce. She reacted just like you."

I glared into my hands. "She didn't want your half naked arse near her either?" I guessed.

Alec snorted. "No, she did. She was just shy and virginy about it."

"Virginy isn't a word and I'm not shy, I just don't want to see you half naked."

Lie.

Huge, big, fat, fucking lie.

Alec chuckled again as he moved away. "I'm moving back into the bathroom now, kitten. You can uncover your eyes and stop blushing."

I sat up when the bathroom door clicked shut.

I felt my cheeks and they were indeed hot.

Damn him!

"I'm not blushin', you just made me mad that's all!" I shouted.

He replied with a laugh that made me curse him.

I angrily bent to pick up my items off the floor. I picked up a black bikini and black cover up, some flip flops, sunscreen, and sunglasses.

"Do not step into this room until I tell you to!" I shouted to Alec.

"Yes, ma'am."

I glared at the bathroom door and didn't take my eyes off it as I quickly changed. I was in the middle of putting my bikini knickers on and screamed when the handle of the bathroom door twisted.

"Not yet!" I yelled as I dove onto the bed, hiding myself with pillows.

Alec's laughter got my attention. "Sorry, I just wanted to see if you would freak out and you did."

I growled as I pulled on my bikini knickers then put on my

cover up. I smiled maliciously when it fell to my knees. I tied my hair up into a messy bun and then slipped on my sunglasses and pink flip flops before I grabbed my beach bag from my suitcase. I crammed towels, sunscreen and other beach necessities into my bag.

"Okay, you can come out now," I shouted.

The bathroom door opened and out stepped Alec in just knee length shorts. I widened my eyes and was thankful I had sunglasses on.

"*That* is what you're wearin'?"

Alec shrugged then froze when he saw me. "Please tell me you have a decent swimsuit on underneath that curtain."

I gasped. "It's a cover up!"

"It's plain, shapeless and makes it look like you have a big butt... and not in a good way."

It did?

I pushed past him, annoyed that he said my arse was big in a bad way.

I heard him moving around in the room behind me just as I stepped out into the hallway. I took the elevator down to the lobby while Alec took the stairs. When I reached the lobby he fell in line beside me. I smiled and waved to the lad at the desk who instantly smiled and waved to me. His smiled dropped though when an arm snaked around my shoulder.

"Look at his face," Alec snickered.

I moved his arm from my shoulder when we got outside. "Stop being such a dick."

Alec pulled a face at me, so I turned and walked ahead of him and took one of the three paths that the signs said led to the beach. I picked the one that didn't have many people on it.

"What did you call that thing you're wearing?" Alec asked from behind me.

"A cover up," I said without turning around.

He snorted. "What exactly is it meant to cover up? When the sun hits it, it goes see through."

I gasped and turned around. "Are you jokin'?" I asked.

He shook his head.

"I'm going to kill Aideen, she said it was matte black!"

"Why are you wearing it? You have a bikini on underneath - I can see it."

I flushed. "I'm... I'm just not comfortable with meself."

Alec looked at me, bemused.

I grunted. "I'm not happy with me body, and I doubt anyone else will be, so I'm not puttin' it on view for everyone to see."

Alec just shook his head at me. "You're such a girl."

I gaped at him. "Excuse me?"

"Yeah, you complain about your body when you have to know how good you look."

I gaped at him. "I have no idea what you're talkin' about."

Alec pinched the bridge of his nose and held up his hand. "What I'm about to say doesn't change the fact that I only want to fuck you, okay?"

"Okay," I replied, unsure of where this conversation was going.

He took in a breath and blew it out. "You're beautiful," he said real fast. "There, I said it."

I stared at him for a moment then shoved him hard causing him to stumble backwards. "I just told you I'm self-conscious and you decide to make fun of me by tellin' me you think I'm beautiful? You're such an arsehole!" I turned and stormed away.

I stopped a few meters away from the shoreline when I got onto the beach and set down my beach bag. I took out my huge towel and lay it down on the sand. I sat near the middle of the towel, raised my sunglasses over my head and looked out at the ocean and let a huge smile spread over my face.

I noticed the shadow next to me and out of the corner of my eye I saw twat face sit down on the other half of my towel.

"You like the ocean, huh?" Alec's voice murmured.

I shrugged. "I just think it's all pretty lookin'. I don't know why, but it makes me smile."

Alec was quiet for a moment then said, "I do think you're beautiful. I wasn't making fun of you."

I glanced to him and he just looked right back at me. He didn't grin or smirk or make any facial expression that told me he was fibbing, so I shrugged.

"Okay, well... thank you," I replied before turning away.

"You still don't believe me, do you?" he asked.

I shrugged. "I'm eighty-twenty on it right now, but it doesn't matter. Looks don't mean anythin' other than lustful attraction from one person to another - it's what's on the inside that counts. You know, a thing called personality?"

Alec snorted. "Something you seem to lack."

I smacked him on the arm making him hiss and rub it.

"I have a personality, a grand one. It's *you* who is the arrogant arsehole here with the pathetic excuse for a personality, not me."

"Are you trying to insult me? I can't tell," he asked, sarcasm dripping from his tone.

"Let's just say that you're so lucky mirrors don't base looks on personality."

"Why?" Alec asked.

I devilishly grinned. "Because if they did, you would be one ugly motherfucker."

Alec glared at me for a few seconds before a grin spread across his face.

I was annoyed by this - I wanted him to feel like shite over that insult, not happy about it.

"Why are you smilin'?" I snapped.

He continued to smile before laying down on his back. "No reason, kitten. No reason at all."

I angrily crossed my arms. "I hate you so much, you know that? I don't think I've ever met such an annoyin' arsehole in me entire life."

"I'm honored," he chirped, mocking me which made me seethe in anger.

He closed his eyes as I turned away from him and rooted through my beach bag until I found the book I was currently reading. Ironically, it was the book Alec was reading in my apartment the day he moved in.

Fifty Shades of Grey.

I opened the cover, flipped to page fifteen - where I left off - and began reading. An hour or so passed and I had gotten about a hundred and twenty pages in when I felt movement beside me and then felt a breeze over my shoulder.

"What are you reading?" Alec asked in a groggy voice like he had been sleeping.

It didn't surprise me - we were out on the beach for a long while.

I shouldered him away from me. "Nothin'," I replied.

"No, it's something. The redness in your cheeks shone so brightly they woke me up."

I ducked my head. "It's hot out here, what do you expect?" I muttered.

He didn't say anything for a moment, so I relaxed a little, but that ended a second later when he dove on me knocking me sideways onto the sand.

He pulled me onto my back, straddled me and sat on my belly making me grunt. He wasn't fat at all but he was still heavy as fuck. I screamed when he reached for my hand that held my book.

The book that *did* have me blushing like a schoolgirl.

"I just want to see the title," Alec grunted, leaning forward adding more of his weight onto me making me gasp as the air was knocked out of me.

I struggled under him when he got the book and flipped it shut. I felt myself turn crimson when a devilish smile spread across his face as he read the title.

"You brought *this* book as your vacation read?" he asked, grinning. "You're a dirty girl, aren't you?"

"Get off me right now or I'll shout rape!"

Alec laughed as he moved off me. "Shit like that goes on in this book and the girl likes it, right? She likes it rough, right? I didn't get very far into it but it seems some kinky shit happens."

I blushed again. "Shut up, Alec."

He chuckled as he leaned back on his elbows looking at me. "Look at you all hot and bothered. I bet your panties are soaked."

I felt myself choke on air; I was horrified and I had no doubt my face matched what I was feeling.

Alec burst into laughter. "You *are* a virgin."

I was so embarrassed but tried to play it off by flipping him off. "I am not a virgin, playboy. Okay!"

Alec raised his hands. "Okay, sorry." He smiled. "Go ahead and finish your book, don't mind me."

I flushed again making Alec smile. "No, thank you. I'll read it later."

"When we're in bed?" he asked and wiggled his eyebrows.

I gasped at how casually he said that, as if us going to bed together was a natural thing.

"No!" I managed to shout making him laugh again.

My whole body felt hot. It did a moment ago from the book and the scenes that took place in said book, but now I was so embarrassed that I could feel the heat radiating from me.

"I'm going for a swim," I said and stood up.

"In the curtain?" Alec asked me, pointing to my cover up.

I looked away from him. "No, I taking me cover up off so just... just turn around, and don't look, okay?" I mumbled.

"Of course, I am a gentleman after all." He turned around and put his back to me. I hesitantly lifted the hem of my cover up and lifted it over my head. I slowly stepped away from Alec and when I was sure he wouldn't turn around I turned and walked towards the water.

When I heard a loud wolf whistle though I froze and looked over my shoulder. Alec was now turned around and grinning and me while whistling and blowing kisses in my direction.

He was making fun of me, the dick!

I gave him the finger, which he smirked at before he lay back down on the towel under him, and threw his arm over his eyes in an effort to block out the sunlight. I forced myself not to cover myself with my hands as I walked towards the waterline. I dipped my toes into the water and jumped back a little - it was cool.

I don't know why but I held my breath and I dipped my foot into the water again, I pulled it back out a moment later and exhaled. I was such a wuss but I didn't care. I wanted to take my time and let myself get used to the temperature.

The arsehole that slammed into the back of me had other ideas though. I was about to whirl around and punch whoever slammed into me until I realised that my feet weren't on the ground anymore.

I heard Alec's laughter and that turned my panic into anger when I realised it wasn't a stranger.

"You dickhead put me down!"

I widened my eyes when Alec walked us out into the ocean, until my lower half was under water.

"Stop!" I screeched.

Alec loosened his grip on me so I turned myself and wrapped my limbs around his body.

"Don't go out any further, I can't swim very good."

"I've got you kitten, don't worry," Alec murmured and kissed my cheek.

I pressed my face to the side of his as he did this, which made him laugh. He rubbed his head on mine and allowed the water to sway us from side to side.

I relaxed after a moment and pulled back from Alec when he gripped my behind. "You should be holdin' me up by my waist."

"That's true but I wanted to feel your ass."

I laughed. "You're so blunt that it's funny."

I turned and looked behind Alec and out to the ocean. I furrowed my eyebrows and focused on a black spot in the water then widened my eyes when a fin broke the surface of the water, but just as quick as it appeared, it disappeared.

"Alec," I whispered, not taking my eyes off the spot where I saw the fin.

The hands on my arse squeezed me as his lips touched my ear. "What is it, kitten?"

I cleared my throat and in the calmest voice I could muster I said, "I think... I think I saw a fin in the waves behind you."

Alec slowly pulled back from me and asked, "A fin... as in a *shark's* fin?"

I shrugged my shoulders. "Either that or a dolphin, could belong a small whale too-"

I gasped, cutting myself off after the air was knocked out of me and water took its place. I was thrown backwards into the water and flung my limbs around in a panic when I sucked water down instead of air. In seconds, I broke the surface of the water and coughed and spluttered until I was greedily sucking air down into my lungs.

"Shark! Big fucking shark! We're all going to die! Swim for your lives!"

I could barely stand up in the water so I moved my arms and legs until I got my footing and stumbled forward enough until the water was below my waist. I rubbed my face as I turned my body fully in the direction of the beach. I narrowed my eyes and shook my head as I saw Alec haul his arse out of the water screeching like teenage girl while he waved his arms around like it was nobody's business.

The bastard left me to die!

He threw me to the shark-dolphin-whale so he could save himself.

So much for him being a fucking gentlemen.

Chapter Twelve

"Keela, are you still mad at me?" Alec asked as we walked up to our room after a long day of lying on the beach and eating in the local cafes.

I looked ahead as I sang, "Twinkle twinkle little star-"

"How I wonder what you are?"

"-I wish I could tie you down and run you over with me car."

Alec groaned. "Okay, I get it, you're still mad."

I clicked my tongue and tapped my foot against the floor as I waited for Alec to open the door when we reached our hotel room.

"You've had the entire day to cool off. How can you still be pissed at me?"

Because I'm female and can hold a grudge till the end of time?

"You left me to die, Alec. You literally threw me to what you thought was a shark just so you could save yourself. Some gentleman you are," I said and shook my head in astonishment.

I cannot believe he was still questioning why I was angry with him, it was plain as day why I was mad.

"Excuse me for not wanting to die. It's very sexist of you to insinuate that I should be the one to throw myself to a shark just to save you just because I'm a man. It's also very selfish of you, I mean, why can't you sacrifice yourself to save me?" Alec asked and stared me down with those big blue fucking eyes of his.

I huffed and placed my hands on my hips before crossing them across myself. "It's just the gentleman thing to do. I bet Nico would throw himself to a shark to save Bronagh."

Alec held up his hands. "I'm sorry to disappoint you kitten, but

I'm not my brother. I can't just punch a shark in the face and win."

I screeched. "I'm not askin' you to fight a shark, I'm askin' you not to throw me to one just to save yourself!"

Alec used both his hands to push his hair back out his face, but it was pointless because it still fell back and framed his face.

"It was a fight or flight situation and my flight instinct took over."

I sarcastically laughed. "Yeah, I know it took over. *I* was the one left to be shark food, remember?"

Alec shook his head in frustration. "We don't even know if it was a shark!"

"No we don't, but it *could* have been, that's the point!"

Alec was about to open his mouth to reply but instead settled on biting his lower lip as he lifted his arms and gestured to my neck with both of his large hands. I snorted because the feeling was mutual - I wanted to choke him too.

"You're the most frustrating woman I have ever spent time with. You're driving me crazy!"

I opened my mouth to snap off a snarky reply, but the ringtone from Alec's phone cut me off. It was on the bed and before he could get it, I dashed onto the bed and rolled off on the other side like a ninja. I lifted the phone to my ear then and answered it.

"Hello playgirl hotline, Keela speakin'. Alec is busy with a client right now, but what can *I* do for you today?" I purred.

Alec narrowed his eyes and set his jaw while I grinned on the other side of the bed.

"Um hello, Keela. I'm Damien, Alec's brother."

The twin I haven't met.

"Hey Damien, we haven't met but I'm Keela, your brother's fake girlfriend."

Alec shook his head and scrubbed his face with his hands.

"You're Alec's *fake* girlfriend? Why?" Damien questioned.

I sighed and lay down on the bed. "It's a long story."

"I've got time gorgeous."

I smiled. "You don't know what I look like, how do you know if I'm gorgeous or not?"

"Because my brothers, especially Alec, don't date anyone - fake or not - who is less than stunning."

I awed out loud.

"You're *so* sweet."

The bed suddenly dipped on my left as Alec climbed onto the bed and filled the space next to me. I looked at him and yelped as he pinched up my underarm causing me to drop his phone. He caught his phone with his free hand, grinned and rolled over to his side of the bed.

He put the phone to his ear and said, "You talk to her for less than thirty seconds and already she thinks you're *so* sweet? You and Dominic will get an ass whopping if you keep that shit up."

I heard laughter coming through the receiver of the phone which made Alec smile.

"What are you up to, bro? Are you okay? I miss you."

I felt my insides melt at Alec's admission to missing his younger brother. I've never heard a man openly say something like that before. It was really cute and I liked it. A lot.

I crawled over Alec to get to the other side of the bed simply because I was too lazy to get up and walk around. Mid-crawl Alec caught my arm and pulled me down on top of him. He grunted when our chests connected with a thud, I looked down to tell him off, but I froze because my face was inches from his. I licked my lips and not a second later Alec kissed my lips with lighting speed which made me hiss and him smile as I pushed away from him.

I sat up and found I was straddling him.

I was sat directly on top of his groin and could feel everything because he only had a pair of swimming trunks on. Thin swimming trunks at that.

"Me? Have you not talked to the guys? I'm in the Bahamas."

I looked at Alec and found his head was lifted up and his eyes were locked down to where I was sitting on him. I looked down and spotted my bare thighs that were on display thanks to my cover up riding up my thighs.

"Like Keela said, it's a long story bro."

I grazed against Alec when I shifted a little and it caused him to hiss as he brought his hand up to my hip. He looked up and locked eyes with me, I smiled at him teasingly, but the smile vanished when I felt the area under me being to harden.

"Damien, you know I love you, right? I really do bro, but I can't concentrate on this conversation when I have a sexy redhead grinding her pussy on me."

Oh. My. God!

I adjusted my body by a fucking inch, that did not count as grinding!

"I'm not grindin' anythin' against you!" I shouted. "Ignore him Damien, he is just mad because I won't sleep with him!"

With that said I climbed off Alec and stormed into the bathroom.

"No, wait! Come back please! My cock is throbbing here!"

I smiled at the whimpering tone in Alec's voice as I closed the bathroom door with force.

"I hate women!"

I laughed out loud at that.

As I relieved myself in the toilet, I decided to take a shower when I was done so Alec could have some time to talk to his brother since he didn't get to see him very often. I took my time and my shower took at least thirty minutes, I was completely relaxed and ready for bed as I wrapped myself up in a towel.

I exited the bathroom in a large hotel towel tightly wrapped around me. I looked at the bed as I walked towards the wardrobe and smiled at Alec who was glaring at me.

"You think you're so funny, don't you?" he snapped.

I put my back to him as I opened the wardrobe.

"I don't think it, I *know* it."

"You're a teasing little bitch is what you are, why did you do it?"

I played the innocent maiden.

"I've no idea what you're talkin' about, good sir."

I heard movement then gasped when a hand gripped my upper arm a moment later and it spun me round.

"You know *exactly* what I'm talking about. You straddled me, rubbed your pussy against me, got me hard then left me high and dry."

I ignored his crude words and frowned at his tone.

"I didn't do any of that on purpose Alec. You're puttin' way too much thought into this."

Alec snarled, "I don't think I am, kitten."

I felt bad and sighed. I didn't mean to make him mad, I meant to tick him off, not piss him off.

"If it counts for anythin', I'm sorry."

Alec stared down at me with hard eyes before they slowly but surely softened.

"I'll accept your apology if you do something for me?"

I eyed him. "No sexual acts."

Alec laughed. "No, nothing like that."

I raised my eyebrow. "What then?"

"I want to go dancing."

"Dancin'?"

Alec grinned and nodded his head. "Dancing."

"Thank you, Jesus," I called out as the elevator doors opened on the fourth floor of the hotel.

It was currently almost three in the morning and I was just getting back to my suite after going dancing with Alec. We left our hotel room at seven with the intentions of leaving the hotel but there was a party going on in the ballroom of the hotel and that was where we ended up. Alec was still down at the party dancing with a bunch of ladies, young and old, while I escaped and came up here. I couldn't stand up anymore and was in desperate need of a bed.

My feet were absolutely killing me.

I yawned loudly as I dragged myself down the hallway to mine and Alec's room. When I reached the door, I slipped my key card into the door waiting for the light to flash green so I could enter.

When it did flash green I all but fell in the door, I managed to stay on my feet, but not for long. I tripped over something and went face first onto the ground.

I groaned out loud as my sore thigh throbbed in pain from the impact. I struggled to my feet and felt around the wall for the light switch, when I found it and flipped it on I cursed.

Alec's suitcase was lying open on the floor. The bastard didn't even have the decency to put it out of harms – my – way. I angrily pushed it towards the wall with my foot then kicked off my heels, unzipped my dress, shimmied out of it then removed my bra. I felt free and let it all hang loose, not caring that I wasn't sucking anything in anymore.

I turned to the wardrobe and opened it, I hadn't drunk anything at the party but my eyes were blurry from being so tired and I couldn't see worth a shit.

I slammed the wardrobe doors shut and considered going to bed in just my knickers but Alec flashed across my mind and I groaned. The fucker would be coming up here to sleep eventually and I couldn't be naked.

I sighed and looked towards the bed, but caught sight of his big black case on the floor. I moved towards it before I could stop myself I reached into to it – it was already open – and picked up the first thing I touched. It turned out to be a white t-shirt.

I checked the size on it and saw it was an Extra Large. Alec wasn't fat, far from it, he was muscular and probably needed the extra room in his clothes to well, breathe.

Before I could stop myself, I put the t-shirt on and smiled when it fell to the middle of my thighs. I reached around to my arse and felt it just covered my bum cheeks. I usually wouldn't ever settle on just wearing this when I knew I was going to be around someone but I was so tired that I didn't give a shite. I moved to the bathroom, picked up my wet wipes and washed as much makeup from my face as I could before I gripped handfuls of my hair and tied it up into an awful looking messy bun.

I left the bathroom, hit the lights and fell face first onto the bed before wiggling my way under the covers. I took in a deep breath and sighed as I closed my eyes and fell into a peaceful slumber.

Banging interrupted that peaceful slumber. I sat up with my eyes still closed and didn't move. I was still kind of half asleep and didn't know whether to lie back down or stay sitting up.

"Keela? Wake up!" Alec's voice called out.

I groaned and moved the covers off of me so I could stand up.

"Let me in!" Alec shouted again then pounded on the door some more.

I held my hands out as I moved towards the door feeling my way along the walls until my head bumped the door, making me stumble back a little.

"I'm comin', hold bloody on!" I shouted, annoyed.

I blindly searched for the handle of the door and found it after a few seconds. I pulled the door open and looked upwards to meet Alec's blue eyes. He was casually leaning against the door frame with his arms folded across his chest. He looked like a vision, a vision of sex.

"Well, aren't you a sight for sore eyes." He smirked.

I could only imagine how my face and hair looked.

"Bite me," I snarled before turning and walking back towards the bed and checked the clock on one of the nightstands, it read thirteen minutes past four in the morning.

I heard a sharp intake of breath just as the light flicked on. I crawled on the bed and got back under the covers and rested my head on my pillow.

"What are you wearing?" Alec voice asked.

I thought about it for a second then opened my eyes.

"Uh... a t-shirt," I replied.

"Is it mine?" he asked.

I didn't know if he sounded mad or amused.

"Yeah," I mumbled.

He was silent for a minute then I heard items hit the floor. I knew he was undressing and it made me tense a little. I wanted to turn around and look at him but I mentally scowled at myself and made sure I stayed in the position I was in.

"Why are you wearing my t-shirt to bed?" he asked.

I shrugged and closed my eyes again. "I couldn't find me shorts or tank top so I just picked this up. I'll get you a new one if that's what has your knickers in a twist."

Alec snorted. "I don't need a new one, I've about ten more of them with me. I was just curious as to why you were wearing my clothing to bed. You do hate me after all."

"I hate you, not your t-shirt."

This made Alec laugh as he moved the covers aside so he could get in after he turned off the light.

"Jesus," he breathed.

I groaned.

"What now?" I asked.

"I can see your ass," he replied.

I instantly turned on my back and turned my head to glare at him. "Don't look!"

He held his hands up. "I can't miss it, it's right there."

I narrowed my eyes and he saw.

He rubbed his temples. "Forget I said anything, go back to sleep."

I rolled my eyes and noticed then that he was in just his boxer briefs.

I widened my eyes. "You cannot sleep next to me like that!" I said and pointed my finger to his body.

What the hell happened to my pyjama trousers condition?

He looked down at himself before looking back up at me with a raised eyebrow. "I usually sleep naked, I figured you wouldn't want that-"

"Damn right I wouldn't!" I snapped.

"Which is why I am wearing these," he continued and gestured to his boxers.

"Just turn off the light."

Alec bowed to me just before he turned off the light. I gave him the finger to which he laughed at. When the light clicked off he moved back towards the bed and it dipped down on his side when he got onto it.

He lay down and pulled the covers over himself, tugging them away from me a little. I tugged them back; he pulled them a little which just caused me tug on them again.

This went on for about twenty seconds until he laughed and said, "*Stop* taking all the covers!"

I growled. "Get stuffed, I was here first."

"This is our bed, not just yours."

I huffed. "Just stay on your side. Don't cross over onto my side and I won't murder you in your sleep, okay?"

I could practically feel Alec's grin radiate from him and it pissed me off.

"Understood."

"Good," I hissed and turned on my side, tugging the blanket with me.

He snorted and didn't tug on the blanket again and that made me relax. It was warm as hell but I still needed to cover myself with the covers, I couldn't sleep with nothing covering me.

I thought I would have been unable to sleep half naked with Alec next to me but surprisingly I hardly even thought about it as I closed my eyes again.

When I woke up it was because wind on my face stirred me. "Close the window," I mumbled, snuggling deeper into my pillow.

I heard a groan just as I felt my pillow move. I furrowed my eyebrows but didn't open my eyes. I groaned a little when I felt movement between my legs and gasped in alarm when something hard pressed against me... there.

I opened my eyes and screamed when I saw a face that wasn't Storm's there. The eyes on the face snapped open just as hands that were already around me tightened.

"It's me, Alec!"

I stopped struggling and screaming and looked to the face again. I recognised him now and relief instantly flooded me, I thought I'd had a one night stand or something.

Relief left when Alec moved and a groan left my lips again. He looked at me, then down to our intertwined bodies and let a smile take over his face.

"Couldn't help yourself could you, kitten?"

I knew his leg was between my legs and it was brushing up against me. I've always been sensitive; the littlest of touches always got me going, but I did my best not to let Alec know that.

I glared at him as he moved his leg into me again.

"Get off me," I said breathlessly.

He smirked and pulled me closer to him. "You don't sound like you want me to," he said just as he turned and somehow moved me under him without moving me.

What the hell?

"Alec," I said in a breathless voice.

It was meant to come out in a warning tone.

"You were saying my name in your sleep," he said as he looked down at me.

He held himself up on his elbows, taking most of his weight off me.

"I was probably trying to kill you and-"

He snorted. "You said it while you groaned, it was sexy as hell. Watching you dream about me as you panted."

I felt my entire body turn red. "You're making that up, I hate you! I wouldn't dream about you, like... like that!"

Alec brushed his nose on mine making me snap my teeth at him which he smirked at. "Oh but you did, Keela."

I didn't believe him.

"I hate you," I said in the firmest voice I could manage.

He bucked against me grinding his groin against mine. He was between my legs and the only barrier keeping him from being in me was my knickers and his boxers.

"I hate you too," he smiled but then growled, "that doesn't stop me from wanting you though."

I felt my eyes widened. "You can't be serious-"

He kissed me.

He *really* kissed me, not just a peck or a stolen kiss this time. His lips were on mine and his tongue forced his way inside my mouth. I said his name but it came out as another fucking groan and it didn't take long to realise I was kissing him back.

I wasn't just kissing him back though, oh no, my legs where wrapped around his waist and my hands where behind his head and neck pulling him as close as he could get. I didn't want to kiss or touch him, but obviously my body had other ideas.

"Say it," he growled onto my lips.

Say fucking what?

My mind was like mush - I couldn't comprehend what he wanted me to say. There was a battle going on inside my head; one side couldn't believe what I was doing and told me that I had to stop, while the other side was chilled out and telling me to get laid and that me and Alec should fuck our problems out.

Literally fuck them out.

"Say it, Keela," Alec's voice growled again getting my attention.

"Say what?" I asked, breathless.

"That you want me," he said and he reconnected our lips. "Tell me you want me to fuck you. Say 'fuck me, Alec'."

The rational side of my head told me to tell him to fuck *off*, while the other side - I'm dubbing the slutty side - was hooting and singing a song that just repeated of the same line.

Fuck me, Alec!

"Fuck me, Alec," I mumbled then groaned when he pushed himself off me again.

"Louder," he snarled.

I swallowed my pride, gave the rational side of my mind the finger and looked him directly in the eyes. "Fuck me, Alec," I said before pulling his head back to mine.

He growled into my mouth and used one of his hands to trust my borrowed t-shirt upwards, exposing my breasts. I gasped when his mouth left mine and then latched onto my left nipple. He suckled and bit on me a little before switching to the right nipple. I grinded my lower half into him, and he shuddered.

"These need to go," he snarled as he sat up, removed my legs from around his waist, hooked his hand around my black lace knickers before yanking them down my legs and clean off my feet before throwing them somewhere behind him.

He lost his boxers in record time and moved back over me before stopping.

"What?" I asked as I lifted my hips upwards and started to grind myself on him.

He closed his eyes as my juices made it easy for him to slide through my folds and upwards towards my belly button.

"I don't have condoms," he said in a strained voice.

My heart broke. I didn't have any either, I wasn't planning on having sex with anyone on this trip, especially Alec. I was about to tell him this was a sign that we weren't meant to have sex when he suddenly used his hand to guide himself to my entrance.

"I'll pull out," he said before he rocked into me.

I screamed out in pleasure at the sensation of being so full. Alec's eyes rolled back a little before he pulled out a little and repeated his earlier actions.

"My God," he groaned. "So fuckin' good."

I agreed wholeheartedly.

He set a steady pace of thrusting and retreating before he leaned back down on his elbows and brought his face back to mine.

"Do you like that?" he asked.

Was that a serious question?

"Yes!" I hissed as I opened my legs further for him.

He made me scream again when he rocked into me harder than he had before.

It felt incredible, too fucking incredible.

"I can't take that, don't-" I screamed when he did it again.

Every trust after that he seemed to apply more power to and each time it made me scream and cry out. I felt myself trying to get away from him because what he was making me feel pleasure so intense that I couldn't take it, while at the same time I was forcing myself to stay put so it could last forever.

"Good girl," Alec purred just as his teeth latch onto my bottom lip.

I started to pant when a warm feeling started to swirl around my core.

"Right there," I said then screamed as a blanket of pleasure and ecstasy crashed over me.

I felt my hands fall back to the mattress when Alec put his hands on my shoulders. I opened my eyes as he smiled at me. "Wake up, kitten," he said.

I looked at him in confusion then widened my eyes he started to become blurry. I squeezed my eyes shut.

"Wake up, kitten!" he shouted.

My eyes snapped open to find the t-shirt I was wearing was stuck to me with sweat and between my legs was pulsing. I instantly sat up and looked around. Alec sat up now as well from his side of the bed.

"You were shouting in your sleep and moving around a lot," he yawned.

I felt myself turned red.

"I thought you were awake because you were saying my name and- Why is your face so red?" he asked, rubbing the sleep out of his eyes.

I felt myself heat up even more as I jumped from the bed. "No reason, it's just hot in here," I lied.

He looked at me for a moment then looked to my shaking legs before he looked up at my face. I looked down myself as well and nearly died when I saw my inner thighs were wet and it was easily visible.

"It's sweat!" I blurted.

Alec looked at me for a few more seconds before a smile stretched across his face. It was the smuggest smile I have ever seen on someone's face.

"Stop fuckin' smilin'. It's sweat, that's all!" I bellowed.

Alec's teeth where showing now because he was smiling that wide. "You dreamt about me, didn't you? You were shouting my name, it woke me up. You were gasping and-"

"Shut up!" I screamed and ran into the bathroom hearing him laugh behind me.

I wanted to die, I wanted the ground to open up and swallow me whole.

"Did I come as well or did you finish before me?" he asked through a belly rumbling laugh.

I picked up a towel and screamed into it.

I was so utterly mortified that I felt like crying.

What the fuck was wrong with me? Why did I dream about

Alec like that, why? I knew I fancied him but dammit, I hated the bastard. Now that he knew I dreamt of him, the fucker would be smug about it for the rest of this trip and possibly the rest of his life.

I sat down on the floor and buried my face in my hands trying to think of something else, anything else.

"I'll call room service and tell them to send someone up later to change the sheets!" Alec shouted from somewhere in the hotel room.

I screamed into the towel again and he burst into laughter.

"I'm so happy," he announced in a sing-song voice.

I wasn't - I was far fucking from it.

CHAPTER THIRTEEN

I closed my eyes and sighed when I heard my phone ring from somewhere in the room. I didn't want to deal with Aideen, but I had to know if Storm was okay so I sat up from the bed, listened for my phone then followed the noise to the wardrobe.

"Is Storm okay?" I asked as soon as I answered the phone.

"This is Storm. Aideen is dead because I ate her."

I felt myself smile.

"I'm sure she deserved it."

"Cow," Aideen muttered then asked, "how did you know it was me?"

I sighed. "Because you're the only person who ever rings me."

"Babe, that is pretty pathetic."

I snorted. "Tell me about it."

Aideen chuckled. "So, how is the Bahamas? I hope it's pissin' down rain because it is here."

I turned my head to the right and looked through the open windows and out to the stunning view of the blue ocean and an even bluer sky.

"Hope again, it doesn't look like rain is on the cards here, just heat and sunshine."

"I hate you."

"Don't be jealous."

Aideen huffed. "Jealous of you in paradise with prince charmin'? Why would I be jealous of that?"

I groaned at the mention of him and felt my cheeks heat up as I remembered how he laughed at me.

No, no fucking way.

We were not discussing the fucker. I didn't want to think about him.

"Can this conversation remain Alec Slater free, please? Tell me about me baby, does he miss me?"

"I don't know, I'll ask Storm later if he feels like talkin' to me."

I snickered. "Smartarse."

"We know I'm a smartarse, let's bypass that already known information and tell me why we can't talk about Alec sexy-as-fuck Slater?"

She was no help, no help at all.

"Aideen," I whined.

"Don't Aideen me, tell me... Unless you killed him, then I don't want to know. I can't vouch for you if I know you did it."

I furrowed my eyebrows, pulled my phone from my ear and glanced at it before shaking my head and placing it back against my ear.

"Wow."

I heard Aideen's sharp intake of breath before she said, "Oh, my God! You didn't deny killin' him! Forget what I said before about not tellin' me, tell me!"

I couldn't help but laugh at her, she was so dramatic and crazy that it was nothing but funny.

"I didn't kill anybody. Alec is perfectly fine and in the same condition as he was when he left Ireland... He might be a bit happier now though."

"Why would he be happier? Also, let me just add that I'm happy you didn't kill him that would have been a terrible waste of delicious man meat."

Mother of God.

"There is somethin' wrong with you, you're not normal."

Aideen snorted. "Normal is overrated, now answer me question. Why is he happier? Did you shag him?"

What the hell?

"No! Why would you even ask me that?"

There was a long pause.

"Because I know you're attracted to him even though you don't want to be. You're fightin' that attraction so you don't dive into bed with Alec, shag him, then wake up feelin' used."

I looked down to my now shaking knees and sighed.

"Am I that obvious?"

"To me? Yes. To Alec? No."

I blew out a breath.

"Thank God for that at least, I can't handle him knowin' I fancy him after what happened this mornin'."

I admitted out loud to Aideen that I fancied Alec, there was no going back from that now even if I want to because she wouldn't forget I said it.

"If you make me ask what happened I'm comin' through the phone and bitch slappin' you."

I swallowed and closed my eyes. "It's *so* embarssin'."

"It's you, Keela, anythin' that happens to you is never less than embarrassin'."

I huffed. "Thanks a bloody lot."

Aideen laughed and then waited for me to tell my horror story.

"I had a dirty dream about Alec and he knows about it," I blurted out and closed my eyes.

Things were silent for a moment, and when that moment was over, hollering and wolf whistling blared through the receiver of my phone.

"You had a wet dream? Get in there, babe. Woot woot! Keela had a dirty dream. A d-i-r-t-y dream about-"

"Aideen, please! You're not helpin'!"

"Oh, stop it! This is funny, find your sense of humour and laugh at this!"

I groaned. "I can't, I can't find anythin' funny about this. He knows I had a dirty dream about him Ado, he knows and he *laughed* at me!"

Aideen's laughter and chuckling paused.

"He laughed at you or laughed at your reaction to havin' a dirty dream about him?"

I opened my mouth to answer her but closed it as I thought on what she said.

"That's exactly what I thought. You just assumed he was laughin' at you and you flipped."

I frowned. "You make it sound like snappin' at him is somethin' I do often-"

"You've done nothin' but snap at him from the moment you met him. You forget he is there as a favour to help you. He doesn't have to be there, Keela. He doesn't have to have anythin' to do with you and yet he is there with you. Cut him some slack. I know you're wary because he wants to shag you but give him a break, at least he admits what he wants from you instead of goin' behind your back to use you. I'm also pretty sure sayin' he wants to fuck you is just his way of sayin' he is interested in you."

I frowned.

"I hate that you're right."

"Of course you do, no one likes bein' wrong."

I sighed.

"Great, the next step is actin' on your attraction."

I rolled my eyes. "I hate Alec."

"You're attracted to his looks, but hate him as a person, that is possible."

"That is so shallow, likin' someone for their looks."

Aideen snorted. "Then the majority of the human population is shallow because most of the time that is what attracts people to others first, their looks."

I didn't reply because I knew she was right.

"I guess," I mumbled.

She sighed dreamily. "Was he good?" she asked.

I gasped. "It was a dream, no actually it was a nightmare."

Aideen burst out laughing. "It was a dream, not a nightmare.

I've had lots of dreams about Alec-"

"He wasn't next to you when you had said dream though."

"That's why you're freakin' out? Because you think he knew what you where dreamin-"

"He did know. He laughed his arse off at me when he seen-" I cut myself off with a cry.

"Did we not already address this? How do you know he wasn't laughin' at your reaction-"

"He saw the... evidence." I winced, covering my face with my free hand.

Aideen was quiet for a second before bursting into laughter. "You came? Like *really* came over a dream? Shite, you *literally* had a wet dream."

"It's not funny!" I shouted. "I had a sex dream about Alec, what about that is funny?"

"It's not funny at all, nothing about me getting laid in a dream but not in real life is funny," his voice said.

I closed my eyes for a moment before turning my head and looking in the direction of the hotel room door. Alec stood in the doorway with a plastic bag in one hand and a bunch of flowers in the other.

"Are those flowers a sorry for laughing at me?" I asked, curiously.

"No, they are to brighten up the room because a dark cloud is hanging over it thanks to your panties being in a twist over something stupid."

"Don't you talk about me knickers, you big bastard. Don't you fuckin' dare!" I snapped making Alec and Aideen burst into laughter.

I wanted to shoot them both.

I looked away from Alec and focused on my phone.

"You shouldn't laugh with him, you're me friend, back me up!"

"No, because he is right. Your knickers are in a twist over somethin' stupid."

I narrowed my eyes and sighed out loud. "Okay, maybe they are in a twist but for a very good reason! I feel like I've committed the biggest sin ever."

Alec snorted. "You had a wet dream, big deal."

Ahhh!

I hung up on a laughing Aideen then dove under the covers of the bed and wished death upon myself. Alec's laughter followed me and I tried to plug my fingers in my ears to make it go away but it wouldn't.

He dove on the bed then, making me grunt as he applied some of his weight down on me.

"Get off, you weigh a ton!" I complained.

Alec moved around then until he was lying next to me. "Look, I know you're embarrassed about what happened this morning, but I have something to cheer you up."

Curiosity got the better of me, so I slowly peeked my head out from under the covers. Alec was looking at me and began grinning while he held up the plastic bag that was in his hand when he entered the room.

I looked at the bag. "What did you buy me? A time machine?" I asked.

He snorted. "No, just some things to make you feel better," he said as he handed me the bag.

I took the bag from him and looked inside. I smiled when I eyed a box of chocolates.

"Thanks, but I'm on a diet and can't eat-"

Alec held up his hand and shook his head. "No, I got you these chocolates as a peace offering and you're going to take them, and you will eat them, and you will like them."

Who did he think he was?

"And if I don't?"

Alec smirked. "If you don't, when your mom gets here, I'll tell her that you had a wet dream about me and destroyed the bed sheets."

"Bastard!" I screamed and dove forward and swung my hands at him.

Alec grabbed me and laughed as he fell onto the bed, pulling me with him. I struggled to get off him when I sat up.

Alec gave me a wink before looking at where I was seated on him. "Does this remind you of something? A certain dream maybe?"

"No, because you were on top in the dream-" I widened my eyes in horror at what I just said. "Shut the fuck up, Alec."

He laughed as I rolled off him.

"I hate you," I said into my pillow.

He threw his arms over me. "No, you don't. You may not like me, but you don't hate me. We're friends after all and friends shouldn't fight like we do."

I grunted. "Friends, huh?"

"Yep."

I sighed, caving in. "Okay, we're friends. Now will you get off us?"

"Us?"

I rolled my eyes and said, "Me."

"But you said us."

"Us means me as well."

Alec tilted his head at me. "You know something? I've been living in Ireland for three years and the Irish still make me scratch my head when they say certain things."

I shrugged my shoulders. "It can't be that bad since you still live there."

"Even if I hated the people I'd still live there."

I raised my eyebrows. "Why?"

"It where my family is, where home is... I like the view, too."

I chuckled. "I like it too, it's pretty."

"You're pretty."

I deadpanned, "Stop that."

"Stop what?" Alec smiled while giving me the 'fuck me' look.

"*That*! Stop tryin' to seduce me."

Alec blinked his eyes, stared at me for a moment then laughed. "I'm sorry, I didn't even realise I was hitting on you."

"Maybe because you flirt with people so much it has become second nature to you, just like breathin', you do it and don't even notice."

"It's a skill."

"It's a pain in the arse, that's what it is."

Alec waggled his eyebrows at me. "I know something else that can be a pain in your ass-"

"Alec, I swear to God, if you finish that sentence I will shove me foot so far up your arse that you will need a surgeon to remove it."

Alec stared at me blankly, unblinking then mumbled, "You're even more creative with your threats than Bronagh."

I inwardly smiled. "I'm sorry for threatenin' you, and while I'm at it, I'm sorry for bein' such a bitch to you. Why don't we start over. Hey, I'm Keela Daley, nice to meet you."

Alec smiled at me and took my hand in his. He lifted my hand to his mouth and kissed my knuckles before he said, "Nice to meet you, Keela Daley. I'm Alec Slater."

I sighed as I blew out a breath, which caused Alec to chuckle.

"So, Alec, what do you like to do for fun? Keep it PG."

Alec smiled, then shook his head and said, "I like animals. When I'm back home, I help out with the local shelters that the DSPCA runs. They have very limited funds so volunteers are always welcome. I donate money as well, but donating my time is something I enjoy. What about you, what do you do for fun? You can get as explicit as you want with your answer, just throwing that in there."

I wanted to laugh at the ending to his sentence but I didn't because I was too busy processing the fact that he volunteers at animal shelters because he enjoys it.

That just added to how attractive is was.

"Um, I like to write. It's nothin' as cool as volunteerin', but-"

"Don't do that, don't put something you like to do down. Don't even compare it to something someone else likes to do. It's yours so put it on a high pedestal."

I blinked.

"What?" Alec asked as I stared at him.

I cleared my throat and said, "I've never had someone, besides Aideen, be so direct with me before."

Alec shrugged. "Spend a little time with me and you can see how direct I can be, kitten."

I raised my eyebrows. "Was that suggestive? I can't really tell."

Alec chuckled. "Never mind, let's get back to you, what do you like to write."

I felt my cheeks heat up with the spotlight suddenly on me and my writing, I was about to take an out when Alec leaned and gripped my chin with his fingers and said, "Don't even think about it, kitten. You started this conversation and I'm seeing that we finish it."

Well, excuse me.

"You have to understand that this is a sensitive topic for me, only Aideen knows I write and now you. You're still new-"

"I'm trying to get in a little wear and tear with you so I'm not so new anymore. The more we talk, the more that happens. You talk, I'll listen. Tell me about your writing."

I furrowed my eyebrows together and asked, "Are you serious? You really want to talk and listen to me?"

Alec frowned at me. "Why is that so shocking to you? People converse daily-"

"You have only talked about sex since we met. I'm honestly haven' trouble separatin' that part from 'serious' you right now."

Alec smiled. "You don't know me, kitten. You know what I want from you but that's it. You don't know me at all."

I felt like he was challenging me.

"Well, maybe I want to get to know you. Maybe I want to get inside your mind and figure it out too. I want to understand you."

Alec reached his hand up to my face and ran his fingertips over my cheek.

"You'd lose your mind trying to understand mine, kitten."

"Don't be cryptic with me, I like you better when you're straight forward."

Alec drew back his hand and laughed. "I like your honesty kitten, don't ever lose it."

"I don't plan on it."

"Good. Come on, we can finish this conversation later, I want to go out."

"And do what?"

Alec pulled me from the bed and onto my feet then into a hug. "Now that we're friends, let's go get our hair done."

I pulled back and gave him a look.

He smiled at me. "You need a wash and blow dry."

I rolled my eyes then looked up to the Heavens. If I didn't kill him by the end of this trip then I would believe that miracles really did exist.

CHAPTER FOURTEEN

"I got my hair done because you hounded me for the last hour, but I'm not gettin' a tattoo and you can't make me."

Alec groaned out loud for the tenth time in thirty seconds.

"For the last time, *I'm* getting inked, you're just going to sit there and *be quiet*. I won't be long-"

"No, you're not leavin' me out here on me own, what if one of the artists *thinks* I want to get a tattoo and then they force me into gettin' one?"

Alec rubbed his eyes with both hands before he focused on me. "Sweetheart, I don't think anyone could force you into something you didn't want to do even if they tried."

"Whatever, I'm comin' into the room with you."

Alec groaned out loud again but instead of arguing, took my hand and interlocked it with his. "Come on then."

Victory!

I huddled close to Alec as we moved closer to the reception desk in the tattoo parlour. Okay, it wasn't exactly a reception desk, but it was clearly the place to go when you wanted to talk to the person in charge. The man in charge just so happened to be a six foot tall black man who was covered in tattoos.

"What can I do you for, mon?" Ink God asked Alec.

I smiled, he said 'mon' instead of 'man'.

It's pretty self-explanatory why I have dubbed the man Ink God.

He. Was. Stunning!

"I'm looking to finish my sleeve. I've a patch of white skin on my tricep that I want covered and blended."

Ink God nodded his head. "Let's have a look at what I'm workin' with."

I noticed the man's Bahamian accent caused him to drop his G's and I liked that because I did that when I spoke too.

Alec was complying with Ink God and opened his hand and tried to pull it from mine, but when I didn't let go he laughed and kissed my head. "I'll give it back to you in a second, promise."

I flushed with embarrassment when Ink God chuckled and tried to cover it up by coughing. I let go of Alec's hand and stood idle next to him as he took off his t-shirt. When he was bare chested, he bent his elbow then lifted his arm up in the air, showing the ink free part of his arm. Ink God looked it over few times before nodding his head.

"Thirty minutes, tops. You got a design in mind?"

Alec nodded his head and stuck his hand inside the pocket of his shorts, pulled out his phone, tapped on the screen then turned it to Ink God. Ink God didn't say anything, he only put the phone down, got some see through paper then started drawing on it.

I was bored just standing there so I turned my head to look around the shop and when I spotted a huge wall with nothing but tattoo designs on it, I moved towards it without evening realising. I flicked my eyes over hundreds of beautiful designs. I smiled when a slight breeze hit my back just before a body pressed into mine.

"See anything you like?" Alec asked as he lowered his mouth to my ear and kissed it.

I shivered making him lightly chuckle.

I cleared my throat and said, "I like loads of them, they are gorgeous."

"Why don't you get one then?"

"Because tattoos are not somethin' I can take back after few days if I change me mind. They don't have a thirty day guarantee."

Alec turned me to face him. "You're one of those chicks who keeps the receipt for everything, aren't you?"

Were there some women who didn't keep their receipts?
"Of course, I wouldn't trust anyone who didn't keep the receipts for the items they buy."

Alec chewed on his lower lip. "I don't."

I snorted. "You're datin' me now honey, that will change."

A smile stretched across Alec face as he lifted his hand and brushed loose strands of hair out of my face.

"I like you, kitten."

I smiled. "I don't believe you."

"I do, I like you a lottle. It's like a little, except a lot."

I rolled my eyes. "You can't take cute sayin's from the internet and try to make them yours."

Alec gasped. "I would never! I made that up-"

"I've seen the little penguin picture with the lottle word on it, you're lyin'."

Alec grunted. "Fine, whatever. I saw it on Facebook somewhere, but it's cute and it fits how I feel about you."

"I smell bullshit."

Alec smiled. "You know I'm serious."

"No, I don't believe you," I whispered.

Alec raised an eyebrow. "You want me to convince you?"

"I don't think anythin' you do will convince me."

Was I flirting?

"You think so?"

"Oh, I know so."

Yes, yes I was.

"You really shouldn't challenge me, little girl," Alec said in a low, threatening voice that I didn't find scary, only sexy.

"Or what?" I asked, keeping direct eye contact with him.

"I'll accept and see that I complete the challenge to the best of my abilities."

I swallowed. "Prove it-"

His mouth was on mine before I could finish my sentence.

Alec has kissed me a once or twice before, but those were pecks on the lips and were mostly to annoy me. But this kiss, this kiss was something else entirely. I felt it not only in my mouth but in other parts of my body as well.

"Alec, stop," I mumbled into his mouth.

He lifted his hands from my waist and placed them on the side of my face, holding me in place connected to him. He applied more pressure to the kiss, and swirled his tongue around mine, thoroughly kissing me. My hands were frozen on his bare biceps and I don't know whether my grip was to keep him from getting closer to me or to keep him from moving away from me.

I felt him pull back from me, and the little nip he gave to my bottom lip was the jolt I needed to come back down to Earth, because after that kiss I was somewhere miles away.

"Keela?" Alec whispered.

My eyes were still closed as I hummed in response.

"I don't like the word 'stop', but I do like hearing you say my name."

I blinked my eyes open and through my thoroughly kissed daze, I smiled.

"You're a really good kisser."

Alec laughed and kissed my forehead. "Kitten, you have no idea. Just wait till I get you back to our room."

I blinked and snorted at his cockiness.

"You're a good kisser, a *really* good kisser, but don't think that will be enough to get me into bed."

Alec winked. "We sleep in the same bed."

I playfully swatted his shoulder. "You know what I mean."

Alec chuckled. "Yeah I know, and I already accepted that challenge back home. As you just found out, I'm very good at completing challenges."

I raised my eyebrow. "What challenge did you just complete?"

"I convinced you that I like you."

He did?

I rolled my eyes. "You convinced me that you're a good kisser, that doesn't mean you like me."

"I'm here pretending to be your boyfriend with the possibility of getting *zero* benefits from you. Trust me kitten, I like you. I like you a whole lottle, remember?"

I groaned. "You should *not* be able to say things like that."

"Why?"

Really?

"Because it's too bloody cute, that's why."

Alec smiled. "Yeah? Well, it's true."

I was wary, I wanted to believe that someone like Alec could even remotely think of liking someone like me, but I couldn't because my mind and heart wouldn't allow me to.

"Yeah, yeah, Romeo."

Alec frowned at me. "Why do you do that?"

"Do what?"

"Play off what I say to you as if it's a bunch of lies? I'm a very honest person Keela. If I say I like you, then I fucking like you!"

I jumped with fright and took a step back as my eyes filled with tears. "Why are you shoutin' at me?"

"Because I don't like that you think I'm playing you. I'm not, I'd tell you if I was."

I forced my tears not to fall as I narrowed my eyes. "You aren't playing me? Did you or did you not tell me that while you were here it wasn't for romance, but only for you to fuck me?"

Alec set his jaw and glared down at me. "I did say that, but that was before I knew you."

"You don't know me Alec, you've been in my life a few fuckin' days."

"Is a few days not enough to know someone? I already know you kitten. You're moody in the mornings, afternoons and sometimes in the evenings. You wet your toothbrush after you apply the paste, which is weird by the way. You like One Direction way too much for a grown woman, their song "Little Things" is your favourite. I know that because you have played it more than any of their other songs. You want to be really skinny but love food too much to fully stick to the diet you're on. *Coronation Street*, and *Eastenders*, are your favourite soap operas, I know that because you set your Sky box to record all the episodes that you will miss while you're here. You love Storm like a mother loves her child, and really hate when Aideen calls him names. You also love Aideen like a sister and cherish her friendship."

I stared at Alec for a moment before I said, "Knowin' me routine doesn't mean you know me."

"I know *you* not just your routine. I probably don't know how many cousins you have, what your mother's maiden name is or who your first kiss was, but I do know the little things that make you who you are. You bite your fingernails when you're nervous, you talk to yourself and answer yourself when you think no one is listening, you make up your own lyrics when singing along to songs you don't know, and cry easily when people shout at you."

I blinked, still trying to hold my tears back. "I do not."

"You're also the most stubborn human on the planet."

"No, I'm not... you are," I mumbled and then sniffled.

I was going to cry.

I was actually going to cry in a tattoo parlour because Alec listed shite I didn't know he knew about me.

I was a mess, a colossal mess.

"Why are you upset?"

"Because you being very deep right now with all this 'lottle and like' talk, Can't we just talk about this some other time?"

Alec eyed me, but nodded his head. "Okay."

"Thank you."

"You and your girl finished, mon?" Ink God called out.

I flushed with embarrassment and quickly wiped my eyes with the back of my hands.

"Yeah bro, we're good," Alec said then turned and moved back over towards Ink God.

I followed silently, making sure my eyes never landed on either

ALEC

man, but instead roamed around the parlour. I looked over my shoulder when the door of the parlour open and in walked four girls. The oldest looked to be about twenty.

I moved away from Alec and walked towards the large sofa across the room. I wasn't really interested in listening to Alec and Ink God hammer out a design for Alec's tattoo. I sat on the chair and inwardly groaned because it was the definition of comfortable.

"Look at him."

I looked to my left and raised my eyebrows.

All four of the girl's eyes were on Alec and it was then that I realised he was still shirtless. I narrowed my eyes at the group and folded my arms across my chest.

"He is so fit," one of the girls whispered.

"Fit doesn't do him justice, he is bloody stunning," another one whispered then giggled.

I rolled my eyes.

Of course they would have to be English. I think they were from London based on their accents and that didn't make me feel better, because not only were they all really pretty, but their accents were really cool and nice to listen to.

When Alec and Ink God were done talking, Alec turned and looked for me but when he found the girls in my place, he smiled. It wasn't a suggestive smile either it was a polite smile.

"Hey ladies."

"Hey," four voices sang in unison.

Fucking bitches.

"Have you seen my girlfriend?" Alec asked.

My eyebrows jumped up to my hairline.

"Girlfriend?" the girls repeated dolefully.

Each girl looked around then and their eyes soon landed on mine, they looked at me with me envy... and I liked it.

"I'm here," I said, waving to Alec who looked over the girls and to me.

He smiled and held out his hand. "What are you doing back

there? Come on, you wanted to come into the room while I get this done, right?"

I nodded my head and got up from the settee. I walked towards Alec and was surprised when the four girls separated and allowed me to walk through them.

"Me legs got tired," I said when I took his outstretched hand and interlocked it with mine.

"I'm not surprised, they probably weigh her down."

I felt my jaw drop open as I let go of Alec and spun around.

"Which one of you said that?" I snapped and took a step forward only to be lifted backwards when arms closed around me.

"Easy, kitten."

I struggled in Alec's arm as he turned and walked off into the back of the parlour with me in his arms.

"Don't tell me to take it fuckin' easy, she basically just called me fat!"

"And it was a stupid thing to say considering you aren't fat. If you were fat I wouldn't be able to carry you."

"Bullshit! You have arms the size of a tank, you can easily lift heavy things."

Alec laughed. "Okay, that's true, but I can't hold them for long periods of time and I'm perfectly fine with carrying you right now."

I grunted and gently smacked at Alec's arms and it caused him to sigh and set me down on the ground like I wanted.

"Fat or not, what one of those slappers," I shouted the word 'slappers' loud so said slappers could hear me, "said was just uncalled for, and fuckin' mean. I would never call somebody names like that."

"You called me names when you first met me."

I screeched and pushed on his shoulders. "You were a pervert and you baited me! Wait, whose fuckin' side are you on here anyway?"

Alec grinned mischievously. "Yours, always yours."

I regarded him. "Good answer."

Alec bit down on his lower lip, grinned then leaned down to kiss me. I allowed him to do so because I wanted to kiss him again, but as his lips touched mine he made his eyes cross and it caused me to burst out laughing.

"Do you take anythin' serious?" I asked.

Alec snaked his arm around my waist and used his free hand to grab my behind.

"You."

I cast my eyes downwards as a sly smile curved around my mouth.

"Why do you take me seriously, Alec?"

Alec squeezed me. "Because you're my girl."

I bit down on my lower lip so hard that it hurt, I did that so I wouldn't smile with delight at hearing Alec call me his girl. It made me happy, and it shouldn't. We weren't a real couple, and we both had to remember that.

"I can see you fighting a battle against me in your head and I'm putting a stop to it right now. What do you say to this; instead of us being fake let's be real, okay? Let's really be a couple for this vacation and feel whatever we feel and however we feel."

I laughed. "Are you serious?"

"Serious as a heart attack."

I looked up into Alec's blue eyes and focused. "Is this another ruse to get into me knickers?"

"No."

I smiled, hoping to draw out a laugh from Alec indicating he was playing with me but he face remained expressionless.

"You really are serious, aren't you?"

"I said I was a serious as a heart attack, how much more serious can I be?" he asked.

Wow.

"I don't know what you want me to say."

"Say you'll be my girlfriend."

"Have you ever asked someone to be your girlfriend before?"

"No, I've never had a girlfriend."

I swallowed. "And you want me to be your first?"

Alec laughed. "Yeah, I want you to be my first. Will you be my girlfriend?"

This felt weird, not bad weird, but not good weird either.

I wanted to shoot him down and say no, but I thought about what Aideen said to me on the phone and realised she was dead right. Alec was here to help me so I should let him and for him to help me I'd have to bend - not literally - to him and meet him half way.

"Okay."

"Really?"

"Yeah, really."

Alec furrowed his eyebrows. "Who are you and what have you done with Keela?"

I laughed. "I'm not goin' to fight you on this."

Alec raised his eyebrows then glanced around the room. "Am I being punked?"

I laughed. "No, I'm just agreein' to be your girlfriend."

"For real, no joke?"

"No joke."

Alec looked liked he was both happy as well as confused.

"Well, okay then. We're a couple."

"We're indeed."

"Will you let me get to second base before we go to bed now that we're dating for real?"

I rolled my eyes. "Just go get your tattoo before I change me mind, you dirty fuck."

Alec waggled his eyebrows. "I'd give you a dirty fuck, kitten."

I grinned. "I don't like bein' dirty, I'm clearly a good girl."

Alec snorted, then turned around and walked in the direction of the room Ink God disappeared into. He stopped by the door though and looked over his shoulder as he said, "There is no such thing as a good girl, kitten. Good girls are just bad girls who haven't been caught."

He disappeared into the room and left me staring at the spot where he stood moments ago. I licked my lips, balled my hands into fists and forced myself to ignore the shivers that Alec's words caused to shoot up my spine.

I hated that a simple sentence from him could cause me to overthink and feel so... turned on.

"Are you coming, kitten?" Alec called out, his tone welcoming.

Well, fuck.

If he wanted to mess with my head with his alluring voice and body, damn him I would do the same!

"Yeah," I replied with a firm nod, "I'm comin'."

CHAPTER FIFTEEN

"I lost Alec."

"How the fuck can you lose a six foot four God?" Aideen asked me, her tone bemused.

I could imagine her confused face as I switched my phone to my right ear.

I shrugged my shoulders as I walked in the direction of my hotel. "We were in a tattoo parlour and he was gettin' inked and it took ages, a lot longer than the tattoo man said. I got bored and decided to go out to the market to have a look around but when I got back to the parlour he was gone. The man who tattooed him said Alec had finished getting his tattoo and went to look for me. I couldn't find him when I went back to the market so figured I'd go back to the hotel, and we'd meet up when he comes back."

Aideen clicked her tongue. "You can't ever sit still, can you?"

I scrunched my face up in annoyance. "Eh, hello, it was *borin'*! I was just sittin' there while Alec was gettin' a tattoo so sue me for goin' for a walk. I told him I would be back soon so technically it's his fault for not stayin' put."

"You'd say anythin' to put the blame on him."

I felt my jaw drop open.

What was she, Alec's cheerleader?

"Either you're hard up for me fella, or you are sidin' with him to piss me off."

"*Your fella?* Since when is he your fella? I thought all this was fake, or was there another reason you have been stressin' that fact since he agreed to help you?"

I rolled my eyes. "Who pissed in your cornflakes? He is me fella since an hour ago when he asked me to be his girlfriend for real. It might only last until we get back home but he asked me and I said yes, so there you go."

"Are you jokin'?"

I shook my head. "Do I sound like I'm jokin'?"

"I can't tell, you're sarcastic ninety-nine point nine percent of the time."

I felt a small grin curve around my mouth. "Well, this is the point one percent of the time that I am bein' serious."

"Fuck. Off!"

I laughed. "That's not nice."

"Are you really fuckin' serious? Don't play with me."

I covered my mouth to smoother my laughter.

"I'm not playin', I swear on Storm's life."

Aideen gasped. "Oh my God!"

"I know!"

"I *told* you he liked you. Didn't I tell you?"

I nodded my head even though she couldn't see me. "Yeah, you told me."

"I fuckin' *love* bein' right!"

I snorted and quickly lowered my head as I passed the doorman on the way into my hotel so he couldn't hear the unlady like sounds that were coming out of my mouth. However, keeping my head down cut off my vision of what was in front of me so when I literally walked head first into somebody, I didn't see coming.

"Ow!" I yelped as I fell back and landed on my arse with a thud.

My head stung from knocking it off the body in front of me but the real pain was in my behind, the concrete floor that kissed my arse saw to that.

"Fuck! I'm sorry, are you okay?"

I froze.

All the pain in my head and behind fell away when I heard that voice.

I knew that voice.

I *hated* that fucking voice with every fiber in my body.

I removed my hand from my throbbing head and looked up.

Jason Bane was staring back down at me and when his eyes landed on my face they widened ever so slightly indicating he recognised me. That look vanished as quickly as it appeared though and what replaced it caused me to curl my lip in disgust.

Jason grinned down at me looking smug as fuck.

"Keela, you made it... here let me help you up-"

"If you touch me, I swear to God I will go fuckin' crazy!"

Jason's flashed his pearly whites as he smiled at me stumbling up onto my feet.

I cleared my throat and once I got my balance I quickly bent down to pick up my phone. The screen was back on my home screen which told me my call to Aideen had been disconnected. But I didn't want to show any sort of emotion in front of Jason so I bit my inner cheeks and shoved my way past him.

"Damn it Keela, don't be like this-"

"I'm not bein' like anythin', I'm goin' to me room. Now fuck off."

I slapped my hand against the elevator button and angrily folded my arms across my chest and muttered obscenities.

Why did I have to bump into Jason of all people, and why did it have to be at a time when Alec wasn't next to me?

I tensed up when Jason's came up beside me. "That's just rude, I'm only tryin' to make sure you're okay. Come on gorgeous, don't be mad at me still. I've said sorry for what I did."

No. He. Did. Not.

How dare he mention it.

How dare he call me gorgeous.

How fucking dare he think saying sorry suffices what he did!

ALEC

"You think sayin' sorry makes up for what you did to me, you fuckin' scum bag? I swear on all that is good in this world that if you don't turn and walk away, I will put me fist down your throat."

Jason's chuckle didn't help douse my rising temper, it only added fuel the flames.

"I've never seen you this... heated before. I kind of like it."

"Go and fuck yourself!" I spat, and surged forward when the elevator doors open.

The people who were in the elevator glared at me when I shoved into them as they exited the steel box. I repeatedly pressed onto the button for my floor, but when Jason got into the elevator and the doors started to close I tried to get out. The bastard moved in front of me and blocked my path.

"What are you doin'? *Move*!"

The doors of the elevator closed as Jason frowned down at me. "Keela, please. Can we talk?"

I humourlessly laughed. "You can talk to yourself because I don't care for a single word that leaves your mouth."

"People make mistakes every day, Keela. Are you goin' to hate me forever for makin' a mistake?"

Was he serious?

"Yes, Jason, hatin' you forever is exactly what I intend to do."

Jason shook his head and stepped forward. "You hate what I did, you don't hate me."

I took a step back. "No, I'm pretty sure I hate you *and* what you did."

He took another step forward. "Are you sure about that?"

I stepped back, and jumped with fright when my back hit the wall of the elevator.

"Yes, I'm sure."

Jason stepped forward again until his chest was a hair's breadth away from being pressed to mine. He placed his hands on either side of my head and leaned down.

"I don't think so. I think you're hurt and upset, which you have every right to be, but I don't think you hate me. I think you still love me, isn't that right gorgeous?"

The doors of the elevator opened on my floor, and no one got on or off so the doors shut and head back down to the lobby leaving me alone with Jason, again.

I swallowed. "Don't call me that. Please, just get away from me."

"You didn't answer me question."

I turned my head to the left and looked away from Jason's face. "I don't love you. I love me boyfriend, who is no shape or form you. He is a real man who takes care of his woman."

Jason, who was in the middle of moving his face down to my neck, froze when I finished speaking.

"You have a boyfriend?" he asked.

"Yeah, I have a boyfriend."

Jason raised his head and used his left hand to grip my chin and turn my head to face him. The smile on his face caused me to narrow my eyes.

"I must say gorgeous, I'm very impressed. You plucked up the courage to come to me weddin', and also brought along a boyfriend."

I rolled my eyes. "I'm only here because I'd rather put up with your disgustin' self and me slutty cousin, rather than listen to me ma moan for the rest of me life."

Jason laughed. "Glad to see you still have your sense of humour."

Sense of humour?

I was being dead serious with him.

"Why are you so close to me? Back off."

Jason raised his brows. "Once upon a time you loved me bein' this close to you. You loved me *gettin'* close to you and whisperin' dirty things to you, it always resulted in you fuckin' me."

I shivered in disgust.

"That was the past. You only repulse me now, Jason."

If he was insulted, he didn't express it.

Jason smiled. "Tell me about your lad."

"Why?" I questioned.

"Because I want to know the name of the lad whose girl I'll be fuckin' throughout this week."

I felt my jaw drop open just as the doors to the elevator opened. "You're unbelievable! Stay the hell away from me!"

"And if I don't?" Jason asked, a smug grin plastered on his face.

"If you don't-"

"If you don't, I'll kick your fucking ass."

I jumped like a fish out of water and quickly put all my strength into pushing Jason away from me. Jason moved, but did it with a lazy attitude.

When I moved away from Jason I stared at Alec who was focused on Jason with his eyes narrowed to slits. I moved forward, and when I was close for him to do so, Alec took me by the arm and gently put me behind his back.

"I don't personally know you, but my brothers know you, and they don't like you. My girl knows you, and she doesn't like you. From what I've seen and heard from you, I don't like you very much either. So here is how this is going to go down, you're going to go about your business during this trip and stay the fuck away from my girlfriend. If you don't, I'm going to enjoy making you sorry. Do you understand me, kid?"

"Who are you brothers?" Jason asked.

"Dominic and Damien Slater."

"What?"

I peeked my head out from behind Alec and looked to Jason who was glaring at Alec, he flicked his eyes down to me and snarled, "You're with a Slater?"

He spat out the word 'Slater' like it left a bad taste in his mouth.

"His name is Alec, and yes, I am with him."

Jason glared at me until Alec moved, and blocked me with his body.

"Eyes on me you little shit, only me."

"Little? Are you fucking with me? What about me is little?"

"According to my girl, your dick."

I covered my mouth as an unexpected laugh escaped it.

"Fuck you, man!" Jason snapped.

I lowered my arms, and put them around Alec's waist then popped my head out from behind him and said, "That's my job."

Alec laughed as Jason leaned over and hit a button inside the elevator. He glared at us both until the elevator doors closed. I blew out a large breath and removed my arms from around Alec so he could turn to face me.

"You go off on your own for five minutes and somehow end up in close quarters with your ex... I can't bring you anywhere, can I?"

I smiled at Alec. "Bite me."

Alec waggled his eyebrows. "Anytime, sweetheart."

I stuck out my tongue, trying to be funny, but Alec dipped his head and latched onto my tongue with his teeth before I could pull away.

"I was okin', d-hon' yew bi meh."

Alec gave me a little nip then let go of my tongue and laughed before he gave me a long closed mouthed kiss.

"You're too cute."

I swirled my tongue around my mouth before I rolled my eyes.

"I'm a lot of things buddy, and cute isn't one of them."

I pressed the button for the elevator, and folded my arms across my chest while Alec put his arm around my shoulders and chuckled. "I can't wait to meet everyone that is attending this wedding."

I looked at him, bemused. "Why? None of them like me and that means that won't like you... They will probably try to make this week hell for us."

"Exactly, it will make things even more interesting."

I stepped into the elevator with Alec when the doors opened and smiled when I thought about how Alec could actually make everything with my family, and Jason's, interesting. I didn't share his enthusiasm on the subject, but I couldn't deny that it would be an interesting week.

A very damn interesting week.

Chapter Sixteen

When I opened my eyes on the third morning of our trip to the Bahamas, a nipple was practically pressed into my left eye socket. I peeled my face away from the hard chest I was lying on, and looked upwards.

Alec was still asleep, but he was starting to stir thanks to my movement.

"Alec," I muttered. "Wake up."

He did and noticed how close we were. My leg was in-between his, and I was half on him and half on the bed while wearing a t-shirt and pyjama shorts.

He raised his eyebrow at me and I shrugged because I could think of nothing else to do.

Alec grinned. "I didn't know you were the type of girl to crawl on top a guy when she wanted him."

I rolled my eyes at his teasing and said, "You don't know what type of girl I am, playboy."

Alec poked me in the cheek with his nose and said, "Tell me then, what type of girl are you?"

I thought about it for a moment then murmured, "A realistic one."

Alec smiled. "I could have guessed that, kitten."

I shyly smiled then moved back from Alec and snuggled into my pillow. He remained on his side, looking at me so I took the opportunity to ask him something that had been on my mind since I found out what his old job was.

"What was it like bein' an escort?" I asked.

Alec eyes widened a little before a scowl took over. "You mean with the sex, and money-"

"No," I cut him off. "I mean was it a fulfillin' job or a lonely one?"

Alec stared at me for about twenty seconds without responding. I was about to say something when he suddenly cleared his throat and said, "No one has asked me that before."

I frowned. "Really? Not even your brothers?"

Alec smiled. "We don't talk about our jobs to each other, we never talk about business when we're together."

"Why not?"

"Because business is all we ever heard about growing up, so when we're together we leave it out of our conversations. Some things from work may still be on our minds, but we don't bring that shit into our house."

Wow.

"This may seem stupid, but if you ever want to talk to me about anythin' you can. Aideen says I'm a good listener."

Alec looked at me, his eyes unblinking as he said, "Thanks kitten, I'll keep that in mind."

I smiled.

"So, what type of job was it?"

Alec cast his eyes down and chewed on his lower lip, he didn't looked at me as he said, "I guess it was a lonely one. I don't want to sound pathetic, because most of the time is was great. I got wined and dined on by some very wealthy and important people. I even got laid a hell of a lot, but because I was an escort nobody ever really treated me like a person. I was treated more like an object. I like money, and I really like sex but I like conversing with people too and that rarely happened unless they wanted dirty talk while I was fucking them."

My heart broke.

It literally broke in two.

"Alec," I whispered. "Why would keep a job like that? The pros of that job do *not* outweigh the cons. If I knew you back when you still had that job I would slap the shite out of you!"

Alec looked up at me and smiled. "Why?"

"Why what?"

"Why would you slap the shit out of me?"

Really?

I huffed. "Because I wouldn't let you work in an environment that treated you like dirt. You're a good fuckin' man and should be treated with the damn respect you deserve. It makes me mad that you willingly put up with that shite-"

I was cut off when Alec surged forward and pressed his mouth against mine. He gripped onto the sides of my face with both his hands and pressed my head back into my pillow. He kissed me hard and fast, but after only a few moments he slowed the kiss down to a painfully slow rhythm that only caused me to groan. While it was sexy and satisfying I wanted it hard and rough and to leave me floating.

"Thank you," Alec breathed against my mouth when he detached his mouth from mine.

I swallowed and pecked his lips before I said, "What for?"

Alec kissed me once more before he pulled back and said, "For caring."

Wow.

I blew out a breath onto Alec's face and it caused him to smile.

"Anytime," I murmured, feeling slightly in a trance.

Alec laughed and kissed my nose. "What are you doing to me?"

I blinked as I looked to him. "I don't understand what you mean."

"I've only known you a few days and you have already made an impression on me. *Nobody* has ever made an impression on me. You've worked your way under my skin and you've done this by pissing me off."

I blew air out of my nostrils.

"Yeah, well you make me mad so it's your own fault if I annoy you."

Alec chuckled. "See? This is what I'm talking about. You're crazy."

I widened my eyes. "I'm not crazy."

"Yes baby, you are."

"No, I'm not.

"Yes, you are."

"I hate when lads do this!" I snapped.

Alec rolled back onto his side to look at me. "You hate when we do what?"

"Call a woman crazy to make her crazy just to validate you telling her she's crazy."

Alec's eyes crossed indicating he was confused.

"You have a way with words, kitten."

"Bite me."

"Tell me where and I will be happy to oblige."

I scoffed in disgust. "You can be so repulsive."

Alec grinned. "You will get used to it."

I snorted. "I don't think a few days are enough for me to get used to how repulsive you can be."

"A few days? Kitten, there is no time frame on our relationship."

I raised my eyebrows. "Wait a second, you're sayin' if we're still civil after this trip that you still want to date me?"

Alec shrugged. "Why not? I like you, and I'm finding being in a relationship fun. I don't know what Dominic and Ryder complain about all the time."

I felt a huge smile take over face. "They have both got some mileage in with their girls, give us a few days and you will probably want to ring my neck."

Alec snorted. "I'm remembering Dominic's Man Bible here so I'm just going to nod my head and agree with you."

I reached over and patted his head. "Good boy."

Alec snickered as he swatted my hand away from his hair.

I relaxed back onto my side.

"Can I ask you a question?" I asked.

Alec smiled. "You just did."

"Don't make me beat you to death."

Alec coughed and rubbed his face, trying to hide a smile but failing.

"Sure, fire away."

"Do your brothers have... similar jobs to what you used to do?"

Alec stared at me and looked like he was trying to decide on whether or not he wanted to answer my question.

"We all worked for the same man, but they weren't in my... field of work. We were sorted into jobs that our talent and skill set could be of use."

I raised my eyebrows. "What talent or skill set is require to be an escort?"

"I have a big cock, so I guess that is my talent. I can make people come easily, so that would be my skill set. I know how to pleasure the human body, I've had a lot of practice since my teen years."

I swallowed. "Don't take this the wrong way, but I think you might be the biggest slut I have ever met."

Alec burst out laughing.

"I think you may be right, kitten."

I shook my head. "You and your family are so exotic compared to me. I'm borin'."

Alec reached out and playfully knocked my chin with his knuckles. "I don't think so, you're a writer, you make it possible to live several lives in the space of a few hours. Your mind is more exotic that you realise, sweetie."

I blushed.

"You think so?" I asked.

Alec winked. "I know so."

I smiled. "Well, thank you."

"Since we're on the topic of your writing, what genre do you write in?"

I felt my face go super nova red.

"You're so pretty when you blush, kitten."

I covered my face with my hands. "Comments like that don't help, Alec."

I heard his chuckling, and for some reason it calmed me down.

"You gonna answer my question like I did yours?"

I groaned.

Way to play fair.

"Fine, I've only started writin' me first book and it is in the contemporary romance genre... with a little erotica mixed in."

Alec waggled his eyebrows at me.

"Wooooo."

I covered my face again when Alec started teasing me, but it only made him laugh and pull me closer to him.

"I'm only playing."

"Uh huh."

"What is the book going to be about?" Alec asked as he played with my hair.

I licked my lips and said, "It's goin' to be about a sweet girl who gets mixed up with a bad lad and they have to deal with a lot of shite before they can be together. I haven't worked out all the details yet, but that is what I am goin' for."

Alec kissed the top of my head. "It sounds like our relationship."

I chuckled. "You aren't a bad lad, Alec. You may be dirty minded - and mouthed - but you're a good person."

Alec hugged me to him. "Thanks, kitten."
I looked at him and smiled. "We're totally bondin'."
Alec grinned. "Yep, bonding while we're almost naked. It's the best moment."

I rolled my eyes. "Shut up."

He rolled his eyes back at me. "Yes, sweetie."

I burst out laughing. "You sound like a man agreein' with his wife just to keep her happy."

"I suppose I am."

"So we're actin' like a married couple now? Great."

He snorted. "We have been bickering since we met so we're practically already married."

"There is more to marriage than just bickerin', you eejit."

"Yeah, like what?"

I gave him a look that told him he was a moron.

"Eh love, maybe? That's why people get married - they are in love with each other and want to spend the rest of their lives together. I don't think the bickerin' starts until a few years after marriage."

Alec grinned. "Let's say we get married in the future, okay? I give it an hour before you and me are bickering," he paused then laughed. "Actually, I guarantee that you would find something to argue about at the altar."

I punched him in the chest making him wince then howl with laughter.

"Just because I fight with you all the time doesn't mean I do it with everyone else. No one gets under my skin like you do, Alec Slater."

"Really?" Alec beamed.

I stared at him slack-jawed. "You seem proud."

"I am," he replied.

"Well don't be, I'm a dangerous person to those who get to me, a *very* dangerous person."

Alec smiled at me. "Good thing we're datin' then, wouldn't want you to harm me in some way."

I laughed. "You're an eejit."

"An eejit who is dating you, but doesn't fully know you. Let's rectify that now."

I was curious. "How?"

"Twenty questions, obviously."

I smiled. "Okay, I'll go first. What is your favourite colour?"

"Green."

"Mine is pink, you go."

Alec scratched his chin. "What is your favourite thing to do besides writing?"

"Easy, reading. What about you?"

Alec ran his finger through my hair. "Being at the DSPCA with the animals."

I sighed. "You know it's really not fair that you're hot; you just have to help underprivileged animals as well, don't you?"

Alec chuckled. "You'd love it, I'll bring you there sometime when we go back home."

I felt my stomach burst into butterflies.

"Yeah, I'd like that."

Alec gave me a little squeeze then said, "Who was the first person you had sex with?"

"Ask me a different question, I'm not answerin' that one."

Alec grinned. "It's twenty questions, you have to answer. As Bronagh would say 'It's like, the law'."

I turned my head so he wouldn't see me smile.

"I don't have to do anythin' I don't want to, playboy."

Alec pinched my calf. "Answer it, you big baby."

"Fine... it was with Jason... and I was twenty-two."

Alec stared at me for a long time without blinking.

I lowered my head. "I know, it's embarrassin'."

I looked up when Alec touched my cheek.

"It's not embarrassin', he manipulated you."

I shrugged. "I'm over it."

"Are you?"

I chewed on my inner cheek and shrugged my shoulders. "I'm over any feelin's I had but I'm still mad at him. He used me."

"Look on the bright side, at least it's your cousin that is stuck with him and not you."

I know that was a good thing but I found it hard to find the bright side of anything.

"I'm not that much of an optimistic person Alec. I don't look on the brighter side of things"

"Why?"

"Because growing up I had no bright side to look at and I didn't imagine about a different life because that would have just been teasin' meself."

Alec placed his hand on my intertwined ones. "You had it tough grown' up?"

I slightly smiled. "I had everythin' growin' up. I lived with a parent who was wealthy and would buy me nice things. I was never hungry, thirsty or cold. I had a roof over my head, and a good education. On paper, I had a great childhood."

"And off paper?"

I chewed on the insides of my cheeks for a few seconds before I spoke. "Off paper I grew up in a loveless home. My mother is just a woman who gave birth to me, nothin' more. She doesn't love me, and she never has. She loves her money, all her materialistic things, and she loves Micah."

I spat out Micah's name and looked away as my eyes filled with tears.

"Keela," Alec whispered.

I shook my head. "I'm not jealous over my mother favourin' Micah instead of me. I am just so mad about it. I mean, I'm her daughter and she doesn't want me, she never has," I whispered then quickly wiped my eyes. "I'm sorry, I'm bein' stupid."

"Stop that. If this is how you feel, then it's not stupid. I'd be pissed off if my mother loved one of my brothers more than she loved me, but like you, my mother loved things she bought, not the beings she created."

I blinked my eyes and turned to Alec who was lying on his side on the hotel room bed, watching me.

"Your ma wasn't lovin'?"

Alec humourlessly laughed. "She was loving, just not to me or my brothers."

I blinked again shocked that someone who was so different to me shared something so personal in common with me.

"And your da?"

Alec shrugged. "My dad wasn't loving in the traditional way, but he showed his fondness for us by keeping us around I guess you could say. My mother ignored us and probably would have giving us all up for adoption had my dad not needed sons for the business."

I frowned. "You mentioned the business before. What business?"

Alec stared at me for a long moment before he said, "I don't want to tell you, you will think less of me"

I felt my shoulders slump. "Alec, I'm sorry, I hate that you think that. I don't, and won't, think less of you. I actually like you."

"You like me?" Alec smiled.

I reached over and playfully shoved his shoulder. "I wouldn't have agreed to be your girlfriend if I didn't like you is some way, even if it is only tiny bit."

Alec stuck his nose up at me. "You only like me for my voice, eyes, and my ass. I remember that conversation on the plane."

I burst out laughing and rolled forward onto his body. He laughed and rolled onto his back while pulling me onto his chest. I grinned as I sat upright and made his groin my seat.

"I like this view," Alec murmured as he trailed his eyes from where I sat on his body until they reached my eyes.

I snorted. "Because you're a dirty man."

"You love that about me," Alec said, his eyes burning into mine.

I looked away from his gaze. "I'm fifty-fifty on that right now."

"Oh, really?" Alec asked, his tone playful.

I smiled and looked back to him. "Don't even think about whatever you're thinkin'."

Alec's eyes crossed. "You confuse me."

I laughed and leaned down until my face was an inch from his. Alec straightened his eyes and smiled at me, but he didn't move.

"Why aren't you doin' anythin'?" I whispered.

Alec waggled his eyebrows. "I want you to kiss me first this time."

"Why?"

"Because it will show me that you do in fact, like me."

"A whole lottle?" I asked, grinning.

Alec smirked. "Something like that."

I lowered my head further until my lips almost brushed Alec's.

"Keela," he whispered.

"Hmmm?"

"Kiss me."

I smiled. "Why?"

"Because I need to taste you."

All playfulness vanished and before I knew it, I pressed my mouth to Alec's and buried my hands into his hair being careful not to pull it with my fingers. Alec's hands went straight to my behind and squeezed the living daylights out of each bum cheek.

"Arse. Pain," I groaned and tried to deepen our kiss, but Alec drew back and looked up at me.

"Are you calling me a pain in the ass?"

I blinked, pulled back and then laughed. "No, well, yes. You're hurtin' me arse right now by squeezin' so I guess you literally are a pain in the arse. Ha!"

Alec narrowed his eyes at me before he squeezed me hard again. I opened my mouth to either squeal or scold him, but he took my open mouth and used it to his advantage by sticking his tongue inside it. I groaned and let my eyelids shut while I used my hands to grip onto his biceps.

"Unless you plan on riding me bare back stop grinding against me, kitten," Alec said when he pulled back from our kiss and placed his cheek against mine.

My eyes were still closed and my heart was pounding. "I didn't even realise I was doin' anythin'."

"It's the effect I have on you."

If I ever needed a sentence to sober me up, that was the one.

"Are you takin' penis enlargement tablets?" I asked with a straight face.

Alec's eyebrows touched his hairline. "What? Why the hell would you ask me that?"

"Because you're bein' a bigger dick than usual."

Alec burst out laughing and slapped my arse which caused me to yelp.

"Bastard!" I growled.

I tried to slap Alec or claw one of his eyes out. I wasn't really sure which one I was going for, but it didn't matter because Alec grabbed my hands which prevented either one from happening.

"Not my face!" Alec shouted through his laughter.

"You're so fuckin' vain!"

Alec smiled at me then kissed me on my mouth.

He actually kissed me.

I latched onto his lower lip and bit down which caused him to whine in pain until I let go, which I did a few moments later.

"That was uncalled for!"

"You will get over it," I said and ruffled Alec's hair before I climbed off his body.

"Where are you goin'?" he asked.

"The weddin' is in a few days, and after runnin' into Jason last night I want to get everyone else out of the way."

Alec rolled to his left then got up from the bed and stretched.

"Is there anyone at this wedding who you're looking forward to seeing?"

I smiled. "Me Uncle Brandon, he is me Ma's brother, and he is brilliant."

Alec smiled. "I like seeing you happy, your uncle means a lot to you?"

I nodded my head. "He means everythin' to me. He always made me feel wanted, unlike Micah and me Ma. Micah's ma died when we were kids, she was nice and treated me nicely. Unlike

Everly, Micah's Stepmother, who is nothin' but a cunt to me. I never told Uncle Brandon about her and her bitchiness, because his face always lit up around her. I didn't want to cause problems since he was happy with her."

Alec frowned. "You're his niece, I'm sure would want to know-"

"Everly hasn't bothered me for years. I've handled her since I was a child, it's fine."

Alec shook his head. "You shouldn't have to 'handle' anyone, Keela."

I shrugged my shoulders. "It is what it is."

Alec moved towards me and halted my movements when he took hold of my arms. "Things are different now, you will be treated with respect, I guarantee you that."

I chuckled. "What will you do? Pound on everyone who isn't nice to me?"

"If I have to, yes."

I raised my eyebrows. "I never pegged you for the violent type."

Alec brushed my hair back out of my face. "I'm not, that trait is left to Dominic, Kane, and my other brothers, but where you're concerned, I'll make an exception."

"Thanks?"

Alec laughed as he reached over a grabbed my red sundress that was hanging from the wardrobe door and placed it against my chest. He then turned me in the direction of the bathroom and slapped my arse.

"Go get ready," Alec said

I cursed him as I stomped forward into the bathroom with his chuckling following me. Once in the bathroom I removed my pyjamas from my body then had a very quick body wash in the shower to clean myself up from the sweat that was stuck to my body. After that I dried myself with the hotel's towels and put on my dress. I groaned when I realised I forgot a bra and underwear.

"Alec?" I called out.

"What?"

"Will you do me a favour?"

"Wash your back? *Yes*!"

I laughed. "Steady on, pervert. I need you to grab me some underwear and a bra, from the small drawer in the wardrobe."

"On it."

"Somethin' comfortable!" I shouted.

"Got it."

I looked at my fingernails and picked out the dirt from under my nails while I waited. I opened the bathroom door when Alec knocked on it.

I tilted my head to the left when Alec held up garments that I have never seen in my entire life.

"They aren't comfortable."

Alec dropped the smile that was on his face. "You haven't even put them on yet."

"I have no clue how to put the bloody things on which tells me they are goin' to be uncomfortable."

Alec swirled the knickers around on his left index finger.

"Let me guess, Aideen bought and packed your underwear?"

I growled, "The slut."

Alec laughed. "Just put them on, they are sexy, and knowing you're wearing them under that pretty dress will have me hard all day."

I swallowed. "And you want to be hard all day?"

Alec smirked. "I want you teasing me all day, and wearing these panties under your clothes will do that all on their own. Teasing is foreplay to me kitten, make a note of that."

Got it!

I licked my dry lips and whispered, "Noted."

Alec chuckled. "Good girl, now put them on."

I took the garments and after a few moments, in reality this was really five minutes, I got the knickers on correctly and shimmied them up my legs.

"Are these boy shorts or a thong, I can't tell the difference because they are rammed into the crack of me arse!" I shouted.

Alec burst out laughing and suddenly entered the bathroom which caused me to jump with fright and pull my dress down.

"Dude, knock!"

Alec gave me a bored look and twirled his index finger in the air. I tilted my head and looked at him, after a moment I gasped.

I think he wanted me to turn around and to show him me knickers.

"Drop dead!" I snapped.

Alec smiled and continued to indicate for me to turn around.

I stomped my foot on the ground like a child. "We're datin', but you can't just expect me to turn and around and show you me arse!"

Alec looked like that was exactly what he expected.

I glared at him to which he only grinned back.

"Prove to yourself that you can be comfortable enough with me to do this. I'm your man kitten, now show me your ass."

I hated that the words made me giggle because it was not the time for giggling.

"You're makin' me feel like a teenager!"

Alec only smiled at me and waited.

I blew out a huge breath.

Okay, I can do this. I wasn't just showing my arse to a stranger, I was showing it to my boyfriend... who was still a bit of stranger to me.

"Dammit," I muttered to myself as I forced myself to turn around. "If you laugh at me, spank me or do anythin' like that I will murder you in this bathroom. Understood?"

"Yes."

I could tell by Alec's tone that he was smiling which wasn't a surprise, all he did was smile.

I blew out a long breath as I reached down and gripped the hem of my dress. I slowly, and I mean slowly, pulled the dress upwards. I wasn't going slow in order to tease Alec, I was going as slow as I could to delay him seeing my arse.

When I felt the cool air on my buttocks, I knew he could see everything.

"Did I put them on wrong?" I asked.

Alec didn't reply to me, and that made me nervous.

"Alec, say somethin', I'm embarrassed enough as it is. Please don't make it worse!"

More silence then, "Your legs go on for days."

What?

"I meant somethin' about the underwear."

I heard him hiss as his hands touched my arse.

"Perfect," he whispered.

I was both flattered and annoyed.

"I'm a little paranoid with you that close to my goods, so could you please-"

I yelped when I felt a tongue suddenly swipe across my right bum cheek. I looked over my shoulder and downwards and could just see Alec kneeling behind me, his eyes level directly in front of my arse.

"What the fuck are you doin'?" I snapped.

Alec hands clamped down on my hips holding me in place in front of him.

"Alec! What are you *doin*?" I screamed the last word when he squeezed my hips.

I tried to move away from Alec but he had a good hold on my hips so when I moved, I stumbled and my upper body fell forward. My hands waved around until I caught myself on the ground which was lucky. It didn't make me feel better because I was still directly bent in front of Alec with my arse, and now my vagina in his face.

I was panicking, and also very mad. I had no idea what Alec was doing, but when my underwear was yanked to the side and a tongue plunged into my body, I got a very good fucking idea.

"Oh my God!" I growled.

Alec's right hand moved from my hip, and came up in between my legs.

"Don't touch me there- Oh my GOD!"

Alec's fingers gently massaged the area around my clit and I didn't know what was worse; the fact that he was doing this to me or that I wanted him to do it correctly by touching me directly.

"Fuck!" I hissed when Alec's tongue plunged into my vagina once more.

I couldn't believe this, he was literally tongue fucking me... and I liked it.

I didn't realise until that moment that I had my eyes closed. I opened them and because I was in an upside down position I could see Alec fucking me with his mouth.

I could literally see his tongue plunging in and out of me.

My body was hurting because I hadn't stretched like this since gymnastics back when I was in school, but it wasn't to the extent that I had to stand up.

I watched as Alec pulled his head back and move his fingers to my entrance were he dipped them inside me a few times. He bit down on his lower lip when my inner muscles squeezed around his fingers. When he was satisfied that his fingers were coated in my juices, he moved the back up to my clit and began his proper assault on my clit.

"Oh, fuck!" I shouted when Alec's fingers bore down on my clit and rubbed with a violent speed.

I cried out when I felt a bite on my behind, it was sobering but didn't draw my body's focus away from what Alec's fingers were doing to me. The pain of Alec's bite somehow mixed with the pleasure his fingers were giving me and it caused my eyes to cross and my teeth to sink down into my lower lip.

I could feel the sensations rack through my body and for a few moments, it caused my breath to falter.

My entire body shuddered when Alec's left hand removed itself from my hip and his fingers slowly pushed inside of my body.

Another bite was delivered to my bum and it caused me to cry out in delight.

"I can feel how close you are, kitten. Do you want to come?"

Yes!

"Yes, please!" I cried and pushed my behind back into Alec's hands.

"Here we go, baby," Alec said as the fingers on my clit pinched then rubbed faster than before.

My body couldn't decipher that the pinch was supposed to hurt, it only used the spike of pain and mixed it in with my pleasure. That spike pushed me over the edge and was the cause of my legs buckling and my body falling to my knees.

My clit throbbed, my eyes were heavy, and my lungs felt like they were going to explode.

"Holy fuck," I gasped when I found my voice.

My breathing was rapid as I greedily sucked down air into my lungs.

I was breathing like I just ran a marathon.

"Are you okay?" I heard Alec's voice ask me.

I didn't answer him, I only lay my body down on the cool tiles of the hotel bathroom floor. I heard Alec stand up over me, and was aware that I didn't feel him remove his hands from my body I felt as though they were still on and in me.

"Keela, are you okay?" Alec voice repeated, his tone louder.

I closed my eyes. "I don't know."

Alec cleared his throat. "Is that a good thing or a bad thing?"

Was that a joke?

"Right now it's a good thing playboy, a *very* good thing."

Alec chuckled. "Well, good. Do you want me to help you stand up?"

I shook my head. "Just leave me here."

Alec laughed. "Excuse me?"

"My legs are tinglin', me vagina is pulsin', and me entire body feels like I'm on a floatin' cloud. Leave. Me. Here."

"You're welcome."

Dickhead.

"Bite me," I murmured.

"I did... twice," I could practically hear Alec's smirk when he spoke.

I groaned then, knowing he wasn't going to leave me alone.

"Okay, you can help me up."

I didn't move and it made Alec laugh.

I smiled when I felt him over me, I squealed when he put his hand under my armpits and heaved me up until I was on my feet. I leaned into him and put my arms around his waist as I closed my eyes and sighed.

I felt so relaxed.

"I want to go to bed."

Alec chuckled. "No can do gorgeous. You said you wanted to seek out the rest of you family, so let's get to it."

I groaned. "That was before you attacked me with your tongue."

"Are you complaining?"

Was I?

"Hell no, that was the best orgasm I've ever had."

Alec placed his hands on my shoulders and held me out in front of him. I opened my eyes and snorted at the shocked look on his face.

"That orgasm was nothing compared to what I will do to you."

I swallowed and felt a little brave.

"So why did you stop?"

Alec's lip curved ever so slightly. "Because I told you, you will beg me before I fuck you."

I rolled my eyes. "You're a pussy."

Alec reached down and patted my vagina through my dress making me gasp.

"This is my pussy."

I raised my eyebrows. "That's a little possessive, don't you think?"

Alec leaned his head down to mine and kissed down my jawline. "I'm possessive with what is mine." He moved his head up to my mouth sucked my bottom lip into his mouth before releasing it with a pop. "And until I say otherwise kitten, you're *mine*."

Chapter Seventeen

"Will you stop looking around, you're going to make me paranoid if you keep that up."

I snapped my head in Alec's direction and growled, "I can't help it. I feel like everyone knows what you did to me."

Alec smirked as he lounged on his sun chair. "Unless anyone was in the bathroom while I tongue fucked you until you came, they won't know."

I jumped off my sun chair then reached down and took off my flip flop and began to beat Alec with it. Alec was on the verge of crying with laughter while I was beating him with my shoe and that only annoyed me further. I wanted to kick him in the nuts, but Alec reached up and put his arms around my waist and pulled me on top of him before I could.

"One of these days, I *will* hurt you."

Alec chuckled. "I don't doubt that, kitten. You're a little hell cat."

I huffed as I rested my head on Alec's chest.

If you would have told me a few days ago that I would actually enjoy being near Alec, I would have laughed in your face. Things have changed though, and I don't just mean because he gave me an orgasm, I mean we have changed when we're together. We still argue, sure I attack him every so often, but I love being in his company now. Especially when he doesn't add a sexual innuendo into everything he says.

I smiled when Alec's hands found their way to my hair, and slowly began to run through it.

"Am I hurtin' you?" I asked as I adjusted myself on top of Alec's body.

"No, it feels good with you being on top of me and I don't mean that in a dirty way."

I smiled. "I know what you mean."

"Yeah?"

I nodded. "Yeah."

I felt him kiss the crown of my head, and it made me smile even more.

"I wonder what Aideen and Storm are up to," I murmured.

"I wonder what my brothers are up to."

I chuckled. "FaceTime one of them, then I'll do the same to Aideen."

I moved off Alec's body, but instead of getting up I laid next to him on his chair. Alec reached down into his shorts and took out his iPhone 5.

"Oh, God, that is so unhygienic."

Alec snorted. "Sorry, mom."

I pinched his nipple making him yelp as he pressed on the screen of his phone. I lifted my sunglasses to the top of my head so I could clearly see the screen of his phone. The glare of the sun wasn't a problem because our spot was under the shade of an umbrella, my skin can't handle direct sunlight. I'm too fare and burn way too easily.

"Who are you callin'?" I asked.

"Kane," Alec replied.

After a few moments of FaceTime ringing Kane, his face appeared on the screen.

"Have you fucked Keela yet? I have a bet with the guys on when you will crack her, my guess was today."

Oh, for the love of God.

"Are all of the males in your family digustin' dickheads?" I snapped, and shoved Alec who had his eyes closed and was shaking his head.

"Nice one bro," he said to Kane who had his hand over his mouth.

He knew he was so busted.

"Keela, I'm sorry."

I narrowed my eyes at the screen of the phone. "You should be, you wanker."

Alec snorted next to me and received an elbow in the side for it.

He hissed. "I don't know why you're hitting me, I didn't do anything."

"You're laughin'!"

"Only because you're so cute when you're mad."

I snarled, "Stop callin' me cute."

Alec snapped his teeth at me. "Or what?"

"I'll bite a chunk out of you."

Alec waggled his eyebrows at me. "Like I bit you?"

I felt my face flush.

"Guys, I'm still here, knock off the teasing shit. I don't like it unless I'm involved somehow."

Alec snorted, and looked from me to his phone. "Is Aideen still the cause of your blue balls?"

I felt a smile stretch over my face when Kane grunted.

"She wants me, she just doesn't know it yet."

I rolled my eyes. "She is a lesbian."

Kane glared at me. "I know she told you to say that to me and I know you're both lying. No lesbian can kiss a man the way she kissed me."

I laughed. "Unless she thought you were a butch girl."

Alec bit into his fisted hand while Kane all but blew a fuse on the other side of the phone.

"Stop it! I know she has some sort of script for you to read off. I'm not buying it, she is not gay. Not. Gay. Okay?"

"Okay." I nodded.

"Okay as in she is not gay?"

"No, okay as in okay I'm agreein' with you."

ALEC

Kane rubbed his temple. "You're hurting my head."

Alec snorted. "I feel you, bro."

I rolled my eyes.

Men.

"What is the weather like back home?" I randomly asked Kane.

He deadpanned, "What do you think it's like here?"

I beamed. "Ha! It's sunny and fuckin' roastin' here!"

Kane narrowed his eyes at me. "You're a teasing little shit, aren't you?"

Am I?

"Yeah, she is," Alec chimed it.

I gasped. "How am I teasin'?"

"What are you wearing right now, under your dress?"

I felt my face heat up. "You told me to wear them though!"

"Wearing what? What are you wearing?" Kane's voice shouted making Alec laugh.

"Never mind, it's only for me to know."

Kane scoffed. "You and the guys suck. What is the point in having hot girlfriends if I can't-"

"I'd watch how I finished that sentence, little brother."

I perked up when Ryder appeared behind Kane.

"Hey Ryder!" I waved.

He moved closer to the screen. "Hey beautiful, having fun?"

"Yes! I ran into my ex last night and Alec threatened to kick his arse, it was brilliant!"

Ryder, Kane, and Alec chuckled at me.

"How are my girls?" Alec asked his brothers making them snort.

"Out shopping, with Dominic and Alannah. I guarantee little bro will come back here close to tears, they always make his life hell when Bronagh asks him to go shopping with them."

I chuckled. "It can't be that bad."

Alec nudged me. "Bronagh and Branna together while out shopping is like shopping with fifty Aideens."

I widened my eyes and said, "Poor Dominic."

"Exactly," Alec chuckled, and kissed my forehead.

Both Ryder and Kane shared a look before looking back to the camera.

"Is that saran wrap on your arm?" Ryder asked Alec.

Alec looked down to his arm and nodded. "I got the space on the back of my tricep filled in."

"With what?" Kane asked.

"The tribal love, live, and loyalty tat that Dominic has."

Ryder groaned out loud. "Dammit, now we're going to have to get it."

"Why?" Kane asked.

"Because dipshit here and Dominic will make it seem like we have no love for them if we don't get one too, since the tat represents us, and our bond. Am I right?"

Alec nodded his head. "Dead right."

Ryder grunted while Kane muttered, "Fuck."

"What's the big deal? You're both cover in tattoos."

"Exactly," Ryder said. "I'm running out of space."

I chuckled.

"How long till the wedding?" Kane asked me.

I shrugged. "Three days. I'm hoping to bump into someone I know out here so we will know if there are any parties we have to attend before the wedding. After last night's encounter with Jason, I'm so ready for everyone else."

Kane was about to say something else when a violent cough tore from his throat. He coughed for at least twenty seconds before the fit subsided.

"Jesus, are you okay Kane?"

Kane nodded his head while Ryder shoved him.

"No he isn't, he is coming down with we what we all think is the flu."

I frowned. "I'm sorry Kane, I wish I could make you feel better."

Kane looked at me with tired eyes and smiled. "Well, you could show me-"

"Don't finish that sentence, I'll fly home just to kick your ass if you do."

Kane laughed but only for a moment before he rubbed his head.

Ryder sighed. "Go to bed man, you have a fever and shouldn't be up."

"Yes mother," Kane grinned.

Ryder shook his head. "It's your funeral, when Branna comes back and sees you're up she will hurt you and then she'll hurt me for not keeping you in bed."

I snorted, Branna and her sister ruled the brothers.

"Alright, alright. I'm going back to bed, keep your panties on. Hey Keela, I'll talk to you soon sweetheart and you too, bro."

"Love you, man," Alec said.

Kane snorted. "Love you too, bumboy."

Alec snickered and Ryder grinned as he shook his head and took Kane's phone from him. I rolled my eyes, brothers called each other the weirdest names.

"Did you make him go the doctor?" Alec asked Ryder.

"Nah, he is sure it's the flu. He has a fever, a cough and is sweating like a pig, he'll be fine in a few days. You know he is loving all the attention from the girls. He pretended to pass out this morning just so Branna would lie down with him in his bed, the bastard."

I burst out laughing. "He is funny."

"He likes to think so."

"How is everything else, good?" Alec asked Ryder.

Ryder nodded his head. "It's good man, things are quiet just the way we like them."

"Good, that's very good."

I had no clue what Ryder and Alec were talking about so I looked down at my nails and began picking dirt out of them. I was momentarily disgusted because for someone who had short nails, I always had loads of dirt under the damn things.

"I have to go let Tyson out in the yard for awhile. The pup isn't house broken yet so I have to do it since Kane has gone back to bed."

I looked up and awed, "You're doggy sittin'? That's adorable."

Ryder narrowed his eyes at me and said, "You're lucky you're cute, Keela."

I threw my free hand up in the air. "I'm not cute, why do people keep sayin' that to me!"

Ryder laughed. "Have fun you two... but not too much."

Alec chuckled. "Bye bro, love you."

"Love you, too. Bye, cutie."

"I'm goin' to cut you when I get back home."

Ryder hung up laughing at me.

I looked at Alec who made a show out of looking up at the huge umbrella that shaded us from the sun, but he didn't have to go through the trouble of hiding his smile, I could still see it on his handsome face.

"Your family is crazy."

Alec looked down at me and nodded his head. "I know."

I chewed on my lip as I reached down to my beach bag and pulled out my own iPhone 5.

"You could just use my phone to call Aideen."

I snorted. "You would give her number to Kane."

Alec gasped, "I would never."

I gave him a 'really' look, which made him shrug his shoulders.

"Okay, I probably would give it to him."

I snapped my fingers. "Exactly."

I pulled up FaceTime on my phone and selected Aideen from my contacts.

After a few rings she answered.

"I hate your devil creature."

Do people not just answer the phone with a 'hello?' anymore?

"Also, thanks for hangin' up on me last night, bitch."

I winced. "I can explain about that."

"Sure."

"I can."

Aideen rolled his eyes then muttered about how much she hated Storm again.

I sighed. "What's wrong now?"

"He sat on the remote and *deleted* me recordin' of *Keepin' up with the Kardashians*."

I looked at Alec who was looking at the screen of my phone with an odd look on his face.

"It was clearly an accident," I said, looking back to my phone.

"Nothin' is an accident when it comes to that animal," Aideen spat.

Jesus, give me patience.

"Maybe he was fed up listening to Kim's annoying voice," Alec suggested with a sly grin on his face.

Aideen got that 'oh no he didn't look' on her face.

"Are you serious? Her voice isn't annoyin'!"

Aideen loved Kim Kardashian.

Alec scratched his head. "Damn Ado, it's a joke not a dick, don't take it so hard."

I gave my phone to Alec to hold as I burst out laughing and clapped my hands together which I'm sure made me look like a demented seal.

"What are you laughin' at?"

I coughed and rubbed my face. "Me? Nothin', nothin' at all."

Alec chuckled and put his arm around my shoulders, I looked at him and smiled.

"Oh my God. You *shagged* him! You fuckin' shagged him!"

I hurt my neck turning my head so fast back to glare at the screen.

"Lower your bleedin' voice, we didn't have sex!" I hissed to Aideen and quickly rubbed my neck with my hand.

Aideen narrowed her eyes. "I don't believe you! Somethin' is different about you."

I sighed and looked at Alec when he nudged me, he waggled his eyebrows at me which only caused me to groan.

"We did some... stuff, but *not* sex."

Aideen squealed. "Kane owes me a tenner."

I stared at Aideen, slack-jawed while Alec cracked up laughing beside me.

"You bloody traitor! You took part in a bet about how long it took me to buck Alec?"

Aideen snorted. "Please, who do you think came up with the idea?"

Oh my God!

She came up with the idea?

Some best friend she is!

"You're so dead when I get me hands on you!"

Aideen stuck her tongue out. "Come and get me, mama."

She defined what a bitch was.

"I can't believe you. You can kiss your cover goodbye because the next time I talk to Kane I'm tellin' him how much of a big, fat, cock lover you really are!"

Aideen gasped. "You wouldn't!"

"I would, blow job lips, trust me."

Aideen covered her mouth and screeched.

"You promise not to call me that anymore!"

I smirked when I looked over to find Alec was in a fit of laughter next to me.

"Please..." he laughed, "continue!"

I looked back at Aideen who was fuming but silent.

Just the way I liked it.

"You're evil," she hissed at me.

I grinned. "I was raised by the Devil, I picked up few things up."

"I'll say," Aideen muttered.

I chuckled. "I miss you."

"I miss you, too. Has anythin' happened? Besides hanky-panky with one of the Slater God's of course."

"Slater God?" Alec snorted.

I ignored him and nodded my head to Aideen.

"Guess who I ran into last night."

Aideen chewed on her lower lip for a moment then guessed, "Micah?"

I shook my head and said, "The bastard himself."

Aideen gasped. "No!"

"Yes."

"Dude."

"I know."

"Wow."

"Yup."

"When you say you ran into him, do you mean literally or-"

"Literally."

Aideen snorted. "I expect no less from your clumsy arse."

I grinned. "Do you want to hear the best part of the run in?"

"There is a best part?"

I smiled. "Oh yes."

Aideen frowned. "Spit it out then, don't leave me suspense."

I cleared my throat and said, "Alec threatened to kick his arse if he didn't stay away from me. Jason was pissed, but you should have seen his face when he found out Alec was a Slater. It was priceless! He was all like, 'You're with a Slater?!' He practically spit when he said Slater."

I burst out laughing and slapped my leg in delight.

"You should have recorded it, I would pay good money to have seen his face!"

I nodded my head. "I'd love to see it again."

"Eh, you will. Whenever he sees you with Alec, he will get a stupid angry look on his face and it serves the usin' bastard right."

I snapped my fingers. "Amen, sister."

"Oh man, I need to hang out with some guys," Alec groaned from my left.

I looked at him as he scrubbed his face with his hands.

"So leave, I'm not keepin' you next to me."

Alec looked down to my legs that were resting over his. I raised my eyebrows because I was shocked, I didn't even notice that I put them there.

"You're me leg rest it appears."

Alec looked at me, his blue eyes shining. "I don't mind."

"Oh my God. Puke. You're more attractive when you're bein' a dick."

I chuckled and looked at Aideen who was now yawning.

"Late night?"

Aideen shrugged. "It's nearly ten in the mornin' here, but I didn't get to sleep till around five. Storm kicked me to death last night and no matter how many times I pulled him out to the sofa, he always snuck back into the room. Your dog can open doors Keela, that's fucked up."

I chuckled. "That's me baby."

Aideen rolled her eyes then widened them as she looked past me and Alec.

"Oh, shite."

"What?" I asked.

"Look over your shoulder."

I furrowed my eyebrows, but did as Aideen said and looked over my shoulder. I instantly hunched down when I spotted who Aideen had spotted.

"She has her cousins with her from her ma's side, I can't face her with them there."

Aideen's face came closer to the camera. "You can, and you will. You have Alec and he has your back, right?"

I looked to Alec, expecting him to back me up, but his head was turned in the direction of my cousin.

"I'm guessing that's Micah? Damn, she looks nothing like I

thought."

I shoved him. "Hey, pick a side, hers or mine."

Alec held his hands up in the air when he turned back to me. "Yours, always yours."

"Oh my God. You're so cute that it's disgustin'."

Alec looked at my phone and touched his chest with his hand. "Thank you, Aideen."

Aideen pumped her eyebrows. "Anytime, hot lips."

I groaned. "Both of you shut up, what am I goin' to do about Micah?"

"Say hello," Aideen said then scratched her neck.

Huh? I know I wanted to get seeing everyone out of the way, but why did I have to be the one to say hello?

"What? Why would I say hello to Micah?"

"Because I'm standin' behind you, cuz."

Chapter Eighteen

I dropped my phone to my lap and froze.

Micah was behind me.

Holy fuck, Micah was behind me!

"Aren't you goin' to give me a hug, cuz?"

I cringed as I forced myself to get to my feet. I hung up on Aideen, and even though I knew she would give me shite about out about it later, I had to because Aideen has no filter when she speaks. She also hates Micah so it was guaranteed that she would have at least cursed at her and I didn't want that because I was the one in close quarters to her.

I blew out a breath as I turned to face Micah.

I was glad that I was wearing sunglasses because Micah wouldn't have been able to see the way my eyes widened when I saw her. She looked incredible; her hair was as red as mine, her skin was lightly tanned, and her figured was fucking amazing.

"Hey Mi, you look great."

I leaned forward and put my arms around my younger cousin, giving her a squeeze.

"You too Kay, you lost weight."

I flushed. "Yeah, a bit."

Almost three stone, but who's counting?

"More than a bit, you were huge when I last saw you."

I set my jaw. "Yeah, I know."

Micah smiled. "I'm glad you could come, Kay. I know this might be awkward for you after everythin' that happened but I'm glad you're here. I know Jason is too."

Yeah, we know why he is happy I am here, the dirty bastard.

"I'm happy too, we can put all that happened behind us."

Lie.

Micah's two cousins chuckled then which earned a smirk from Micah.

"Your ma said you were here with a boyfriend. Where is he? I'd like to meet him."

Oh, fuck yes!

I could tell she thought my mother was lying about me having a boyfriend - her tone and smug look gave it away.

I was on the verge of bursting with joy when I stepped to the left and turned to my side, gesturing to Alec as I did. He was turned around and watching my encounter with Micah, but when I moved and gave the girls a clear view of him, he stood up from his sun chair and turned to face us.

He had on a pair of knee length shorts and that was it.

Seeing him shirtless would usually irked me, but right now I couldn't have been happier with him being half naked.

"This is Alec Slater, me boyfriend. Alec, this is me cousin Micah, it's her weddin' we're here for."

Alec smiled, his dimples creasing his cheeks, and I took the opportunity to look at Micah and her cousins. I wanted to do a happy dance because the three of them of them stared at Alec with their mouth's hanging open.

He'd rendered them speechless.

Success!

"Ladies, nice to meet you."

Silence.

I looked down as I smugly smiled.

This was fucking perfect.

I looked up as a throat was cleared.

"I'm Kerry, and this is me sister, Clare. We're Micah's cousins from her ma's side of the family.

I flicked my eyes to Kerry Brennan, then to her twin sister

Clare. The Brennan twins weren't identical, but the bitches were both blessed with pretty as can be genes. They both had huge tits as well.

"Nice to meet you both, I'm this little one's boyfriend."

I smiled when Alec put his arm around my shoulder and pulled me to his side.

I chuckled when I looked at Micah who was flicking her eyes between myself and Alec, the shock plain as day on her face. "Alec Slater, as in Dominic and Damien Slater's brother?"

"Yeah, they are my little brothers."

Micah's eye twitched. "I went to school with your brothers."

"I know, they told me all about you... so did Bronagh."

I bit down on my lip when Micah's face went red, but not with embarrassment, with anger.

"I see, well, it's nice to meet you. I think I've seen you around me estate a few times, it's good to meet you in person, thanks for comin'."

Alec smiled. "No prob, I'm happy to be here. Congratulations by the way, marrying your high school sweetheart, that's cute."

Cute.

I snorted, but covered it up with a cough.

Nothing about Jason and Micah were cute. They were a sexy couple, a mean couple, a fucked up couple, but not a cute couple.

"Thanks, we're happy. Have you seen Jason yet, Keela?"

I looked to Micah when she said my name and nodded my head. "Yeah, I bumped into him last night. He seemed... happy I could make the weddin'."

Micah smirked. "Yeah, he really is thrilled you can be here, we both are."

Yeah, right, like I believe *that*.

"*I'm* thrilled to be here. I still can't believe you're both gettin' married, it's crazy."

Micah grinned. "It's weird how things worked out, right?"

Why was she grinning?

"Yeah, and in the Bahamas of all places."

Micah shrugged. "Yeah, the weather isn't reliable back home and I love it here. I came twice when attendin' weddings before, it's perfect."

I smiled. "It's beautiful, you made a good choice."

"I know."

Bitch.

"So, the weddin' is on Friday, are there any parties or dinners we have to attend?"

"There is a welcome dinner tonight followed by a party. Most of the guests arrived last week. Your ma will be the last to arrive on Thursday."

I nodded my head. "Sorry I didn't know about the schedule, I only found out about the weddin' at the last minute. Me ma arranged everythin' for us to come out here."

Micah waved me off. "It's grand, you aren't the only one gettin' used to things. I still forget when and where I have to be, me ma has to remind me."

Her ma?

Bleh.

"How is Everly? I haven't seen 'er in ages."

Micah shrugged her shoulders and grinned, "You know me ma, she doesn't change."

Wonderful.

"Yeah," I said, forcing a chuckle.

"So," Micah said and gestured between Alec and myself. "How long are you two together."

My mind went blank.

Fuck, how long did Alec say we were dating when he was talking to my ma?

"Three months, and a few days give or take," Alec answered Micah and gave my side a little squeeze.

"Is it serious?" Micah asked Alec, staring directly at him without blinking.

It freaked me out a little.

"We live together, so yeah it's serious."

"Lucky bitch," Kerry muttered under her breath, but I caught it and it made me smile.

"I'm happy for you both," Micah said, her face expressionless.

Yeah, you look happy for us.

"Thanks," I smiled and gave Alec's delectable body a squeeze.

"Well, I'll see you both later at the welcome dinner, it starts at seven in the ball room of the hotel."

I saluted Micah. "We'll be there."

Micah nodded her head, smiled then turned and walked in the direction of the free sun chairs on the opposite side of the swimming pool. Kerry and Clare moved slowly making sure they took in all of Alec's body along the way. I suddenly felt possessive of his body, so I flattened my palm across Alec's stomach then slide it downwards until it was over his groin. I squeezed his softened member making him yelp and me laugh at the Brennan sisters who were now stalking after Micah looking pissed off.

"Can I have my cock back, please?" Alec hissed.

I loosened my grip on his penis and gave it a few strokes, which caused Alec to look down at me with widened eyes.

"What are you doing?" Alec asked.

I smiled. "Makin' Micah's cousins jealous."

Alec put his hand on my arm and pulled until my hand was back on his stomach. "You making *them* jealous is making *me* hard, have a heart and leave my cock alone."

I snorted then got up on my tiptoes and puckered my lips.

Alec smirked as he lowered his head and touched his lips to mine before he slid his arms around my waist and held me in front of him while he kissed me.

"You're so sweet," he murmured onto my mouth.

I licked my lips and said, "Strawberry lipgloss."

Alec licked his own lips and hummed.

"I like it."

I smiled. "Let's go back to our room?"

"For sex?" Alec asked, his tone hopeful.

Yeah, I wasn't caving that easily... not on full vagina penetration anyway.

"No, so we can decide on what I should wear to the dinner party tonight. It will be the first time I see everyone together and I want to look good."

"If you want to show everyone how hot you are, go naked, that'd make me stop and stare."

I stared at Alec with creased eyebrows. "You should really think before you speak, a lot of the time sayin' nothin' is really the best option."

Alec cheerfully smiled like what I just said didn't bother him.

I grabbed his hand and pulled. "Come, let's go."

"What? Now?" Alec stared at me in horror. "It's only the afternoon... will deciding what to wear take hours?"

Was he joking?

"To find the right outfit? Yeah!"

Alec let go of me and lifted his hands to his face. "I don't like giving opinions on clothes, I never give the right ones and always end up pissing somebody off."

I gave his shoulder a sympathetic pat with my free hand.

"It will be fine, I won't get mad."

Alec looked down at me, his eyes sceptical.

"Do you promise?"

I waved him off. "Yeah, yeah, of course."

Alec didn't budge and it irritated me.

"You have to say I promise, otherwise it's not a promise."

He sounded like a little boy.

I blew out a large breath and turned to face Alec, I looked up at him and smiled. "I promise not to get mad over an opinion you give when I try on clothes, okay?"

Alec nodded his head. "Okay."

Alec walked with me then in the direction of the hotel, but he

looked pained already.
"Cheer up, buttercup, this is gonna be fun!"

CHAPTER NINETEEN

"This is not fun, you lied to me."

I smiled as I pulled on the tenth dress that Aideen had packed into my suitcase.

"This is the last one playboy, nearly there."

I heard Alec's dramatic sigh before he said, "Why the fuck did Aideen pack so many dresses? This our third day here, and we're leaving on the seventh day, what was she thinking?"

I adjusted my dress until is sat nicely on my body.

"She was thinkin' variety, honey."

"Variety my ass, you look hot in every one of those dresses you tried on, there was no need to pack so many."

I shook my head and smiled.

He was such a man.

"I'm glad you think they all look nice on me-"

"Hot, I said they were *hot* on you."

I laughed. "I'm glad you think they were *hot* but I want to be comfortable in what I am wearin', that's the reason I'm tryin' on so many. I mean the fourth one was so short you could see me bum cheeks, it is definitely in the no pile."

"That was my favourite," I heard Alec grumble and it me chuckle as I exited the bathroom.

"Okay daddy, what do you think of this one? Yes, no, or maybe?"

Alec folded his arms across his chest and tilted his head to the side as he examined me from head to toe. He stuck his index finger in the air and rotated it in a circle.

I happily turned around in a slow circle for him until I was facing him again.

"What's the verdict?"

Alec gave me two thumbs up. "I like this one best. It has some length to it but still showcases how long your legs are. It hugs your ass showing that you do actually possess one, and it's tight around the chest making your tits look bigger than they are. Plus it's green and I love the colour green."

I wasn't sure whether to be happy with his assessment or pissed off with it.

"Are you saying me arse is small? I know me tits are, but I thought me arse was a decent size."

Alec shrugged. "It is a decent size, I mean it's not a Bronagh Murphy sized ass, but it's still a nice ass. I like it a lot."

I narrowed my eyes and folded my arms across my chest. "You like your little brother's girlfriend's arse?"

Alec opened his mouth to answer me then immediately closed it.

He was silent for a moment until he said, "This is a trick question, I know it is."

"It's a straight forward question."

Alec shook his head. "No, it's not. You're trying to trap me in a corner until I give an answer that will give you enough reason to hit me... I know how your mind works."

I boldly walked towards Alec until my knees touched his. I then reached my hands out and placed them on his shoulders as I leaned my head down until I was very much in his face.

"How does me mind work, Alec?"

Alec licked his lips as his eyes flicked down to my chest, before finding their way up to my eyes.

"In mysterious ways?" he guessed.

I tried not to smile, I really did, but I couldn't help it.

Alec leaned forward and pressed his lips against the side of my mouth.

"I love your smile."

I slid onto his lap and looped my arms around his neck as I said, "I love your smile, and your dimples."

"I'll add that onto the list with my eyes, ass, abs, and voice."

I snorted. "You're so cocky."

Alec licked my lower lip. "I love when you say cocky."

I giggled. "Give it a rest, it's your turn to try on clothes to see what looks best."

Alec's nose scrunched up. "I'm wearing shorts, and a white tee."

"Yeah but a V neck, a tank top, or a crew neck?"

Alec looked at me like I grew an extra head. "You've got to be kidding me."

I raised my eyebrows. "Do I look like I'm kiddin'?"

Alec really looked at me then groaned. "For God's sake."

I win.

I smiled as I stood up. "Go on, get."

"Is this what having a girlfriend entails? I lose my freedom?" Alec asked as he stood up.

I snorted. "That and *much* more, honey."

Alec shook his head and turned away from me as he picked up a bunch of clothes from his suitcase then walked towards the bathroom.

"I finally see what Ryder and Dominic are talking about," he muttered to himself.

I smiled. "I heard that."

"You were meant to."

I chuckled as I shimmied out of my dress and placed it on a hanger then I hung it on my wardrobe door to keep it crease free. I picked up a pair of knee length leggings and one of Alec's t-shirts and put them on. I jumped onto the bed then and relaxed.

"Do you have a bucket list?" I randomly asked Alec.

I heard him muttered something so I said louder, "Do you have one?"

"Do I have one what?" Alec shouted.

"Do you have a bucket list?" I repeated.

Alec popped his head out of the bathroom and grinned. "I have a fuck-it list, does that count?"

"There is somethin' wrong with you, you have an erect dick for a brain."

"Are you calling me a dick head?"

I bit down on my inner cheeks to keep a smile at bay.

"I hate you."

"No you don't, you want to dislike me but you can't and it kills you."

That was the most accurate thing I have ever heard him say.

Alec disappeared back into the bathroom, and I stayed put on the bed until he was ready to model for me. After a few minutes he emerged from the bathroom in a white V neck t-shirt and a pair of knee length shorts.

"I'll wear the flip flops I bought at Pennys back home. Do you approve?"

I pictured the outfit with his flip flops and mentally nodded my head.

I did approve of what he wanted to wear, but I wanted him to twirl for me before I said anything so I simply lifted my hand, stuck my index finger in the air, and rotated it in a circle.

"Are you fucking with me?" Alec snapped.

I continued to rotate my finger in silence.

"Women," Alec muttered before he stuck his arms out wide and slowly turned his body in a circle.

When he was turned back in my direction, I scrunched up my face and said, "It'll do."

His face was priceless.

"It'll do... *it'll do*? Come here, now!"

I screamed with laughter as Alec dove on the bed and grabbed at my body with his hands. He pinned my hands down at my sides and all but crawled up onto me. He let go of my hands so he could use his own to hold himself up off me. You know, so he wasn't *completely* smothering me.

"Can you breathe?" Alec asked, smiling down at me.

"Kind of," I wheezed.

Alec chuckled and rolled off me. He shook his head when I dramatically gasped for air.

"Were you born a bitch, or does it just come natural to you?"

I rubbed my chest. "I'd say born one, being a cunt may come natural to me."

Alec shook his head. "I'm still amazed that some women use that word so freely over here. In the States most women freak over it."

I snorted. "It's only a word, I wouldn't get bent out of shape over a word."

Alec shrugged. "I guess so."

I sat up on the bed, and criss-crossed my legs.

"I'm kind of nervous about the dinner tonight."

Alec turned on his side to look at me. "Why?"

"Everyone knows that me and Jason were involved, but I'm positive that they don't know he was usin' me. I know Everly and Micah, they will have turned all of this around on me. Everyone will probably think I seduced me cousin's boyfriend. I'm dreadin' what people might say to me... or think of me"

Alec reached out and placed his hand on my knee. "No one will verbally attack you, I'll make sure of that."

I smiled. "You've got my back?"

"Always."

CHAPTER TWENTY

"Stop biting your nails."

I looked at Alec as we walked down the stairs of the hotel. We were making our way to the ballroom for the welcome dinner, Alec really didn't want to take the elevator and because I needed extra time to mentally prepare myself for seeing my family, I took the stairs with him.

"I can't help it, I'm nervous."

Alec tied his hair back out of his face with a bobbin then took my hand, and intertwined it with his. "It's going to be fine, you'll see."

I blew out a huge breath when we reached the bottom of the stairs.

"I hope you're right," I muttered and walked out into the lobby from the stairwell.

Alec lead me to the ballroom. The doors were closed, but a man was outside with a stand that had a list on it.

"This is a private function. I'm sorry."

"We're here for the dinner, we're guests."

"What is your name, miss?" the man asked.

I cleared my throat. "Keela Daley."

"Ah, yes, Keela Daley and plus one."

"I'm plus one, nice to meet you," Alec said to the man.

The man grinned as he walked to the doors, opened them for us before he gestured us in with his hand.

"You're both to be seated at table two. Enjoy your meal."

I smiled at the man and tugged Alec behind me as I walked into the ballroom. I was a little surprised that the room wasn't dark like Micah's and Jason's personalities. It was all white with blue splashed throughout. The lighting was mostly bright neon blue, which I thought was really cool because it matched the decor perfectly.

I grunted. "I hate that I like the room and the colours."

"The food might be crap though."

He was trying to make me feel better by giving me hope something would suck about the dinner.

He was brilliant.

"So... where is table two?" I murmured a loud.

There were at least fifteen tables that I could see and they were all full with people. They sure managed to get a lot of people here on such short notice.

Rich people.

"The head table for the bridal party is table one, and that's at the head of the room. You will be at the table closest to that."

I turned around to face Alec, my eyes wide. "Why would they seat me so close to them?"

Alec shrugged. "You grew up with Micah, maybe she considers you close to her?"

Yeah, right.

"No way, she wouldn't have me here at all if she got her way. This is Everly and me ma's doin'."

Alec lifted his hand to brush his knuckles against my cheek and said, "It doesn't matter who seated us at that table, let's just go and sit down... Okay?"

I nodded my head and followed closely behind Alec making sure not to look at anyone seated at the tables we passed. I swallowed nervously when we reached our table and noticed every person at the table was an immediate member of Jason's family.

Oh, fuck me.

"Hello Keela, you look lovely," Jason's father, Mr. Bane said as he stood up to greet me.

I think Mr. Bane was the only genuine member of the Bane family.

"Hello Mr. Bane, it's lovely to see you again." I smiled as I shook his hand.

I then gestured to Alec. "This is Alec Slater, me boyfriend."

"Nice to meet you, sir," Alec said as he shook Mr. Bane's hand.

"And you, son. These are my daughter's Krista, and Koda, and my son Jonathan. My wife will be along in a moment, she is in the restroom."

Jason's bitchy sisters were the first to jump up and greet Alec and not with handshakes either, those sluts went in for hugs.

"Nice to me you both." Alec smiled then turned to Jonathan when he stood up. "Nice to meet you, bro."

Jonathan just smiled as he shook Alec's hand.

Alec turned to Koda when she complimented his hair.

I wanted to listen to what she was saying to him, but Jonathan touched my arm, getting my attention.

"Hey Keela," he said, and gave me a hug which was very shocking because I *knew* Jonathan hated me.

I was about to say hey back to him when he put his mouth by my ear and whispered, "It's nice to have a shameless slut at the weddin'. Can I count on you to spread your legs if I don't get lucky with any decent women tonight?"

The nerve of him!

"Go fuck yourself!" I growled, and promptly pulled back from the hug.

Jonathan only grinned at me as he retook his seat.

I brightly smiled to Alec when he looked at me, he watched me for a moment before he pulled out my chair that was right next to Jonathan. I badly wanted to ask Alec to switch with me, but it would have been rude so I bit the bullet and sat down next to Jonathan. Alec took his seat next to me and smiled to everyone.

"I'm glad you're all dressed casual, we were a little worried about it... and by we I mean Keela."

Mr. Bane chuckled. "Shorts and t-shirts are all I can wear over here, it's too bloody hot for anythin' else."

Alec chuckled, and I smiled.

I looked down to the menu just to avoid having to converse with anyone at the table. It didn't matter that I was silent though because Alec wouldn't shut up. I glanced up and noticed he had Mr. Bane chuckling, Jonathan asking questions, Krista staring, and Koda drooling.

It really looked like the girl was drooling.

Just... ew.

"Knacker," I muttered.

"What was that Keela?" Jonathan asked.

I looked up at him, then the rest of the table and found everyone's eyes on me.

I nervously laughed. "I said I'm knackered. Must be the heat gettin' to me."

Alec leaned over and put his hand on my back. "You okay?"

I nodded. "I'm fine."

He stared at me for a moment before he straightened himself back up and looked down at his menu. A few minutes passed when the waiter came by to take our table's order. Alec ordered something that had steak in it so I got the same, simply because I didn't understand what the rest of the food on the menu was. The names were too fancy for me to know what the hell I would be ordering.

"Steak is in what we ordered, right? I heard you say steak."

Alec looked at me and nodded. "Yeah it's steak, mashed potatoes, vegetables, and gravy."

"Oh thank God," I said and breathed a sigh of relief. "I didn't know what any of the names meant. I just heard you say steak and got the same."

Alec laughed. "You're so cute."

I narrowed my eyes at him. "Every time you call me cute playboy, I will bite you."

Alec looked me dead in the eye and said, "You're a cutie-mac-cute face, cutie pie."

I couldn't keep down the burst of laughter that erupted from me. I quickly put my head down against Alec's shoulder until I was sure my face wasn't red anymore.

"I'm sorry, he made me laugh," I said when I showed my face to the table.

Alec and Mr. Bane were chuckling, while Kirsta and Koda were giving me dirty looks. Jonathan, the nasty son of a bitch was just smirking at me. I didn't realise why until I felt something brush up against my left leg. I looked at Jonathan who was now talking to his father. I knew it was him touching me with his foot because Alec was on the opposite side of me.

I moved my legs away from Jonathan, but bumped them into Alec making him jump a little.

"You okay?" he murmured.

For a spilt second I wanted to tell him what Jonathan said to me and that he was trying to play footsies with me under the table. I didn't know how he would react and because I did not want any attention on us I smiled and said, "Fine, I just want to be close to you."

Alec playfully gasped. "You aren't one of those really clingy girls, are you?"

I smirked and said, "Yes, I'm goin' to be stuck to you forever."

"I'm sorry, did you say you're going to suck on me forever?"

I snickered and swatted his shoulder. "You're dirty."

Alec leaned down and kissed my cheek. "You have no idea, kitten."

I looked down and smiled to myself. I repositioned my legs in front of me but felt my smile drop from my face when a foot touched my leg again, this time it began to rub up and down.

I ground my teeth to keep from saying something to Jonathan, and to keep from kicking the bastard as hard as I could. I literally bit my tongue and put up with it. I managed to put up with it for at least five minutes before I couldn't take it anymore.

"Excuse me, I've to use the rest room," I said and stood up, making sure I stomped down on Jonathan's foot as I turned.

He yelped.

"Oh, sorry."

Jonathan glared at me while I walked in the direction of the restroom - I was beyond happy that I'd hurt him in some way for touching me. I found the ladies restroom and froze when I found Mrs. Bane looking into a large mirror fixing her lipstick.

She looked at me through the reflection.

"Keela," she nodded curtly.

I nodded back. "Mrs. Bane."

She left the restroom without another word or glance in my direction and I thanked God for it. She greeted me by name which is more than I expected to get from her so I considered it progress.

I shook off the encounter then went into the toilet stall and relieved myself. When I was finished, I exited the stall and washed my hands. I checked my appearance in the mirror, nodded to myself then turned and headed back into the ballroom and to my table.

Alec was looking down at his phone as I reached the table. I raised my eyebrows as I sat down.

"What?"

"It's about fucking time, Keela!" Alec snapped lowly.

He shoved his phone into his trouser pocket and stood when I moved to take my seat next to him. He gripped the back of my chair and pulled it out for me. I was shocked as hell - he was displaying manners and was acting like a... gentleman. I was about to thank him when he slapped my arse as I positioned myself to sit down.

I rolled my eyes and tried not to react because honestly, I should have seen that one coming.

"You're a pervert," I muttered lowly as I moved my seat closer to the table.

He grunted as he retook his own seat. "Be thankful I didn't leave a mark, you deserved it for leaving me out here on my own for hours."

Hours? I was gone five minutes at most.

"I'm back now so why are you complainin'?" I asked, sighing.

"I was bored... and Jason's sisters keep hitting on me."

See, sluts!

"I'll give on the girls annoyin' you, but it couldn't have been that borin'-"

Alec cut me off with a wave of his hand and said, "It was. Trust me."

I gave him a look and asked, "On a scale of one to ten, how bored were you?"

He looked me dead in the eye and said, "I read the terms and conditions for the new iOS update on my phone. Twice."

That bored?

"Jesus," I said.

Alec dramatically nodded his head.

I chuckled at him. "Well, I'm back now... and just in time for dinner it seems."

Waitors arrived and began placing plates with different meals in front of the people seated at the tables. I inhaled the smell of the food and heard my stomach growl.

Oh, I was going to enjoy this.

When dinner was over, music started to play and the large dance floor that was to the far right started to fill up with both young and old people. Mr. Bane and Koda got up to dance and so did Jonathan who took his mother to the dance floor. I was ecstatic over because I was one more toe stroke from knocking the cunt out.

Alec asked me to dance as well, but I told him I couldn't move and that I had to let my food digest. He only laughed at me. Since I declined to dance with him, Krista Bane made sure to ask him to which he accepted.

"You don't mind, do you?" he murmured to me.

Did I mind?

"No, I don't care."

Yes, yes I did.

Alec hesitated. "When you say you don't care is that Man Bible code for you really *do* care? I'm not very good at reading people so I don't know what you're trying to say."

Men.

I rolled my eyes. "It's not code for anythin'. Go dance, whatever."

Alec snapped his fingers at me. "Whatever is another way for woman to say fuck you, I remember that one."

I was going to strangle him.

"Alec you're startin' to annoy me."

He chewed on his lower lip. "It's only a dance."

"Go dance then."

His smile was only annoying me further.

"Keela, you don't have to be jealous, it's *only* a dance."

I nodded curtly.

Alec chuckled, then leaned down and kissed my cheek.

"I won't be long."

Damn right you won't be long.

"Okay."

I sulked as I watched Alec take a beaming Krista by the hand and lead her to the dance floor. The music was fast, so they didn't actually have to touch each other while they danced and I felt a bit better about that.

"Jesus, what is wrong with me?" I muttered to myself.

How the hell could my feelings and attitude change so rapidly towards Alec? A few days ago I would have been delighted for anyone to take his attention away from me, but now... now I don't want his attention on anyone else *but* me.

Maybe I *was* being clingy with him.

Fuck!

It has only been five days since I met him. Three of those days I was hostile towards him, and now we were in the early stage of dating where everything is perfect and I was the picture of happiness.

Once again, it has only been *five fucking days* since I met him.

Why was I allowing myself to get emotionally attached to him? Especially after what happened the last time I allowed myself to be emotionally swept away by a man.

I was not comparing Alec to Jason - because Jason is a wank stain and Alec was not - but there *was* a similarity at how fast I let myself get lost in both men. Jason emotionally cracked me in about two weeks, and Alec in just two days.

Was I a hopeless romantic, or just hopeless?

Hopeless.

I was definitely hopeless.

After all, I fully knew this could come crumbling down at any given second so why did I agree to be Alec's real girlfriend? Why couldn't I have just said no?

Because I was a fucking eejit who thought with her vagina instead of her head.

I was so bloody stupid.

I mean, let's just look at how Alec came to be my boyfriend. He was a retired escort for crying out loud! He was doing me a favour by coming with me to this wedding, and here I was mad that he was dancing with someone when we both know dancing with women is nothing compared to what he can do with them.

Sexually, I've only had a taste of Alec - or he has only had a taste of me - but be that as it may, I *knew* he would ruin me for any other man. I just *knew* it.

I liked Alec, I didn't like when his arsehole trait came out to play, but I did enjoy his company and how he made me feel anything other than homely.

This confused me because unlike my relationship with Jason, I knew there was a higher percentage of things that could go belly up with Alec and yet I still wanted to be with him.

What. The. Fuck?

"I hate being a woman," I muttered out loud earning a chuckle from my left, which caused me to jump with fright because I didn't hear anyone sit down next to me.

"I didn't mean to startle you, miss?"

"Daley," I replied to the middle aged, American man who was sat in Jonathan's seat.

"Miss Daley... a relation of the bride?"

I nodded my head. "Yes, Micah is me younger cousin."

The man smiled at me and I noticed the creases around his eyes deepened. He was a good looking man, tanned skin, dark hair with an impressive beard.

"I'm afraid I don't know the bride, only her father."

I raised my brows. "You're a friend of me uncle?"

The man nodded. "Yes, well more of a business associate, than a friend."

I smiled. "Can't mix business with pleasure, huh?"

The man chuckled. "Precisely."

I continued to smile as I looked out at the dance floor where everyone was having fun dancing.

"Shouldn't you be out there dancing and having fun?" the man from my left asked.

I shook my head. "Nah, I just ate and unlike everyone else, I need time before I can move again."

The man laughed. "When you can move, I'm sure Alec will happily take your for a twirl on the dance floor."

I looked to the man and said, "You know me boyfriend?"

The man looked shocked, extremely shocked. "Alec Slater is your *boyfriend?*"

What the hell was that tone supposed to mean... did this man think Alec was too good for me, too?

I openly frowned at the man who quickly cleared his throat and said, "Forgive me, I think out loud sometimes... Yes, I know Alec. I am an old friend of his."

Now it was my turn to be shocked.

"From America or Ireland?"

The man chuckled. "America... we go way back."

Wow.

"Really? Might I ask your name?"

"Of course sweetheart." The man smiled wide.

"My name is Marco, Marco Miles."

CHAPTER TWENTY-ONE

"Nice to meet you, sir, I'm Keela."

Marco smiled as he accepted my outstretched hand and raised it to his mouth were he kissed my knuckles.

"The pleasure is all mine, Keela."

I smiled. "Alec will be so surprised to see someone he knows here."

Marco chuckled. "Trust me sweetie, he will be more than surprised to see me."

I grinned. "A good surprised or a bad surprised?"

Marco wiggled his fingers. "I'm going to go with the latter, but Alec is a free spirit so I can't really be sure."

"I doubt that, sir. Alec is always happy, I doubt anythin' could upset him."

Marco looked out to the dance floor. "You'd be surprised."

What?

"I'll excuse myself so I can seek out your uncle, business can't wait today it seems." Marco smiled.

I nodded to him. "It was nice to meet you, sir."

"Marco please, just Marco. I'm no sir, sweetie."

Umm, okay?

"It was nice to meet you, *Marco*."

Marco bowed his head to me and said, "Until our next meeting."

With that said he moved away from me and got lost in the crowd of people. I spent a minute or two trying to spot Marco again but he wasn't anywhere to be seen.

"Well, *that* was weird."

"What was weird?"

I jumped at Alec's voice.

"You frightened me!" I snapped and smacked Alec who was now laughing at me as he retook his seat.

"Sorry, kitten."

I waved him off. "It's okay, I was in a world of me own."

Alec nodded to my belly. "Is there still a threat of your stomach exploding?"

Smartarse.

I shrugged. "Press on it and you can find out."

Alec pulled back from me. "Uh, no thanks."

I snickered and said, "So how was dancin' with Jason's tramp of a sister?"

Alec raised his eyebrows at me. "Is she a tramp for dancing with me or for another reason?"

"For dancin' with you and for another reason," I replied.

Alec shook his head. "Damn, who would have ever guessed *you* would be possessive of *me*."

"Not me," I muttered.

Alec nudged my leg with his knee. "I like it," he said.

I rolled my eyes. "Yeah? Well, I don't. We're only datin' two days and have known each other five. It's too soon for either one of us to feel possessive."

Alec snorted. "Not in my world, kitten."

"Your world is mess up."

"That is already known knowledge," Alec teased.

I tried to keep a straight face, but I caved and giggled when he leaned into me and kissed my face.

"I could eat you up."

I raised my eyebrows.

"Oh, really?" I asked suggestively.

Alec narrowed his eyes. "Don't even think about whatever it is you're thinking."

I crossed my eyes. "Your words confuse me."

"Bitch," he murmured and latched onto my neck with his teeth making me convulse with laughter.

Alec pulled away looking very pleased with himself, so for some weird reason I leaned forward and flicked his ear with my fingers.

"Oh dear God! That hurt!"

I almost choked on air from laughing so hard.

"You're damn evil. Small, but evil."

I shrugged. "You speak the truth."

Alec rolled his eyes and rubbed his ear. "What were you thinking about when I frightened you?"

"Huh?"

"You said something was weird."

Oh, Marco.

"Oh, an old friend of yours is here at the weddin'! How cool is that?"

Alec dropped his hand from his ear and turned to face me. "An old friend of *mine*?"

I nodded. "Yeah, he said you by name."

Alec furrowed his eyebrows together. "Did he say what *his* name was?"

I nodded. "Yeah, his name is Marco Miles. Do you know him? Because he knows you, he said you both go way back."

Alec stared at me for a long moment without blinking or saying anything. I was about to repeat my sentence because I didn't know if he heard me or not, but he suddenly reached for my hand and held it tightly in his.

"We're leaving, right now."

I pulled my hand back from his hold. "What? Why?"

Alec was on his feet and looking around our surroundings before I even finished my sentence. When he looked back down at me his eyes scared me.

"Alec, what's wrong?"

He licked his lips and said, "Marco is not my friend Keela, he is my old... boss."

Excuse me?

"I don't understand."

"I know and I know I'm probably scaring you right now, but you need to leave with me before he comes back."

I felt my heart start to pound against my chest.

"I don't know why you're freakin' out, but it's okay... He is off with me uncle somewhere, you don't have to worry about him."

Alec instantly retook his seat and placed his hands on my cheeks.

"What does your uncle do for business, Keela?"

I tried to look down, but Alec wouldn't allow me. "Baby, this is important."

I sighed. "I honestly don't know what he does for business. Me uncle is very private and never spoke of business around myself, or Micah... But I know whatever he does, it's not exactly legal."

"You said your uncle's name was Brandon Daley, right?"

I nodded. "Yeah, that's his name."

Alec shook his head. "I've never heard of a Brandon Daley, and if he is in business with Marco I should know him."

I bit down on my lower lip. "I don't think me uncle is involved in the escort business, Alec... No offence."

Alec looked at me and his eyes wavered. "Marco was my boss Keela, but he was also my brothers' boss."

What?

"I don't understand, you said your brothers had different jobs-"

"They did, but we all worked for the same man. Marco has a hand in a lot of different trades."

I laughed. "Are you sure? Because he was nice to talk to, he doesn't look like a man who would-"

"Manipulate a family by using the life of one brother to control the rest?" he snapped.

I jumped when Alec's hand encircled my arm.

Ow.

This was the first time he had ever snapped at me and handled me to the point where I got scared.

"Alec, you're hurtin' me... let go of me arm," I said, my voice firm but also cracking.

Alec looked down to his hand, but before he could say a word or remove his hand, a man appeared next to him and sucker punched him in the gut.

"Oh my God!" I screamed.

Alec bent forward and grasped his stomach with both hands. His mouth was open, but no sounds came out and that freaked me out.

"Keela!"

I jumped up and swung around when I heard my named being bellowed.

I relaxed a little when I saw my uncle Brandon, but frowned when I noticed his pissed off look as he stalked in my direction.

I held up my hands in front of me. "I didn't to anythin'. This *wanker*," I said as I looked to the man who hurt Alec, glared at him, then looked back to my uncle, "punched me fella for no reason!"

"Your *fella* had his hand on you!" my uncle snarled.

When he was close enough to do so, he took me by the hand. "Let's do this in private."

"But what about Ale-"

"Timmy, bring him too."

My uncle smiled then and looked to the many guests who were staring at us.

"Shouldn't you all be drinkin' and dancin'?"

Everyone laughed and went back to their conversations as if they didn't just witness my boyfriend getting assaulted.

"What the fuck is goin' on?" I snapped.

My uncle glared down at me. "Watch your mouth or I'll smack it."

I looked down, fully aware he would follow through with his

threat if I cursed again.

"Sorry," I mumbled.

My uncle didn't say anything, he simply walked towards the double doors on the far side of the room and pulled me along with him. I looked over my shoulder to see where Alec was and found him also being pulled along by the prick who had hurt him.

I let go of my uncle's hand when we entered a large empty room with a huge table at the centre of it.

I guess it was a conference room.

"Take a seat, sweetheart," my uncle said to me.

I huffed but did as I was told and sat down.

I looked at Alec when he stumbled then fell into the seat next to me.

"Are you okay?" I asked him.

"I'll let you know," he murmured, his face twisted in pain.

I frowned then snapped by head in my uncle's direction when he sat three seats up from me at the head of the table.

"Care to explain why a strange man assaulted me boyfriend in front of the entire family?"

Uncle Brandon bared his teeth and snapped, "Because he was hurtin' you!"

I rolled my eyes. "If he was hurtin' me *that* bad I would have hit 'em meself... I'm not a child, I am an adult and I know how to take care of meself."

Uncle Brandon laughed and rubbed his chin. "You know how to take of yourself? Is that why you're datin' a whore?"

I bristled. "I don't know what you're talkin' about-"

"Oh I think you do, baby girl."

I tried to keep eye contact but failed and looked down to the table's surface.

"You couldn't have brought a decent man to my daughter's weddin', Keela? You wish to disrespect me that much after I have done nothing but love and care for you all your life."

Excuse me?

"Disrespect *you*? Are fuckin' serious right now? The only thing disrespectful about this *sham* of a weddin' is that you're allowin' your slutty child to marry a wanker who fucked me over!"

I jumped when my uncle slammed his hands down onto the table.

"You listen to me, Keela Daley. I will smack that attitude right out of you if you speak like that to me again. Do you understand me?"

I narrowed my eyes at my uncle and snarled, "Yes, I understand."

My uncle shook his head and laughed, "Dammit, baby girl you have me temper that's for sure."

I rolled my eyes and folded my arms across my chest.

My uncle smiled at me but dropped any trace of amusement when he switched his gaze to Alec.

"Slater? You're aware she is my niece? That's a bold move, boy."

Alec cleared his throat and rasped, "I didn't know she was your niece, Brandy. I swear it."

Brandy?

What the hell?

"You *know* me uncle?" I asked Alec, shocked laced throughout my tone.

"Yes," Alec replied without looking at me.

I stared at him in disbelief. "You *lied* to me, you told me less than five minutes ago that you didn't know who he was!"

"You said your uncle name was Brandon Daley... I only know him by Brandy."

I furrowed my eyebrows in confusion.

"I don't understand any of this... Uncle, what the hell is goin' on?"

My uncle clasped his hands together and said, "Alec is goin' home. Tonight."

"What? No he isn't! He is stayin' right here with me."

My uncle's eye twitched in irritation.

"You're goin' to defy me?" he asked, giving me time to change my mind.

I quickly thought it over and I knew I shouldn't go against him but I was too mad to care.

"Yeah, I am. You can't just poke your nose into me life and try to change things. I'm twenty-three, not thirteen!"

My uncle let out a loud belly rumbling laugh, the sound almost drowned out the noise of the door behind me opening and closing, but I heard it.

"You can hear the arguing from outside... I'm glad I don't have any kids."

I looked over my shoulder and glared. "What the fuck do *you* want?"

"Keela," my uncle said in warning tone, but had a smile on his face, "be nice to Mr. Miles."

"Ha! Fat chance of that."

Marco chuckled as he took up the seat next to my uncle.

"No it's fine, I think I deserve it."

I scoffed. "You think? I thought you were a nice man."

Marco smiled. "I know you did, which is a worry for your uncle."

I narrowed my eyes. "Why is it a worry?"

"Because you take people at face value and that's dangerous, it doesn't take much for someone to charm you."

"Are you tryin' to say I'm easy?"

Marco burst out laughing and even my uncle shook his head while smiling.

"No, I'm saying you're gullible and you trust people too easily."

I opened my mouth to snap off a snarky reply, but when I happened to glance to my left to Alec, I seen he was sitting upright now and he shook his head at me.

"You don't want me to speak to him?" I murmured.

Alec shook his head again.

Okay.

He knew Marco better than I did.

I ignored Marco and refocused on my uncle. "If Alec goes home, so do I."

My uncle narrowed his eyes at me. "You're purposively bein' difficult, Keela."

"Yes uncle, I am."

My uncle didn't break eye contact with me for a few moments and I made a point not to blink to show him how serious I was. It got a little hard to keep my eyes open so when my uncle sighed and looked down, I blinked so many times in ten seconds that I might have set a new world record.

"Keela, I don't want you mixed up with anyone in *my* world."

I swallowed. "Alec isn't in *your* world anymore."

Marco laughed and rubbed his right shoulder. "Yeah, him, his brothers, and a certain bitch made damn sure of that."

I didn't know what he was talking about so I looked at Alec and said, "What is he wafflin' on about?"

Alec's hand suddenly touched my thigh and his thumb gently rotated in a circle as he said, "I'll tell you everything later, I promise."

I nodded my head to him, then looked back to my uncle. "He is stayin' with me."

My uncle's jaw set as he watched me. After a moment he flicked his eyes to Alec and said, "I want to speak to you without her present."

Her?

"*Her* can hear perfectly fine," I snarled.

My uncle grinned when Marco chuckled and said, "Are you sure she is not your daughter?"

My uncle cut his eyes to Marco then softened them when he looked back at me.

"She is my niece by blood, but my daughter by every other means... I can't be angry when she acts like me, can I?"

Marco chuckled and shook his head.

I looked my uncle in the eye and said, "I want your word that you won't have dickhead Timmy, or anyone else, lay a finger on him."

My uncle sighed. "You have my word."

I looked to Marco and spat, "He doesn't like you for a reason, so leave him alone or I'll bite a chunk out of your hairy face."

Marco raised his eyebrows in surprise. "Damn, I could use someone like you for-"

"Don't make me punch you Marco," my uncle cut him off making Marco laugh.

"Noted, and noted," Marco said to my uncle then to me.

I eyed him and my uncle.

My uncle gave me the nod to leave the room and I felt sick because I did not want to leave Alec alone with him and Marco.

I turned to him. "Will you be okay?"

Alec smiled. "I can take care of myself kitten, but having you defend me is pretty awesome, I won't lie."

He nodded down to his groin, and when I looked down and saw the bulge of his penis, I rolled my eyes.

"Only you could find something in this situation to get hard about," I whispered making him laugh.

I made a move to get up but Alec grabbed onto my wrist and pulled me back down to my chair.

"Kiss me before you go," he whispered.

I didn't know what to say, so I did as he asked and kissed him. I placed my hands on his cheeks and pressed my lips against his and got lost in feeling his mouth and tongue on mine.

"Slater!" my uncle's voice growled.

Alec pulled back from our kiss with a sigh, before he moved his head from mine he kissed my nose and said, "I'll be okay."

"You better be," I whispered.

He smiled and kissed my nose once more before he let me go.

I stood up and turned to face my uncle and Marco. I looked my uncle in the eye and said, "You gave me your word. Don't forget it."

My uncle nodded.

Marco blew me a kiss and waved at me. I narrowed my eyes at him suddenly taking a huge disliking towards him. Before I turned I gave his disgusting self the finger and that made everyone laugh, even Alec.

I left the room and re-entered the ballroom where guests were dancing and drinking like nothing serious was happening in the room next door.

I was going to go sit down at our table and wait for Alec, but I suddenly felt a hand on my left arm halting my movements.

"Keela, sweetheart. You look... put together."

I looked to my left and wanted to die.

"Hello, Everly."

CHAPTER TWENTY-TWO

"How are you, darlin'?" Everly asked me.

The smile on her face was as small and as fake as the botox in her face.

"I'm... not too bad Everly, thanks. How are you?" I asked and looked over my shoulder at the double doors of the conference room that Everly was leading me away from.

"I'm fabulous, sweetheart. My little girl is gettin' married after all."

I swallowed down a snort.

Everly was a wicked stepmother - not a mother, not even to Micah.

"Where is this boyfriend I've heard about?" Everly asked me as we walked.

I jammed by thumb over my shoulder and said, "In that room with Uncle Brandon."

Everly smiled. "Your Uncle is probably just givin' him a talkin' to."

I rubbed my neck. "I hope so."

"What is your boyfriend's name?" Everly asked.

Why did she care?

"Alec Slater, he is- Ow!"

I pulled my hand back from Everly's grip and held it to my chest.

She pinched me.

She *actually* pinched me.

"What the hell was that for?" I snapped.

Everly looked like she was in her own world before she looked back in my direction.

"I'm sorry, hun."

She didn't fucking look sorry.

I rubbed my stinging palm and followed her when she began walking again.

"How long have you been with Alec?" Everly curiously asked over her shoulder.

She was interested?

"A little over three months now."

She didn't reply.

I closed my eyes when I realised Everly was bringing me to the head table. I opened my eyes and smiled when I was greeted with smiles and hellos.

"Where is Alec, Keela?" Krista Bane asked.

She was sitting on her brother's lap because there were no free chairs at the table. Loads of people were at it, Jason's siblings as well as his mother, Everly, Micah, and her bridesmaids, the Brennan sisters.

"He is havin' a chat with me uncle, he will be along soon enough."

Krista smirked. "I hope so."

Bitch.

I raised my eyebrow. "Yeah, you can ask him for another dance. I'm sure he won't mind dancin' with a little mutt in heat."

Whoa, were did that come from?

"Keela!" Everly bellowed.

Everyone at the table - and I mean everyone - gawked at me.

"Yes, Everly?" I asked, sweetly.

"You watch your mouth!" she hissed.

I looked her up and down. "Or what?"

Her face went red with anger.

"Or else I'll have to have a *talk* with you, cuz," Micah's voice chimed in.

I looked at her and laughed. "We aren't kids anymore Mi, your sly threats don't worry me."

Micah furrowed her eyebrows when I looked at her.

"What is with you... you're actin'... different."

I was... I really was.

I shrugged. "I don't feel like bein' a doormat to people anymore."

Micah looked surprised for a moment then smiled. "Good for you."

Huh?

Everly angrily folded her arms across her chest and spat, "Wait till I tell your mother about this."

I looked to her and laughed. "I'm twenty-three Everly, me ma can't do anythin' about me not taken shite off a Bane."

Jason laughed. "You really *are* feisty now!"

Micah cut her eyes to Jason and glared at him.

I completely ignored Jason, Micah, and Everly as I glanced over my shoulder hoping to see Alec, but I didn't.

"I don't want any arguments this week."

I looked at Everly and said, "You won't hear a peep from me."

Everly nodded then looked to the rest of the table. "I expect the same from each of you."

Everyone mumbled okay and it made me shake my head. Everyone at this table was an adult but yet mumbled and grumbled like a bunch of children when Everly put her foot down.

"Brilliant, now everyone get up. The photographer will take a group picture."

I did not want to get in a picture with any of these people, but to save myself from an argument I kept my mouth shut.

"Keela move to the back in front of the lads since you're the tallest girl," Everly said to me.

Oh, crap.

"Okay."

I stood behind Micah and the girls, and between Jonathan and Jason who both towered over me.

"Fancy seeing you here," Jonathan murmured to me.

I glanced to him. "Go fuck yourself."

Jason laughed while Jonathan glared down at me.

"Leave her be, the new Keela might hit you when she is mad."

Might?

"More like will," I said.

I felt Jason's eyes on me and noticed how different I felt.

I used to love his gaze on me and now... now it gave me shivers of disgust.

"Eyes forward, groom," I muttered.

Jason chuckled. "Yes, ma'am."

"Is everyone ready?" the photographer asked.

"Yes," we replied.

"Smile!" the man shouted.

I smiled along with everyone else and for a spilt second it felt like I was part of a real family picture, that was until a hand touched my arse.

"Whoops, my bad."

I turned and glared at Jason. "Don't do it again, I'm warnin' you, Bane."

Jason smiled. "Understood, Daley."

He was trying to be funny but I just found him annoying.

"Oh, here's daddy."

I looked over my shoulder when Micah's voice chirped.

Uncle Brandon was walking in our direction, but Alec wasn't with him.

I panicked and rushed forward.

"Where is he?" I asked.

My uncle put his hands on my shoulders.

"He has gone up to your room, he said join him when you're ready."

I was ready now.

I made a move to walk away to go upstairs when Everly shouted, "Brandon, get a picture with your girls."

Damn.

"Great idea, sweetheart."

I sighed and my uncle frowned.

"You don't want a picture with me?"

Oh, for the love of God.

"Don't frown, you should not be allowed to frown. That look isn't fair on an old man's face."

My uncle gasped. "I'm forty you cheeky little shite, that's not old."

I laughed and so did my uncle as he looked down at me. I turned to my right when a flash went off and found the photographer smiling at us.

"Sorry, but unexpected pictures are the best."

I smiled then looked to my uncle. "I want a copy of that one."

"You got it, baby girl."

I smiled and my uncle beamed down at me then kissed my head.

"I only want what's best for you... You know that don't you? I love you, Keela."

I smiled. "I know you do and I love you too."

I looked to Micah when she came up beside me then switched to the other side of my uncle.

"Make this a good picture you two, the last picture we have of the three of us is from years ago when we were kids."

I glanced at Micah surprised that she knew that.

"There would be more pictures of us all together if I could stand to be around you."

Micah cleared her throat and looked down. "Yeah, I know."

No smart reply?

"Can you two please just get along? I'd like to be in a room with me girls without an argument starting between the two of you for once."

I nudged his side. "We wouldn't be Daley's if we didn't argue about everythin'."

My uncle laughed. "Right you are, sweetheart."

We each looked to the photographer when he stood a few feet in front of us.

"Ready?"

"Keela," Everly murmured in a low voice while gesturing to my tummy with her hand. "Suck it in."

I flushed with embarrassment and nodded to my auntie before sucking in. I bloody hated sucking it, after a while it just got uncomfortable and just plain hurt.

"What are you doin'?" My uncle asked me.

"I'm just standing here waitin' for the man to take our picture," I replied.

"No, you look constipated or somethin'."

I couldn't suck in anymore so I gave in and let my gut relax.

"I was suckin' it in," I murmured to my uncle.

Uncle Brandon looked at me like I had ten heads.

"Why?"

I shrugged. "'Cause me belly sticks out."

My uncle looked at me for a few seconds longer then shook his head. "You don't need to 'suck it in', you're perfectly fine the way you are."

I smiled. "You're just sayin' that 'case you're me uncle."

"No, I'm sayin' it because it's the truth. You're beautiful Keela and it's time you realised it."

I felt my cheeks heat up.

"Thank you."

My uncle kissed my head and said, "Who told you that you have to suck it in anyway, your mother?"

Micah heard what my uncle said and listened in.

"Um, no... Everly just told me to suck it in a minute ago."

"Everly!" my uncle snarled making Everly jump. "Don't be

tellin' Keela she has to suck it in, she doesn't have to do anythin' like that."

"Hun, I just want her to look her best in the weddin' album. A chubby stomach isn't attractive."

Thanks very fucking much!

I'd had it with Everly and her mouth and I was about to turn and walk away when Micah reached over and stopped me by taking hold of my hand.

"Don't you move," she said to me then looked at Everly. "Leave her alone, she looks great."

What. The. Fuck?

"What is goin' on here?" I asked Micah.

She looked at me a shrugged. "Looks like you aren't the only one who is turnin' over a new leaf, cuz."

I widened my eyes. "You *want* to change?"

Micah nodded. "Yeah, I'm gettin' married. I can't act like a spoilt brat for the rest of me life. Besides, you're me family and we should stick together not tear each other down which is what I've always done to you. But I'm workin' on makin' it up to you."

I was suspicious. "How?"

Micah laughed. "By not bein' a miserable bitch all the time."

I didn't trust her obviously, but I was open to the idea of her not being a bitch anymore because that would make everyone's life easier.

"Okay," I said to Micah.

Myself, Micah, and my uncle smiled as the photographer took our picture.

"The dinner was lovely, but I'm goin' to get goin' on up to me room."

Micah was whisked away by Everly for more pictures so my uncle nodded his head to me and said, "Have fun... but not too much. I don't want to have to hurt Alec."

I didn't know whether he was joking or not so I just smiled and gave him a tight hug.

"I'll see you later."

I moved through the crowds of people in the ballroom until I was in the lobby.

The nice, quiet, and spacious lobby.

I took the lift up to my floor and when the doors opened I reached down and took off my heels.

"That's so much better," I murmured to myself.

I walked down the hallway in my bare feet with my heels in my hand. I didn't bring a bag with me but I had put my key card in the back of my iPhone case earlier.

Once the keycard was in my hand I put in the into the card slot in the door and when the green light flashed, I pulled down the handle and opened the door.

"You don't understand. She is Brandy's niece, his fucking *niece*! Do you realise how serious this is? Bronagh fucked around with Micah who is his daughter, if he'd interfered back when they fought we could have been destroyed... He won't make the same mistake now that he knows I'm with Keela."

I frowned and quietly closed the door behind me so I didn't interrupt Alec.

He had his back to me and was on his phone talking to someone.

He had no idea I was in the room.

"I don't know bro, but I *have* to do this otherwise Brandy will have all our balls. Literally."

I stepped forward.

"You have to do what, Alec?"

Chapter Twenty-Three

"Keela!" Alec shouted and swung in my direction.

I dropped my heels to the floor and folded my arms over my chest.

"Answer me question. What do you have to do to keep your balls?"

Alec swallowed and looked anywhere but my eyes.

"Um... I have to treat you right otherwise your uncle will hurt me, he said so."

That was why he was going crazy?

"Alec, he was only jokin' with you. He is just puttin' fear into you to make sure you treat me right."

I laughed and Alec smiled, but it was so small I barely saw it.

"Who are you talkin' to?" I asked.

Alec licked his lips and said, "My brothers."

"All of them?" I asked.

He nodded. "Yeah, Damien is on the call so I can hear and speak to him too."

I frowned. "Why are you ringin' them?"

Alec rolled his neck on his shoulders and grunted, "Shut the fuck up!"

I narrowed my eyes. "Excuse me?"

Alec waved his hand at me. "Not you baby, I'm talking to my brothers."

Oh.

"Why are you shoutin' at them?"

Alec sighed and glared at his phone. "Because they are being *very* fucking difficult and giving *stupid* advice."

I was lost.

"Advice? For what?"

Alec gazed at me for a long moment before he said, "Advice on what to do with this... new information."

New information?

"Do you always speak in riddles? I've no clue what you're on about. *What* new information?"

Alec pinched the bridge of his nose then looked at me and said, "You're Brandy's niece Keela. Your uncle is part of my old life and with Marco being here... It's just not good to mix a Slater in with Marco Miles... The results are never pleasing."

My head was starting to spin with confusion.

"What is your deal with Marco Miles? Can you just *tell* me because me head is really startin' to hurt tryin' to figure all this out."

After a moment of listening to his brothers Alec suddenly narrowed his eyes and snapped, "Fuck you Dominic! You told Bronagh, so why can't I tell Keela?"

I moved over to the bed and sat down when Alec began to pace up and down the room.

"Yeah, well you aren't here with him. I am. You weren't in a room with him staring at you. I was."

I raised my eyebrows when Alec's voiced cracked.

"Again bro, that is shitty advice."

"What advice are they givin' you?" I asked.

Alec turned to face me and said, "They want me to come home. Tonight."

I forced away the sudden wave of saddens that washed over me.

"Oh... well, you can if you want. You don't have to stay here... it's okay."

I looked down to my fingers and knotted the together.

I heard Alec sigh. "Kitten... look at me."

I couldn't.

I shook my head. "It's honestly okay. You don't have to stay here, don't feel like you have to... I... I release you from your favour... There... You can go back home."

Oh God, I was about to cry.

"I'm not going back home."

I looked up. "You're not?"

Alec smiled as he crawled onto the bed. "You think I would leave you? We have a deal, I said I would escort you to your cousin's wedding and I will... Plus I've a few challenges yet to be completed with you."

I laughed when he waggled his eyebrows.

"Cut the bullshit, Alec! It's too dangerous for you to stay there with Marco on the scene. Think with the head on your fucking shoulders for once."

Wow.

Dominic Slater was pissed, so pissed I could hear him clearly without putting the phone to my ear.

"That's why I'm staying bro, I'm not leaving her in a place where *he* is."

All of his brothers swore.

"He is not a threat to her. Her uncle is Brandy for fuck sakes. That prick is just as fucking dangerous as Marco!"

What?

"I don't know what has you all riled up, but do *not* insult me uncle again, do you hear me Nico? That is me *blood* you're talkin' about."

I heard a growl. "Your blood has never been kind to my blood so why should I be nice?"

A dark look fell over Alec's face. "Because she has no idea about Brandy or who he is. Don't speak another word, I mean it Dominic."

Silence.

"I... *We* just want you to be safe. It not like we can drive to where you are to back you up. You're in a whole other country Alec."

Alec sighed. "If it was Bronagh would you leave her?"
Nico replied less than a second later, "Not a chance."
Alec smiled. "Exactly. Keela is my Bronagh, bro... I'm staying."
There was a collective group of sighs.
"Stick to Keela, he won't go near her because of Brandy."
Alec smiled and looked to me. "I plan to stick her."
"Oh, for fuck's sake," Ryder's voice muttered.
"Can you focus?" Damien's voice asked.
"Fuck that, get balls deep bro," Kane's voice rasped making the brothers mutter curse words.

It barely sounded like him, he must still be feeling sick.

"I'll call you all tomorrow. I've some explaining to do to Keela."

Oh thank God.

I don't think my head could handle being this confused for much longer.

"Call us when it's done."

When what's done?

"Okay," Alec said then hung up his phone.

I fell back and sighed.

"You're the most confusin' man I have ever met."

Alec crawled onto the bed next to me.

"I'm sorry, I don't mean to confuse you."

I turned on my side to face him. "So get talkin'."

Alec turned on his side to face me. "I don't know where to start."

"How about at the beginnin'?" I suggested.

Alec nodded his head. "Okay, are you ready?"

I shrugged my shoulders and said, "As ready as I'll ever be."

CHAPTER TWENTY-FOUR

"Remember when I told you my mother loved her materialistic things and my dad was only fond of us for our use in his business?" Alec asked me.

I nodded my head. "Yeah."

"Well, that business was a business my dad ran with Marco."

Whoa.

"Your da is like Marco?" I asked.

"Was," Alec murmured. "My mom and dad were exactly like Marco, but they got too greedy on a deal and tried to double cross Marco. He knew all about it and killed them both."

Holy Christ!

I covered my mouth with my hand. "I'm so sorry."

Alec shrugged. "It is what it is. I didn't exactly like them, but they were my parents... you know?"

"Of course, I'd question your mental state if you didn't feel something when they... when they died."

Alec swallowed. "I was a little sad about it, not to the point where I cried, but it still brought me down. Damien took it the worst. My little bro always thought our mom and dad would change their ways one day and love us like parents should... It took him a few years after their murders to realise they were the same people in death that they were in life... scum."

Fuck me.

"So what happened afterwards... with Marco?"

Alec licked his lips. "Well, we were a part of the business at that point. Me, Kane, and Ryder at least. Before everything went down we did petty things like small drug runs, weapon runs, and watch duty at the compound we lived in. We all hated it and only did it because we couldn't leave."

I frowned. "Why couldn't you leave? You were old enough to branch out on your own, right?"

"Yes, we were. Me, Kane, and Ryder at least. I was twenty-two when my parents were killed, Kane was twenty, and Ryder was the eldest at twenty-five. "

"So you were old enough to leave... why stay?"

"Because the twins were fifteen at the time of my parents murders. They were even younger when we all started working with dad and Marco. The three of us could have easily left because we were adults, but we didn't because we wouldn't leave without the twins. It wasn't an option, it was never even brought up or thought of. We knew we just had to keep our heads down and work until the twins were older so we could take them and leave. We had a plan to move out of New York after the murders. We wanted out, but something happened with the twins that kept us in New York... kept us tied to Marco."

I had a feeling I wasn't going to like whatever the 'something' was.

"What was it? What happened with the twins?"

Alec sighed. "They got in an... altercation with Marco's nephew Trent over Damien's girlfriend Nala. Things were said, punches were thrown... it was typical kids fighting it out until... until a gun was brought into the mix."

I gasped. "Who had the gun?"

"Trent. According to Dominic, Trent was going to kill Damien and would have if Nala hadn't jumped on Trent and knock the gun out of his hand."

I shook my head in astonishment.

"You still with me over there?" Alec asked.

I nodded my head. "Yeah, I feel like I'm in some sort of crazy mobster film, but I'm with you. What happened to the gun after Nala knocked it away from Trent?"

Alec frowned. "It somehow ended up in Damien's hand. Understand that this was right after my parents were murdered, everything was very fresh and raw and Damien was a wreck. All it took for Damien to shoot Trent was one insult from him directed at my father."

I flung both of my hands over my mouth. "Omigod."

Alec nodded. "Yeah."

Damien *shot* somebody?

"Did Trent live?"

Alec's brow creased. "We thought he died, I mean, Marco... that bastard *told* us he died."

I was confused.

"Wait... so Trent didn't die, but you were told he died... why?"

Alec laughed. "That's the question of the hour."

I patiently waited for Alec to continue to speak.

"Marco helped my dad groom us for getting neck deep in the business one day. All our lives we were brought up around violence, sex, drugs, and numerous crimes. While kids our ages went to school and tried to talk to girls, we were homeschooled and fucking our tutors."

I widened my eyes.

"How old were you when..."

"When I lost my virginity?" Alec finished my unanswered question.

I nodded my head.

He scratched his chin and said. "I was the same age as Dominic and Damien I think, I was either thirteen or fourteen. I wasn't any good at it until I turned sixteen and actually had a decent sized cock. It was tricky, I had to learn how to hold back instead of ejaculating early when I got excited otherwise my partners would smack me. The women in the compound taught me and my brothers how to please women from an early age. Thanks to them, each of us strongly believe in a woman coming first, and last. I was apparently very good... and that opened me up to a whole new world with a lot of... variety."

I grimaced. "Ew."

Alec laughed. "I know... sorry."

I shivered. "You lost your virginity nearly a whole decade ahead of me. Wow."

Alec smiled and playfully clocked my chin. "My experience will only mean a better time for you."

My face flushed but I quickly refocused. "Okay, back to your story. Why were you told Trent died when he didn't?"

Alec lightly gnawed on the inside of his cheek. "We were told that to keep us in dark. If we knew Trent was alive, Marco wouldn't have had the hold he did over Damien's head. We could have left."

"Wait, wait, wait. Are you sayin' Marco *pretended* his nephew was murdered by Damien just so he could make you and your brothers do something for him?"

Alec looked down and nodded.

"That sick son of a bitch! What did he make you do?"

Alec kept his eyes downcast. "He made me an escort."

I widened my eyes in horror. "You were *forced* into that job?"

Alec looked up at me and shrugged. "Pretty much. Marco gave us jobs and told us once we do them and keep him happy he wouldn't avenge Trent's death by hurting Damien."

What a scumbag!

"You were an escort and I heard from Aideen that Dominic was a fighter... was that his job?"

Alec nodded. "Marco looked at the CCTV of what happened that night and once he saw Dominic defend Damien by beating the shit out of Trent he decided he wanted to try his hand in the underground fighting world, thus Dominic became the star fighter to represent him. He was the people's favourite at every spot he fought in because he was so young and tough. A lot of times I thought he would die because even though he won his fights, he would be so busted up afterwards that even breathing hurt him."

I swallowed down the bile that filled my mouth.

"That's disgustin'."

Alec nodded. "It is."

I was almost afraid to ask my next question, but I had to know.

"What jobs did your other brothers have?"

Alec scratched his chin and said, "Ryder ran weapons and drugs the odd time or two for Marco. Kane was what Marco called his bruiser. He did the dirty work on people who didn't pay their debts to Marco or people who simply pissed Marco off. Out of all the jobs his was the worst because Marco was pissed off at someone everywhere we fucking went, and Kane had to hurt these people who knew it was coming. They would defend themselves with weapons because they had nothing left to lose... it was a bloody job. Literally."

Holy Christ!

I gasped. "So that's why he is covered in scars?"

Alec nodded. "Yes, his body isn't a pretty sight but it's just looks, he is really a great guy. I don't know half of the things he has seen or done, but he always manages to be happy."

I thought of Kane's scars and cringed.

"And Damien? What did he do?"

Alec smiled. "Luckily nothing. The deal we had with Marco was that we worked for him and Damien was to be left alone. Completely."

My heart melted.

"That is an amazin' thing you and your brothers did for Damien."

"He is our brother, we would do anything and everything to protect him."

I smiled. "I've never seen a bond like one you and your brothers have... it's beautiful."

Alec smiled so wide his dimples dented deep into his cheeks.

"Yeah, we have a pretty solid bond. It's the best thing we have to show from our shitty childhood."

I can only imagine.

I chewed on my lower lip. "So you worked for Marco to keep Damien safe... When did you find out that Trent was alive and Marco lied?"

Alec clenched his hand into a fist and rubbed his knuckles. "Two and a half years ago, it'll be three in December."

I widened my eyes.

So recent.

"So you worked for him as an escort for-"

"Three years."

Wow.

"How did you find out about Trent and the lie?"

Alec snorted. "This is where the story gets even weirder."

I lightly smiled. "I doubt I will be surprised after everythin' you just told me."

Alec anxiously looked at me. "I wouldn't count on that."

Oh.

I swallowed.

"Two and a half years ago Dominic met Bronagh and decided he was done with Marco and done fighting for him. We wanted out too and agreed that we had more than paid our debt to Marco... Me and my brothers made him a lot of money, and money was all Marco cared about. With all of us in agreement we contacted Marco and told him we were done and any jobs left we had in Ireland would be the last."

Alec frowned. "He agreed that we worked our asses off for him - some more than others - and that he was happy to let us go free. We should have known the bastard wouldn't leave us alone that easily. Marco is like a spoiled toddler in some ways, we were his prized toys and under no circumstances was he letting us go."

I tensed. "What did he do?"

Alec shrugged. "He flew to Ireland and with the help of Trent he kidnapped Bronagh, Alannah, and Damien in order to force us back into work."

Jesus Christ!

He said that so casually.

"No way," I whispered.

"Yes way. It was messed up... Anyway, long story short we went to where Marco had them, killed his guards then freed the girls and Damien. They were all beat pretty bad and both of the girls had concussions and ended up passing out. We used that to our advantage and got to work of disposing of Marco guards and Trent. Damien took care of him."

I widened my eyes. "So he really did end up killin' him?"

Alec looked to me and his gazed hardened. "Don't judge him Keela. Trent revealed some things that sent Damien - and us - into a fit of rage."

I raised me eyebrows. "Like what?"

Alec looked pained as he said, "We found out Nala was raped and murdered by Trent because she found out he was alive and not dead like we were told. Damien also revealed that she was pregnant with his kid at the time of her murder."

I gasped. "Omigod!"

Poor Nala!

"Yeah, later that night when we got home Damien explained that he and Nala were too afraid to tell anyone about the baby. They thought if they ignored it then it would go away. They were babies who were going to have a baby, you understand how scared they must have been?"

I have no doubt they were scared, I would have been terrified.

I nodded my head. "Of course."

"Anyway, it made sense why Damien was so torn up when we left New York. He asked about Nala of the time, but her family cleared out of the compound after Trent's supposed death. He had no way of contacting her and trust me, the kid tried everything."

Poor Damien.

Alec smiled then. "It seems stupid now, but at the time when got back to our house Ryder smacked Damien across the head and told him he knew better and he should have worn protection. I still think it's funny, his protective instinct came surfaced to lash out at Damien even though we had just killed a bunch of people."

I swallowed. "How did none of you get caught?"

"The spot we were at was up in the mountains and it was after hours. The cameras were turned off with a few wires cut and besides us and the thugs the place was empty. Behind that mountain were the club is located are more mountains and endless fields. We wrapped everyone up, loaded them into the back of the Jeep and then Ryder and Kane drove up to the mountains and buried them.

I winded my eyes. "What if someone finds them? People get discovered all the times up the mountains."

Alec shrugged. "It won't matter. Ryder had acid and got rid of their finger prints, hair, teeth... I think they burned them too just to be sure that-"

"Omigod! Okay, I get it, no more details."

Alec winced. "Sorry."

I shook away the disturbing images of what Ryder and Kane had to do to those bodies.

"It's okay, I asked."

Alec remained quiet while I thought things over.

Okay, the Slater brothers killed people, but it was bad people they killed... and they only did it to defend themselves and their family. They aren't bad people.

"I've a question," I murmured.

Alec nervously licked his lips and said, "Fire away."

"Why didn't you kill Marco?"

Alec was quiet for a moment then said, "We were going to kill him. Dominic was so up for it... but Marco promised if we showed him mercy then he would leave us alone. He spewed to us that he helped raise us and saved us from countless beatings when we upset our father. I remembered one time when I spilled coke in my dad's

SUV and he pulled me out of the car and punched and kicked me around the courtyard of the compound we lived in... He wouldn't have stopped if Marco hadn't intervene. I felt like I owed him something so I told Kane not to shoot him."

Alec sighed. "It took awhile to convince Dominic and Kane, but when I asked them not to sink his level and act like him or our dad... they let him go."

I was perplexed.

"Wait, you *believed* 'em? After everythin' he did, you believed he would just forget about Damien murderin' his nephew?"

Alec looked and me and said, "Yeah, we did."

Wow.

"I don't think I would have believed him," I murmured.

Alec reached out for me so I moved closer to him.

"I have my doubts now and then wondering if we did the right thing by letting him live. Today is a day when I really question if we did they right thing by letting him walk free. But no man should have the life of another in his hands - I know we did the right thing, it sucks right now though."

I frowned. "Why?"

"Because he is here and he is connected to you by your connection to your uncle... I don't want him to have anything to do with you Keela, I don't want you mixed up in anything that Marco has a hand in."

I put my hand on Alec's cheek and said, "Me uncle has kept his life private from me and Micah our entire lives. He isn't about to tie me to anythin' Alec, believe that."

Alec was still wary, I could tell. "I don't know... Brandy... Your uncle... he isn't exactly the nicest man or the most trustworthy."

With his family he is.

"Whatever happened with you and him is in the past, he is me uncle and I love him, please don't tell me somethin' that will make me question that."

Alec firmly nodded his head. "Okay."

I snuggled into Alec and held him tight.

"Thank you for tellin' me... I know that wasn't easy for you."

Alec flattened my hair down with his hand and began to stroke it.

"It was actually nice to be able to tell someone everything... we don't talk about it at home."

Understandable.

I sighed. "I used to think I had it hard growin' up, but you just made me realise how easy me childhood was."

Alec kissed the crown of my head. "Don't compare, what you went through was hard for you but it shaped you into the person you're today so at least there are benefits to having things rough. It makes you stronger."

"I guess," I murmured.

We were silent then, all I could hear was Alec's breathing.

"Thank you for standing by me when your uncle was against me downstairs... that meant a lot to me, kitten."

I looked up at Alec and smiled. "Of course, you've got my back and I've got yours."

Alec smiled down at me. "Always."

I flicked my eyes from Alec's eyes to his mouth and I could see his breath catch in his chest.

"Stow those heated eyes kitten, a man can only take so much of that look before he acts upon what his body wants."

I kept my gaze on him as I said, "So act."

"What?" Alec whispered.

My insides began to heat.

I leaned my head up to his and smiled. "I want you."

Alec bit down on his lower lip and pulled my body fully up against his.

"Say it."

I flushed. "Say what?"

"I told you I wouldn't fuck you until you begged me, but right now I'll settle for you just asking me."

Oh.

"If you want me to touch you, to kiss you.... to love your body, then *say it*."

I widened my eyes.

You want this, you want him... fucking say it!

"Alec," I whispered and locked my gaze with his. "Fuck me."

CHAPTER TWENTY-FIVE

Within seconds of my demand, Alec's mouth was on mine and his hands were on my body. The pressure of Alec's kiss was borderline painful but I wouldn't have changed anything about it because it was animalistic, and right now, animalistic was *exactly* how I felt.

"You have no idea what I'm going to do to you, do you baby?" Alec asked when he let up on his kiss.

He lips brushed against mine and I shook my head.

"I'm going to take you places you've only dreamed of, kitten... I can't wait to make you purr."

Oh fuck me that was hot.

"I didn't know women could purr," I teased, trying to get a handle on the situation.

Alec smiled down at me. "You're such a smartass kitten, I'll make you purr just wait and see."

I stuck my tongue out and slide it across his lower lip. "I look forward to it, playboy."

Alec growled. "Hmm, what to do with you first?"

I swallowed. "Kissin' me is good... for now."

Alec smirked. "I plan to kiss you all over beautiful, but first get up."

I blinked. "Get up?"

I was lying down on the bed - this was as horizontal as he was ever going to get me.

"Yeah, get up."

Okay.

I did as I was told and sat up then stood up off the bed.

"Okay, now what?"

Alec's lip curved and he gestured me closer with his index finger.

I walked forward two steps and stopped when my knees touched the bed. Alec sat down and put his legs on either side of me so I was now standing between his legs. He rested his hands on my shoulders and looked at me.

"How does the dress open from a zip or buttons?"

I grinned. "Buttons at the back but I did them up first and just put it on over my head. I can take it off the same way if you want?"

Alec leaned forward and brushed his nose against mine. "How partial are you to this dress?"

Huh?

"Um, I mean I like it, but I won't go out of my way to wear it again. Why?"

Alec smirked. "Because I've always wanted to do this."

Once again, huh?

"You've always wanted to do what?"

"This."

A screamed caught in my throat when Alec moved his hands under my arms and around to my back where he gripped my dress and quickly pulled down. I widened my eyes at the sound of buttons hitting the floor, then my jaw fell open when the shoulder straps of my dress fell off my shoulders and the front of my dress dropped down with the rest of the material to my ankles.

He... he ripped off my dress!

"You're so fucking sexy!" I gasped when Alec's fingertips dug into my behind and gripped my cheeks.

Alec buried his face in my breasts and groaned.

"This may be my favourite place."

I looked down and couldn't help but snicker as I said, "Your favourite place on my body?"

Alec shook his head making my boobs jiggle.

"No, my favourite place as in my favourite place to be anywhere."

I felt my eyelids drop as I gazed down at Alec, my heart starting to pound against my chest. I felt his fingers slide around to my back, and not a second later my bra was unhooked as the straps fell down my arms.

I automatically cupped my breasts, holding my bra in place.

Alec grinned as he gripped the fallen straps of my bra and tugged. He didn't say a word, he only looked into my eyes and they told me to trust him... so I did.

I let my hands fall to my sides and closed my eyes.

"Keela," Alec whispered.

I flushed with embarrassment. I was a B cup at best so I knew my chest was nothing to fawn over.

"I'm mortified right now," I said and resisted the urge to cover myself with my hands.

Alec didn't reply and that didn't help settle my suddenly upset stomach.

I was about to open my eyes and abandon the idea when suddenly I felt a breath on my chest. I opened my eyes and looked down just as Alec placed a kiss in the centre of my chest.

"You're perfect."

I opened my mouth and gasped when he moved his head and covered my right nipple with his hot mouth. I sucked my lower lip into my mouth, closed my eyes and tilted my head back.

"Oh my God," I breathed and arched my back as shivers shot up and down my spine.

I blinked my eyes open when Alec switched breasts and encased my left nipple in his mouth then used his hand to massage my right breast and tug on my nipple every few seconds.

I hunched myself forward because the sensation felt a lot like someone sucking on my sweet spot, it was so nice, but also felt like I was about to keel over. I couldn't take it.

Alec laughed after he released my nipple with a pop.

"You have sensitive nipples."

I looked at Alec through hooded eyes. "It would appear I do."

Alec dropped his smiled and brought his face close to mine. "You look like you want to take a bite out of me."

I snapped my teeth at him and said, "More than a bite."

Alec rubbed his lips together causing his dimples to dent his cheeks and without a thought I lifted my hands and trailed my index fingers over each dimple.

"I love these."

Alec smiled wide and his dimples deepened. "They're all yours."

I put my arms around his neck. "All mine. I like that."

Alec put his arms around my back and without warning he leaned backwards then turned to the side and rolled me under his body. He lifted some of his weight off me so I pushed myself into a straight position and shimmied up the bed until my head bumped into the headboard.

Alec followed.

He placed his hands on my knees and kept eye contact with me as he spread them wide. I felt my already hot body grow hotter with his intense gaze on me. The sensation of pins and needles, without the pain, spread down my legs as Alec ran his hand from my knees to my thighs.

"Your panties are green... my favourite colour."

Knickers.

I smiled. "Me bra was green too, to match my dress... you know, the one you *ripped off me like a caveman*."

Alec smirked then silently reached for the hem of my underwear. He tugged and ever so slowly pulled my knickers down my legs until they were free of my feet. Alec balled them up and threw them over his shoulder.

"Won't be needing those," he murmured.

I chuckled then froze when Alec stared directly at me... there.

"What the hell are you strain' at?" I asked, suddenly self-conscious.

Alec flicked his eyes up to me and said, "You're a natural redhead."

What?

"Yes, I'm a natural redhead. What does that have to do with- Omigod, don't tell me I forgot to shave!"

I instantly lifted my head to look down between my legs, I feel back in relief when I spotted the tiny strip of hair that I always leave. I never like going bald, I always leave a little strip.

"I like the strip of hair, it's different from what I usually see."

I gave Alec a look and he winced. "No talking about previous experiences - got it."

I smiled then tilted my head as Alec gazed at me.

"What?"

"I want to kiss you."

So kiss me.

I leaned my face up to his but he smiled, shook his head and pulled back.

What?

"I don't want to kiss you here," he pointed to my mouth. "I want to kiss you here."

I widened my eyes when he ran his fingertip down my stomach, passed by navel and stopped just above my slit.

"Oh, that's okay. I don't like that so you don't have to-"

"You don't like that?" Alec cut me off, his eyes wide. "Ex-fucking-cuse me? Did I or did I not tongue fuck you the other day till you came?"

I swallowed.

"Yes, but your mouth was never on my clit, your fingers were."

Alec frowned. "What's the difference?"

"Well, with a tongue it feels nice but hurts after a while so I'd rather you didn't-"

"Hold the fuck on. How does it hurt?"

I flushed. "Can we just forget about this and-"

"No we cannot. Explain how it hurts."

I was going to smack him if he cut me off one more time.

I huffed in annoyance. "I don't know, Jason was the only person to ever do it to me, it starts out feeling good then it gets really good then it hurts."

Alec sat back on his heels and frowned at me. "Does it hurt for long?"

I shook my head.

"No, it eases off after a few minutes."

Alec smiled. "That sounds like your orgasm built up but crashed when the final touch wasn't executed correctly."

I stared at him. "Are you sayin' that-"

"Jason can't eat pussy for shit." He laughed.

I frowned. "So if you-"

"Eat your pussy." Alec grinned.

I grunted. "Yeah, if you do that it won't hurt?"

Alec laughed. "No it won't, it will feel amazing. Enough talk, I'll let my tongue do the talking for me."

"Your tongue always does the talkin' for you, that's its function."

Alec rolled his eyes. "Ha, ha, ha."

I smugly smiled.

Alec sat up, moved down the bed then lay flat on his stomach.

I covered my face with my hands when Alec's face was at vagina level.

He just looked at it and licked his lips.

"Stop strain' at it, a clown isn't goin' to pop out and make balloon animals for you."

Alec laughed then went silent.

I bit down on my bottom lip when I felt a cold breeze spread over my clit. I wanted to close my legs but Alec wouldn't allow it.

"Don't be interrupting me, I like to take my time when I kiss."

I groaned. "You can't kiss me there!"

Alec chuckled. "A pussy wouldn't have lips if you weren't

meant to kiss them, kitten."

Oh.

"Are you ready?"

I uncovered my face and nodded my head.

"I'm ready, show me what you got, playboy."

"Yes, ma'am." He smiled then spread me with his fingers and placed his tongue directly on my clit.

I took deep breaths in through my nostrils and out through my mouth when his tongue began to swirl around.

Oh, yes!

"Ahhh," I groaned in delight when a little jolt of pleasure caused my lower half to twitch.

I opened my eyes and looked up at the ceiling then I bit down onto my lower lip when Alec lightly sucked on my clit.

"Oh, God!" I felt my clit began to pulse and each pulse triggered my pelvis to automatically buck into Alec's face.

I couldn't help it, my body did it involuntary.

I lifted my hands to my hair and pulled to try and give myself a different sensation to focus on because the throbbing and heat in my core was starting to become unbearable in the most delicious of ways.

"Oh... fuck..." I moaned when Alec suddenly shook his head from left to right giving my core an extra burst of heat.

I started to panic, this has never happened to me before. It was all too much to handle. Having my clit tongued felt good, but never *this* fucking good.

My breathing was now rapid, my forehead beaded sweat, my chest was rising and falling like it was no bodies business and the hotspot between my legs suddenly felt like it was on fire.

"Alec!" I cried out and pulled my lower half away from him but only for a moment.

He shot forward and took hold of my waist to keep me still.

"Just one more taste," he growled.

From my clit to my entrance he licked slowly, savouring me.

He dragged his hands from my waist and dug his fingertips into my hips when I tried to scramble away from his talented mouth. I gripped the bed sheets when he dipped his tongue inside my entrance. He swirled it around and caused the fire in the pit of my stomach to spread.

Oh my God!

His tongue withdrew from me and returned to my clit were he bore down and sucked. I bucked against his mouth and trashed my head from side to side.

"Yes, yes, yes," I begged then arch my back when my core exploded and wave after wave of pleasure flooded my body and touched every nerve ending.

I stayed in my arched up position for fifteen or so seconds then dropped when the waves of pleasure subsided and only little pulses of aftershocks remained.

"Oh... my... God," I breathed.

"You're welcome."

I placed my hand over my hammering heart. "Holy God in Heaven."

"Holy God in your hotel room you mean."

I raised my hand to my head and wiped the sweat off my face. "Jesus Christ."

"That's Mr. Christ to you, young lady."

"Holy Mary Mother of God," I whispered and closed my eyes.

"She's a good woman, makes a mean meat loaf."

I took few deep breaths, more than a few actually. I think it took me a couple of minutes to open my eyes. For a second I wondered if I had fallen asleep but when I lifted my head and found Alec still between my legs and smiling up at me that wonder went away.

"Did that hurt?"

The smug bastard knew it didn't.

"No, that was... incredible."

Alec kissed my lightly pulsing clit then crawled over to the spot beside me.

"You taste sweet."

I looked at Alec and blushed.

He laughed. "Don't get all shy on me now, little kitten."

I playfully rolled my eyes. "I'm not shy, but sayin' I taste sweet is-."

"Sexy."

I opened my mouth to say something different but Alec arched his brow and silently dared me to speak.

"Fine, I taste sweet and it's sexy."

"Damn fucking right."

I was caught by surprise when Alec leaned over and covered my mouth with his and forced his tongue into my mouth. I could taste myself on his lips and tongue, I didn't know what it tasted like but it didn't taste bad and that relaxed me.

I closed my eyes and groaned, then quickly lifted my arms to circle them around his neck, holding him tightly to me. Alec kissed me slowly and thoroughly, and when he pulled away I moaned in protest.

"Come back," I murmured.

Alec brushed his nose against mine. "You want another taste of yourself?"

"Hmmm."

Alec leaned down and sucked my lower lip into his mouth. He released it a second later.

"What did you call that orgasm I just gave you?"

I looked up at him with heavy eyes and said, "Incredible."

Alec grinned. "Yeah? Well I call it number one."

CHAPTER TWENTY-SIX

I stared up at Alec. "Number one?"

Alec grinned and nodded his head. "Judging from the look of you I'm going to aim for three... I think you would die from any more than that."

I don't care if he was teasing, I felt so exhausted that I wholeheartedly agreed with him. If one orgasm made me this tired, I can only imagine what a few more would do.

"Three is fine with me... but you should know I feel like I need a nap already."

Alec laughed. "You know that only carters to my ego, right?"

I shrugged, uncaringly. "I'll say somethin' later to knock your ego down a peg, don't worry."

Alec chuckled and lay on his side looking at me. It was in that moment that I realised he was fully clothed, whilst I was laying spread eagle on the bed... butt ass naked.

"You're wearing too many layers for my likin' Mr. Slater. Strip."

Alec smirked as he got to his knees and gripped the hem of his shirt.

"Wait, I want do it."

Alec froze then reached his hand down to me and with little effort pulled me up into a sitting position. I then got to my knees and turned to face him. I reached up and lightly pecked his lips with mine then looked down as I reached for the hem of his shirt. I gripped the hem in my hands and lifted.

"Your body is perfect... how do you maintain it?" I murmured as Alec helped me by shrugging out of his shirt when I lifted it high enough.

"Do you really want to know about my diet and exercise regime or do you want to touch me?"

Touch, I vote on touching.

"Touch you," I whispered then reached my hand out and traced his abs with my fingers from the top all the way down to his drool inducing V line.

"These are so sexy. I always want to lick them and follow the treasure trail."

I heard Alec's intake of breath.

"Feel free to lick any part of me, kitten."

I looked up at Alec and smiled. "Okay, lie down."

Alec turned and instantly fell down onto his back, it caused the whole bed to shake.

I laughed and threw my leg over his body, straddling him.

Alec placed his hands on my knees and ran them up to my thighs, he grinned up at me but frowned when his phone rang.

"I'm sorry," he sighed.

I glanced to my left and picked Alec's ringing phone up off the bedside locker.

"I'll deal with whoever it is."

Alec wasn't paying attention to me, he was too busy staring at my body.

I smirked as I tapped on the screen of the phone and placed it to my ear.

"Hello."

There was no sound.

I frowned and pulled the phone away to look down at it to make sure I didn't hang up. When I did, I screamed and dropped the phone when I found Kane Slater looking back at me with a smile stretched across his face.

"What?" Alec asked, panicked.

I pointed to the phone just as Kane hoarsely shouted,

"Dominic, come here!"

"What for?" Dominic voice replied.

"I saw Keela's tits!"

Alec's eyes flared as he grabbed his phone from the bed.

"I'm going to fuck you up, Kane!"

I heard Dominic laughing then, "Is your fever back? Are you hallucinating?"

"No, I'm not seeing things. I *really* saw Keela's tits."

Alec growled at the phone. "You're a dead man walking Kane!"

I heard muffled sounds from the phone then, "Fuck, you really saw them? I wanna see them! How come he gets to see them and I don't?"

Oh, my fucking God!

I had small boobs, they were *not* a pair you complain about wanting to see.

Trust me.

"You two are sick in the head!" I snapped.

I heard the brothers laugh then Kane said to Alec, "I clearly interrupted sexy time."

"Yes, you did. What did you even want?" Alec snapped.

"To ask you what the password is to your Netflix account. I'm sick and want to watch some movies."

Awe.

"Jesus, Kane! It's Britney Spears," Alec growled.

I covered my mouth when Kane and Dominic burst out laughing.

"Your password is Britney Spears?" I asked, snickering.

Alec rolled his eyes. "Yeah, she is hot and has a killer ass."

Laughter ceased from the phone. "That's true, her tits are perfect too... not as perfect as yours Keela."

I rolled my eyes.

Men.

"Is that all?" Alec asked.

"No, how do Keela's tits feel?"

"Fuck off!"

Alec pressed on the screen of his phone just as both Kane and Dominic shouted, "Balls deep, bro!"

I glared at Alec who turned off his phone and put it on the bedside locker.

"Your brothers are disgustin'."

Alec tried to hold back and smile and failed. "They are funny though."

I shook my head then squealed when Alec reached up and cupped my breasts. "I don't blame them for wanting to see these puppies though."

"I have small-"

"Small, but perfect. Big tits don't always mean a nice pair. I've seen some huge tits and trust me, I prefer the smaller ones."

He did?

"Oh," I murmured.

Alec grinned. "No more interruptions or talking, I remember you saying you wanted to suck my cock."

I raised my eyebrows. "I said that?"

Alec smirked. "Probably not but you thought it."

Cocky bastard.

I looked down to the buldge in Alec shorts and shimmied my way down until I was sitting on his knees. I didn't look at Alec as I reached for the hem of his shorts because I would have died of mortification. I've only done this a handful of times before and each time I stopped because I was afraid of swallowing when it came to the point of no return.

I blew out a breath and relaxed as I removed his shorts.

You can do this, it's Alec this time, you can do- Ohmigod, it's huge!

I sat back and stared down at Alec's goods.

"What the fuck? That is a forearm not a fucking cock!"

Alec laughed, I looked up as he put his hands behind his head.

"I told you it was my talent."

I rolled my eyes. "Yeah, and pleasin' the body is your skill set, I remember... But Jesus, Alec, I'm not tryin' to cater to your ego, you're huge. I think that would do some damage actually."

Alec widened his eyes and quickly sat up, this caused his erect cock to hug his abs.

I couldn't help but stare at it.

Alec placed his hands on the side of my face and lifted my head until I was looking at his.

"Trust me, you will be fine."

I swallowed. "Thats easy for you to say, you don't have somethin' that big goin' inside your body."

Alec nervously laughed. "Well, about that,-"

"I mean, *look* at it!

Alec sighed. "Let me tell you this, I have had-"

"Does that completely fit inside women?"

Alec opened his mouth to speak but closed it instead.

I frowned. "Sorry, I interrupted you, what were you goin' to say."

Alec stared at me for a moment then said, "It's nothing that can't wait, let's get back to my package."

I snorted. "Your extra-large package."

Alec snorted. "It's not that big, it probably just looks like it is because it's massive in comparison to Jason's cock."

I looked up and laughed. "Does it make you feel better that he is smaller than you?"

Alec only grinned back at me.

I looked back down at him and nodded my head. "Okay, I can do this... lie back."

Alec did so with a shit-eating grin on his face.

I could do this.

I lowered my head and when I came face to face with the monster I decided to make it my pet. I reached my hand up and wrapped my fingers around the head and squeezed a little.

Alec hissed. "Easy... it may be big, but it's sensitive."

Noted.

I licked my lips as I began to stroke up and down. I looked up at Alec and saw he was biting his lower lip as he watched me.

He was gorgeous.

I focused on what I was about to do, and flicked my tongue out swiping it over the head of Alec's cock. I did it twice more before I took the head in my mouth and lightly sucked.

"Damn, Keela."

I hummed in response and took more of him into my mouth. I went as far as I could until my gag reflex kicked in and I had to withdraw. I calmed myself and took Alec into my mouth as far as I could each time but not far enough to make me heave.

"Keela take me all the way in, you won't choke."

Yes I fucking would.

"Do it slowly baby, nice and slow."

No.

"Please?"

Fuck, fine.

I did as told and slowly took Alec into my mouth and when my gag reflex kicked in I stopped but didn't pull my head back.

"Good girl," Alec murmured. "Now take in the last bit."

The last bit was another inch or more!

I slowly pushed my head forward allowing more of Alec to fill my mouth, I couldn't try to fit anymore of him into my mouth because I really would choke and I wasn't doing that for anyone.

I was about to pull back when Alec said, "It's easy, baby. You hold your breath for a moment then bring my cock to the back of your throat, swallow and withdraw so you can breathe again, then you repeat."

What?

Seriously, *what?*

How the fuck did he expect me to hold my breath and swallow when I had his cock half way down my throat?

That was asking for a panic attack.

I placed my hands on Alec's thighs and scraped him with my

nails to get his attention.

He hissed a little but looked away from my mouth and to my eyes, he saw my panic and reached forward with his hands, brushing his thumb over my cheek.

"Nothing will happen to you, I promise. When you swallow your throat muscles will contract around me, that's all."

I'll take your word for it.

I tried to swallow but didn't put enough into it, the second time I held my breath and focused on swallowing properly which earned a loud groan from Alec.

"That's it, baby."

See, I knew I could do this.

I fell into a rhythm and pretty soon taking Alec fully in my mouth wasn't bad, I swallowed every third or fourth time instead of every time because I didn't want to become breathless and Alec who groaned each time seemed happy with that. I placed my hand on the base of his cock and worked it up and down in rhythm with my mouth.

"Yes," Alec moaned. "Suck harder, baby."

I sucked harder and worked faster, while I was pleased it was making Alec feel good I wished he would hurry up and come already because my arm was starting to cramp and my jaw ached.

"I'm going to come in your mouth baby, get ready."

Oh hell no.

I removed Alec from my mouth but continued to stroke him.

"I can't swallow," I said, looking up at Alec.

His face was twisted in pleasure.

"I thought you said were a good girl."

I looked up at him and glared. "I *am* a good girl!"

Alec smirked and reached forward as he fisted my hair in his hand then pushed my head back down to his cock as he said, "Good girls swallow, kitten."

"I don't know, I mean, what if makes me get sick-"

"Keela."

"And I puke all over you-"
"Keela."
"And you get mad-"
"Keela!"

I jumped with fright. "What?"

"Could you stop talking long enough to suck my cock?"

Was he for real?

I blinked. "Seriously?"

Alec nodded his head. "Is it a possibility that in the near future, and by near future I mean in the next thirty seconds, that mouth of yours will serve its purpose by wrapping itself around my cock? If not, I'm going to have to ask you to leave because you're giving me a headache."

What. The. Fuck?

"Are you jokin'?" I asked, shock laced my tone.

He *better* be joking or I would kill him.

Alec raised his eyebrows. "Does it look like I'm joking?"

If you kill him, you'll go to prison.

"You're lucky I'm horny, I'd slap the shite out of you otherwise."

Alec wasn't in the mood for joking around it seemed.

"Okay fine, I'll swallow!"

I widened my eyes when Alec suddenly thrust himself back into my mouth and buried his hands in my hair as he pumped his hips up into my face.

He was fucking my face.

Literally.

I moved my hands and placed them on the bed since the object I'd previously held onto was currently jackhammering in and out of my mouth. Alec didn't thrust far enough to make me uncomfortable, but he did it enough for him to spurt into my mouth.

My eyes crossed and shivers racked me as the salty taste of Alec spread over my tongue and dripped down the back of my throat.

Fuck all those porn stars who make swallowing come look like it's the most delicious thing they have ever tasted.

"Holy fuck!" Alec shouted.

He was still lightly pumping upwards into my mouth and when he fully withdrew I quickly swallowed and took some deep breaths in and out of my mouth.

"Oh my God," I whined, "that couldn't have been saltier."

Alec slowly laughed. "You will get used to it."

Will I now?

I wiped my mouth with the back of my hand and looked up at Alec who was lying spread eagle on the bed, and I smiled.

That was me ten minutes ago.

"Did I do okay?" I asked.

Alec opened his eyes and nodded my head. "Yeah, baby. You will be even better the next time because you will know how far you can take me."

I smiled, happy I did a good job.

"Come here to me."

I crawled up Alec's body feeling each hard muscle as I rubbed against him.

"Hi," Alec smiled when my face hovered over his.

I smiled back. "Hey."

Alec leaned his head up and flicked his tongue against my lower lip, after that he sucked my lip into him mouth and hummed.

When he released it he said, "It doesn't taste that bad."

Fuck.

He tasted himself on my mouth... that was *hot*.

"Can we have sex now?" I breathed.

I watched him in a trance as he reached down and picked up his shorts and took his wallet out from the pocket. He took a silver foil packet from it then used his teeth to rip the packet open. I licked my lips as he rolled the condom from the tip of his still hard cock to the base.

Alec grinned. "What way do you want it?"

Anyway that gets you inside me.

"Whatever way you want," I whispered.

Alec placed his hand on my back and slid them down to my behind.

"I like it kitty style."

I raised my eyebrows. "I know you're more experienced than me but what is kitty style? I've only ever heard of doggy style."

Alec grinned. "Kitty style is a lot like doggy style, only with scratching and biting."

Oh.

"You up for the job, kitten?"

I swallowed. "Yes."

Alec leaned up and kissed me long and deep before he sat up and lifted me off him.

"Turnaround," he growled.

A wave of need crashed into me as I turned and gave Alec my back.

"What are you goin' to do?" I asked as my heart pounded against my chest.

He fisted his hands into my hair and tugged making me hiss as he brought his mouth to my ear and whispered, "I'm about to fuck you like I hate you."

Oh, fuck!

He took one hand from my hair and brought it between my legs.

"After I'm done with you kitten, you will feel me here," he said as his fingers circled my entrance, "for days."

Oh.

"Are you ready?" Alec asked, his voice low and husky as he positioned himself behind me.

Was I?

"Yes," I whispered.

Instead of lining himself up, he slowly pushed forward allowing his cock rub and push up my slit and against my clit.

Oh, please.

I reached around and grabbed the first pillow I found and brought it to my face. I didn't have to beg out loud for him to get inside me because he lined himself up then gripped my hip, digging his fingers into my flesh.

"My cock has been craving this pussy from the moment I laid eyes on you," Alec hissed as he slowly slide inside me, inch by agonising inch.

I widened my eyes.

"You just came, *how* can you still be this hard already?"

Alec smirked. "I told you I had skills, rapid recovery is one of them."

Fuck!

I felt him stretch me, and it felt both foreign and incredible. I panted as he pressed me down to the mattress with his hands on my shoulders then pinned me that way so I couldn't move.

"Face in the pillow, I don't want anyone to hear you scream."

Oh.

"Now, Keela," Alec snarled and stilled.

I felt goose bumps break out all over my body at his command.

I quickly placed my face against the pillow, but not hard enough that it cut off my breathing.

"I can feel every part of you stretching around me, baby."

Me too.

I clenched my hands into fist when Alec's pressed forward with a little bit of a thrust.

"Almost there baby."

I jumped when his pelvis touched my behind.

Oh my God, he was buried in me to the hilt.

"I told you that you could take me... This pussy was made for me, kitten."

I groaned in response then gasped when Alec pulled out and slowly thrust back inside of me.

I took some deep breaths and slowly pressed back against Alec as he trusted forward. A shivered racked through my body and I moaned out loud.

Yes!

I clenched around Alec when another shiver shot up my spine. Alec groaned. "Fuck, do that again."

Do what?

Clench?

I did as told and clenched around Alec, he groaned again and thrust forward with more pressure this time and it made me gasp. I opened my eyes when his fingers moved from my shoulders and bit into the flesh around my hips.

"So." Thrust. "Fucking." Thrust. "Good!" Thrust.

I turned my head into the pillow and screamed as Alec switch from slow and steady to fast and furious. I gripped the sheets around me and held on for dear life.

"Yes, yes!" I shouted into the pillow.

I yelped when Alec's left hand left my hips and fisted my hair instead. He pulled my hair, which brought my head up from my pillow and caused my back to curve.

So hot!

"Keela... you feel amazing, kitten."

Alec's growl only heightened my pleasure.

I pushed back against him as hard as I could and he grunted and slapped my arse.

The unexpected sting caused me to scream, I quickly found my face shoved back down into the pillow not a second later.

"Your screams are *mine*, no one else's."

His, my screams were his.

"Me clit, touch me clit," I cried into the pillow.

Alec slowed his thrusts as he reached around and placed two fingers on my clit and rubbed. He face was by my ear, biting it as I leaned my head back for him.

"Fast or slow?" he whispered.

Fast.

Always fast.

"Fast!" I gasped then growled when the pace of Alec's fingers reached the one I yearned for.

I trashed under him, the faster he rubbed my clit and trusted into my body, the faster he brought me to the edge. I panted when I started to fall over it, the pulses in my clit came in rapid sessions and my hips automatically bucked back against Alec's pelvis.

My eyes crossed, I sucked my lower lip into my mouth and I bore down on Alec's fingers. I held my breath then cried out as my entire body flushed in ecstasy.

Yes!

Alec removed his fingers from my clit and slowed his pumping until I got my breath back.

"Oh my God," I whispered.

I closed my eyes and took in some deep relaxing breaths while my body came back online. My head felt light as I snuggled into my pillow. Everything felt perfect. Then Alec trusted forward as hard as he could earning a surprised gasp from me.

"I'm still here, kitten."

Holy crap, I could't stay awake!

"I can't move. I'm too tired, I-"

"We have to build up your stamina, kitten."

Yeah, we can do that after I wake up.

"Okay," I murmured.

Alec chuckled and gripped my hips pulling my body back into him. He then placed his hand on the top of my back and dragged his nails all the way from the top of my spine down to my arse and if that didn't hurt enough he leaned forward and bit my shoulder.

Kitty style.

I yelped and pushed up to all fours.

"Stay like that while I find it, baby."

Alec rotated his hips as he moved in and out of me, each movement caused me to shudder.

I hissed when Alec pulled of me completely then filled me with his fingers. It felt good, but I had no idea what the fuck he was doing.

"What are you doin'?" I asked

My body twitched when Alec's finger stroked a part of me that made my eyes cross.

"Omigod!"

"Found it," Alec whispered.

"Found what?" I shouted as he rubbed his finger over the sensitive spot again.

"Your g-spot."

I didn't even know he was looking for it.

"Keep doing that. Oh, God!"

Alec pulled his fingers out of me much to my displeasure.

He lay down on his back and patted his thighs when I looked at him.

"Get on top, you will feel each stroke better this way, I promise."

I trusted him as I slowly crawled on top of his body.

"You're gorgeous," I whispered as I looked down at my view.

Alec looked up at me as he had one hand on my hip and the other on his cock guiding it into my body. He bit down on his lower lip as I sunk down onto him. I groaned and tilted my head back.

Christ.

"That's it, kitten.... Now fuck me."

I straightened my head and gazed at Alec through my hooded eyes. I lifted my body up then plunged back down making his hard body twitch beneath mine.

"Fuck," he said then reached both of his arms back and gripped onto the top of the headboard.

I fell into a quick paced rhythm as I bounced on Alec. He was right, every pump of his cock inside me touched my g-spot. It was soul shattering good.

I was in heaven from the sensation but also lost in confusion.

The feeling in my core was different than the one I felt when I rubbed my clit - it felt amazing, but foreign.

"What are you doin' to me?" I groaned.

Alec began pumping upwards meeting me thrust for thrust.

"Don't hold back. I'm close, baby."

I reached forward and gripped onto Alec chest as I put all of my energy into bouncing on him harder and faster.

Much faster.

"Fuck, yes!" he growled.

I was blindsided by the sudden urge to urinate then completely taken back by the pulsing that racked through my body.

"Alec!" I screamed.

Alec growled as I stopped moving. He sat up and grabbed hold of my body then flipped us so I was under him and he was hovering over. He pounded away between my thighs and buried his face in my neck, latching his teeth onto my flesh.

My back was arched and my mouth was agape as a tsunami of pleasure rippled throughout my body. I was mildly aware of liquid squirting from me but I wasn't bothered by it and neither was Alec.

He gave three last hard pumps before he tensed and shuddered. His pelvis was still lightly, bucking against me. It was only for a few more moments until Alec withdrew from me completely.

He was relaxed.

So relaxed that he was crushing me.

"Can't breathe," I wheezed.

Alec chuckled and quickly rolled off my body and to the empty space beside me.

I mustered up enough strength to lift my head up and look down at myself.

"What are you looking for?" Alec asked, breathlessly.

I flushed. "I felt like I had to go the toilet, and I felt... you know... something' come out."

Alec glanced to me and chuckled at my facial expression.

"You came. Literally. You squirted, it's perfectly normal during a g-spot orgasm."

It was?

"Oh, okay," I whispered then leaned my head back.

Holy God.

I tried to swallow but found my mouth was too dry.

"Are you okay?" Alec asked me.

Was that a serious question?

"I've never felt this good in me entire life, but I'm so tired."

Alec laughed. "Close your eyes, kitten. Go asleep."

And you know what? I did just that.

I woke up some time later still naked, and still tired.

Alec was next to me, awake and playing on his phone. When he saw that I was awake and looking up at him, he put his phone down and smiled at me.

"Hello beautiful."

I smiled.

"Still tired?"

I nodded my head. "My body is the picture of relaxation."

Alec smirked. "You're welcome."

Dick.

I rolled my eyes but smiled.

Alec nudged me. "That was romantic, right?"

What?

"The sex."

The sex was romantic?

"Tellin' me you're goin' to fuck me like you hate me is *hot*, not romantic."

Alec frowned. "I thought it was sweet and romantic."
Really?
"You couldn't be sweet and romantic even if you tried." I stated.

Alec looked offended. "I can fucking too be sweet and romantic!"

I snorted. "Prove it!"

He raised an eyebrow and asked, "Right now?"

I nodded. "Right now."

Alec chewed on his bottom lip while he thought, and I found myself staring at his lip and the teeth that caged it. I died a little inside when I realised I was jealous of those teeth.

There was something wrong with me if his teeth could get me going.

Alec suddenly jumped and snapped his fingers to get my attention. "I've got a poem that will charm your panties off!"

Knickers, they are called KNICKERS!

I gave him an amused look. "Go on then Romeo, let's hear it."

He cleared his throat and said, "Roses are read, violets are blue; I'm using my hand, but I'm thinking of you."

I felt my jaw drop open.

I could do nothing but stare at him in total shock at what he said and at his logic for thinking it was sweet and romantic. Alec took my expression the wrong way and his ego expanded because of it. He stood up and stretched before looking back down at me. "Told you I could be sweet and romantic," he said smugly then strutted off into the bathroom like he was a runway model.

I watched him walk way and after he was gone from my line of sight I allowed myself to smile, a real smile. I chuckled then and shook my head, if he is the only person who can get a genuine smile and laugh out of me then I was well and truly fucked.

Five minutes passed by until Alec emerged from the bathroom with a towel wrapped around his lower half. There were beads of water all over his body but he was more concerned with drying his hair as he went to work on it with a towel.

Alec caught me looking at him and winked.

"Are you still in a romantic daze from my poem."

Oh, puh-lease.

"That 'poem' was not romantic. Honestly honey, you're about as romantic as a penguin."

Alec threw the towel he used to dry his hair at me, which I caught.

"If I were as romantic as a penguin, you would be head over heels in love with me."

I raised my eyebrows. "What are you talkin' about?"

"You compared me to a penguin by saying I'm not romantic, but penguins are extremely romantic animals."

I stared at Alec wondering if he hit his head whilst in the shower.

"You're such a weirdo."

Alec shook his head, his hair swaying from side to side as he did this.

"No, I'm serious. Penguins are romantic animals."

I folded my arms across my chest and arched an eyebrow. "Explain."

He cleared his throat and said, "Penguins only fall in love once and once they mate, it's for life. No cheating or divorce with these animals. When a male penguin falls in love with a lady penguin he will search the entire beach he lives on until he finds the perfect pebble to present to her. He will only give her the best because she deserves the best and he knows that. If people were like penguins, the world would be a completely different place. A better place."

I looked at him with wide eyes and murmured, "Where did you learn that?"

He shrugged and said, "The Natural Geographic Channel."

I swallowed. "You like that channel?"

He nodded. "Yeah, and the Discovery Channel and the History Channel... I like documentaries."

Holy shit.

The need to kiss him suddenly overwhelmed me, and I had to press myself back against the headboard of the bed.

"You're full of surprises, you know that?" I whispered.

Alec smiled. "Yes."

I looked away from him and rolled to my side so I could stand up from the bed. I don't know why, but I grabbed the small towel Alec threw at me and held it up in front of myself. It covered my breasts and privates, but the rest of my skin was still on show.

Alec tilted his head and folded his arms across his chest.

"Are you serious?"

I shrugged.

"I was inside you less than an hour ago, how can you be shy?"

I shrugged again.

Alec chuckled and lifted his hands and covered his eyes.

"Escape to the shower, I won't look."

Doubtful.

I walked forward and turned to my side as I slide by him, when I turned to enter the bathroom I yelped when a stinging slap was delivered to my behind. I swung in Alec's direction and glared.

He only grinned. "I said I wouldn't look, I never said I wouldn't spank."

I shook my head and hid a smile as I turned and entered the bathroom.

"I saw that smile which means you can't be mad at me."

I rolled my eyes.

That was male logic for you.

I reached into the shower and turned it on. It was already warmed up from Alec's shower so I stepped under the spray and stayed put until every inch of me was soaked with water.

I washed my hair twice, before I conditioned it. I washed my face and body with Alec's shower gel because it smelled awesome, then I proceeded to stand under the shower spray just because it felt nice. After a few minutes of standing under the spray I turned the shower off, squeezed the excess water from my hair with my hands then stepped out onto the bathroom tiles.

I picked up the only remaining towel from the towel rack and wrapped it around myself. I snuggled into it for a moment then used the towel to dry myself off. I towel dried my hair a little then wrapped the towel back around my body as I re-entered the bedroom.

I stopped and stared at Alec who was dressed in a blue tank top and navy knee length shorts. He had just finished blow drying his hair with his hair dryer.

Yeah, he had his own hair dryer.

"Why are you dressed?" I asked as I walked to the wardrobe and scanned for a t-shirt and shorts that I could wear to bed.

"Because we're going to the welcome party."

Excuse me?

I turned to face Alec who was now tying his hair back with a bobbin.

"We went to the welcome party."

"No, we went to the welcome *dinner*."

I frowned. "I thought you didn't want to be near Marco or me uncle."

Alec swallowed. "I don't."

"So then we can stay here-"

"No," Alec snapped.

I jumped with fright.

Alec sighed and walked over to me placing his hands on my shoulders. "I'm sorry, I didn't mean to snap... I don't want to go to the party, but I *do* want you to be included in everything."

I smiled. "Alec, I hardly get on with me family, it's really okay."

"No, we will have fun. I promise."

Why was he pushing this so much?

"Are you sure?" I asked.

Alec relaxed his shoulders and said, "Yes, of course."

Something wasn't right about this.

"Okay then, let me get dressed," I murmured.

I turned and began looking through the wardrobe. I grabbed a teal dress that I tried on earlier and liked. I got a bra and some knickers then headed into the bathroom. I sighed when I realised that I had to dry my hair, I really didn't want to go through all that again after it took me forever to get ready for the dinner.

I groaned in annoyance.

"What's wrong?"

I looked to my left when the bathroom door opened.

"I don't wanna dry me hair... I'm tired."

Alec laughed. "So braid it."

I rolled my eyes. "I can't do a French plait on meself, only on other people."

Alec shrugged his shoulders. "So I'll braid it for you."

I looked at him with raised eyebrows. "You know how?"

Alec grinned. "When you're around Bronagh and Branna long enough they make you learn these things... Besides, I like playing with other people's hair."

"Yeah, but only when you're tired."

Alec waggled his eyebrows. "I *am* tired."

I turned away and smiled.

"I know you're smiling when you turn away like that, stop trying to hide it," Alec laughed.

I continued to smile as I brushed my hair out, applied my strawberry body lotion and got dressed. I towel dried my hair until it was only damp then I sprayed some summer fruit mix onto my hair to give it a nice smell.

I headed back into the room with a skinny white bobbin in my hand and sat on the floor in front of Alec who was sat on the side of the bed.

"Do you have a comb?" he asked.

I shook my head.

"It's cool, I'll use mine."

He leaned over and grabbed his hair comb then carefully

brushed my hair out with it.

"One braid or two?"

"One, please."

He then went to work on putting a French plait in my hair, and for the most part it went pretty smoothly until he got to the hair at the back of my neck.

"Ow, Alec!"

"I'm sorry, but it has to be tight."

He tugged my hair and again I yelped, "Ow!"

He sighed. "Nearly done you big baby."

I folded my arms across my chest.

I'll big baby you, you big bastard.

"*Voila.* All done."

I reached up and placed my hand on my head, the hair was in a very tight French plait, not a single hair hung loose. I got up and went into the bathroom to check it out.

"Wow, nice job."

"You're welcome," Alec called from the bedroom.

I smiled and got to work on my make-up. I didn't want to wear foundation because I wanted to let my skin breathe since I got slightly sun burned from the past few days of exposure to the sun.

I simply put on some mascara, filled in my eyebrows with brow power, and applied some lip gloss. I debated on whether to add more to my face when I leaned into the mirror.

I had a patch of light freckles sprinkled over my nose, and under my eyes.

Should I cover them?

"Damn it," I muttered and went back into the bedroom.

Alec was playing on his phone whilst he was lying down on the bed.

"Do I need to put on foundation or powder?" I asked him.

He looked up at me and shook his head. "No, you look beautiful."

My stomach burst into butterflies at his unexpected

compliment.

"Oh, thank you."

Alec smiled. "Why do you ask anyway?"

I leaned down and pointed to my nose. "I have freckles on me nose and under me eyes from the bloody sun."

Alec put his phone down and took my face in his hands then kissed my nose and my now closed eyes.

"I like them, don't cover them up."

"Okay," I murmured as my face flushed.

"Are you ready to go?"

I sighed, pulled back then went and slipped on a black pair of heels.

"Yep, I'm good to go."

Alec stood up and looked down at me, making a point of showing me he was still taller than me.

"Can you walk in those things?" he asked.

I looked down at my feet then back up to Alec's face.

"We shall see."

CHAPTER TWENTY-SEVEN

"I *cannot* walk in these fuckin' things!" I snapped as I grabbed onto Alec's arm to steady myself for the third time since we left the hotel room.

Alec laughed as he slowed his pace to match my own.

"Do you want go back up and put your flat shoes on?" he asked.

I would never admit defeat!

I shook my head. "No, I'll be fine."

Alec snorted. "Just hold onto me."

The problem was going to be letting go of him.

Alec and myself entered the ballroom where dinner was served earlier, and I instantly spotted my family at the bar.

"Typical," I muttered.

"What's typical?" Alec asked as I gripped his arm and steered us towards the bar.

"That is where me family always end up at functions."

Alec laughed. "You're all Irish, I expect nothing less."

I rolled my eyes but said nothing.

"Keela!"

I plastered a smile across my face when Everly's plastic face came into view.

"Stay next to me, Everly will talk the ears off you about herself otherwise."

Alec said nothing, he only nodded.

"Darlin', you look adorable."

I looked adorable?

Fuck you too, lady.

"Thanks Everly, you look cute."

Everly cast me a cold stare before she flicked her eyes to Alec and smirked.

She actually smirked.

"And who is this handsome devil?"

Here we go.

"This is Alec Slater, me boyfriend. Alec, this is me Auntie Everly."

Evil stepauntie.

Everly held her hand out to Alec and he took it in his and brought her hand to his mouth and kissed it.

What the fuck was that about?

"Everly," he murmured. "Nice to meet you."

"And you Mr. Slater," she said keeping eye contact with him - she never once blinked.

Alec lowered her hand then released it. "Please, call me Alec."

Everly smiled. "Alec."

I stared between Alec and Everly and felt like they knew something I didn't.

"Can I get you both a drink?" Everly asked us, snapping out of her staring competition with Alec.

I removed my hands from Alec's arm with a pull.

I was suddenly mad at him and I had no idea why.

"No, I'm can get me own but you can get Alec one. He might enjoy that."

I walked forward then to the bar and got the bartender's attention.

"Vodka and coke, please."

I felt a hand on my lower back and then a breath by my ear a few moments later.

"What was that?"

I turned to Alec who was very close to me.

"You tell me."

Alec frowned. "I don't understand."

I did, it just hit me.

"You flirted with me auntie, right in front of me."

Alec blinked then laughed.

His laughing pissed me off.

"Go fuck yourself!" I growled and turned my back to him.

Where the hell was my drink?

Alec was still laughing when he slid his arms around my waist and leaned his head down to rest his chin on my shoulder.

"I was being polite, I wasn't flirting."

Whatever.

"You kissed her hand and looked at her like your adored her or somethin'."

Alec was silent for a moment then his kissed my cheek. "I adore you, no one else."

I snorted. "Yeah right."

Alec pressed his groin into my behind and I hissed.

I was tender and the bastard knew that.

"I adore *you* kitten, trust me on that."

I didn't reply, but I did perk up when the bartender suddenly appeared in front of me. I happily took the drink and ordered another one - it was an open bar after all.

"Keela," Alec murmured.

I turned to him and looked up. "Yes."

"Don't get drunk out of spite, if you're annoyed at me let's talk it out."

I laughed. "It's very big headed of you to think I would get drunk just because you annoyed me."

Alec grinned down at me. "You annoyed yourself by thinking I flirted with your aunt when I didn't."

Dickhead.

"I may not be an expert like you when it comes to sex, but I know flirtin' when I see it."

Alec sighed. "We've only been here five minutes and you're already arguing with me."

"Because you're bein' a dickhead."

"I didn't do anything."

"Keep tellin' yourself that buddy."

"Okay fine, I'm sorry for whatever I did to upset you."

I narrowed my eyes. "So you admit you did somethin'?"

"Keela! What do you want from me? I say one thing and you get pissed. I try to fix it and you get even more pissed. You're so damn confusing - you should come with a fucking instruction manual!" Alec bellowed.

I snorted. "At what point in time would you ever read an instruction manual?"

He looked like he wanted to strangle me. He took a deep breath and looked away from me then up to the ceiling.

"God, give me strength."

I turned my head and made a move to walk off but Alec wouldn't let me.

"Where are you going?"

"To congratulate the groom." Alec's eyes narrowed and his face turned to stone.

Why did I say that?

"Keela do *not* threaten me, it will not work out in your favour. Do you understand me?"

I looked down.

What I said was a dickhead move and I knew it.

"Say you understand or things will get bad between us fast."

Shite.

"I understand."

"Good, I'm not a fucking tool. Don't ever try and make me jealous with another guy because it will only hurt you in the end."

What the fuck did that mean?

"How would it hurt me?"

Alec looked me dead in the end. "Because I don't stick around for bullshit like that to be thrown in my face."

"Got it," I mumbled.

Alec lowered his head to mine and kissed my lips. "Stop this. We had an amazing day today, please don't ruin it by arguing."

I looked up and nodded my head.

He was right.

Alec smiled and kissed my lips once more.

We both turned as my Uncle Brandon came over to us, Everly next to him.

"I told you she was here."

My uncle smiled. "I wasn't sure you would come back down."

I shrugged. "I wasn't goin' to, but Alec convinced me."

"Did he now?"

Things got a little tense then as my uncle and Alec stared at one another.

I didn't like the tension so I snapped, "You both need to cut the bullshit and pretend to be nice to each other. It will make these encounters a lot fuckin' easier."

"Keela!" Everly snapped.

"What?"

"You're a lady, you shouldn't curse," she said in a snotty tone.

I smiled. "You're a prude and you should mind your own business."

Everly glared at me. "I'm not a prude and just because I don't like putting curse words in every sentence doesn't make me one!"

"You are a prude if any curse word bothers you, and do you want to know why? Because they are exactly that, just words. For example, 'fuck' isn't a bad word and the only reason it is considered a bad word is because society has branded it as one. I could call you a flower and mean it in the meanest possible way, and it will have the same effect as a 'bad word' because I am putting an emotion behind it."

"You're stupid."

I shrugged. "You're a cunt."

Alec face palmed himself while my uncle set his jaw.

"Keela Daley," he growled.

"Don't say my name like that, I'm twenty-three years of age. I not a bloody child and I'm not *her* child, so tell her not to chastise me."

"You two and Micah will be the bleedin' death of me."

I sighed but I didn't apologise.

"Let's go greet more people, we still have so many to get around to."

Uncle Brandon narrowed his eyes at me. "We will continue this another time."

"Can't wait."

He sighed as Everly led him away.

"Fuckin' bitch, I can't stand her."

Alec didn't say a word as he took my hand then led me to the dance floor. When I realised what he had planned I widened my eyes and tried to pull back.

"I can't dance."

"Everyone can dance," Alec smiled.

I shook my head. "I mean I can't dance with another person. I've never danced with someone else... I'll step on you or somethin'."

Alec turned to me and smiled as he held out his hand.

"Give your first dance to me, kitten."

I looked up at him, hesitant to place my palm in his.

He smiled at me. "I promise I'll be gentle with you."

Oh damn.

How could I refuse that?

"I'm goin' to make a holy show of meself."

Alec laughed. "You won't, I've got you."

A fast song was playing but as soon as we stepped on the dance floor "Rude" by Magic! came on and Alec grinned.

"Reggae. Nice. We can slow grind."

What the fuck did that mean?

"I don't know how to slow grind."

Alec smirked. "It will be my pleasure to show you, Miss Daley."

I couldn't help but snort, he sounded like a Sir I've read about in books.

I moved close to Alec then raised my eyebrows when he turned my back to him and pulled my body back against his. He put his mouth my by ear and said, "Look at that couple."

I looked to the couple he was talking about and widened my eyes at the girl who was grinding her arse into a fella's groin, but did it while dancing in front of him.

"You think I can move like that?"

"I know you can."

He had more faith in me than I did.

"Okay, sure."

Alec laughed and placed his hands on my hips and ever so slightly rolled his pelvis into my behind. I placed my hands on Alec's and copied what the girl in front of me was doing. No one stopped and stared because everyone was doing their own thing on the dance floor and I quickly fell into a comfortable rhythm.

I smiled when Alec sang in my ear the chorus of the song.

"Why you gotta be so rude, don't you know I human too?

What you gotta be so rude? I'm gonna marry *you* anyway."

I laughed when he changed the word 'her' to 'you'.

I closed my eyes and leaned my head back against Alec's chest as he sang in my ear. His voice was so relaxing that if he wasn't careful, I would fall asleep standing up.

He seemed to sense this because he took hold of my right hand and spun me out away from his body then pulled me back to him so the front of my body was pressed against his as we danced swaying side to side. I laughed up at him as he continued to sing the song without a care in the world.

He grabbed my hand to spin me out again, but this time it didn't go as smoothly because I stumbled a little in my heels and crashed into a man's back.

Fuck.

"I'm so sorry!" I squeaked and grabbed onto the man's arm just in case I knocked him over.

Luckily the man didn't fall, he actually turned around and laughed down at me.

I stopped myself from letting my jaw drop, not only was this man taller than me, but he was also gorgeous... *extremely* gorgeous.

"It's fine beautiful girl, are you okay?" he asked.

He was another American, but instead of focusing on his accent, I focused on what he just said.

Beautiful girl?

I felt my cheeks flush. "Yes, I'm fine. Thank you."

The man smiled and stuck his hand out. "I'm Dante Evans."

I swallowed and slowly placed my hand in Dante's. "Keela Daley."

His eyes lit up. "Ah, so you're the infamous Keela Daley."

Infamous?

"Why infamous?" I asked.

The man brought my hand to his mouth and kissed my knuckles before he replied, "You are apparently the reason why my boy isn't in the game anymore."

What is he talking about?

I pulled my hand back from Dante and took a step back only to knock into another person. I was about to say sorry until I felt hands slide around my hips holding me in place.

Dante looked to the hands then looked up over my head and smiled.

"Speak of the devil."

What was going on here?

I tilted my head back and looked to Alec. "You know this man?" I asked.

He nodded his head and without looking away from Dante he said, "He is an old... colleague."

From his escort days?

I looked back to Dante as he chuckled, "An old colleague... is that all I am to you?"

Alec's fingers dug into my hips as he snarled, "Don't."

I looked to Dante as an evil smirk appeared on his face. "Oh, this is interesting... she doesn't know?"

I frowned. "Know what?" I asked Dante.

Alec suddenly moved and pulled me behind him. "I'll kill you."

Dante laughed. "For telling your girl who you really are? Why haven't you told her? Are you ashamed?"

I could feel the anger radiate from Alec.

"I'm not ashamed."

"Then why not tell her?"

"Because I just met her a few days ago and we hit it off really fucking well. It's not something you spring upon a partner."

What the fuck were they talking about?

I moved from behind Alec and got back in front of him. I fisted his t-shirt in my hand and pulled to get his attention.

"What is goin' on? What are you keepin' from me?"

Alec looked nervous, very nervous.

Dante laughed from behind us. "Go ahead Alec tell her, and while you're at it tell her who I am to you."

"Was," Alec snarled.

"Fine, tell her who I *was* to you."

"Somebody better tell me somethin' because I'm gettin' mad."

Alec looked down to me and sighed. "I'm sorry to do this here, I tried to tell you earlier," he said as he lowered his voice, "Before we had sex but you wouldn't listen."

I swallowed. "You don't have an STD do you?"

We used a condom, but I still had his junk in my mouth without one!

Alec frowned at me while Dante laughed behind me.

"No, I don't."

Thank God.

"Then what do you have to tell me? Who is Dante?"

Alec licked his lips and said, "Dante used to be my partner on jobs."

"How so?"

Alec sighed. "Can we go upstairs and talk?"

"No, I want to talk here."

"Okay, fine," he murmured but took my hand and lead me from the dance floor and to the side of the room.

"Dante and I... we used to be involved."

"I don't understand, how were you involv-"

I cut myself off and widened my eyes when realisation hit me and I took a step back. Alec began to look distressed so he took a step forward and held me close to him.

"Please don't think differently of me. Please Keela."

I was so confused.

"Alec, are you gay?"

CHAPTER TWENTY-EIGHT

"What? No I'm not gay, why would I be with you if I was gay?"

I frowned. "You could be pretendin'."

"Keela, I'm not pretending with you. I swear I'm not."

I nodded my head. "So if you're not gay then what are you?"

Alec looked at me and said, "I'm bisexual."

Oh, God.

He liked the V *and* the D.

Now all those random sayings from his brothers about him being a bum boy and his job having variety, and his expert knowledge on giving head made sense!

"That's just greedy," I muttered.

Alec stared at me for a moment then laughed, he full on laughed. Hard.

"You have a gift, you can turn the most tense conversation into the funniest."

I lightly smiled. "I'm blessed."

Alec chuckled then kissed my forehead. "You aren't disgusted by me then?"

I gasped. "Disgusted because you like men and women? No, of course not. Is that why you didn't tell me, because you were worried I'd look at you differently?"

Alec shrugged. "When we met you didn't lead with telling me you were straight, so I didn't lead with telling you I'm bisexual. It shouldn't matter."

"It doesn't matter."

Alec smiled. "I'm glad you feel that way... Most people aren't so accepting but I'm going to be criticised for whatever I do, or whoever I do, so why should I give a shit? I am content and happy with who I am. No one else's opinion matters."

He was dead right.

"I don't care that you're bi... but I am worried."

Alec frowned. "Why?"

I hesitated.

"Kitten, why are you worried?"

Just spit it out!

"Do you go through a phase of which gender you prefer to be with more? What if you're in the vagina stage now, but the dick stage tomorrow and want a lad instead of me?"

Alec burst out laughing which I thought was rude.

"I'm serious."

Alec laughed harder.

"Alec!" I snapped and punched his arm.

He didn't flinch from my hit, but he did calm himself down enough to speak.

"Baby, I'm with you because I like you. Sure I'll think other men and women are attractive, but that doesn't mean I'm about to up and leave you for them. I mean, if you think some other guy was attractive would you leave me just to take a tumble with them?"

I shook my head. "No."

"Exactly, it works both ways. Even with bisexual people."

I nodded my head then shoved him when he smiled.

"Stop teasin' me, I didn't know."

Alec leaned his head down to mine and kissed my lips.

"You're ador-"

"I'll break you if you finish that sentence."

Alec laughed and kissed my mouth hard.

I pulled back from him and randomly asked, "How do you decide which gender you like in the moment? Do you flip a coin or somethin'?"

Alec snickered. "No, I just go to whoever I am attracted to the most."

"How do you decide though?"

"I do what the voices in my underwear tell me to do."

Wait, what?

"You mean the voices in your head?"

Alec smirked. "Yeah, the voices in my head."

I furrowed my eyebrows together and stared at him.

Why was he smirking at me?

He was confusing me.

Wait.

Voices in his underwear.

In his head.

The head in his underwear.

I gasped. "You dirty bastard!"

Alec burst out laughing and tried to kiss me again but I held off.

"Why are you kissin' me so much, perv?"

"Because you're perfect."

I rolled my eyes.

His standards for perfection were shockingly low.

"Okay, now that I know your sexuality has variety tell me about your variety, specifically Dante Evans."

Alec growled. "I don't want to talk about him."

Oh, he would talk.

"He is here and seems to think you're no longer an escort because of me so get to talkin'."

Alec grunted. "I used to double team certain clients with Dante... and sometimes when we were on our own, I would fuck him."

I swallowed.

"Was he your boyfriend?"

Alec shook his head. "No, I told you that you were my first-"

"First girlfriend, not first partner."

Alec grinned. "You're a smart little cookie, but either way, you're my first *partner*. Dante was - and I mean this - just a way to pass the time when my dick got hard."

I gasped. "Alec! That's not nice."

Alec chuckled. "Sorry, mom."

I shoved him. "I'm serious, you can't use people like that."

"He used me as much as I used him, baby."

I widened my eyes when a thought entered my head.

"Did he... um..."

"Did he what?" Alec asked curiously.

I flushed. "Nothin', never mind."

Alec's face was the picture of amusement.

"No, tell me."

"Fine," I muttered. "Did he ever fuck you?"

Alec raised his eyebrows. "No, I only ever fucked him. I'm a batter, not a catcher."

"Oh, I see."

I swallowed nervously then.

"Does that mean you will want to do that to me? Because I've never done that before, but I'll try it for you if you want."

Alec's face softened. "You know most girls would freak out or be jealous when their boyfriend reveals he is bisexual. You worry about if I want to fuck your ass or not, and tell me you'll try it if I want to."

He looked over every inch of my face.

"God, I'm a lucky bastard."

He took my face tightly in my hand and covered my mouth with his. I placed my hands on his biceps and squeezed them as I kissed him back. I got lost in his kiss, my mind clouding over with need for him.

I could kiss him forever.

"Get a room."

I jumped and pulled away from Alec only to spot a grinning Dante standing next to us.

Some privacy maybe?

"Go away, Dante."

Dante smiled to Alec. "That's no way to treat an old friend."

"Friend?" Alec growled. "We were *never* friends."

Dante sighed. "Are you mad because I'm here on a job or that you're aren't on the job with me?"

Say what?

"I'm giving you ten seconds to walk away," Alec growled.

"He's givin' you ten, but I'm givin' you five. Get lost or I'll put me foot up your arse."

It took me a second to realise what I said and who I said it to.

"And it'll be a studded boot I wear so it won't feel good," I clarified.

Dante burst out laughing and even Alec tried to hide a smile but failed.

"I see why you like her. Long legs and a smart mouth, you must be in Heaven."

Alec put his arm around me. "I am, now leave."

Dante grinned. "Until tomorrow."

Until tomorrow?

He turned and left so I turned to face Alec and asked, "What's tomorrow?"

Alec swallowed then shrugged. "Probably another dinner or party he will hound us at."

I chuckled. "I'll wear studded boots to keep him at bay."

Alec laughed then looked to our left when our names were called.

It was Everly waving us over to a large table.

"Damn," I muttered.

Alec nudged me forward until I started walking. "It won't be that bad."

You have no idea.

At the table was Everly, Micah, Krista, Koda, the Brennan sisters and their mother, Mrs. Bane, and a few other girls whom I've never met.

Alec was the only male.

I know everyone has met him but I didn't know what to say so I introduced him again.

"Everyone this is Alec, Alec this is everyone."

"Hey," he smiled.

"Heeeeey Alec," everyone chorused, smiling wide at Alec.

Was I invisible?

I sighed and nudged Alec to sit down on the only spare seat, I sat on his lap and wanted to smile when all the women at the table glared.

Even the married ones.

"So Alec, do you have any brothers?" Kerry Brennan asked.

Alec looked to her and nodded. "Four."

"Do they look like you?" Clare Brennan asked.

Alec chuckled. "The twins probably look like me the most."

"*Twins?*" multiple voices echoed.

Alec nodded his head then got his phone out and tapped on the screen a few times and turned it around.

"This is all of us when we were all together about two and a half years ago."

Jaws dropped.

I muttered to Alec, "You would think you were all good lookin' with how they are carryin' on."

Alec pinched my thigh. "Bitch."

I chuckled then looked to Micah who was examining her nails.

"Are there any planned parties or anything for tomorrow?"

Micah looked up to me and nodded. "Just another party tomorrow night."

I nodded my head and glanced to the bar, I wanted another drink so I stood up.

"Do you want a drink?" I asked Alec.

He shook his head.

I shrugged, I'd just get myself two drinks then.

I turned and walked in the direction of the bar. When I got there I had to wait for the bartenders to finishing serving people. I got a barman's attention, and he got me two vodka and cokes.

With my drinks in hand I turned and walked back to the table Alec was at. I raised my eyebrows when I got back to the table and heard the girls talking.

"I want a *good* man, how do you suggest I get one?" Krista frowned.

What the hell were they talking about?

"If you want a man, and not this perfect image of a man you have in your head, then you have to lower your standards." Alec shrugged.

Krista frowned. "How do I lower my standards?"

Alec grinned. "Tequila."

I laughed while everyone took Alec's advice literally and fled from the table to the bar to order shots of tequila.

I looked at Alec as I sat next to him.

"You have probably just got half the males in here laid tonight."

Alec smirked. "Just doing my part to help my fellow man."

I laughed and moved my chair closer to his and he draped his arm over the back of my chair then smiled when I turned to face him.

"Why do you look excited?"

I beamed. "Because I want to ask you a question."

"Shoot."

"If you could sleep with any man in the world, who would it be?"

Alec stared at me before he allowed a huge smile to take over his face. "Why are you excited to ask me that?"

I shrugged. "To see if we have the same taste in men."

Alec laughed, shook his head then chewed on his lower lip as he thought on my question.

"Jamie Dornan."

I gasped and smacked his shoulder. "Oh my God. I'd shag him

too! Nice bloody choice."

Alec looked like he was about to burst into laughter, but he kept it under control.

"What about you?" he asked me.

I placed my elbow on the table and my chin in my hand as I thought.

"Hard question?" Alec grinned.

"There are just a lot of fit famous men that I'd like to buck." Alec laughed.

I snapped my fingers. "Matt Bomber, but then that's kind of weird because Ryder is the spitting image of him."

Alec scrunched his face up in disgust. "What the hell, Keela? You have just ruined Matt Bomber for me!"

I burst into a fit of giggles.

"My bad."

Alec shook his head then smirked. "If you could have sex with any *female* in the world who would it be?"

I tilted my head and smiled. "You're wrong if you think this creeps me out. Me and Aideen have a to-do list of famous women who we would buck if we got the chance."

Alec's eyes widened. "A *to-do list*?"

I smirked.

"Name some," Alec murmured.

I cleared my throated. "Emma Watson, Mila Kunis, Jennifer Aniston, Jessica Alba, Miranda Kerr, Emma Stone, Alyssa Milano, Jennifer Lawrence, Scarlett Johnson, Keely Cuoco, Sophia Bush-"

"I said name some!" Alec laughed.

I shrugged.

"Are you sure you're straight? Because that's a hell of a fucking list."

I laughed at Alec's dark expression then squealed when he reached for me and pulled me onto his lap.

"I want to fuck you so bad right now," Alec growled into my ear.

I pulled backed from him. "Because I listed some famous people I would buck?"

"I got an image in my head of you rolling around with another woman and it has me hard as fuck."

I wiggled my arse over Alec's bulge making him squeeze my hips to the point of pain.

I laughed and picked up one of my vodkas and coke, downing it in a few gulps.

I turned back to Alec and said, "If I get drunk enough tonight that might just happen."

"Really?" Alec asked, wide eyed.

I nodded. "If it would make you happy then yes, it would."

Alec swallowed as he leaned down and brushed his nose against mine.

"Thanks baby, but I won't be sharing you with another man or woman. You're mine and I don't share. Ever."

My pulse spiked.

"I like that," I murmured then leaned my head down to his and kissed him lightly.

I jumped when a flash went off on my right.

I looked to an apologetic photographer who shrugged and said, "Sorry."

He turned and trotted off snapping pictures of other people along the way.

"Who do I talk to about getting a copy of that?"

I snorted. "Probably me auntie... Where is she anyway?"

Alec shrugged. "She went off somewhere with Jason's mother and the other woman when you went to the bar."

I reached for my third drink, or was it my fourth?

I shrugged to myself and picked it up either way and took a gulp of the yummy tasting liquid.

"I think you should take a break from drinking."

I laughed.

"I'm serious."

I laughed again.

"Can you ever do what you're told?" Alec snapped.

I laughed so hard I almost farted.

"I'm not obedient so... no," I giggled.

"This is wrong."

I looked to a distraught Alec and asked, "What is wrong?"

"God promised men that obedient women would be found on all corners of the Earth. I've been all over the Earth, and I call bullshit on that!" Alec snapped as he glared directly at me.

I snorted. "I hate to burst your bubble, but God also made the Earth round, he's got jokes."

Alec paused and glanced and me then to the sky. "Well played man, well played."

I laughed again then hiccupped.

I squealed when the beat to "The Best" by Tina Turner began to play.

"Oh my God! I *love* this song!"

I got up and made a beeline for the dance floor without Alec and almost broke my neck in the process thanks to my damn heels.

"You're simply the best!" I screamed and shimmied my way around the dance floor.

I looked to Alec who was smiling wide as he pointed his phone in my direction. I didn't care and continued to dance on my own. I squealed when Micah's face appeared in front of mine. She too was singing the song and jumping around so I joined her and found it hilarious. I forgot that I couldn't stand her and grabbed her hand as we twirled around and bumped into people.

I glanced to my left when a flash went off and I noticed my Uncle Brandon was instructing the photographer by pointing at myself and Micah.

He looked so happy.

I pulled her close to me and through my dizziness I focused on her face.

"I don't like Jason and I don't like that you're marryin' him but we're family, we have to get on better Mi."

Micah's eyes glassed over and she pulled me into a hug.

"I love you."

I hugged her back. "I love you too, Mi. You drive me mad but I do love you."

We both wiped our eyes and laughed as we continued to dance around. We both sang our hearts out and danced around like fools when "Gangnam Style" blared throughout the ballroom. Mid-way through the song I had to stop because I was tired, I looked for Alec but he wasn't at our table.

He wasn't anywhere to be seen.

"I'm gonna go find Alec!" I shouted to Micah who nodded her head and continued to dance around.

I manoeuvred my way around people who were dancing until I was free from the dance floor. I slightly stumbled my way in the direction of the table I was sat at before I got up to dance. I came to the conclusion that I was drunk when I sat down and giggled to myself.

I don't know how long I was sat down my own, but I drank four of the drinks that were sat on that table and they only caused my head to spin faster than it already was. I eventually put my arms on the table then rested my head on my arms.

"Keela, come with me."

I blinked my eyes open and frowned.

I knew that voice and I knew I didn't like it.

I closed my eyes. "Go away."

"Come on, gorgeous girl-"

"What the fuck did I tell you? Leave her alone you piece of shit. You're trying to pick up girls at your own wedding? Have you no shame?"

I heard a chuckle. "I'm in an *open* relationship with me soon to be wife, she is cool with it... I don't know what shame is man."

I heard a grunt then a gasping sound.

"You b-bastard."

"I did that discreetly, but if you want a more public ass kicking, just let me know."

More gasping.

"Fine, k-keep her."

"I fucking intend to."

Silence.

"Kitten, you're a lightweight."

I smiled. "Alec."

"I'm here."

I felt myself being moved, and then suddenly I was lying on a hard body.

"I want to have sex with you... again," I giggled.

Alec's body lightly vibrated as he chuckled.

"I better get you up to bed."

I purred, "Yes, please."

Alec laughed as he stood and lifted me into the air. There was a lot of noise for the next few minutes then a sudden silence.

"Am I dead?" I asked.

"No, you're in an elevator."

"You're afraid of lifts."

Alec sighed. "I know, but I'm not carrying you up four flights of stairs."

I laughed and I don't know why.

I heard a pinging sound then we were moving again.

"I can walk... see."

I made my legs walk.

"What are you doing?"

"Vertical walkin'."

Alec laughed. "Pitch Perfect?"

"Amazin' film."

Alec mumbled to himself as he struggled to open our hotel room door, but he eventually got it open. He walked inside and lay me down on our bed when he was close enough to do so. I felt my heels slipping off my feet and it caused me to groan in delight.

"Throw them devil objects in the bin!"
"No, you might hurt me tomorrow."
"The bin I say. Do what you're told, peasant."
I said all this with my eyes closed as I lay on the bed.
"Yes, Queen Keela."
I giggled.
My upper body was sat upright, then my dress was being lifted from my body.
"Take me bra off."
"Yes, your highness."
My bra was removed and like a dead weight I dropped back into my pillow and groaned in delight.
"Have your way with me, stable boy."
"Oh my God."
I spread myself out. "It's your lucky night."
"Yes, ma'am it is... but are you sure you want to slum it with the stable boy?"
Was that laughter I heard?
"Yes, I'm sure."
That was *definitely* laughter.
I heard movement then the bed I was on top of dipped down.
I rolled over and plastered myself against a hard body, I opened my eyes and smiled up at the beautiful figure next to me.
"Hi." He smiled down at me.
I grinned. "Hey."
He brushed my hair out of my face.
"Do you come here often?" I asked and he laughed.
"Go to sleep, kitten."
Kitten?
The beautiful figure was Alec.
My Alec.
"Alec," I murmured as I closed my eyes.
"Yes, beautiful lady?"
I sighed. "I love you."

Silence.

I felt myself begin to drift off when a voice whispered, "Please forgive me."

I hummed as I fell deeper into darkness.

"Don't hate me... he is making me do this."

The whispering muted and faded to black along with everything else.

CHAPTER TWENTY-NINE

"Alec?"

My call was met with silence.

"Me head," I groaned.

What the fuck happened last night?

I can't remember past getting drinks from the barman then downing them at the table with Alec next to me.

What the hell did I drink to have such a headache?

"Oh Jesus, please take the pain away and I'll never drink again."

More silence.

"Alec!" I snapped.

Please answer me, I need painkillers.

I lazily reached my hand out to shove Alec but I felt nothing.

I opened my eyes and instead of a pretty dimpled smile beaming at me, I noticed a piece of paper sitting on Alec's pillow. I groaned as I grabbed the paper then rolled over onto my side and opened it.

Good morning, beautiful, you were out cold when I woke up so I decided to go down to the gym for a few hours. I put water and painkillers on the locker next to you. Take two pills and drink a lot of water, I'm sure you will have a hangover. Go to the buffet downstairs and have some breakfast when you are ready, see you later. P.S. You drool when you sleep.

- Alec xx

He was a gem as well as a dickhead.

L.A. CASEY

I groaned and closed my eyes as I rolled over and slowly sat up. When I was sure I wouldn't collapse, I opened my eyes and reached from my painkillers and water. I swallowed down two tablets and drank three quarters of the litre jug of water.

"Hmmmm. That's better," I murmured.

I looked down to myself and rolled my eyes when I noticed the only article of clothing I had on was a pair of knickers.

"Please God don't tell me I embarrassed myself last night," I grumbled.

I slowly stood and zombie walked into the bathroom.

I was tired, smelly and had a killer headache. I needed a shower. Badly.

I turned on the shower then after a moment I stripped down out of my knickers and got in the shower. I spent a long while scrubbing my body and my hair then spent even longer standing under the spray of the shower. I wasn't sure how long I spent showering, but when I got out and wrapped myself in a towel I felt so much better.

I bent down to pick up my dirty underwear then glanced around the bathroom, it was a hell of a lot cleaner than when we left the room yesterday and the towel rack was topped off with fresh towels too.

I walked back out into the room and threw my underwear into a plastic bag. I noticed the bedroom looked cleaner too.

Did someone come in while I was asleep and clean?
That was not cool!

I was mortified in case the cleaning staff came in and cleaned while I was out cold and drooling on the bed. I searched around for my phone and found it on the floor near the wardrobe. I picked it up and ignored my email inbox as I opened up my contact list. I found Alec's name and hit call.

The phone rang twice before it was answer.

"Hello?"

No one answered me but I could hear talking in the

background.

"Hello, Alec?" I called out louder.

No reply.

The eejit must have hit answer while the phone was in his pocket or something. I was about to hang up and ring him again when I heard a familiar voice... a familiar female voice.

"Are you sure she is going down to breakfast?"

Everly?

"I'm not certain," Alec replied to Everly.

"Well, ring her and find out, I don't fancy a studded boot up my ass."

Dante?

What the fuck was going on?

"I'll ring her now-"

I panicked and hung up on the call to Alec.

My stomach was rolling.

Why was Alec with Everly and Dante, and why were they asking if I was at breakfast?

I felt sick.

I jumped when my phone rang and Alec's face flashed across my screen.

I answered it and hoped he wouldn't ask where I was.

"Hello?"

"Hey baby, where are you?"

I swallowed and decided to lie, just to see what would he would say.

"Goin' down to get some food... where are you?"

Please don't lie.

"Still in the gym, I'll finish up here soon then go back to our room and shower then I'll join you. I'll be about an hour... okay?"

Oh my God.

"Okay," I whispered.

Silence.

Alec took a long moment before he said, "See you later, kitten."

"Yeah, bye."

I hung up and covered my hands with my mouth.

I quickly stood up and ran to the wardrobe and grabbed knickers, a bra, a tank top, and shorts. I put them on without even fully drying my body. I was shaking as I grabbed a bobbin and threw my hair up into a soppy wet messy bun.

What was happening?

My mind came to a conclusion but I wouldn't believe it.

I sat on my bed and waited.

If Alec came up here with Everly and Dante, I didn't know what I would do.

I hoped I was being paranoid and the conversation I overheard meant something different but my hopes and stomach dropped when I heard voices right outside my hotel room door!

"Oh, Jesus!" I whispered and jumped to my feet.

I spun around in a circle looking for somewhere to hide just as the noise of the hotel room door opened. The wardrobe was the only thing big enough in the room to fully conceal me so I darted forward, opened the doors, stepped inside and gently closed the doors behind me.

I instinctively hunkered down and covered my eyes with my hands. I don't know why I did this, I knew if anyone opened the doors they would clearly see me, but in my head they wouldn't see me if I covered my eyes - so covering my eyes is what I did.

"She isn't here."

I frowned at Alec's voice.

"It's excitin' that she could come back at any moment... right?"

I clenched my hands into fists around my eyes at Everly's voice.

"Exciting? She might just kill you *and* me, Everly. This is risky, not exciting."

If they were going to do what I thought they were going to do then Dante was right, I would kill them all.

I was about to get out of the wardrobe and confront the three of them, when through the cracks of the wardrobe I saw Alec grip them hem of Dante's t-shirt and pull it over his head then rid himself of his own t-shirt.

"Let's get this over with."

I froze and stared at Alec for a moment then flicked my eyes to Dante who was staring at Alec as well, and I mean *really* staring at him. Alec raised his eyebrows at Dante who stepped towards him and reached out with his index finger and proceed to trace Alec's V line with his fingertip. I widened my eyes and covered my mouth with my hands, forcing back a gasp that was about to escape my mouth.

"Will you bottom?" Dante asked Alec.

Alec gripped onto Dante's finger and brought it to his mouth, he flicked his tongue over the fingertip before sucking it into his mouth. When Alec released it with a pop, Dante was leaning towards him, head first, almost like he was swaying.

"I never bottom. Ever. You know this," Alec said, his tone firm.

Dante groaned. "I want your ass though."

Alec smiled, his dimples standing at attention. "The only ass that is getting fucked here is yours and Everly's. If you don't want that then leave. No *hard* feelings."

What?

Fucking what?

My head was pounding and I'm not sure if it was from what I was hearing or if it was from my hangover.

"No, I don't want to leave... I'll bottom."

I curled my lip in disgust at Dante, he was panting and sounded almost desperate for Alec and Alec enjoyed it, his face was smug and his body language indicated he loved the attention Dante was giving him. I knew this because I could see Alec's erection tenting his shorts.

It caused my stomach to roll.

"Good boy, now strip," Alec said to Dante.

Alec flicked his eyes to Everly and arched his eyebrow. "You too, ma'am."

Oh, God.

I wanted to leave, to get out of this room but I couldn't.

I couldn't move a muscle in my body.

I opened my hands and blocked out what I was seeing, but I quickly had to make my fingers earplugs when I heard a very pleased, male groan. It wasn't Alec who was groaning, I could tell that much.

Oh, please no!

I wish I kept my eyes closed because when I opened them and saw Alec on his knees with Dante's cock in his mouth I could have puked everywhere. I flicked my eyes upwards away from what Alec was doing and found a naked Everly on her knees on the bed pressed against Dante's upper body as she kissed him.

I looked away, utterly disgusted.

I closed my eyes and kept my ears plugged with my fingers. After a few minutes went by I opened my eyes again and a silent whimper racked through my body.

Everly was on her back, her legs were spread with Dante face buried between them while Alec was behind Dante as he thrust in and out of his body. I forced myself not to look at where Alec became one with Dante - I couldn't even stomach Everly and Dante - so again I re-closed my eyes.

Why was he doing this?

Alec was cheating on me... he was *really* cheating on me, with my auntie and his ex-fuck buddy none the less.

I don't know how much time went by before I opened my eyes again. This picture was even more stomach turning than the one before because Alec was now between Everly's legs while Dante was hovered over her face, thrusting in and out of her mouth.

I forced my eyes shut and swallowed down the bile that rose up my throat.

I bit down on my lower lip when I started to shake and tears began to fall from my eyes. I kept my eyes shut and my ears plugged for the longest time. I only reopened them when I felt a vibration.

I opened my eyes and through my tears I could see only Alec was on the bed, Everly and Dante were gone. Alec was still shirtless, but now he had on shorts.

He was sat on the edge of the bed with his head downcast but he spoke, and it caused my eyes to go wide.

"You can come out, Keela... I know you're in there."

CHAPTER THIRTY

He knew I was in the wardrobe.

He knew?

I kicked the door open with my shaking foot and struggled to get to my feet because pins and needles attacked my legs after being in a hunched down position for so long.

"You knew I was there all along and yet you..."

I couldn't even say it.

"I'm sorry."

He was sorry?

I stalked forward, balled my hand into a fist and swung. My fist connected to Alec's cheek and his head was forced to the left with a loud crack.

I pulled my hand back and Alec looked forward again but didn't move to stop me.

I slapped him across the face with my left hand then again with my right.

He still didn't move to stop me and I wished he would.

I used both my hands to shove him in the chest as hard as I could.

"I hate you!" I screamed as I slapped his chest. "I hate you! I hate you! I *hate* you!"

I felt tears stream down my face.

"What did I do?" I cried. "What did I fuckin' do?"

Alec swallowed but said nothing.

"Why, Alec? *Why?*"

He was cold.

"Why would you do this to me?"

He remained silent.

"I don't know you at all," I whispered.

I stared down at him for a long movement before I turned. "Keela?"

I couldn't look at him as I shakily walked to my locker and picked up my bag that was on the floor.

"Keela, I'm so sorry."

I was surprised when laughter came from my mouth.

"No, you aren't."

I heard him move and when I felt him behind me, my pulse didn't spike nor did my breath quicken... my stomach rolled in revulsion.

"You make me sick."

I heard his sharp intake of breath.

"Please," he whispered.

"I don't want to be near you. I don't want to be in the same proximity as you... you make my skin crawl," I spat.

I heard him take a few steps back.

"Keela, please."

I swallowed and wouldn't allow myself to feel any sympathy for him, he was the one in the wrong here, not me.

"I want you to leave."

Silence.

"What?"

Was he deaf?

"I want you to leave. Go down to the bar, go back to Ireland, go wherever the fuck you want to go, just get away from me."

He didn't move.

I squeezed the handles of my bag.

"Alec, please, leave me."

He still didn't move.

I turned to face him and glared at him, feeling nothing but

anger and betrayal.

"What are you still doin' here? Get the fuck out!"

Alec blinked then slowly nodded his head.

He blindly walked over to his suitcase and grabbed a t-shirt then put it over his head and stuck his feet in some flip flops. I numbly watched his every action through unblinking eyes.

"Will you be here when I get back?"

Depends on how long it takes me to pack.

"I don't want you to come back. I don't *ever* want to see you again."

Alec swallowed. "But-"

"But? There is no fuckin' 'but'! There is nothin', do you hear me? *Nothin*'!"

Alec flinched like I struck him again.

I turned my back to him because I knew I was about to cry and I refused to let him see.

I heard his slow footsteps walk away from me then the door opened and close, but instead of breaking down in tears I turned to the left and spotted his suitcase. With a wave of anger I rushed to the suitcase and grabbed a handful of Alec's clothes then I threw them around the room in a fit of rage.

I tripped over my own two feet and fell to the ground. My phone landed next to me on the floor so I picked it up and dialed Aideen's number. I tried six times but she never answered. I threw my phone on the bed and I stayed on the floor as wave after wave of sobs crashed into my body. I laid there on the ground and cried till there were no more tears left in my body.

I hated Alec Slater.

Hated him.

CHAPTER THIRTY-ONE

I didn't react when the door of the hotel room opened then closed an hour later.

I heard slow footsteps then a deep inhale.

"Keela, can we please talk? I need to explain. You need to know- Wait, what are you doing?"

I smiled as I continued to pack my suitcase.

This should be good.

"How can you explain fuckin' me cousin's stepmother, *and* your ex-fuck buddy, or should I say your very *current* fuck buddy?"

I shoved my clothes into my suitcase, suddenly not caring about anything being neat or tidy.

"Keela, what are you doing?" Alec asked from behind me.

I laughed. "I'm waitin' for you to explain what I witnessed this mornin'."

I jumped with fright when I was suddenly picked up from behind, and turned in the direction of the hotel room door. Alec let go of me when I scratched the back of his hands with my nails.

I swirled around and pointed my finger at him. "Don't you dare touch me. Do you hear me? You make me sick!"

Alec didn't look mad or angry in anyway... he actually looked extremely calm.

Good, at least one of us was.

"I'm sorry, but I need you to focus on me so we can talk."

I threw my hands up in the air and shouted, "Did it ever occur to you that maybe I don't want to talk to you, Alec? Did it ever occur to you that I don't want a single fuckin' thing to do with you?"

Alec swallowed. "I understand that you're upset and you have every right to be-"

"Upset? You think I'm upset? No, I'm not upset because bein' upset would mean that I actually have to care and I don't! I don't fuckin' care about you or who your put your dick into!"

Alec's jaw set. "You aren't doing yourself any favours by getting yourself worked up, Keela. You're only going to say things you regret."

I humourlessly laughed. "Thanks for that Doctor-fucking-Phil but trust me, I think gettin' a few things off me chest will make me feel ten times better!"

Alec took a step forward. "Keela, I'm telling you to rein it in. Now."

How fucking dare he tell me what to do!

I rushed forward and shoved his chest as hard as I could with both of my hands.

"You don't get to tell me what to do, you cheatin' scumbag!" I screamed.

I was so mad at Alec. I was enraged, but what pissed me off even more was that he barely moved an inch, and I'd shoved him as hard as I could.

Fucking tank of a man!

"I didn't willingly cheat on you, Keela! Will you just fucking *listen* to me?"

He didn't willingly cheat on me?

"I'm sorry, did me auntie or your boy toy physically *force* your cock inside their bodies? I'm findin' that hard to believe since you were on fuckin' top of both of them!"

The image of the three of them on the bed flooded my mind.

Alec lifted his hands and ran them through his hair. "I don't mean it like *that*, I meant-"

"No, no, let me finish. I find this very intrestin'. You say you didn't *willingly* cheat on me, yet you were on top when you penetrated me auntie and your boy toy. I'm failin' to see how none of that was done willingly *unless* gravity somehow failed you, and your cock just happened to fall into their bodies. I actually think I seen somethin' like that on the Discovery Channel-"

"I don't find you funny!" Alec cut me off with a growl.

I laughed. "Really? I find meself to be quite hilarious. It's not surprisin' you don't find me funny since you seem to get your kicks from fuckin' people over by fuckin' others."

Alec scrubbed his face. "I can't talk to you when you're like this."

"So leave, get the fuck out. I told you not come back here anyway."

Alec sighed and shook his head. "Okay, but I *will* be back in a few hours when you cool off. We really need to talk, you don't know the full story."

"I'm sure I don't," I said and pushed by Alec and got back to repacking my suitcase.

Alec lingered behind me for a whole minute in silence before he sighed and left closing the door gently after him. I think I managed a whole two minutes before tears left my eyes and spilled down my cheeks again.

I angrily wiped my cheeks but the tears kept on coming.

"Stop cryin'," I breathed and covered both of my eyes with my hands.

He doesn't deserve your tears.

I wiped my eyes, exhaled a large breath, and pressed on with packing my clothes into my suitcase. Every so often when a tear fell from my eyes I made sure to wipe it away as quick as it fell.

This was my own fault.

I knew very well what I was getting into when I asked Alec to come to the wedding, and I was fully aware that dating him for real was a stupid idea. This situation just proved how correct and idiotic I was.

I mean, we were dating two days before he slipped and dove cock first into another woman's vagina... as well as a man's arse. I shivered in disgust just thinking about Alec with Dante. I wasn't homophobic, I knew I wasn't, seeing him with Everly made me just as sick as him being with Dante.

"You've only known him a few fuckin' days, what do you expect? You *don't* know him," I snapped to myself.

I hated that saying it out loud upset me all over again, because even though it was only a few days of being with him, I thought I knew Alec... or knew enough of him to trust him.

Either way I was wrong.

Very wrong.

I came to the wedding of the lad who fucked me over, only to get fucked over at said wedding by me date, who was meant to make the lad who fucked me over jealous. It blew up in my face, big time.

Twenty or so minutes passed by when finally I got all of my belongings into my suitcase.

"Thank God," I muttered.

I frowned when I heard a knock at the hotel room door.

I thought Alec said he would give me a few hours to cool off?

"Go away, Alec! I don't want to speak-"

"It's not Alec."

I widened my eyes.

Uncle Brandon?

I walked to the door, looked through the peephole and when I saw it was my Uncle Brandon I opened the door.

"Hey," I said, forcing a smile.

He smiled back at me. "Hey, sweetheart... Can I come in? I need to talk to you."

He did?

"Oh, sure, come in. Sorry about the mess, Alec's things are everywhere."

Yeah, because you threw them all around the room like a mad woman.

"Don't worry about it."

I closed the door after my Uncle Brandon entered the room. I sat on the bed while he sat on the comfy chair in the corner of the room.

"So, what's up?" I asked and nervously played with my fingers.

"Why is your suitcase on your bed... and packed from the looks of things?"

I looked at my suitcase next to me and felt my shoulders slump.

"I'm going home today."

I looked at my uncle and expected him to be shocked that I was missing Micah's wedding, or at the very least mad but he wasn't. He looked... understanding.

"I don't blame you."

What... I... Just... What?

"Excuse me?"

Uncle Brandon smiled. "I said I don't blame you. I'd be on a plane headin' back home right now if I was you."

What. The. Hell?

"Uncle... what are you talkin' about?"

Uncle Brandon frowned. "Everly told me about what happened this mornin'."

I picked that moment and time to feel humiliated.

"She did?" I murmured.

"Yes, and since she didn't have my permission she will be punished for it severely. You have my word on that."

I widened my eyes to the pointed of pain.

"Permission?"

Uncle Brandon sighed. "This is why I wanted that lad to go home before he could cause any damage. The reason I know Alec Slater is because I paid for his time and Dante's time to entertain Everly when I was too busy when we went away on business."

"What?" I whispered.

"I'm afraid it's the truth."

They've been together more than once?

"That's why they acted weird when I introduced them. They already knew each other... very well. I feel sick."

"I'm sorry honey, like I said before she will be punished for this."

"She will?"

"Yes, I will personally see to it that she is very sorry for hurtin' you."

Wow.

"What are you goin' to do to her?" I asked.

Uncle Brandon smiled and it gave me chills.

"You let me worry about that, sweetheart."

Oh Christ.

"You aren't gonna to kill her, are you? I hate the woman but I don't want her to die!"

Uncle Brandon stared at me for a long moment before he burst into laughter. I sagged back in relief then grabbed a pillow, and threw it at my uncle who caught it.

"You should have seen your face!"

I growled. "That's not funny! I know you're into some shady shite, so murder obviously entered me mind."

My Uncle Brandon tossed my pillow back to me and tilted his head to the side.

"What do I do for business, Keela?"

I shrugged my shoulder. "I don't know, but if you're involved with Marco Miles, it can't be good."

Uncle Brandon looked curious. "Alec told you about Marco?"

I chewed on my lower lip and shook my head. "Yeah, but he didn't go into a lot of detail. He did tell me the type of 'business' Marco runs and some stuff that the brothers used to do."

Uncle Brandon sighed. "You will be happy to hear I don't have my foot in any sex rings or weapon cartels."

That did make me happy, but only a little.

"And drugs?"

Uncle Brandon smiled. "I'm involved with them."

I gasped. "Uncle Brandon, that's against the law! What if you go to prison?"

My uncle laughed. "Sweetheart, I've been doin' this since before you were born. I'm a powerful man, prison isn't on the cards for me. Trust me on that."

My uncle was a drug trafficker!

"Oh my God," I whispered.

"You understand why I kept you and Micah out of that part of my life, don't you?"

I nodded my head. "Yes I do, but still... I feel like I don't know you anymore."

Uncle Brandon frowned and leaned forward on his chair. "I'm still your uncle Keela, and I love you. You're very important to me, like a daughter."

I felt my eyes well up with tears, so I quickly looked down.

"I love you, too."

"And because you're so important you me and in order to keep you out of harm's way, I want you to do somethin' for me. Okay?"

I looked up and wiped away the tears that fell from my eyes.

"What do you want me to do?" I asked.

Uncle Brandon looked me in the eyes and said, "Stay away from Alec Slater and his brothers, okay?"

I furrowed my eyebrows in confusion. "I don't plan on ever speakin' to Alec again, but why do I have to stay away from his brothers? They are nice, a close friend of Aideen's is datin' the eldest brother so I would eventually bump into one of them-"

"Keela," my uncle cut me off. "You're to stay away from the Slater brothers, do you understand me?"

What the hell?

I narrowed my eyes. "What will you do if I don't?"

Uncle Brandon sat forward and narrowed his eyes before he hissed, "I'll kill them."

Chapter Thirty-Two

I felt like I was kicked in stomach, because the wind was suddenly knocked out of me.

"Don't test me Keela, you're to *stay away* from that family. You're puttin' yourself, *and* them in danger because if anythin' happens to you I'll kill the lot of them."

I was going to be sick.

"I can't believe you're sayin' this right now," I said, then grabbed my stomach as I began to heave.

"Fuck," Uncle Brandon said when he got up and grabbed me by the arm.

He got me to my feet and brought me into the bathroom where I puked into the toilet for a solid minute. I was still heaving but nothing was coming up anymore, so I grabbed some tissue and wiped my mouth.

"Is there anythin' else I should know about this family? I don't have a secret siblin' who kills people for a livin' do I?"

Uncle Brandon laughed as he helped me up to my feet. "I'm as criminal as you're goin' to get, sweetie."

I shook my head. "How could I have not had an inklin' that you were into somethin' so... illegal?"

Uncle Brandon pushed my hair back out of my face. "Because it was kept from you. I'm not known as Brandon Daley unless it's with family, or other bosses. Everyone else involved in the business knows me as just Brandy."

I snorted because the pop singer Brandy popped into my head.

"You find this funny?"

I laughed. "I find this fuckin' hilarious, I mean me uncle is a *gangster*."

Uncle Brandon cringed. "I prefer the term business man."

I laughed again, hard.

Uncle Brandon rubbed his head and led me out of the bathroom.

"You want the next flight home, I presume?"

I looked up and nodded. "Yeah, I have to get out of here."

Uncle Brandon nodded then took out his phone, tapped on the screen and put it to his ear. "Afternoon Andrea, I need the next flight out from the Bahamas to Dublin... Three hours? That's perfect. Make it for Keela Daley and put her in business class. Fax the e-ticket to my hotel."

When Uncle Brandon hung up, he turned to me and smiled. "All set."

I gaped at him. "Just like that?"

He nodded. "Just like that."

I eyed him. "Is Andrea forced to work for you? Is she some kind of prisoner?"

Uncle Brandon looked at me as amusement twinkled in his grey eyes. "Andrea is just me assistant, Keela."

I raised my eyebrow. "For your shady business, or your legit business?"

Uncle Brandon chuckled. "Both."

Fuck me.

"I like Andrea! How can someone so sweet, willingly work with a criminal?"

"Because I'm a nice criminal... and I pay her well."

Gah!

"I cannot believe this."

Uncle Brandon didn't say anything and out of nowhere I started crying.

"Baby girl."

"I'm sorry," I wailed, "but me b-boyfriend cheated on me with me auntie and his e-escort partner. Then you tell me you're into some s-shady shite, and Aideen won't answer her p-phone, and I really m-miss Storm. This is the worst day in me entire l-life."

My uncle remained silent and I couldn't stop talking.

"Why did he do this to m-me? What did I do wrong?"

I picked up a dirty t-shirt and wiped my running nose.

"I thought he cared a-about me."

I cried so hard then that I almost made myself sick again and this really upset my uncle.

"Sweetheart, please."

I felt his arms come around me and I quickly wrapped mine around him and cried into his chest.

"I'm goin' to make this better, I swear it."

I shook my head. "Don't hurt him, please."

My uncle sighed but I felt him nod his head.

"I have to leave, I need to go home."

My uncle kissed my head then stood up. "Okay, I'll help get your things downstairs."

I nodded my head as he grabbed my suitcase and heaved it off the bed. I stood up and grabbed my side bag making sure I had my passport, money, and my phone. I looked around the room and all that was left were Alec's things, mine were packed away.

I grabbed a pen and note pad that the hotel provided and scrawled a message on it for Alec to read.

I don't know why you did this to me, but I hate you for it. Stay away from me.

I put the note pad on his pillow then glanced around the room once more before I sucked it up and left the room. My uncle was outside waiting for me and we went down to the lobby in silence. He picked up my e-ticket at the front desk while I waited outside for him. He sighed when he got me settled into a taxi outside the hotel.

"I would say tell Micah I'm sorry about missin' her weddin', but I can't stand Jason."

My uncle chuckled. "He is about to be me son-in-law, how do you think I feel?"

I lightly chuckled.

"I'll see you durin' the week when I'm home, okay?"

I nodded my head. "Okay."

"Call me if you need me."

I smiled. "I will, bye."

"Bye, baby girl."

I silently cried all the way to the airport and I had a face like a slapped arse through check in then through security. I felt like everything was happening around me at super speed while I waited in the waiting area of the airport for my gate number for my flight. I didn't realise I was tired, but I dozed off and awoke when a female voice announced my flight was now boarding.

Fuck!

I quickly grabbed my bag and joined the queue for my flight. I was dying to get home as I was settled on the plane, I managed to calm myself knowing it wouldn't be long before I got there and I could see my Storm.

CHAPTER THIRTY-THREE

"Keela?"

I ignored the saddened expression on Aideen's face as she opened my hall door to me.

"Hi," I murmured.

She stared at me.

"How was your flight?"

I shrugged out of my cardigan. "Long."

Aideen swallowed. "Are you hungry?"

I shook my head.

Aideen chew on her lower lip. "Thirsty?"

I shook my head.

She swallowed. "Your uncle rang me... he told me what happened. Alec rang too-"

I held my hand up cutting Aideen off.

"Don't mention him or even say his name."

Aideen nodded her head. "Okay, babe."

I walked passed the kitchen and stopped when I looked into the sitting room. I was only mildly surprised to see the Slater brothers and both of the Murphy sisters staring back at me.

I looked back at Aideen.

"Make them leave."

Aideen's face dropped. "They are here to see if you're okay-"

"I am okay, I'm perfectly okay. Tell them to leave."

Aideen stepped forward to me. "Keela."

I took a step back. "Where is Storm?"

Aideen rubbed her neck. "I had to bring him to the kennel for the day. Just so we could figure this out with him out of the way."

I was livid, Storm was the one being I looked forward to seeing!

"Which kennel? I'm goin' to get him."

"Keela, stop it. Storm is okay, we can get him later. Let's just talk-"

"You want to talk now? I wanted to talk *fourteen hours* ago when I called you a million times after *their*," I pointed at the brothers, "scumbag of a brother fucked Everly and some other scumbag in me bed. I don't want to talk anymore. I want Storm."

"Kay, I'm so sorry. I left me phone here when I was out with Kane."

"You were with one of them?" I growled. "Bit of advice honey, they are not the nice people you think they are. Trust me."

"Hey, that's bang out of order Keela. The brothers didn't make Alec cheat on you."

I snapped my head in Bronagh Murphy's direction and snarled, "Say one more word, I fuckin' dare you. Unlike your sister or Nico, I *will* knock you fuckin' out."

Dominic stood up and put his arm around Bronagh, which made me laugh.

"I wonder if she will let you touch her once she finds out who was in the Bahamas with me and Alec."

All the brothers stood up then.

"Keela, you're angry, do not say anything out of anger."

"I'm not angry Ryder, I'm enraged. I'm disgusted that your *filthy* brother used me and humiliated me in such a way. I guess you can't help it, workin' with Marco made you all stone fuckin' cold. I actually think he is kinder than you all."

Bronagh stared at me for a long moment then said, "What did you just say?"

I shrugged.

Bronagh pushed away from Dominic and came right up to me.

"What did you just say?"

I raised an eyebrow. "Am I supposed to feel threatened by you?"

Bronagh's gaze never wavered. "Keela, please... you said the name Marco."

I frowned.

Her tone wasn't one of anger it was one of desperation.

"Alec told me all about what happened in his past, his brother's past and what happened in Darkness three years ago. Only I was told the truth, where as you were lied to. Marco isn't dead, he is alive and well."

Bronagh's eyes glazed over.

"No," she swallowed. "He is dead."

I shook my head. "I've spoken to him. He is alive."

Bronagh looked me in the eye and gasped.

She saw the truth in my eyes.

"I don't understand."

I heard a whimper. "You lied to me!"

"Branna, please-"

"Don't touch me!"

Bronagh held her hand up then when Dominic approached her.

"Don't."

"Baby-"

"Don't, Dominic. Please."

I shook my head and looked at Kane who looked like shite and found he was staring at me.

"You're all liars."

Kane frowned. "We lied to save the girls from losing their minds with worry, Keela."

"They are both losin' their minds to worry and also dealin' with the knowledge that their boyfriends lied to them about somethin' so important."

"You could have let us tell them!" Nico bellowed in my direction.

I snarled, "You've had over two and a half fuckin' years to do that and you didn't, so fuck you!"

Nico glared at me as the atmosphere in the room shifted.

I looked at Aideen and gestured to the brothers.

"The truth makes bullshitters uncomfortable."

Nico shook his head then turned his attention to Bronagh. "Don't hate me."

Bronagh began crying. "I don't hate you, but how could you keep this from me? How you could you lie about this?"

Nico was either at a loss for words or just didn't want to talk with an audience.

"Let's go home, I'll tell your everything about that night... I promise."

Bronagh nodded her head and walked by me with her eyes downcast. Nico walked by me too, but he paused for a moment and looked down at me, his jaw set.

"Alec cares about you."

I humourlessly laughed. "Is that why he cheated on me?"

Nico glared. "He had no choice."

What the fuck?

"Of course he had a choice, there is *always* a choice."

Nico shook his head. "Not this time."

What the fuck did that mean?

Nico left with Bronagh and was soon followed by a crying Branna and a distraught Ryder.

I looked at Kane and raised my eyebrows when he sat down on my settee.

"Your cue to leave was when your brothers walked out that door."

Kane folded his arms across his chest.

"I'm not goin' anywhere."

I looked over my shoulder to Aideen who looked at me with nervous eyes.

"Aideen is leavin' too so there is no need for you to stay."

I looked away from Aideen's hurt face and focused on an immobile Kane.

I glared. "Get the fuck out of me apartment Kane, I'm not jokin'."

Kane stood up and walked over to me.

"I. Am. Not. Leaving."

I cracked and shoved him in the chest as hard as I could.

"Get out! I don't want any part of him near me, leave!"

I didn't realise I was crying until I sniffed.

I quickly wiped my face but the dam was broken and the flow of tears wouldn't stop. I turned to Aideen and threw myself at her, wrapping my arms around her.

"What do people do this to me?" I cried.

Aideen cried as she wrapped her arms around me, she had a soft heart and cried when she saw other people cry.

"It's goin' to be okay," she whispered.

I shook my head. "It's not... he used me Aideen. He told me he cared for me and he lied. They *all* lie!"

I was surprised to feel a body press into my back and bigger arms wrap around me and Aideen.

"I'm sorry he hurt you, Keela."

I cried harder.

Aideen held me, and Kane held us both.

I don't know how long I cried, but I cried so much that I made myself drowsy on Aideen's shoulder and eventually felt myself being lifted up into the air.

"Her room is down here," Aideen whispered.

I felt like I was floating then I was settled down onto a cloud.

"She is a good girl. I hate that she is hurting over my brother."

"She has a heart of gold, but it's protected by a wall of steel... I don't know who she will trust after she makes it though this."

Silence.

"She looks so small," Aideen's voice sniffled.

"She will be okay, he will explain himself to her. He is already on a flight home from-"

"No, Kane. If she wants to see him then it will be on her terms. She is broken right now, you can't spring him on her when she is this down."

Silence.

"Okay, it will be hell keeping him away from her but I'll make it happen."

"Thank you."

"Let's go, she needs to sleep."

I heard the click of a door then darkness consumed me.

Chapter Thirty-Four

"Keela?"

I pretended I was still asleep so she would leave alone.

"I know you're awake... you aren't snorin' or droolin' anymore."

Bitch.

"Leave me alone."

"Get up."

No.

"Just because I'm awake doesn't mean I'm ready to do things."

Aideen sighed. "How are you doin'?"

"I want a new liver to replace my heart."

"Um, why?"

"Because then I could drink more and care less."

I heard movement then groaned when light flooded my room as my curtains where pulled open.

"What the fuck, Aideen?"

She stalked over to my bed and pulled at my covers.

"It's been two days. I understand you're heartbroken but you need to eat somethin'!"

I held onto my covers for dear life but I just didn't have the strength anymore so I let go.

"I'm not hungry... and I'm *not* heartbroken."

I heard Aideen sigh and could imagine her nose scrunching up in annoyance.

"If you aren't heartbroken then why have you been held up in here for the past two days?"

"Because I'm jet lagged."

Aideen laughed. "I bought that excuse yesterday, but you have slept a collective total of twenty-six hours since you got home so it's time to think up a new excuse."

I snuggled into my pillow.

"Okay, I have cramps in my stomach and can't move. How is that for an excuse? Now fuck off and leave me alone."

I heard Aideen huff. "I'm sick of this, enough excuses! Excuses sound best to the person who is making them up, stop feelin' sorry for yourself!"

I humourlessly chuckled. "No, I'm not done with me pity party yet... Why are you still here?"

"Fuck's sake, Keela! Stop pushin' me away! I know you're hurtin' and I want to help you. I'm not the bad lad here, babe, I'm your friend."

I bit my inner cheeks to stop myself from crying.

I was done with crying.

"I just want to be on my own, Ado... please."

I felt my bed dip then a body mould around mine, spooning me.

"Not a hope in hell, we're in this together. I took an oath as a blood sister to go through what you go through. I took that shite seriously so there is no gettin' rid of me."

I burst out into unexpected laughter and said, "I love that our friendship is based off of really inappropriate humour.

"Me too."

God, I loved this girl.

"I love you."

Aideen kissed the back of my head. "I love you, too."

"I'm sorry for bein' horrible. I know you did nothin' wrong."

"Don't apologise, I know it's your hurt and anger takin', not you."

We were silent for a few moments until I decided I wanted to talk.

"I seen the whole thing."

Aideen gave me a squeeze but remained silent.

"Him, Everly, and Dante were comfortable with each other... They've done it loads of times before. They were like some sort of *thing*."

Aideen gasped. "Does your Uncle Brandon know?"

I nodded. "Uncle Brandon said he paid for her time with Alec and Dante over the years to keep her happy while he was busy with work, which by the was *is* shady and illegal as fuck, but this time he didn't give her his permission so he is pissed about it. I don't know how to feel about it because their relationship is their own, but I can't help but blame Alec. He could have said no Aideen, he really could have."

Aideen stroked my back.

"And if cheatin' wasn't bad enough, he did it with them on the bed we shared. The bed we had sex in for the first time. It makes me feel sick to me stomach."

Aideen held me tightly as my voice cracked.

I closed my eyes and chuckled. "Micah and Jason got married today."

"I know... the stupid bitch."

I laughed, and so did Aideen.

And for a second I didn't feel so broken.

"You're up."

I smiled at Aideen four days later when I emerged from my bedroom.

"I'm up."

She placed her hands on her hips.

"You're showered."

I looked down to myself and then back up.

"I'm showered."

Aideen smiled. "Thank God, you were startin' to reek."

I laughed. "Bitch."

Aideen beamed. "Are you goin' to dry you hair?"

I shook my head. "Can't be arsed."

Aideen gestured to the chair nearest to me.

"Park it and I'll plait it."

I happily did as asked and sat down while Aideen French plaited my hair.

"Have you eaten anythin'?"

I nodded my head. "I had a few slices of toast."

Aideen blew out a relieved breath. "I'm so happy, I thought I was goin' to have to force feed you today."

I chuckled. "I'm fine Ado – I'm washed, feed, and fully clothed."

"Yeah, but how is your head doin'?"

I lightly smiled. "Me head isn't what's hurtin'."

"I know babe," Aideen finished off my plait and cuddled me to her.

"Since you're up and dressed I'm liftin' your Storm ban."

Yay!

"It's evil that you kept him at the kennel away from me."

Aideen came around and shrugged. "I had to take matters into my own hands when you wouldn't leave your room. I knew a Storm ban would get you out sooner rather than later."

Evil cow.

"Well, I'm out now so go and get me baby."

Aideen saluted me. "On it boss!"

I chuckled as she grabbed her keys and literally skipped out of the apartment.

"Bloody weirdo," I said when she left.

To keep me occupied I spent a few minutes tidying up the kitchen and when I had nothing left to do I sat down. I was sat at my kitchen table only a few seconds when a knock came from my door and I rolled my eyes.

Aideen probably forgot something.

I walked over to the door and opened it. "What did you forget this time-"

I cut myself off when the person I was looking at was *not* Keela.

"Hello kitten."

It was Alec.

CHAPTER THIRTY-FIVE

I stared at Alec for a long moment and I noticed he looked like shite, he had bags under his eyes and he looked like he'd lost weight.

He looked how I felt.

I shook my head and tried to slam the door shut, but Alec jammed his foot between the door and the doorframe preventing it from closing.

"Please, kitten-"

"Don't! Don't call me that!"

I pushed against the door as hard as I could trying to force it closed, but Alec pushed back against the door. He was stronger than me and once the door was pushed open he made his way into my apartment.

"Get out!" I screamed.

Alec closed the door behind him and turned the lock.

I walked backwards into the kitchen and looked for a weapon. Alec saw my eyes dart around the room and he frowned as he removed his jacket.

"I'm not going to hurt you Keela, you *know* I'm not."

I laughed. "I don't know you so I've *no* fuckin' idea what you're capable of."

Alec looked vulnerable as he stared at me.

I couldn't look him in the eyes so I focused on his chin instead.

"What are you doin' here? Do you not think you have fucked me over enough?"

Alec looked at me, his gaze uncertain.

"I'm sorry... I needed to see you."

"Why?"

He took a deep breath and said, "Because I missed you."

He missed me?

Oh, that was rich.

I humourlessly laughed. "You missed me? Did you miss me when you were fuckin' Everly and Dante?"

Alec flinched. "I deserve that."

"No Alec you deserve to be hit by a double decker bus, *that* is what you deserve."

Alec nodded his head. "I agree."

I glared at him. "Don't agree with me."

"Okay."

I snarled, "Don't do what I say to appease me either."

Alec opened his mouth to speak but thought better of it and closed his mouth.

He was silent for a moment then said, "I don't know what to do then."

I pointed to the door.

"I do, you can leave."

Alec shook his head. "I'm not going anywhere."

I swore.

"What the fuck is with you and Kane? When I say leave, I mean fuckin' leave!"

Alec didn't move or respond to me and it infuriated me.

"Are you enjoin' this?" I snapped. "Did you just come by to see if I was crying over you? Does it get you off to know what a sick and twisted piece of dirt you are?"

Alec look dejected but I wasn't falling for his sad puppy dog eyes.

No fucking way.

"I'm here because I needed to see you. I told you... I missed you."

"I don't believe you."

Alec swallowed. "I'm sorry."

All the hurt, anger, and sadness that I had bottled up over the past few days exploded out of me.

"What are you sorry for? Tell me exactly?"

Alec didn't speak he only stared at me.

"I'd imagine you're sorry for shaggin' me auntie and that piece of filth of a boy toy. But you have *a lot* more to be sorry for than just that and you have a lot more to answer for."

I began to pace back and fourth.

"I know it was set up and not somethin' spontaneous, you planned it when the three of you realized you where all in the same place. I've thought about it since I got back home, and it all makes sense. At the welcome party when Everly looked at you knowingly and Dante said, 'Until tomorrow' that was all because the three of you *knew* what was goin' to happen. That's why you wanted me to go to that party so bad wasn't it? Did you want to triple check where you would all meet or somethin'?"

Alec looked down and nodded his head. "Yeah, I wasn't sure on the details of the meet so when you were up dancing with Micah I sought out Everly and found out."

I closed my eyes.

"And earlier that day, after the welcome dinner, why did you let it go as far as sex between us when you knew you were goin' to be with them?"

Alec looked up and blinked. "It wasn't just sex with us Keela. I wanted to have you... even if it was just once."

I gasped. "You wanted me body at least once because you knew after I found out what you did I would never want you to touch me again?"

Alec licked his lips and looked back down. "Yes and no."

"What does yes and no mean?" I snapped.

"Yes I wanted to be with you because I knew it would be my only chance, and no because I didn't 'just want your body'... I needed it."

I grimaced in disgust and Alec shook his head.

"I don't mean it how it sounds."

"How do you mean it then?"

Alec shrugged. "I don't know how to word it."

I ground my teeth. "Try."

"I don't know what to say Keela, sorry just comes to mind."

I clenched my hands into fists.

"You're a horrible person, Alec Slater."

"Please Keela, I'm not a bad person, I swear I'm not."

I glared daggers at Alec.

"Your actions tell a different story."

Alec shook his head. "They weren't my willing actions. I had to pop a fucking pill just to get it up... I was revolted before, during, and after the act."

He had to take a tablet?

"I don't understand."

Alec looked up. "Let me explain then."

"No, I don't want to hear it, you have said enough."

Alec's face hardened. "I haven't nearly said enough."

I looked away from him.

"I don't give a fuck what you have to say, just like you didn't give a fuck about me when you fucked other people."

Alec cast his eyes downward.

"Don't you dare act like the victim, don't you fuckin' dare."

Alec looked at me, his eyes were sad. "I'm not Keela, I'm not acting like anything. I'm just sick with myself... I'm so sorry for everything I did to you. I swear on my life that I didn't want it to happen, I really wasn't a willing participant."

My heart started to hurt.

"Then why did it happen Alec? Why the fuck did you stray after only *a few days*?"

Alec look frightened. "I'm afraid you won't believe me if I tell you the truth."

I shrugged my shoulders. "That's a risk you're goin' to have to take because I'm a minute away from callin' me uncle."

Alec's lip curled in disgust. "This is all because of *him*."

Excuse me?

"Are you insinuatin' that you cheated on me because of me *uncle*."

Alec looked me dead in the eye and said, "I'm not insinuating it, I'm stating it. Your uncle made this happen."

I blinked and shook my head not sure if I heard him correctly. "You're lyin'."

Alec shook his head. "No, I'm not."

"You're lyin'!" I screamed.

Alec rushed at me. "No, I'm not!"

I lifted my hands up in front of my face to block any incoming hits.

No hits came because Alec stopped just short of touching me when he saw my reaction to him. He turned then and punched one of my kitchen presses so hard that his fist went through the wood.

"Omigod!" I screamed and covered my ears.

Alec pulled his fist free from the wood and gripped onto the kitchen counter as he took some long deep breaths.

"It pisses me off that you think I would physically hurt you."

"You hurt me emotionally which was just as bad as takin' a punch... I don't see the difference."

Alec turned to face me, his face tense.

"Are you okay?" he asked.

"I'm just peachy, thanks."

Alec scowled. "Don't be sarcastic."

"If you don't want a sarcastic answer, don't ask a stupid question."

Alec sighed. "You're right that was a stupid question."

No shit Sherlock.

"No more stupid questions, but you're going to listen to me Keela. You can decide on what you want to do *after* I've explained myself, do you understand me?"

I swallowed and looked at the hole in my kitchen press.

"Okay," I replied.

"Do you remember the welcome dinner and how your uncle wanted to speak to me in the conference room on my own without you present?"

I folded my arms across my chest.

"Yes."

"When you left the room he told me that no relation of his would ever be in committed relationship with a whore."

I blinked. "Well, you fucked his wife a lot of times, I'm sure he didn't want to keep that trait of yours runnin' in the family."

Alec cut his eyes to me so I looked down.

"I told your uncle that I didn't work for Marco anymore, and Marco agreed that I was no longer his employee, but your uncle didn't care about any of that. He didn't want me to taint you."

"I fail to see how me uncle wantin' to protect me from you made you cheat on me."

Alec shook his head. "Do you really not see where I'm going with this?"

I shrugged. "Should I?"

Alec scrubbed his face with his hands.

"Keela, your uncle *told* me I had to make you hate me. He said I had to do somethin' to push you away from me... He *told* me I had to sleep with Everly and Dante and to make sure you knew about it."

I blinked as Alec's words entered my mind.

I tried to process them, I really did, but it hurt my head and chest.

"Why are you sayin' this?" I whispered.

"Because it's the truth. He told me I had to make you hate me... and I did."

I swallowed. "If that is true, then why didn't you just tell him no?"

Alec frowned. "He said he would kill my family if I didn't do it.

He said cheating on you would make you hate me and never want to see me again. From the looks of things he was right."

I didn't reply.

Uncle Brandon made Alec do this?

He wanted me to be hurt?

"He held me as I cried," I whispered.

"I'm so sorry, Keela. I truly am."

I walked out of the kitchen and down to my bedroom where my phone was.

"What are you doing?"

"Ringing me uncle, I need to hear this from him."

I closed my door to keep Alec out.

I dialed my uncle's number when I had my phone in my hand and fear gripped me.

If Alec was telling the truth then I couldn't trust my uncle anymore, my most beloved family member... But if Alec was lying then I was still going to be left miserable and heartbroken because of his cheating.

There was no good outcome.

"Keela? Hello baby girl-"

"Is it true? Did you make Alec do it?" I cut my uncle off.

Silence.

"What did he tell you?"

I sobbed. "That you told him to cheat on me or you would kill his family."

My uncle swore but he didn't deny it.

"Uncle, is he lyin'? Please be honest with me, I need to know the truth."

My uncle sighed and after a long pause he said, "No baby girl, he is tellin' the truth."

I broke down into tears.

"*Why?* Why would you want me hurtin' like this?"

"Because you deserve better than a whore!"

"He is *not* a whore! He was *forced* to work for Marco because that bastard held the threat of hurting his family over his head, just like *you* did! He would have never done it if you didn't back him into a corner!"

Silence.

"I can *never* trust you again, do you understand that? You have lost the ability to call me your niece. I'm fuckin' done with you!"

I heard my uncle's sharp intake of breath. "I was tryin' to protect you from getting hurt, Keela."

"You caused me to get hurt, Uncle!"

"You deserve better than him!"

"I deserve to decide for meself who is good enough for me! I deserve to be happy and you *ruined* that for me. I hate you for it. You lied to me face! You sat in that hotel room back in the Bahamas knowing good and well what you did and you let me hate him!"

My uncle was at a loss for words so I hung up on him.

I kept my phone in my hand as I opened my bedroom and walked down the hallway and into the kitchen where Alec was still leaning against the kitchen counter top.

"You were right."

Alec frowned. "I'm sorry, Keela... I had to tell you the truth, it was killing me."

I nodded my head.

Alec pushed off against the counter and I think he was going to hug me, but I stepped back letting him know that it was not what I wanted.

"I told you the truth. Why can't I touch you?"

I looked away. "Because I can still see you touchin' them."

Alec looked tense as he whispered. "But I told you the truth."

This hurt.

"I know you did, I know you had no choice-"

"The only choice I had, was to be with you after the welcome dinner and I had to be with you Keela. There was no bad intent or ulterior motive, I just wanted to feel like you were mine. You have no idea how much I feel *for* you."

I swallowed. "It doesn't change anythin', Alec. I can still see you with them and it makes me skin crawl."

Alec stared at me for a long while without speaking and it was during this period of silence that I knew what I had to do. Uncle Brandon would still most certainly want me away from Alec and he would keep good on his word about harming Alec's family if I didn't.

I had to do what he did to me so he would stay away... I had to make him hate me.

"Please, don't leave me again... it nearly killed me when I read your note and realised you'd left the Bahamas."

I forced a bored sigh out of my mouth. "Alec, you hurt me and the only reason for that hurt was because I was startin' to get attached to you. But it's better that we go our separates ways now, feelin's make everythin' messy."

He looked perplexed. "I don't understand, you told me you-"

"I wasn't meself in the Bahamas, I let the thought of us really datin' go to me head but it was a lie."

Alec was lost. "A lie?"

"Yeah, I don't want you, Alec. Everythin' was just a ruse for me family... nothin' between us was real. It was a just a favour, remember? All fake. I pretended to have feelin's for you to make us seem real as a couple because I wanted to one up Jason. You don't really think I could love someone who fucks people for a livin', do you?" I said my voice cold.

"Keela," he whispered.

"Come on, Alec-"

"But I love you."

I almost dropped to the floor at his declaration, but I managed to keep myself upright and still as a statue.

"You love me? You don't even know me!"

"Yes I do, and I do love you."

I wanted to cry, but I chuckled instead.

"Do you not abide by your own conditions? What happened to

number one - no fallin' in love?"

Alec leaned back against the kitchen counter and slowly slid down until his arse hit the floor.

"You're the only person I've ever cared this much about in my entire life," he whispered.

My heart was breaking all over again, and my stomach was threatening to empty at any moment but I had to remind myself why I was doing this, why I was hurting him. I was keeping him alive.

"It was a favour, a job to you-"

"You weren't a job, Keela. It started out as a favour, but that changed... You *know* it changed."

I shook my head. "It never changed. It was always fake. I was fucked over by Jason, do you really think I could have feelin's for you so quickly? Come on, think about it."

Alec remained silent.

"If it was fake then why were you so upset?"

"Because I couldn't believe you slept with me auntie, I hate that bitch."

"That's the only reason?"

"Yep."

I tried to keep my composure when Alec got to his feet and directed a hateful glare in my direction. I began to breathe heavily when he walked towards me. He stopped right in front of me and looked down.

"You feel nothing for me?"

I shrugged. "Disgust. I mean, you fucked Everly and Dante at the same time. Ew."

Alec set his jaw. "You're a hell of an actress, kitten. You really had me believing that you cared about me."

I frowned. "Damn, I'm sorry. I thought you were playin' off of me. I didn't think you would ever love me."

Alec snarled, "I can't believe a fucking word out of your mouth."

ALEC

I cleared my throat. "I don't know why you're so mad, you got a free holiday out of it, you had sex with me, and you had a threesome. You should be happy as Larry."

Alec looked at me with nothing but rage and disgust and I knew my job was done.

"We can have one last tumble if you-"

"Don't fucking touch me, you heartless bitch."

I placed my hands on my hips. "That's just rude and uncalled for. I would like you to leave now."

Alec looked me up and down. "I don't know you."

He used my words against me and they broke my heart.

"I *never* want to see you again. Never."

I felt sick.

I shrugged. "Fine by me."

Alec turned and stalked over to my hall door but before he reached it, a knocked came to the door. I wondered if it was Aideen. I was about to ask who it was when my phone rang and my uncle's face flashed across the screen.

I looked up as Alec opened the door but not to Aideen, it was to Bronagh Murphy.

She sighed when she seen Alec.

"I knew you would be here, your brothers are lookin' for you."

Bronagh came in and closed the door behind her.

Alec put his hand on her shoulder. "Don't get comfortable, we're leaving."

Bronagh frowned. "Why, what happened? Does she not believe you?"

Bronagh knew?

"Let's just say Keela isn't who I thought she was."

Bronagh frowned at Alec but when she looked at me, her eyes were narrowed.

"What did you do?"

I shrugged.

Bronagh opened her mouth to speak when the hall door

suddenly opened and Aideen entered the apartment with an excited Strom.

"Storm," I beamed.

He came right at me and nearly knocked me to the ground when he jumped up on me.

He licked the hell out of me.

"I missed you too, big boy!"

Storm nuzzled his head against me then sought out Alec.

"Hey buddy," Alec smiled and gave Storm's head a good hard rub.

"What's happenin' here?" Aideen asked.

"Nothing, just realising how wrong I was."

Both Aideen and Bronagh frowned at Alec.

"What were you wrong about?" Aideen asked.

Alec looked at me and said, "Keela."

I opened my mouth to defend myself when a loud knock on my hall door got everyone's attention.

Who the hell is *that*?

Alec opened the door again, but this time he answered it to two men, two tall men.

"Who are you?" Alec asked.

A face popped out from behind one of the tall men and smiled, "They work for me."

"Marco," Bronagh gasped and took a step back.

Marco laughed when he saw her. "Oh, this is perfect. Three for the price of two."

I furrowed my eyebrows together. "What the hell are you doin' here?"

Marco Miles switched his gaze from Bronagh to me then to Alec and sighed.

"You had to come see the mouthy Daley bitch the first time you leave your house in four days, didn't you? I'm gonna be in serious shit in Ireland now if Brandon finds out she is harmed."

I didn't know what he was talking about, but I knew it was

something bad so I answered my still ringing phone.

"Keela, don't hang up. I'm sorry, okay? I didn't mean-"

"Uncle, Marco Miles is at my apartment. He said he is goin' to hurt me."

Marco's face went red as he roared, "Get her."

Alec blocked the door with his body and shouted, "Run!"

"Storm!" I screamed and sprinted down to my bedroom, I looked back for Bronagh and Aideen but the men broke past Alec and while two were handling him, Marco had Bronagh and Aideen by the hair. I slammed my bedroom door shut and moved to the window, I pulled it open but it jammed half way up.

"No, no, no!"

I looked to my phone and put it to my ear.

"Uncle, help me!

"Keela, get out of there! I'm on the way-"

I screamed when my bedroom door was kicked open.

"Come here, bitch." one of the men who fought Alec snarled.

"No, please, no!"

I tried to hide my phone so I jammed it into my dress pocket as I turned back to the window. When it was safely in my pocket I tried to get out of the window but I was lifted up from behind before I could squeeze out the half opened window.

I screamed.

Then I heard a loud growl and Storm's bark.

The man who had a hold of my hair screamed in pain and I knew Storm had a hold of him.

Get him, Storm!

"Get off!" the man shouted.

Storm suddenly cried out and I think the man kicked him. It enraged me.

"Don't you hurt him, you bastard!"

The man screamed in agony and let go of me. I fell forward and crashed into the window. I didn't go through the glass but it did crack when my head made contact with it.

I gripped the windowsill and steadied myself. I lifted my hand to my forehead and groaned as pain began to pulse away.

I groggily turned around and I widened my eyes when I saw the scene before me. The man who had me was on the floor and Storm was attacking him, from what I could see Storm had a hold of the man's arm.

The man was using his other hand to bash at Storm's head to try and break his hold. I rushed forward and began kicking the man in the stomach to stop him from hitting my baby. The man swung his legs and hit the back of mine.

I went up into the air and a second later I slammed into the ground back first.

It hurt like hell and I cried out in pain.

"Keela!" Aideen screamed.

"Shut the fuck up!" Marco's voice bellowed, then I heard a loud smack that caused mayhem to erupt in the other room, in the form of Alec and Bronagh's shouts.

I refocused on Storm and the thug who was back to hitting him in the head with his free hand. I rolled onto my front, got up on all fours and began to crawl.

Just before I reached the man's body I watched in horror as he managed to break Storm's hold and knock him back. It was then I spotted the gun that was in the hand of the arm that Storm previously had a hold of.

There was blood all over the man and even though he was in a lot of pain, he managed to lift his gun wielding arm and point it at Storm who was already advancing back at him.

"No!"

Storm lunged towards the man then there was a loud bang. My ears rang and my head got a little dizzy.

"KEELA!"

I heard Alec and Bronagh scream for me, but I ignored them and watched as the man pushed a now immobile Storm off his body and onto the floor next to him. When I saw he wasn't moving I screamed louder than ever before.

He was lying on his side, his breathing was rapid and his leg was twitching.

He shot Storm.

"Storm!" I cried.

I crawled over to him and put my hand on his head. "It's okay, it's okay. You're goin' to be fine-"

Storm's loud whimper cut me off.

Oh, God.

"Help me! Somebody help me, please!"

I wished even Mr. Pervert would hear my calls and come to help, but no one came to my aid. No one.

I put my head down to Storm's.

"You're goin' to be fine, I promise... I'm here."

I looked up to see how bad his wound was when I noticed a growing patch of blood began to soak the floor under Storm.

Oh, God.

Please, no!

"Come here, bitch!"

I fought against the hand that suddenly tangled itself in my hair and screamed for help again. It was the last thing I said as a pulsing pain erupted in the back of my head and caused me to sail into darkness.

CHAPTER THIRTY-SIX

"Keela?"

I groaned.

"Wake up."

I groaned again, but blinked my eyes open. It took a minute for my eyes to adjust to the dimly lit room, but that didn't matter because I suddenly hissed in pain. My head was pounding and I felt like my stomach was about to explode.

"What happened?" I murmured.

"We were kidnapped."

I looked for the source of the voice speaking to me and when my eyes landed on Alec, I almost cried with relief.

"You're okay."

He was sitting against a wall and his arms were tied above his head with some rope that was nailed into the wall.

"Depends on what you mean by okay."

"You're alive."

Alec laughed. "Yeah, I'm alive."

He laughed, but he sounded far from happy.

"Storm," I whispered.

"I don't know Keela, he never came out of your room."

I sniffled.

Please, no.

"Where is Aideen?" I asked, wiping my eyes.

"They left her back at your apartment, Marco hit her and knocked her out so they left her on the floor."

I widened my eyes. "Was she breathin'?"

"Yes," Alec said. "She was just knocked out from the hit."

I nodded my head.

Please let her be okay.

"Where's Bronagh?"

"Next to you."

I looked to my left then my right and gasped when I found Bronagh strung up in the same position as Alec, but she was unconscious. I didn't understand, I wasn't tied down or bound in any way, I was just sat against a wall.

Why?

"He won't touch you, he is neck deep in shit now that Brandy knows he has taken you."

I looked at Alec. "How do you know that?"

Alec shrugged. "I pretended to be unconscious when we got here, so I overheard a few things."

I looked around the dark room we were in and swallowed.

"Did you happen to hear where we are?"

Alec smiled. "I know exactly where we are."

"Why are you smilin'?"

Alec chuckled. "Because I hate irony, and being in Darkness is about as ironic as things can fucking get right now."

I widened my eyes. "Darkness? The club where Bronagh, Damien, and Alannah were held by Marco a few years ago?"

Alec winked. "Good memory."

I frowned at him. "Why are you bein' like that?"

"Like what?"

"Cold."

"Cold? *Me?* I'm barely even lukewarm compared to you, baby."

I looked down. "I'm not cold, Alec."

"You are an ice queen, you heartless bitch."

I flinched and Alec laughed.

"Don't you dare play the wounded little girl, I know who you really are."

No, you don't.

I didn't respond to Alec, telling him I was pretending about all the vile stuff I said back at the apartment would fall on deaf ears right now because he was mad. I groaned as I pushed myself up to my feet. I placed my hand on the cold dark wall to steady myself when my head got dizzy.

That wanker who grabbed me hit me hard.

"We need to find a way out of here."

Alec laughed. "Don't let me stop you from searching for a way out, as you can see I'm a little tied up here."

I ignored him and looked around the room, I slowly walked over to the only door and tested the handle.

It was locked.

"Damn it."

"They won't make things that easy for you, princess."

I turned to face Alec.

"Stop it, hatin' me won't get us out of here. Put a stopper on your feelin's for a minute and focus."

Alec grinned. "Tell me what to do again, baby. I love it when you give me orders."

Damn him.

I stalked over to Alec and bent down until I was face to face with him.

"Hate me all you want, but I need you to focus so we can get out of here. Think of Bronagh."

Alec flicked his eyes to Bronagh's unconscious body and set his jaw.

"This is all your fault."

My fault?

"What? How?"

Alec growled, "If you never came to my house looking for my help we wouldn't fucking be here."

I felt tears gather in my eyes but I blinked them away.

"I had no idea about Marco's existence or about me uncle's business life when I met you. I had no idea any of this would happen! How dare you place the blame at me feet, I didn't put us here... *Marco* did."

Alec hissed at me and it frightened me so I pulled away and fell back onto my arse and yelped in pain.

It really hurt.

"What do you know you *can* feel something."

I turned my head away from Alec as I began to cry.

"Your crocodile tears won't get you any sympathy with me."

I covered my face with my hands and sobbed.

How the hell did this mess happen?

Alec sighed. "Enough, Keela."

I cried harder.

He was being so cruel. This wasn't the Alec I knew, this was a darker side to him.

"God dammit, why are you crying?"

"Because of you!"

"*Me?*"

"Yes you. You're bein' horrible to me."

Alec laughed. "For good reason."

No, not for good reason!

"Look, I lied to you when I said all that stuff back in me apartment. I did what you tried to do, I made you hate me to keep you safe. Me uncle told me if I didn't stay away from you or you family, that he would kill you all. I don't want that to happen so I said all that horrible stuff about us bein' fake so you would get mad and hate me... So you would never want to see me again... So you would be safe."

I pressed my face down into my knees as my tears fell.

"How am I supposed to believe you? How can I be sure that you aren't saying this as some sort of ruse?"

I cried harder. "Because I'm not horrible, I'm a good person! I did what I had to do to keep you safe and you hate me for it!"

Silence.

"Keela."

I ignored Alec.

"Keela!" he called my name, louder this time.

"What?" I snapped.

"Prove what you said in your apartment was a lie, prove you care for me."

What?

"How can I do that? You won't believe a word I say."

"Show me."

Show him?

I wiped my face and my running nose then turned to Alec.

"Show you?" I asked.

He nodded. "Show me... or are you too disgusted to touch me?"

I swallowed.

Before, I could only see him willingly touching Dante and Everly in my head, but now I can only see him being forced into a situation that he had no control over.

He didn't disgust me. Not in the slightest.

I carefully crawled over to him then straddled his body and placed my hands on his warm cheeks and brought my head down to his. I looked into his blue eyes and I rested my head against his and inhaled his scent.

"We're real," I whispered then covered his mouth with mine. I kissed him with every fibre in my body to show him how much he meant to me.

I felt my tears fall as I kissed Alec, they ran down to my mouth and blended into our kiss. Alec passionately kissed me back, and if he'd had the use of his hands, I knew he would be holding me tightly to him.

I slowly pulled back from kissing Alec and rested my forehead on his as I caught my breath.

I opened my eyes and found Alec's blue orbs staring back at mine.

"Hi," he whispered.

I cried. "Hey."

"I've missed you so much, kitten."

He believed my kiss.

He believed *me*.

I sobbed, "I've missed you too, playboy. I'm so sorry for leavin' you. I should have gave you a chance to explain when you wanted to-"

"Shh. It's okay, it's in the past now."

I put my arms around Alec and cried.

I cried until no more tears fell from my eyes.

"You look like shit," Alec said after I calmed down.

An unexpected laugh tore from my throat. "You don't look so hot yourself."

Alec brushed his nose against mine. "Can I ask you a question?"

I lightly grinned. "You just did."

Alec smiled. "You know what I mean."

I pecked his lips. "Yes, you can ask me whatever you want."

"Okay, will you marry me?"

I momentarily forgot how to breathe and began to cough when my lungs protested.

When I got a handle on myself I looked at Alec through wide eyes.

"What did you just say?"

Alec smiled. "Will you marry me?"

I gasped. "Are you jokin'?"

Alec deadpanned. "I've been kidnapped, beaten up, and now I'm tied to a wall - do I look like I'm jokin'?"

I blinked.

No, he looked dead serious.

"We've only known each almost two weeks."

Alec shrugged. "So? We will be *that* couple that does everything in haste."

I laughed. "I can't believe you're askin' me this - and that you're serious."

"When I heard that shot go off back in the apartment I can't tell you the pain that went through me not knowing if it was you who was on the receiving end of the bullet. Life is too short kitten. I want to be with you everyday for the rest of my life."

Oh my goodness.

"Alec," I whispered.

"I also wanted to ask you in case you hit me with it unexpectantly. I'm still pissed you told me you love me first."

I forgot how to speak.

Alec laughed at my facial expression. "Yeah, you said it and that's why I struggled so much when you went off on me at your apartment."

I blinked.

"When did I say I loved you?"

Did I love him?

Alec bit down on his lower lip.

"No more lies, I can't take anymore of them. If you have somethin' that you think I should know about then tell me... Please."

Alec looked directly into my eyes and said, "The night before things went to hell in the Bahamas, you told me you loved me as you were falling asleep. I didn't tell you because I wanted to be the one to say it first."

Oh, my.

It hit me then like a bullet to the heart, I did love him.

I loved him so much it hurt.

"Yes," I whispered.

"What?"

"Yes, I'll marry you."

"Keela," Alec breathed.

"I love you, I love you *so* much."

I kissed him hard and he reciprocated wholeheartedly.

"You're going to be my wife," Alec murmured into my mouth.

"And you're goin' to be me husband."

Alec sighed. "Storm isn't going to take this well."

I laughed and kissed Alec again.

"I don't mean to ruin the moment even though it was a beautiful one, but no one is gettin' married because we're still trapped in a room... and we might die."

Alec groaned when I pulled back from him.

"Way to put a downer on things, Murphy."

I looked at Bronagh and found her smiling at us.

"Congratulations."

I smiled. "Thank you."

Alec nuzzled my neck. "Okay wife, get us free."

I raised my eyebrow when I looked back at him.

He smiled. "Just getting a feel for it."

I playfully rolled my eyes at him then stood up, gripped onto the rope that bound him and pulled as hard as I could, but it didn't budge. I walked over to Bronagh and tried the same with her restraints, but they were solid too.

"Damn it, what now?"

We were all silent as we thought, but when I placed my hand into the pocket of my dress I squealed.

"What?" Alec asked.

I dug out my phone and showed it too him.

"Me dress doesn't look like it has pockets so they didn't search me!"

Alec frowned. "We're underground, it won't work."

Underground.

What?

I pressed on the screen of my phone and jumped when I saw my signal had a single bar.

"I've one bar, who will I call?"

"My brothers, they will help," Alec said.

"Call out a number."

Alec called out a mobile number and I dialed it into my phone.

I held my breath as I hit dial.

I squealed, "It's ringin'!"

It rang once.

Twice.

"Who are you and why don't I recognise your number?"

"Nico? It's me, Keela-"

"The bitch who broke my brother's heart, I know you who are. What do you want?"

Rude!

"I want your help! Me, Bronagh and Alec need it!"

Nico roared for his brothers then focused on me. "What's happened?"

"Marco is here, he kidnapped me, Alec, and Bronagh. Alec says we're in Darkness, please come and help us."

"Is Bronagh okay?" Nico asked, his voice rough.

"Yes, she is fine, but she is bound and so is Alec. I can't get them free."

"Fuck!" Nico bellowed. "Okay, Keela, keep calm and listen to me. Do you know how many men there are?"

"Marco had two with him at me apartment, I'm not sure how many more there are. We're locked in a room."

I could hear Nico filling his brothers in on what was happening and they reacted much like him.

They were pissed.

"Keela? It's Kane, you're doin' great, Red! Can you hear anything from the room you're in?"

I moved over to the door and pressed my ear against it. I could hear voices.

"Yes, I can," I said to Kane then focused back on the door.

I could hear two people talking.

"If shit blows up here, I'm getting the fuck out. Brandy doesn't fuck around when we miss a payment. Can you imagine what he will do when he gets wind that Marco has his fucking niece? It's a death sentence for us all."

There was a groan. "If we leave we're dead, Marco will kill us."

"So we leave during the chaos and trust me, there will be chaos. He won't get out of here alive, but we might."

Silence.

"What if the Slater's get here before Brandy and his men?"

"I don't know, they are just as dangerous. You heard Carter tell us about them and what they did to his brother Trent. He hates them and so does Marco, but they are both blinded by rage and that can get you killed."

"Carter is only a kid. He's back in the US so that little shit's opinion doesn't matter."

"It's only a matter of time before he comes here."

I pulled away from the door and put my phone back to my ear and whispered, "There are two men outside and they are talkin' about getting out of here before me uncle and you and your brothers get here."

Silence.

"Kane?"

I looked to my phone and found the call was ended and my signal bar was now empty.

"Fuck," I hissed and looked to Alec and Bronagh. "The signal is gone."

"It's okay, you did good. They know where we are. They are coming."

I nodded my head and moved over to Alec, snuggling next to him.

It was freezing.

"What else did you hear those men say?" Alec asked.

"They are talkin' about leavin' before your brothers or me uncle gets here. They don't want to die."

Bronagh laughed. "Marco sure has loyal followers."

I smiled and was about to speak when the door to the room was suddenly opened.

"Miss Daley, come with me."

"No fucking way." Alec snarled.

The man who entered the room laughed at Alec. "You're going to step up and stop me from taking her, are you?"

"Touch her and I'll kill you."

The man laughed and grabbed onto my hair, pulling me to my feet.

I screamed.

"Leave her alone, you prick!"

The man laughed at Bronagh and walked out of the room, pulling me by my hair with him.

"Keela!" Alec voice roared.

I could hear him screaming for me even after the door was closed, locking him inside the room again. It was muffled, but I still heard him.

I fought against the man holding me and as punishment for my resistance he turned me to face him and slapped me across the face. I cried out as a burning pain spread across my cheek.

It instantly throbbed.

"Be a good girl and be quiet, the boss wants a word."

CHAPTER THIRTY-SEVEN

"You have caused me a lot of problems, Miss Daley."

I wouldn't look at Marco when he spoke, I kept my head down and my hand placed over my burning cheek.

"Are you listening to me?" Marco asked.

I nodded my head.

"Then look at me."

I swallowed as I slowly lifted my head and my gaze to Marco.

He whistled. "What did you do to receive that welt?"

I shrugged. "Resisted goin' somewhere with a scumbag."

Marco laughed. "You are definitely your uncle's niece, there is no denying it."

Speaking of my uncle.

"He is goin' to kill you, I hope you realise that."

Marco lost him smile. "Like I said before, you have caused me a lot of problems."

I shook my sore head.

"How have I caused you problems? *You're* the one who kidnapped me."

Marco sighed. "I just wanted Alec. That son of a bitch somehow convinced Dante there is a better life out there. One that doesn't require him to be an escort. Dante was a money maker for me and now that he has dropped off the grid, that is a substantial loss for me. I like my money, and if you mess with it, I fuck with you."

I raised my eyebrow. "You want to fuck with Alec?"

L.A. CASEY

"What? No, that's not what I meant."

"But you said you-"

"I know what I said you smartass, but how you took it is not what I meant."

I tilted my head to the side. "How did you mean it then?"

Marco narrowed his eyes at me. "You're in no position to be asking question, Miss Daley."

I rolled my eyes. "You know my name so use it."

Marco grinned. "I take it your uncle's plan for Alec to be out of your life didn't work, am I right *Keela*?"

I set my jaw. "You're correct."

Marco laughed. "Brandon won't like that."

I shrugged. "He will get over it."

"You call the shots do you?"

I glanced around the large room I was in, noticing the booths, the bar and the large open dance floor as well as a darkened section of the club.

"I'm his niece," I said when I looked back to Marco, "there is not much me uncle wouldn't give me. He loves me."

I turned away and glanced around again.

"What are you looking for?"

I shrugged. "I'm wondering where your nephew was when he died."

Silence.

I looked to Marc with my heart in my throat.

"You're a brave cookie, I'll give you that."

I smiled. "You're the one who said I'm a lot like me uncle."

Marco snorted then glanced out to the floor and pointed to the centre of it.

"He died there."

I looked to where he pointed and I expected to see something, a stain of blood or something but there was nothing.

"Why come back here if he died here?"

Marco chuckled. "Darkness is the only place I own in Ireland, I don't own any other property so it made sense to come here."

I was surprised.

"You own this place?"

Marco shrugged. "I bought it the last time I was here, this place has character."

"Your nephew died here, who gives a fuck about character?"

Marco smiled. "You're correct about Trent dying here, but you're mistaken if you think his death meant anything to me. He meant nothing to me in life, he means even less in death."

That was foul.

"You're horrible."

Marco leaned back and gazed at me with a cheerful expression. "You don't get anywhere in my world when you have people you care about. Take your uncle for example; he has his wife, daughter, sister, and you. Any one of you could be used against him if the right people knew about you."

He was trying to scare me.

And it was working.

I wouldn't let him know that.

"It's a good thing you will be dead before you snitch."

Marco's expression darkened as he reached over the table and belted me across the face with a solid object.

I cried out in pain.

"I've had enough of your smart fucking mouth, you little whore. One more word and I'm using the primary function of this gun on your pretty face. Do you understand?"

I whimpered as I pulled my hand away from my stinging eyebrow and spotted blood. I then looked at Marco's hand and saw the gun he smacked me with.

"Do. You. Understand?" Marco snarled.

I nodded my head and pressed my hand against my eyebrow.

God it hurt.

I didn't know which pain to focus on, the one in my eyebrow or the one in my cheek.

"Good girl, now tell me, do you know where Dante is?"

I shook my head.

"Don't lie to me."

I whimpered. "I'm not lyin', the last time I seen Dante was back in the Bahamas."

"Alec never mentioned his whereabouts to you?"

I sniffled. "No, today is the first time I've spoken to Alec since I came home. I have no idea where Dante is or could be. I don't know anythin'."

Marco watched me with interest.

"You're either a really good liar, or you're telling me the truth."

I whimpered as blood escaped the cut on my eyebrow even though I had pressure on it.

"I'm tellin' the truth."

Marco pointed his gun at me and I screamed with fright.

"I'm tellin' the truth, I swear. Please, don't shoot me."

Marco sighed and lowered his gun.

He looked passed me.

"Bring the other two out here."

I heard footsteps then a few minutes later I could hear Alec and Bronagh.

"Keela?"

"I'm here." I turned and looked to Alec when he all but ran in my direction.

Marco pointed his gun at Alec.

"Not so fast Romeo, sit in the middle of the floor with your brother's bitch."

Alec did as ordered but he did it while looking at me. His mouth formed a tight line when he seen me cradle my face.

"Are you okay?"

I turned to him fully and he widened his eyes when me saw the blood.

"It depends on what you mean by okay."

My attempt to lighten up the situation with his own words

didn't work.

Alec stared at me. "Are you okay?"

I tried to be strong, but I broke down and shook my head.

I felt dizzy and my face was so sore.

Alec cut his eyes to Marco.

"She is defenceless you asshole."

Marco snorted. "She wasn't defenceless. Her mouth was her weapon, trust me."

Alec stewed as he looked to me then back to Marco. I could sense he wanted to come to me, but he couldn't and he hated it.

"Why are you doing this?"

Marco growled, "Because you convinced Dante to leave and go start a new life. He was my top earner after you left. All of my businesses took profit loses when you and your fucking brothers jumped ship. I was steadily building everything back up and now Dante is gone. Where is he?"

Alec look pessimistic and that worried me.

"He asked me what my life was like since I left and I told him the truth, it was, and is, fucking great. I didn't convince him of anything. If he left, he did so on his own free will."

Marco wasn't happy, he wasn't happy at all.

"You don't have free will when you work for me," Marco growled.

Alec kept eye contact with Marco. "Then where is Dante?"

Marco snapped, "Tell me here is he! I'm not going to ask you again, boy!"

My already pounding heart kicked into overdrive.

"I'm telling you the truth, I don't know where he is."

Marco lifted his gun and pointed it at Alec.

"I don't have time for bullshit."

"No, please, no!" I screamed.

"Tell me where he is or I'm going to kill your boyfriend."

Oh God!

"Please," I screamed.

"You bastard, don't bring her into this, she only met Dante once!"

I watched in slow motion as Marco rolled his hand over the top of the slide of the gun and cocked it back.

He was going to shoot Alec.

"Plane lists!" I screamed.

Marco paused what he was doing and looked at me.

"What?"

"You could check the outgoing flights from the Bahamas from two days ago. Dante would have to use his passport so his real name will be on a flight list."

Marco looked at me for a moment then smiled.

"Why didn't I think of that?"

Because you're a fucking psychopath maybe?

"Toby, run a search of all outgoing flights from the Bahamas from Thursday of last week."

"On it, boss."

I knew that voice.

Toby was the man who struck me and pulled me by the hair.

I stored that information and visibly relaxed when Marco lowered his gun, but my panic started all over again when Marco's focus switched to Bronagh. I noticed Bronagh had a dark red mark on her cheek, it looked very similar to mine.

"Nice to see you again."

"And you Marco, it's a pleasure as always."

Marco chortled.

I didn't know what their history was so I kept quiet. My head was hurting bad so I lowered it until it rested it on the table.

"Keela?"

I heard Alec's voice, but it took a minute for me to lift my head and look at him.

"Are you okay?" he asked.

I lightly shook my head. "Me head hurts," I said as I pulled my hand away from my eyebrow then put it back, "and the bleedin' won't stop."

Alec paled then looked at Marco.

"Marco, let me see to her cut. She is bleeding."

Marco looked down at me and waved Alec over as he turned back to Bronagh.

"Still dating Nico?"

Bronagh nodded. "Yep, we're still goin' strong."

"I'm happy for you both."

Bronagh snorted. "Yeah, I bet you are."

"Is my boy still fighting?"

"Yeah, but not for money, just for fun."

I tried to focus on the conversation but my focus switched to Alec when he moved into the booth next to me and lifted me head up off the table.

"Hi," Alec said, giving me a small smile.

I think I smiled. "Hey."

"Everything is going to be okay, I promise you."

I nodded my head and leaned against him but he kept me sitting up straight. I lazily watched as he ripped a large piece of fabric off the end of his shirt, then he did the same thing to my dress.

He folded up the fabric from his shirt then removed my hand from my head and pressed it against my eyebrow very hard.

"Ow," I whimpered.

"I'm sorry baby, the more pressure I apply the more it will help stop the bleeding."

I nodded my head.

"Hold this piece over your cut. I'm going to place this strip over that piece then tie it off behind your head, okay?"

"Okay," I said.

Alec did as he said, and it may have looked funny but it worked as a gauze and bandage under the circumstances. I leaned against Alec then jumped with fright when I heard a loud bang.

"What was that?"

"Toby, front door!" Marco bellowed.

"Front door is covered, it not coming from the entrance."

"Where the fuck is the exit?"

He bought a building and didn't know where the exit was?

"Eejit," I muttered.

"It's behind you," Alec said, and from the sound of his voice, he was smiling.

I opened my eyes and looked up at him, he was in fact smiling.

"Why are you similin'?"

"Because my brothers are here."

They were?

"Where?"

"There."

I looked down to Bronagh and followed her line of sight.

Dominic Slater was the first brother I spotted followed by Ryder, and Kane.

I lead my head back against the booth and relaxed.

We were going to be okay.

"Put your weapons down," Marco growled.

"We don't have any," Kane replied

Scratch what I said before we were going to die.

"You don't have weapons? Are you fuckin' around?" Bronagh's voice snapped.

"Sorry bee, I don't deal in that business anymore," Ryder said and for some reason I found it funny.

"A butter knife would be somethin' lads, not nothin'!"

I agreed with Bronagh, I was just too tired to voice it.

"So you come here unarmed... why?" Marco asked.

"Because your issue isn't with us, it's with him."

Him?

"Who is him?" Marco asked.

"I'll give you two guesses, but you're only goin' to need one."

Uncle Brandon!

"Oh, fuck!" Toby said from somewhere behind me.

Yeah, Toby knew what was up.

"I've tried to think of a logical reason as to why you took my niece into a hostile situation, Marco, but I just can't see past your stupid."

I mentally snorted.

"She was in the wrong place at the wrong time, it happens."

"That doesn't apply to what is mine, and *she* is mine."

Silence.

"Take her then, take her and leave."

I opened my eyes and could only see Marco's back with his arm raised.

He was pointing a gun at someone.

"It's too late for that."

Marco shook his head. "It's not, she is still alive. See."

Marco stepped to the left and gave my uncle a clear view of me.

My vision was a little blurry but I could see how pissed my uncle was.

He wasn't nice when he was pissed.

"What. Did. You. Do. To. Her?" my uncle growled.

"I didn't do anything, that was my men-"

"What men? You mean the two pricks who high tailed it up the entrance stairway less than a minute ago?"

Marco glanced around.

"Toby? Thomas?"

Toby and Thomas didn't reply to Marco's calls.

Things were silent for a moment then a loud bang sounded.

I jumped with fright.

"Toby or Thomas, one of them won't be answerin' to anyone," my Uncle Brandon said to Marco.

Marco turned his attention and gun back to my uncle.

"Take her and leave, my problem is with the brothers."

"No, your problem is with me. You see, me niece's lad is one of those Slater brothers, and I'm not tellin' her she can't have him again. I got an ear full the first time so I'm savin' meself a headache and leavin' them be. He is her's and she is mine, and we already know nothin' happens to what is mine."

I think that was my uncle's weird way of giving us his blessing. I smiled and so did Alec's brothers.

"I don't think you understand the concept of having a gun pointed at your head, Brandon."

"And I don't think you understand the concept of have ten pointed at yours, Marco."

I heard multiple clicks then.

I moved my head to see past my uncle and I caught sight of his men.

I counted six, but my uncle said ten guns so I knew the other four were around the room somewhere.

I tried to lean back against the booth, but I slumped forward. I would have hit the table except Alec grabbed my shoulder stopping it from happening.

"Slater, is she okay?"

"I think she has as concussion."

"Keep her awake," my uncle ordered.

I closed my eyes.

"Hey, you heard your uncle, stay awake."

I grumbled. "I'm tired... and me head hurts."

"I know, but we will be going home soon and then you can sleep."

Home.

I whimpered. "Aideen... Storm."

"They are okay. Aideen is awake and Storm is okay, it was a through and through flesh wound. Aideen and Branna are with him at the animal hospital now."

I began crying as relief flooded my body.

Aideen was okay and so was Storm. He was really going to be okay.

Thank God!

"You shot my niece's dog?"

"You sick bastard," Bronagh suddenly said and it made my uncle laugh.

"The girl said it."

"I didn't shoot it, but it attacked my men," Marco said in a defensive tone.

I growled, "He was protectin' me you sick twisted fuck."

"I heard for the past year that you we goin' insane. I wondered if it was the reason why you lost so many business partners and then I heard about your obsession with this family. I didn't fully believe it until now, I mean, shooting a dog? You really are fuckin' crazy."

Marco laughed like a madman. "They ruined me, everything fell apart when they jumped out."

"Your empire was never that strong to begin with if a group of brothers ran the show for you."

"You don't know what you're talking about."

My uncle laughed. "No, I actually do. You've lost everythin'. I did a background check on your finances and they are non-existent. You came to the Bahamas to sell this dump to me for fuck's sake, you even accepted half the price it's worth."

My uncle owned Darkness now?

"You thought Dante might earn you a quick buck too, where is he by the way?"

Everything went quiet.

Very quite.

"You know where he is?"

"I do, he came to me looking for an out so I gave him one."

What did that mean?

"I want him back."

"I'm afraid that can't be arranged. I take employee confidentially very serious."

Oh God.

"You son of a bitch, you pinched him?"

My uncle shrugged. "My niece's interest in Alec got me thinkin' on that branch of business. I thought I'd try my hand in it, hence Dante now being on me payroll"

I gasped.

"Uncle!"

My uncle laughed at me and so did his men.

"Sorry baby girl, it's only business."

I mentally rolled my eyes.

Gangsters.

I heard commotion behind me then shouting, it got everyone's attention.

"Get your fucking hands off me."

The man's voice wasn't Toby's so I guessed him to be Marco's other thug.

Thomas.

I heard Bronagh laugh as she spoke to Thomas and said, "It's not nice bein' pushed around by someone bigger than you, is it?"

Oh, he must have been the one to strike her.

"Fuck you!" Thomas snarled at her then hollered in pain.

I turned back to my uncle who stepped forward and snatched Marco's gun from his hand while he was distracted by Thomas. Marco didn't react though, he just sighed.

"Go ahead, shoot me! I have nothing left."

My uncle smiled.

"That would be too clean, Marco. You kidnapped me niece, that won't go unpunished."

Whoa, uncle Brandon looked feral.

My uncle looked behind him. "Turn the lights on for the back of the club."

I heard footsteps then after a moment the darkened area of the club lit up.

"Lads, help Thomas here up onto the platform."

Oh, Jesus Christ.

"Slater family, the fine man headin' to the platform gave that beautiful darlin' on the floor that pretty nasty mark on her face. Who wants to tell him it's not nice to hit women?" my uncle asked, grinning.

Nico Slater instantly walked forward, he paused by Bronagh and glanced down at her. She looked up at him, her hair fell out of her face showing just how swollen and red her cheek really was.

Fuck, Thomas hit her hard.

"I'll be back in two minutes, pretty girl," Nico said to Bronagh then looked towards the platform, set his jaw and walked forward.

Bronagh groaned, "Here we go again."

I watched as Nico reached his hands up to the platform and pulled his body up in one swift movement.

I swallowed when Nico rid him of his shirt and kicked his runners off. He stood facing a mean looking Thomas in just a pair of dark blue jeans.

Alec's little brother was fucking *hot*.

"Damn," I muttered.

"Are you kidding me?"

I jumped and looked up at Alec.

I smiled then winced. "Damn, me head hurts."

Alec rolled his eyes at me and looked back to the platform. I was waiting for some sort of whistle to blow, but none of the lads were waiting for one to blow. Not Thomas anyway who shot forward and speared Nico to the ground.

"Oh, fuck!" I shouted.

His poor back!

I think I felt Nico's pain because he didn't cry out, cringe or reach for his back at all, he simply wrapped his legs around Thomas's hips then used his power to roll Thomas under him.

I gasped and flung my hand over my mouth as I watched Nico deliver punch after lightening fast punch to Thomas's unguarded head.

"Cover your head!" I shouted.

I felt everyone's eyes on me then.

"Whose side are you on?" Bronagh asked me.

I flushed. "Sorry, I was sort of caught up in the moment."

My uncle laughed at me and shook his head. I looked back to the platform then and winced when Nico stood up and delivered a powerful kick to Thomas's stomach.

Nico paced back and fourth in front of him like a lion stalking his prey and it gave me goose bumps, he was straight animalistic on that platform. I can tell exactly why he won so many fights. He was amazing.

He didn't need to pace though because Thomas wasn't getting up; he was too busy writhing on the ground in pain.

"Dominic!" Bronagh shouted.

Nico looked to her and she said, "You won, babe."

Nico looked down at Thomas and kicked him once more then he hopped down off the platform and jogged over to Bronagh. He stood her up off the ground and hugged her body to his.

I smiled and leaned against Alec before I closed my eyes.

"Keela!" I jumped.

"What?"

I looked at my uncle who shouted my name and glared, "Don't do that."

I put my hand over my hammering heart and shook my head at my uncle.

He nodded to Marco.

"I thought you would like you witness Marco's platform debut."

What?

"What?" all the brothers said in unison.

Uncle Brandon nodded his head and suddenly two of his men grabbed Marco and forced him over to the platform. They got him up on it then kicked Thomas off it. He landed on the ground with a thud.

He was moaning in pain and for a moment I felt sorry for him, but then I looked at Bronagh's face and that sympathy went away.

"Who is fightin' Marco?" Bronagh asked.

"Me," Nico growled.

That seemed the logical choice since he was a fighter but when my uncle looked at Alec with raised eyebrows I broke out in a sweat.

"No," I said.

No way, he was not fighting Marco.

Alec sighed from beside me. "Keela, I have so much hate for that man right now, he has destroyed me family for too long, he has disrupted the Murphy sisters' lives for too long, and he did that to your face. Don't you fucking dare say no to me teaching that prick a lesson."

Holy fucking God.

"I don't want you to get hurt though," I whispered.

"I'll be fine."

"But Nico is the fighter, *not* you."

I started to cry.

"Sit tight and watch, you will see what a man is capable of when he is pushed to the edge."

Alec, please.

Alec got up and walked towards the platform. I stumbled out of the booth after him but arms came around me and halted my movements.

"Let him do this, red."

Kane.

I leaned my head back against Kane's chest because I felt so lightheaded I was afraid I would fall forward. I forced my eyes open just as Alec got up on the platform.

"How long have you wanted to get me into a situation like this, boy?"

Alec clenched his hands into fists. "For a long time."

Marco smiled and cracked his neck then rolled his head on his shoulders.

"Stay away from my ass, I don't swing that way."

That prick!

Alec laughed then pushed the sleeves of his t-shirt up to his elbows.

"The only thing going up your ass old man is my foot."

My uncle, his men and Alec's brothers either chuckled or flat out snickered.

I grinned as well.

Marco glared at Alec then out of nowhere rushed at him. I widened my eyes expecting to see Alec get speared to the ground like Nico did, but when Alec lifted his arms and swung at Marco the most disgusting thing happened.

Alec's elbow smashed into Marco's face and I heard the crunching sound from across the room.

"Oh my God!" I shouted.

Marco fell to the ground and hollered in pain. Alec reached down and pulled him back to his knees before punching him in the face and sending him back to the ground.

Marco turned in our direction and his face was covered in blood. I didn't know were it came from because it was all over his face.

He tried to crawl off the platform but Alec grabbed his legs and pulled him back.

"Stop!" Marco screamed.

Alec didn't.

Alec straddled Marco's chest, gripped his hair in his left hand and balled his right hand into a fist.

"This is for my parents," Alec snapped and punched Marco in the face. "This is for Nala." Another punch. "This is for Bronagh and Branna." Another punch. "This is for Aideen and Storm." Another punch. "This is for my kitten." Another punch. "And this if for me and my brothers you son of a bitch. You ruined our lives." Countless punches.

I felt my eyes well up with tears when Alec's voice cracked.

I looked away when Alec continued to beat Marco long after he stopped moving.

I moved out of Kane's hold and stumbled over to my uncle. I put my arms around his waist and placed my face against his chest and closed my eyes.

"I've got you, baby girl."

I gave him a squeeze.

"I'm sorry for what I did, I made a business choice and allowed it hurt you. I regret it dearly. I would take it back if I could, I swear it."

I didn't say anything as my uncle whispered to me.

"Do you hate me?"

I opened my eyes and looked up at my uncle. "No, I love you. You just made a bad decision, it will be okay. You're only human."

My uncle carefully kissed my sore head. "You're a good girl, Keela."

I smiled and placed my head back against his chest.

"Sir."

I froze when Alec spoke.

"Do I need to waste a bullet on Mr. Miles?" my uncle asked.

I swallowed.

I didn't like how casually he spoke of ending someone's life like that, even if the person who he was talking about was horrible.

I knew I would have to get over it though, after this night was over I knew I'd probably never hear of another incident like this ever again. It was still hard to wrap my head around the fact that my uncle was a gangster. Not only a gangster, he was the boss.

"No sir, you need to waste one on Thomas though. He is still breathing."

Jesus.

I heard footsteps.

"No, please... No." Thomas's voice moaned.

Bang.

I screamed into my uncle's chest and held onto him for dear life.

"Baby girl?" my uncle murmured.

I felt tears fall from my eyes, they slid down my neck and down onto my chest.

"Yes?" I asked.

"Your lad would like a word."

I swallowed. "The blood... I can't."

"He wiped it off."

I took in a deep breath and released as I slowly turned.

I looked up to a now shirtless Alec with his messy hair and a frowning face. He looked so young.

I looked down to his hands and could see some blood, but not enough to make me sick.

Alec watched me with nervous eyes, and I could tell he was afraid that I was disgusted with him and to prove that I wasn't I stepped forward and put my arms around him.

He wrapped his arms tightly around me and kissed the crowned of my head a few times then he sighed a sigh of relief.

I titled my head back and looked up at his tired face.

"Hi," he whispered.

I smiled. "Hey."

"I love you," he murmured.

"I love you, too."

"Ah bollocks, they are in love."

I laughed at my uncle, and so did everyone else. I moved to Alec's side and put my arm around his waist as I faced my uncle with him.

"I don't think I need to tell to look after her."

"You don't sir, I have her covered."

My uncle nodded at Alec then gave me a wink. "Go on and get home, I've got some work to finish up here."

I grumbled, "I don't wanna know."

My uncle smirked.

I turned with Alec and smiled at Nico who was kissing Bronagh. I moved away from Alec and grabbed her hand as I passed her. I tugged her away from Nico and threw my arm around my shoulder.

"You can help me up the stairs while the brothers converse."

Bronagh laughed and put her arm around my waist as we walked.

I looked over my shoulder just as Alec hugged his brothers. I smiled and so did Bronagh when she looked back. We turned and walked forward when the brothers looked at us.

"They caught us," I murmured.

Bronagh laughed then called for help when she buckled a little under my weight. I blinked my eyes open when another arm wrapped around me.

I looked at Alec and smiled as he held me close to his side. Bronagh held onto my arm that was still over her shoulder as she helped Alec walk me up the stairs of Darkness.

"Can you carry me?" I asked Alec.

"No, you have to stay awake."

"I will stay awake, I promise, your voice will keep me awake."

Alec awed.

"You're so sweet - you leave little footprints on my heart."

I glared up at him through my dizziness. "Keep that sarcasm up and I'll be leavin' little footprints on your face."

Alec glanced down at me and smiled. "You're perfect."

"You're a prick."

Alec laughed. "I'm a Slater, of course I'm a prick."

"Truer words were never spoken," Bronagh laughed. We were silent until we exited Darkness and stepped out into the night.

I gazed out at the city and all the lights then glanced up to the dark sky and took in a deep breath.

"I'm glad that's over."

"I'm glad Marco is dead," Bronagh murmured.

I looked to her with wide eyes.

She sighed. "I'm not evil, the world is just a better place without that man."

After my brief encounters with Marco, I could only agree with her.

"I hope Aideen and Storm are okay."

"You heard Kane, Aideen is fine and the pup is okay. Aideen and Branna are with him now."

I lightly shook my head. "That's what I'm worried about, Storm hates Aideen."

CHAPTER THIRTY-EIGHT

"What time did Branna say we have to be there for dinner?" Aideen asked me.

"Five," I replied.

It's half five, the brothers will kill us. Branna won't let anyone eat until we get there."

I looked to a stressed out Aideen and smiled. The bruise on her face was still clear, but it was healing nicely. I couldn't help but feel terrible for her, the bruise and cut she received the night I met Alec was almost healed and now the other side of her face was injured.

Poor girl.

"They will understand, we were with Storm."

"*You* were with Storm since ten this mornin'."

I shrugged. "So? He was shot ten days ago, give him a break. He won't be back to full strength for awhile, it's why he is still at the hospital."

Aideen grunted. "He is milkin' it, I'm fuckin' tellin' you he is. I *saw* him sit up earlier then when you looked at him he quickly laid down and start whimperin' and shite lookin' for sympathy treats. He has easily gained ten pounds in that hospital."

I laughed. "You're losin' it, man."

Aideen grumbled about Storm and it made me smile.

Things were already back to normal.

Ten days ago I was kidnapped and you wouldn't even know it by the way I was acting.

My Uncle Brandon told me 'not to worry' and that he would 'clean up everything' at Darkness. I have no idea what he did with

Marco, Toby, and Thomas's bodies, but I didn't want any idea so I was fine with being kept in the dark.

The first few days after the incident I was very jumpy, and found sleeping at night difficult but the brothers' and my uncles' advice, was to simply 'get on with life' so that was what I was trying to do.

"What are you doin'?" Aideen suddenly shouted then gaped at the car that over took us. "What. The fuck. Are you doin'?"

I snorted and pulled down the visor in front of me so I could look at my face. I winced when I seen my face. I had to get five stitches in my eyebrow to close the cut, but that was nothing compared to the swelling and bruising I dealt with. Thankfully the pain was minimal now and everything looked worse than it felt.

"I'm goin' ten miles *over* the speed limit, is that not enough for you?" she hollered.

I lightly snickered at Aideen and closed the visor.

"Where the hell did these wankers get their licenses?" Aideen snapped to herself.

I bit down on my lip as a car changed lanes in front of us without indicating they were going to do so. Aideen's face got so red I thought her head might pop off her shoulders. I watched in amusement as she lowered her window down and bellowed, "Nice indicator, arsehole!"

I lost it - I literally rolled around in my seat laughing.

"Is that the Garda behind us?" Aideen murmured and checked her mirrors, then gasped. "Fuck, it *is* the Garda!"

I heard the noise of a siren and I laughed harder.

We were getting pulled over!

"Keela, pull up your dress!" Aideen hissed at me as she pulled into the break down lane.

I looked at her and said, "Excuse me?"

She was peering into her rear view mirror while she undid some buttons on her top. "It's two male guards, I'll use my tits and you use your legs. Pull. Up. Your. Dress!"

"You have got to me jokin' me!"

Keela snapped her head in my direction. "Does it look like I'm jokin'?"

No it didn't and that's what I was freaked out about.

"Oh my God!" I snapped when she exposed herself.

Jesus, forgive me.

I shimmied up my dress so *a lot* of leg was showing.

I looked directly ahead and jumped a little when the glass on Aideen's side of the car was tapped.

"Evenin' sir, can I help you with somethin'?"

"Um... well, yeah. Do you know how fast you were goin'?"

"No, sir."

I glanced to my right and noticed Aideen pushed her chest out.

Fucking slag.

"Nine miles over the limit."

Ten.

"Oh, I'm sorry sir. I didn't even realise."

I looked out my window when the other guard walked by and checked the tax and insurance discs in the dash window. He walked back by my window then slowed down and took a longer look at my legs.

I looked up at him and smiled.

He smiled and nodded his head.

Dammit, I was a slag too.

"I'll let you off with a warnin' this once."

"Oh, thank you, sir."

"You ladies have a nice evenin'."

The guards went back to their car, so Aideen took off and kept under the speed limit.

"I feel dirty!" I snapped.

Aideen burst out laughing. "I can't believe it worked!"

I shook my head and folded my arms across my chest and remained quite until we got to the Slater's and Branna's house. Aideen and I jumped out of the car and quickly walked up the garden steps.

The door was flung open.

"It's about fucking time!" Nico bellowed. "I'm starving!"

I rolled my eyes and we passed him and walked down the hallway.

"Don't blame me, blame Keela."

I gasped as I entered the kitchen. "Blame me? That's rich. Who's the one who got pulled over for speedin'? That's right bitch, you!"

Aideen rolled her eyes. "We got out of that situation in less than five minutes."

I glared. "Yeah, but at the risk of losin' our self-respect!"

"How did you lose your self-respect?" Ryder asked.

I snapped my fingers. "I'll tell you how, Aideen used our bodies to get out of a speedin' ticket."

"You didn't!" Bronagh said then burst into laughter.

It wasn't funny!

"It wasn't as bad as she is makin' it out-"

"My dressed was hiked up so high you could see me knickers and your tits were on display for the world to see."

"I don't suppose anyone took pictures-"

"Dammit Dominic, shut up," Bronagh snapped to a smirking Nico.

"It wasn't *that* bad... besides he let me off with a warnin', it was a success."

I rolled my eyes then jumped when I felt arms come around me from behind.

"Hi," Alec whispered in my ear.

I smiled. "Hey."

"How's the pup?"

I beamed. "He is great. The doctor said we can take him home in three or four days."

"I'm tellin' you all that dog is fakin' it."

"He was shot Aideen, give him a break."

ALEC

I walked over and high fived Kane. "Thank you."

Aideen glared at Kane. "You keep out of this, germinator."

I smiled while Kane growled in annoyance.

He has been sick the past two weeks, so Aideen dubbed him the "Germinator" and he hates it.

"Leave him alone," Branna frowned and hugged Kane.

Kane grinned and hugged Branna tightly. "Yeah, leave me alone."

Ryder glared at Kane and shook his head.

"I'll serve dinner now that everyone is here," Branna said.

"Praise Jesus!" Nico shouted.

"Would you stop? You eat every five minutes, you're not starvin'."

Nico groaned. "Stop watching what I eat and how often I eat, it's driving me insane woman."

"Like Marco insane?" I asked.

Alec burst out laughing.

"Not that insane," Nico smirked to me.

"Keela."

I looked at Alec and walked over to him when he nodded for me to.

"What?"

"Hi," he smiled.

I chuckled. "Hey."

"I got you something."

I smiled. "You did?"

Alec nodded and reached into his pocket and took out a small black box.

"Oh my God!"

He got down on one knee.

"Oh my God!"

He held opened the box and revealed a beautiful diamond ring.

"Oh my God!"

He smiled.

"I didn't ask you properly the first time, so I wanted to do it right this time."

"Oh my God!"

Silence.

"Keela Daley, I love you and I'll spend the rest of my life proving just how much I cherish you. Only you. Not even your girl crush to-do list can get in on this. Will you marry me kitten?"

I laughed.

Would I marry Alec?

"Hell yes!" I replied.

Cheers erupted from behind us as Alec slid my engagement ring onto my finger. He stood up, took my face in his hands and kissed the daylights out of me.

When we broke apart, the girls attacked me while Alec's brothers slapped hands and hugged him.

"Congratulations!"

I hugged all the girls, then the brothers.

"Can I call you sis now since you're going to be my sister-in-law?" Nico asked me.

"You can call me whatever you want to."

Nico grinned and just as he opened his mouth, Bronagh whacked him across the back of the head.

"I wasn't going to say anything!"

Bronagh grinned. "Good."

Nico grumbled under his breath then grabbed Bronagh by her arse and pulled her down onto a kitchen chair with him.

I laughed at them then stared down at my ring.

It was beautiful.

"Do you like it?" Aideen asked when she popped up beside me.

"I love it."

"Good, because I helped pick it out."

I shoved her. "You're so sneaky."

She grinned and gave me a hug.

"You know you're me maid of honour, right?"

Aideen began jumping up and down excitedly and so did Bronagh and Branna when I told them I wanted them as bridesmaids.

"You have it easy," Alec said to me when I found him in the home gym a few minutes later.

"How?"

"I have to pick a best man out of four brothers. No matter who I pick, the bastard will rub it in the face of the other three."

I chuckled. "You're brothers, it's to be expected."

Alec sighed then kissed my head when I put my arms around him.

"I'm nervous about seeing your mom tonight, how do you think she will take the engagement news?"

I shrugged. "I don't care how she takes it, we're happy and that's all that matters."

I leaned up to kiss Alec when suddenly Aideen graced us with her presence.

"I have to give you the talk, Slater."

Alec looked up from me to look at Aideen and grinned. "What kind of talk?"

"The don't-hurt-me-friend-or-I"ll-kill-you talk."

Alec nodded his head. "Ah, *that* talk."

I snorted.

"I like you Alec you're a good lad, but if you ever harm me friend in anyway, I will kick you so hard between the legs that your balls will be picking your balls out of your teeth for a week. We clear on that?"

Alec stared wide eyed at Aideen for a moment then flicked his eyes to me and whispered, "Was I just threatened by a leprechaun?"

I nodded my head.

Yes, yes you were.

Alec turned back to Aideen and hesitantly smiled. "Crystal clear, beautiful."

Aideen grinned. "Flattery doesn"t work on me, blue eyes.

Remember that."

"How about chocolate... does that work?" Alec asked.

Aideen froze then murmured, "Dairy Milk, Carmel."

I laughed. "So it's okay for him to hurt me once you get chocolate off him?"

"But it's Dairy Milk, Carmel... that chocolate is amazin'. World war could be forgiven with that chocolate."

I shook my head and laughed.

Aideen frowned. "I'm a bad friend."

"Go help Branna with dishin' out dinner, crazy."

Aideen smiled then pranced off into the kitchen.

"She drives Kane crazy."

"Only because he wants her and can't have her."

Alec laughed. "True."

I smiled up ask Alec and he sighed.

"You know something?"

"What?"

"I love you to Neptune and back."

My heart warmed as I laughed. "You mean you love me to the Moon and back?"

Alec shook his head. "Nah, Neptune is the furthest planet from Earth in our solar system so the greater the distance, the greater my love."

Oh, wow.

I teased. "I thought Pluto was the furthest planet from the sun?"

Alec shook his head again. "Pluto isn't known as a planet anymore; it's a dwarf planet meaning neither planet nor moon."

"How do you know that?" I murmured.

Alec put his arms around me and looked down at my now tear filled eyes. "I told you, I watch the Discovery Channel."

"I'm so hot for you right now," I declared making Alec laugh.

I wasn't joking.

I leaned up and kissed him.

ALEC

God, I was lucky.

When our kiss broke I said, "I love you to Neptune and back, too."

Alec beamed and said, "Good, I expect nothing less from my future wife."

Wife.

"Holy fuck, we're gettin' married."

"Yep, and since it's in serious haste, I say we do everything ass backwards. How do you feel about getting knocked up tonight?"

I burst into laughter. "Slow down, Romeo, let's just deal with the knowledge that we're gettin' married. Babies can come later... *much* later."

Alec shrugged. "Fine by me, I get to keep you to myself for longer."

"Alec, Keela... dinner!"

Alec slapped my behind. "Come on, she gives away seconds when she is in a good mood."

I chuckled and followed Alec into the kitchen. I sat down next him and winked at Kane who was on the other side of me. Everyone was silent then and still as statues, everyone except Aideen who reached for the mashed potatoes first.

"First!" everyone shouted making me and Aideen jump with fright.

"What?" I asked.

"Aideen reached for dinner first so she has to say grace."

Oh, nice.

Aideen groaned. "That's not fair, I didn't know you lot did that!"

"Say grace, please," Nico pleaded and stared at the food on the table.

I snickered at him.

"Okay, fine."

Everyone held hands and lowered their heads.

"Hey God, it's me... Aideen Collins. I know we haven't spoken in a long time, since you took me ma away from me when I was a little girl. The Slater's are making me pray to you so I can eat their food. I don't want to be rude so I'm doin' as asked, I hope this is good enough because I've no idea what else to say to you... Oh, I know, bless this house and everyone it in it. Thanks. Amen."

"Amen," everyone chorused.

I covered my mouth with my hand as my shoulders began to shake.

Alec and Kane were both the first to laugh out loud, and everyone quickly followed suit.

"I hope you don't lead morning prayers in your classroom, Aideen," Alec laughed.

She rolled her eyes. "I pick different kids every day to do that actually."

"Thank God," Kane murmured.

Aideen cut her eyes to him and snarled, "This is exactly why I'm such a bitch to you!"

"What is 'this'? Do you have a list of reasons or something?" Kane asked, amused.

Aideen's eyed twitched. "Yeah, I've two reasons as to why I'm a bitch to you. Number one, you're fuckin' stupid. Number two, see number one!"

I burst out laughing.

"That was just rude," Kane said and shook his head.

We all chuckled and dug into the food Branna made for us, and let me tell you it was *so* good. We discussed random things all through dinner, there was no mention of the previous week's events and that couldn't have made me happier.

"That was amazing, Bran. Thanks." Nico beamed and leaned back in his chair, more than stuffed from the looks of things.

Nico caught me staring at him so he winked and blew a kiss which made me laugh.

"Leave the girl alone, she doesn't want your nasty arse makin' kissy faces at her."

Nico looked at Bronagh and grinned. "Every girl wants my *sexy* ass making kissy faces at them."

Bronagh rolled her eyes. "Is that so?"

"It is."

"Too bad all those girls don't have to deal with your man-child arse."

Nico snorted. "They would happily deal with me if they knew that I have to deal with your phat ass all by myself."

Oh, no he didn't.

"Nico, you bastard, you don't *ever* say a girl has a fat arse. Are you fuckin' serious?" I snapped.

All the males looked to me and groaned.

"A phat ass is a *good* thing!" they stated in unison.

"On what universe is sayin' someone has a fat arse a good-"

"Alec! Sort your woman out and explain it to her. I cannot go through this again, it took me *years* to convince Bronagh I'm not insulting her. I'll fucking cry if I have to go through that again."

"I'll explain later," Alec murmured as he watched the couple across from us.

Bronagh turned to Nico and glared.

"One, two, three, four, five-"

"Dominic leave the room," Ryder murmured.

Nico was already on his feet and all but ran out of the room.

"-Nine, ten." Bronagh finished counting and opened her eyes.

She blew out a big breath and said, "I'm goin' for a run on the treadmill."

When Bronagh left the kitchen, I looked at Alec to find he was rubbing his face with his hands. "What the hell was that?"

Alec removed his hands and sighed. "That was Dominic and Bronagh, kitten."

I raised my eyebrows. "They have short fuses."

"You don't know the half of it."

"Have they ever thought of anger manag-"

"Bronagh starts classes next week," Branna cut me off.

I nodded my head. "Good for her."

"Yeah, but God help that class when Hurricane Bronagh blows through," Ryder murmured.

"I heard that!"

Ryder widened his eyes and shouted, "Just kidding."

I chuckled and looked at Kane and noticed he didn't eat much. "How are you feelin'?"

Kane looked to me with tired eyes and smiled. "Good."

I gave him a frown that he chuckled over. "It's just the flu, I'll be fine."

Branna huffed. "It's been almost three weeks, it's not the fuckin' flu. You need to go to the hospital."

Wow.

He was *that* ill?

"Bran, it will pass-"

"You aren't a doctor so don't try pacify me, Kane."

Kane sighed. "If it will make you feel better, I'll go to the doctor during the week to get seen, okay?"

Branna stared Kane down. "I'm goin' with you."

"Oh for the love of God," Kane muttered. "Fine, okay."

Everyone lightly chuckled, but I got a sick feeling in my stomach when I looked at Kane.

I hoped he was all right and that it *was* just the flu.

Alec put his arm around my shoulders and grinned getting my full attention.

"Welcome to the family, kitten."

ALEC

CHAPTER THIRTY-NINE

"We have to get a bigger place," Alec murmured to me as I wiped down my kitchen table.

We were both in the kitchen and bumped off each other about ten times as we cleaned.

I sighed. "It's annoyin' I know, but we can start looking after I get a new job, I still can't fucking believe I got sacked for staying out a day longer than I said I would. Why would they even want me there on the tills? I'll only scare the costumers with my face bein' so messed up."

Alec frowned. "Why don't you just focus on writing and let that be your job?"

I laughed. "Because I actually need an income to support us. That's why."

"Keela, you know I have a lot of money... right?"

I looked at Alec. "You do?"

He nodded. "We can buy own place outright tomorrow if you want too."

I widened my eyes. "*That* much money?"

"I earned a lot working for Marco and I'm not a huge spender. I have close to four million Euros sitting in my bank account right now."

My finger was around a cleaning spray bottle, and when Alec said that high number, my fingers automatically pulled on the spray trigger.

Holy fuck!

"Why do you live with you brothers if you have so much

money?"

Alec shrugged. "We *each* have a lot of money... and none of us ever lived on our own before. We saw no reason to until Bronagh, Branna, and you came along. Myself and my brothers are very close, we only had each other growing up."

I frowned. "I know, babe."

Alec smiled at me. "Then it's settled we can buy a house soon, preferably in Upton, and you can focus on writing as your work."

I smiled only because I didn't trust myself to speak.

"What's wrong?" Alec asked.

I shrugged.

"Tell me."

I sighed. "I've takin' care of meself all me life. I refused me uncle's help at every turn and banned me mother's. I don't feel right lettin' you just buy a house for us-"

"My money is your money. We're engaged Keela, what's mine is yours and what's yours is mine."

I sighed. "I guess... but it still feels weird."

"This all feels weird because we jumped into things very fast. We will get used to it, just give it time."

I nodded my head.

Alec smiled. "So your book... when do I get to read it?"

I gasped. "You're not readin' it."

"Why not?" Alec asked, hurt in his voice.

I flushed. "Because I don't want you to read the... dirty scenes."

Alec smirked. "Kitten, I'm sure your scenes are things I've done to you-"

"Exactly so you're not readin' them."

Alec snickered. "Don't get your panties in a twist about it."

"I'm not a violent person Alec. God knows I'm not, but I swear to him that if you call knickers 'panties' one more feckin' time, I will strangle you with a thong!"

Alec shook his head as he laughed.

"Come on, I like reading. I won't read it as your man, I'll read it as a bete reader person."

I laughed. "You mean *beta* reader?"

"If that's what you did for your friend Yessi and Mary on their books, then yes, that."

I groaned. "I just finished the first draft, I don't even know if I'm goin' to self-publish-"

"Why not?" Alec cut me off.

"Because what if no one approves?"

Alec arched a brow. "You mean readers or people you know i.e. your mom?"

I nodded my head. "She will slam it when she finds out about it, she doesn't like smut books."

"What is smut?"

I shrugged. "Books that have erotica in them. Sex."

"But your book has romance too, sex is a part of romance."

I laughed. "Not with my mother."

"Baby, I mean this in nicest way possible but fuck your mom. If you want to publish a book about sex and love then fucking publish a book about sex and love. Fuck everyone who has a negative opinion on it. They only hate on your ideas and dreams because *they* have no ideas and dreams. Do this for you, no one else. Do you understand?"

I felt my heart pounding against my chest. I loved him for having so much faith in me.

"I hear you, I really do, but what if I'm not good enough? What if this is impossible? Just writin' a book isn't enough. The fuckin' line I need to cross to actually self-publish might as well be invisible. I can see it, but can't get to it. It's so damn hard."

Alec gripped my shoulders. "Those who can see the invisible can do what seems impossible."

I leaned my head forward and rested it against his chin. "You're amazin'."

"I know."

Smartarse.

I pulled back and stared up into his eyes. "You're gettin' very deep on me."

Alec's hands gripped my behind. "I'll be getting very deep *in* you if you keep looking at me like that."

I couldn't help it, I giggled.

"The only person who can stand in your way is you, kitten, no one else." Alec brushed his nose against mine. "And that's not an option, right?"

I nodded my head. "Right."

Alec smiled. "So I can beta read your book?"

I sighed. "Sure, why not?"

Alec punched the air in delight and it made me laugh, but my laughter stopped when three loud bangs thudded against my hall door.

"Gird your loins, the devil is here," I murmured.

I walked over to my door, looked through the peephole and sighed when I saw my mother's less than amused face on the other side. I opened the door and let her in.

"Hello, mother."

My mother walked inside my apartment.

"Keela, Alec." She nodded.

I closed the door already wishing she was walking back out through it.

"You missed your cousin's wedding, Keela."

I sighed and turned around. "Yes mother, I did."

My mother was furious.

"I can't believe you would be so selfish."

Selfish?

"You don't know what you're talkin' about, mother."

My mother began to pace up and down. "Your uncle tried to make excuses for you. Even Micah was okay that you couldn't be there, but I wasn't. You should have been there."

"Well, I wasn't and you know somethin'? I don't care that I wasn't there. Me and Micah are not close ma, I don't think we ever will be. I can't stand Jason, he is a disgustin' person so when the opportunity came for me to leave the resort I took it. So sue me."

My mother snarled, "You always think about yourself."

I laughed. "No, ma, I don't think about meself enough."

"I can't believe I birthed such an evil cow."

Her words stung but I could do nothing but laugh.

"That is all you ever did. You gave birth to me, that's it as far as bein' a mother goes for you."

"Why you ungrateful little, bitch! I gave you everything growing up!"

I exploded.

"You gave me toys and other materialistic things! You *never* gave me love. You made me feel like a burden, you *still* make me feel like a burden and I'm fuckin' done with it. I'm done with *you*!"

My mother stepped back like I'd slapped her.

"What would you do without me?"

I looked at Alec and smiled. "I will be happy."

My mother looked at Alec then back at me.

"Fine, enjoy your little romance but when it goes belly up and this one leaves you for a better looking woman don't come crying to me."

The fucking nerve!

"I can assure you, you will be the *last* person I ever go to for help or comfort."

My mother took a step closer to me. "You're like your scumbag father, impossible to love."

I wanted to cry but I refused.

"You know what, ma? It doesn't matter what you say or think about me. What matters is the way I feel about myself and I fuckin' love meself!" I said with my chest pushed out and my head held high.

"I love herself as well, just putting that out there."

I stood a bit taller when Alec came to my side and put his arm around my waist.

"This won't last," my mother hissed.

"Get out of me house and don't ever come back."

My mother stayed put.

Alec cleared his throat. "I believe my *fiancée* asked you to leave, ma'am."

My mother was so shocked at Alec's declaration that she only stared at us both.

I moved away from Alec and walked to the door, opening it wide.

"Goodbye, mother."

My mother composed herself and stuck her chin out. She left my apartment and turned to face me before she walked down the hallway. "I won't miss you."

I swallowed. "I feel sorry for you. You're a bitter woman with nobody. I have a fiancé and a new family that means a million times more to me than you ever did. Have a nice life mother, because I sure as hell will."

I closed the door in her face and froze.

Did that just happen?

"Kitten?"

I took a deep breath. "I'm fine, I'm okay."

I turned to Alec and smiled, but at the same time tears fell from my eyes.

"Baby," Alec whispered.

I moved to him and wrapped my arms around his body.

"I'm not sad, I'm relieved."

Alec kissed the crown of my head. "I'm proud of you."

I hugged him tightly. "I'm proud of me too."

We were silent for a few minutes until Alec spoke.

"You know what I think you should do now?"

"What?"

"Forgive Micah and Jason."

Excuse me?

I pulled back from Alec. "What?"

ALEC

"I know it seems crazy, but you just made peace with yourself and released yourself from you mother. It's time to do the same with Micah and Jason. You don't have to like them or involve them in your life, but you should forgive them."

I widened my eyes. "You want me to forgive him for doin' me wrong and forgive her for treaten' me like dirt all me life?"

Alec nodded his head. "Yeah, I do. I care about you so much Keela, and I refuse to watch you become a hateful person because of them. You don't have to like them, but forgive them."

I felt my eyes well up. "But *why*? Why can't I just hate them?"

Alec stepped forward and took me in his arms. "Holding a grudge is like drinking poison and expecting the other person to die. It eats away at you until it consumes you completely."

I frowned.

"Weak people seek revenge, strong people forgive, and intelligent people ignore. Which one are you?" Alec asked me.

I thought about it for a moment then said, "I'm all three. I'm a strong, intelligent person who sometimes has weak moments."

"You know what that makes you?"

I shook my head.

Alec smiled. "It makes you human, kitten."

I processed what he said; it took me a few minutes but I eventually nodded my head.

He was right.

I closed my eyes and thought about Micah and Jason. I thought about how horrible Micah was to me all my life, and how cruel Jason was. Even though nothing would change the past, I just thought about the three simple words that would change how I shaped my future.

I forgive you.

I wouldn't let Micah get me down anymore.

I forgive you.

I wouldn't let Jason have a hold over me anymore.

I forgive you.

I wouldn't let either of them have any impact on my life, none whatsoever.

I forgive you.

I blinked open my eyes and smiled at Alec. "I think it will take some time to be uncarin' when it comes to them, but I forgive them... Besides, Micah said at the weddin' she was workin' on not actin' like such a bitch all the time. There may be hope for her yet."

Alec kissed my forehead. "You're free, kitten."

I exhaled. "I feel it."

"Well, you're semi-free. I put a ring on it after all."

I looked down to my engagement ring and laughed.

Alec nuzzled his nose against mine. "I love you to Neptune and back."

I leaned up and kissed Alec's lips. "I love you, too."

"Come to bed," Alec's voice suddenly broke the silence of the night.

I got such a fright I almost came up off the settee.

The kitchen light flicked on and made me squint until my eyes adjusted.

"I don't like you being with other men, so come to bed. Now."

Other men?

Was he high?

"What are you talkin' about?" I asked, quizzically.

Alec grunted. "The guy's you write about and spend all your time with lately may be fictional, but it counts as spending time with other men so come to bed now."

I let a huge smile take over my face. That was the most adorable thing he has ever said to me.

Besides the penguin story of course.

"I'm beta reading *Something Sweet* by MJ Morphis."

"MJ... Is that Mary, the blonde women on your Facebook page?" Alec asked and I nodded my head.

"Did she write that book that had the nipple butter scene in it?" Alec laughed.

I snickered. "No, that was Yessi's book, *Love, Always*."

Alec hummed.

"What is happening with your *book*?"

I shrugged. "It's being beta read for plot holes and such. I'll put it on me Kindle tomorrow so you can read it, okay?"

Alec nodded his head then flicked his eyes to my laptop.

"What is it?"

He shrugged. "Every time you're on that thing lady, you're 'with your characters'... it's bugging me."

"You're jealous of my characters?" I asked as I saved my work and shut down my laptop.

"They get your attention."

I smiled as I walked towards Alec. "You want all me attention?"

Alec grinned. "All day, every day."

"Until Storm comes home you can have my undivided attention, playboy."

Alec waggled his eyebrows then deadpanned, "What do you mean until Storm comes home? What about after he is home?"

I smiled as I walked by Alec.

"I'll divide things up fifty-fifty."

Alec followed me down the hall to our bedroom.

"But we're getting married!"

I laughed. "Exactly."

Alec groaned as he shut our bedroom door.

"Fine, I'll take what I can get."

I smirked as I turned to face him, my hands placed on my hips.

"So... what do you want do to?"

"I want to play a game," Alec grinned and took a step towards me.

"What game?" I asked, smiling wide.

Alec hummed. "Let's play our clothes are on fire."

I laughed as Alec rushed forward and tackled me onto our bed.

He hovered over me and smiled. "Hi."

I beamed. "Hey."

I took this moment to be thankful. Thankful for laughter, thankful for family, thankful for Alec, and thankful for the life he breathed back into me. He was my savour, my rock, my future husband... and he was drop dead gorgeous.

Damn, I was a lucky bitch.

ACKNOWLEDGEMENTS

I did it. I finally did it. Alec is complete. Thank you, God!

I have a very large crew of people to thank, no, more like a village of people to thank.

As always I'd like to thank God first and foremost, through Him all things are possible.

I wouldn't be where I am today without my daughter; you're the best thing ever to happen to me. I love you with all my heart, mini me.

My family. My crazy family. Everyone from my parents straight down to my second cousins have shown me nothing but love and support. Thank you all for believing in me, and hijacking family events to promote my books; I'm looking at you, ma. LOL. Love you all!

My sister, my crazy partner in crime. I love you so much, and I'm so happy you get to share in this incredible journey with me. You help me with everything; you listen to me go on and on about the same things in my books for months, and you haven't attempted to murder me yet. You're a star.

My crew of superwomen aka my beta readers! Yessi, Jill, Neeny, Dawn - I love my stalker ;) – Kelly, Jodi, and Mary. I love each of you so much, and I am so grateful to have such a force of crazy awesomeness behind me. Thank you for everything you do.

Yessi, my sister from another mister. Getting to know you over the past year has truly made me believe God placed us on different sides of the Earth because people would not be able to handle us together. You're the Hispanic version of me, and I love you. Not many people can handle my personality, but you can because you're just as mental as me!

Jill, not only are you my PA but you're a friend. You're amazing at what you do; you're constantly on the ball, and if weren't for you I honestly don't know what I would do. You're my rock! Thank you for being the amazing person you are, love you!

Mary, my wonderful Mary. You're one of the most-amazing people that I know. You always manage to make me smile, no matter what it is you do. I'm so blessed to have your friendship. I cherish it. I can't wait to give you a big squeeze when I meet finally meet you face to face in September. I'm counting down the days. Love you loads.

Jennifer Tovar, the master behind Gypsy Heart Editing. Jen, thank you so much for spending hours going over Alec with a fine toothcomb to make it as best as it could be. Thank you for all the GIF's and comments, they made going over edits SO much easier!

Mayhem Cover Creations, you have done it again LJ. Alec is the third cover you have created for me, and I am absolutely in love with it. Thank you!

C.P. Smith, my saviour. Thank so much you formatting Alec for me, you"re an angel!

Last, but never least, my readers. I would not be typing the acknowledgments to my second book had it not been for each and every one of you. Thank you for making me dreams come true <3

ABOUT THE AUTHOR

L.A. Casey was born, raised and currently resides in Dublin, Ireland. She is a twenty three year old stay at home mother to an almost two year old German Shepherd named Storm and of course, her four and half year old (the half is apparently vital) beautiful little hellion/angel depending on the hour of the day.

CONNECT WITH ME
Facebook: www.facebook.com/LACaseyAuthor
Twitter: www.twitter.com/LAWritesBooks
Goodreads: www.goodreads.com/LACaseyAuthor
Website: www.lacaseyauthor.com
Email: l.a.casey@outlook.com

NOW AVAILABLE
DOMINIC
SLATER BROTHERS #1

BRONAGH
SLATER BROTHERS #1.5

COMING SOON
KEELA #2.5
KANE #3
AIDEEN #3.5
RYDER #4
BRANNA #4.5
DAMIEN #5
ALANNAH #5.5
THE SLATER BROTHERS #6